TIDES OF FATE

The Origins of Life and Death: Part One

Sean J. Leith

Copyright © 2019 Sean J. Leith.

No portion of this book may be reproduced in any form without permission from the publisher.

First publication: January 2019.

For permissions, contact:
sleith5@gmail.com
https://www.seanjleith.com

Cover by J caleb design.
Maps developed using Wonderdraft.

All rights reserved.

ISBN-13: 978-1-9995476-0-8

To those that believed in me.

Jess, Renée, Dad, Mom, Steph, Scott, James, Jenny, Victoria, Hillary, Caitlyn, Kristen, and all others.

Thank you.

Most of all, a special thanks to those who inspired me to create this world.

Alexander Williams

Eli Washburn

Lucas McArthur

Michael Hayes

Nicky Hayes

William Denis

ORMONT

DRAKKENBANE SEA

SERPENT'S SEA

KATHYNTA

RE

SEA

FEYAMIN

THE WORLD

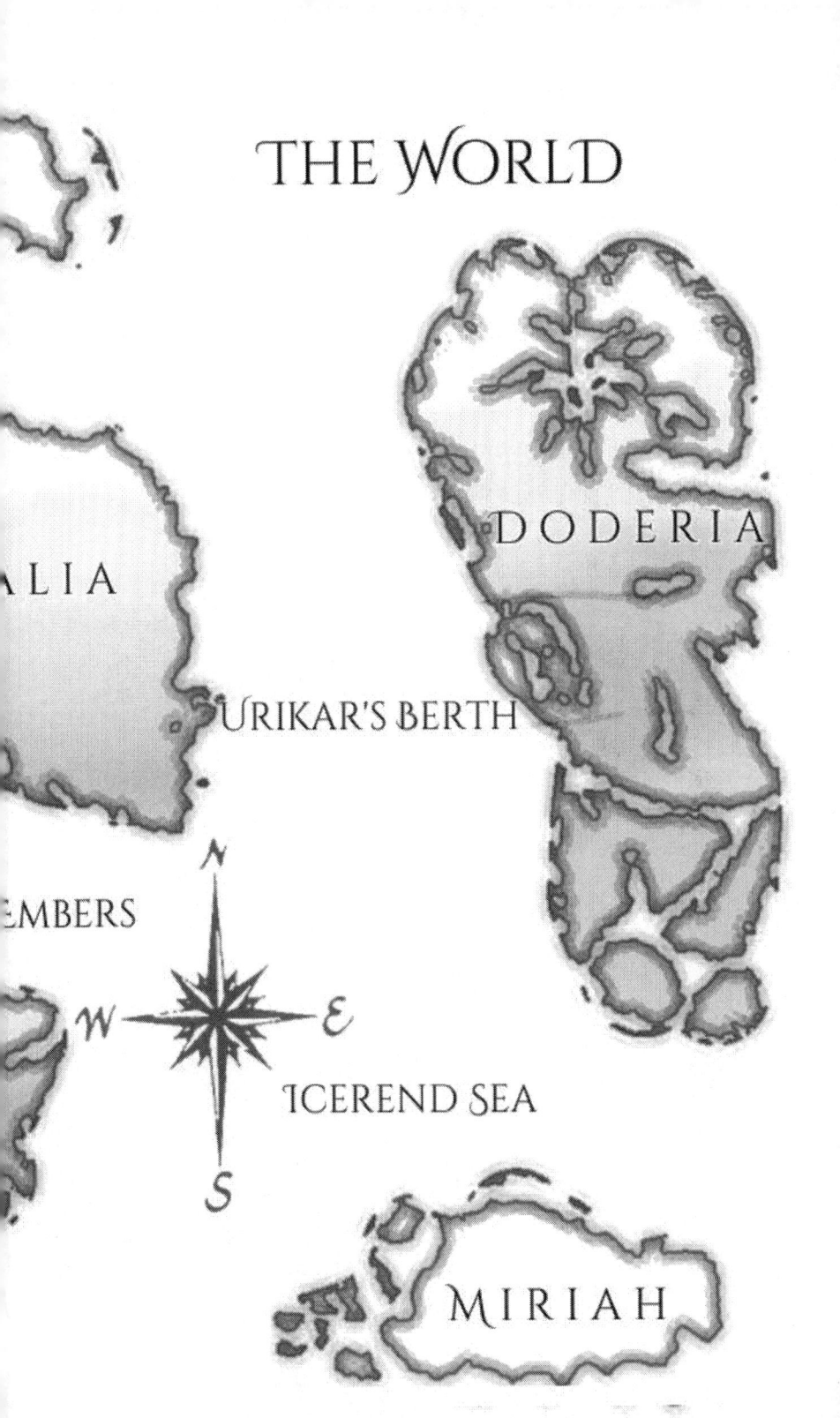

ALIA

DODERIA

URIKAR'S BERTH

EMBERS

ICEREND SEA

MIRIAH

DRAKKENBANE SEA
FROST GIANT'S PASS
SEAWATCH
DARKFIRE HOLD
HILLWATCH
ORDANA
LILAC LAKE
LOUGHRAN
THE CROSSROADS
WOLF CAMP
ROGAN'S MANOR
WYRWOOD
IMPERIUS
DEURBIN
ALENDA
ORBONNE
SOLMARSH
VALKYA
RHONNA
THE DRAGON'S ARCHIPELAGO
DRAGONHEAD
KIRILLIA
MIRAM
PHON
LON
LAYRIA
PORRIS
RAYN
WING
MINDRA
FANG
IRONWANE
CLAW
STONEMAINE
FIRE
EMBERSAND
SCALE
SHELLMIRE
HORN
SPIKEMOUNT
FLAME
MORDAGH'S VOLCANO
SERPENT'S SEA

CLIFFS OF ICARUS
KHOLRAN FORESTS
SERINO
FJORNA
LOTHRAD
ORIÑAS
LOTHRAN
URIKAR'S BERTH
THE TWISTING VINES
ETERNUM
ROCK
N
W
E
S
PLAINS OF AMIRION
GATES
KROTAHKS VALLEY
AMIRION
KWORA
ZENATO CITY
KNIFE
BAY OF GHOSTS
SCORPION'S OASIS
ZENATO
CRESCENT ISLAND
JIGGAD
WATERBANE MOUNTAINS
KIDATO
HERAIA
RCY
DREAD WASTES
SEA OF EMBERS

NECK OF THE SEVEN
SISLA
GRALINE
ELASTON
SHI'DOBA
THISTLEWEED FOREST
EYZORA
KHORIA
BLACKCORE MOUNTAINS
VERGE
DRAGONCLAW
KINGROTO
KITHRA'S VALLEY
FIELDS OF IRON
THE SERPENT'S PLATEAU
THE CIRCLE OF ELEMENTS
ARGONDIA
GARN'S REACH
SERPENTARIUS
SNAKE'S FANGS
BOLERRA'S FLOW
STORMBOUND FOREST
STRIKER'S CLIFFS
THE STORMSPIRE
SEA OF EMBERS

DRAKKENBANE SEA
TORCH OF LATHYRIA
RA
LATHYRIA
FORESTMIRE
HERO'S FALL
STONEHALLOW, EDGE OF FANGS
MAKAN
REMMNIS
MAYNA
THE VALE
CLAN YGGRANDA
CLAN GADORA
KAGROTH, FLAME'S HAND
CHROMATA
CLAN KANNAKASH
CLAN URIKAR
THE FISSURE
THE THREE KNIVES
THE TETHER
ALIN
KALIDOR
KADRANA, THE VENOMLANDS
N
W
E
SERPENT'S SEA

Chapter One

The Rule of Three

Lira Kaar

For the first time, the Loughran militia came to Lira's village of Solmarsh with more than a king's mark on the banner. They wanted every citizen who could lift a weapon, in the name of the new King—and the royal god. The sigil of King Fillion Drayfus—the scroll on a field of bright, fiery orange—was embroidered on the shoulders of every soldier less than a year after his crowning. The violet eye of Lornak, the newly worshipped god, accompanied the King's mark. Lornak was powerless since the war with Shiada, Lira's goddess, but times changed.

My lessons stated he would not be imprisoned forever, she thought. *Fate tells of his return.* Lira stopped sewing to rub her calloused fingers, which hurt from working all day. She pricked herself twice as often as usual. She tightened her grip on the needle to stop herself from shaking. It wasn't her she worried for; she couldn't swing a blade to save her life.

Her brother, Noren, worked in the iron mines, and he was one of the first on the conscription lists. If he didn't die in battle, he could be imprisoned for disobedience. Dark rumors of jailing with no trial, release, or even an execution spread across Loughran like wildfire. Friends went to visit their loved ones in the jails, and they were moved for no reason. It was said many of the conscripts of the army were mysteriously missing from the ranks as well. *They're only rumors,* Lira reminded herself.

But rumors hide a sliver of truth.

The plated steps of many echoed from beyond her front door, and commands being yelled. *They're here.* She wondered where Noren was. He was a little late coming back from the mines. She didn't dare go outside while the soldiers prowled the streets.

Lira stayed inside most of the day, being a clothier. She was far from the priestess she could have been. To her dismay, the church denounced her potential for healing magic. The six-pointed sun branded upon the back of her hand reminded her that she 'wasn't worth the time or effort.' She kept to what she was best at.

"Outta the way, Harvey," a shrill voice snapped from beyond her front door. "I got here first."

A knock pounded at her door. The heavy steps pounded the dirt beyond, and Lira feared drawing a gaze from state soldiers. Her dark skin glowed in the sun gleaming through the window, but with each of the battalion's steps, the light subsided as thick clouds passed over her village.

"I have to get these sweaters to my wife and daughter before I leave, Laura," a male voice pleaded. "They're near my home."

"And ma husband needs the linens before he's gone!" Laura growled. "If I don't hurry, he'll have nothin'. Or he'll get in trouble. Not to mention you still owe me five pounds of fish."

"And the leathers I ordered?" Harvey snarled. "Are those still waiting?" Trent continued with some less-than-kind words, and she only retorted more angrily.

Lira hopped off her chair and placed her needles down. She bounded toward the door in a panic. Swinging it open, the gruff Harvey and portly Miss Pollard turned vicious gazes toward her. A battalion of soldiers wearing the scroll of drayfus marched by. Two turned their gaze toward her, to which she drew her eyes to the ground before speaking to her customers.

Miss Pollard shoved Harvey aside. "Finally! I was worried you'd be taken too, Miss Lira. I gotta get ma linens before—"

Harvey cut in and walked in front of Laura. "—me? You gotta be kidding."

Lira held up her hands to the two. Trying to keep her voice down, she said, "Please, please, don't argue. Why don't you come in and I'll see what I can do. Maybe I can help you work something out?" She gave the best smile she could, today of all days.

She led the two friends inside and started passing through her racks of clothing. She glanced toward Laura and tried to picture her husband. Tall, six-feet and two inches, she reckoned, and picked a linen or two that she'd made previously. Lira motioned to a set of chairs she made earlier that year. "I won't be long."

The two didn't sit down. Glaring at one another was clearly more important. *Everyone is on edge today.*

Lira decided to lend a hand while she searched. What she was best at. Mediating. "Do you need leathers, Harvey?" she asked. "I have a few."

"Three." Harvey grumbled. "But she's the one who owes me."

Lira drew her mouth to the side as she looked from one piece of clothing to the next. "It's very unlike Laura to owe anything to anyone. Is something wrong?"

Laura shuffled in her stance. "Ma husband hasn't been able to do any huntin' recently. With the soldiers comin', he's been tryin' to spend more time with Sara and I."

Lira gave Harvey a look. *Go easy on her.*

Harvey's wife was half a foot shorter than Lira, five feet and five inches, possibly. Picking out a forest green-dyed wool sweater. She eyed it thinking, *perfect!* His daughter Marie was still young, so Lira found something bright and appropriate. Lemon yellow was Lira's favorite color. It made her happy. She felt that was important for a daughter about to lose her father to the force beyond her door. A force ordered by the King—or something more.

After denouncing the rule of the young prince, Lord Drayfus claimed the throne, and kept it with the support of the nobles in the west. Rumors of unrest spread across the land, including the stirring of the savage hordes of the Broken across the sea, vying for Renalia themselves.

"As for the fish," Lira said quietly, picking out one additional linen. "The Trents lost one of their boats. Taken by the soldiers recently for their own uses. So that's why they have less." She went to her sets of order parchment and scribbled a note down.

"Why didn' ya jus' say that?" Laura said, looking to Harvey with a somber eye. "I wouldn' have been so hard on ya if ya just told me."

Harvey just shrugged, eyes at the floor. Ashamed.

When the late King Bracchus Tirilin died, the world groaned. The lack of resources was only the first wake from the sundering of one land into three nations. Rebellion came next under the name of the Scions of Flame—who, luckily, were far from Lira's home.

With a heap of clothing in her arms, Lira sauntered toward them. She placed three sweaters into Harvey's arms. "Make sure these fit," she said.

With her other strained arm, she took three lengths of leather meant for tunics in orders to come and handed them over with a bright smile. "Here."

Before he could reply, Lira turned to place the four linens in Miss Pollard's arms and handed over the note. "Here! Give this to Porra. She owes me a favor. She mentioned they had good luck with their fishing in past days, so she'll get you what you need." Lira just smiled, hoping to help friends through a difficult time.

Stunned, the two customers and friends barely stuttered their next words. "Th—thank you," they both said quietly. They looked at each other with sullen expressions, both apologetic, and fearful of the time to come.

Lira just smiled sweetly in response and gave a shrug. If it made them happy in their time of need, she had no qualms with it.

She felt the same as they—worried for their family. Lira knew that all too well. She leaned in to give each a hug, wishing Laura hope for her husband, and wishing Harvey luck in his battles to come. The light outside faded with the clouds, and Lira lit a few candles and lanterns to see. "Would you like to stay for tea?" Lira asked. Hoping for company in a time of need.

"I wish, Lira, but I need ta get back to ma husband."

Harvey nodded. "My wife and daughter will love these. I can't thank you enough."

Family. Something Lira would soon lose. She scratched the nape of her neck. She wished Noren was home, worrying what the militia might do. Just as she thought it, he burst through the door in a panic.

Laura and Harvey quickly scooted out the door, each giving Noren a somber nod.

Lira rushed toward her brother and gave him a tight embrace. "Is everything okay? What's going on out there?"

Noren's dark skin glistened in the candlelight, and his breaths were quick. "They've come." He rushed over to her large felt chair and collapsed into it. He tried to stifle his shallow breathing. After she followed him over and sat down, he placed his hand on Lira's cheek and gave a woeful smile. "I know you don't want me to leave. But it's for us. I have to. You know I do. Father is still in the Monastery to the south. You won't be alone."

"Father hasn't paid attention to us ever since mother died. I miss him, but he hasn't tried to visit us," Lira mumbled. "I don't want you to go." The faint pattering of rain danced across the wooden roof above. "I like this place, but it wouldn't be the same." She had some close friends but that was it. Calvin Daggart, the man who pursued her, was close to her, but he made her slightly uncomfortable. She had no interest in him, or anyone else, for that matter.

"Stay here, Lira. It's better for both of us, I promise," Noren said. "I've tried to protect you for as long as I can, and now I'm doing the same. I want to keep you safe." He slowly got up and began to pack what clothing he had.

"Why? Why you?" Lira cried. "Why do you have to go?" She shot up and pulled hard on her brother's arm. *I don't need to be protected. I just don't want to be alone.* For reasons she could never explain, she never handled loneliness well.

"They want able-bodied people for the army. With brutal rebels scouring the lands and towns, they need even more than before. If I don't go, they'll throw me in jail. Maybe both of us!" he exclaimed. "I want you to stay safe in Solmarsh. A war against two armies and a savage band of rebels is no place for you." The Scions of Fire, the rebels were called. Their leader was part of a race borne of fire, having a subtle flame flick over his hair. They burned a stronghold not far from the capital a month past but hadn't come anywhere near Solmarsh yet.

She couldn't believe what she heard. *What am I supposed to do? Sit in Solmarsh forever?* She and her brother moved there recently to live near their father in the temple to the south. "What about the rumors of the missing soldiers, or the prisoners?" she yelled. "There are rumors of King Drayfus using dark magic to forward his influence. What if things get worse?"

"Lira!" Noren pulled her into an embrace. "I'm doing this for you. If you stay here, nothing bad will happen. The town is safe," he said in a comforting voice.

I'm not helpless, she thought. She and Noren had been together since birth. She worried that he would become just a memory. Casualties were high during the war, so Noren's chances weren't good. Not only that, but a rebellion began, and Loughran was vulnerable with the militia fighting off both the new nations of Orinas and Zenato.

"I've heard terrible things about the leader of this recruiting regiment, please stay inside." He held her steady. "Look at me," he said quietly. "Please, stay here."

Lira didn't see why she had to. What could possibly happen if she watched him go? Lira hated not seeing family off; every time her father left for work to maintain the trade roads and tend to the repairs, she would follow him down the road. She wasn't going to be taken for the military—she wasn't strong enough.

Lira looked deep into Noren's dark eyes. "Okay, I will," she lied, comforting him for now. She needed to see him off if he was to go.

A bludgeoning knock came from the door. "Open up! Your King demands it!" a man yelled from outside.

Noren looked to the door before turning to her. "Get in the other room and close the door," he ordered.

She nodded quickly and rushed to her bedroom, closing the door. Dark clouds covered the skies outside her window. Thunder rumbled as she heard the front door open.

"Noren Kaar?" the man asked.

"Yes sir. That's my name," Noren replied. "Are you here for recruitment?"

"Don't be cheeky!" the man yelled.

Lira heard a bludgeoning sound, and a body hitting the floor. She covered her mouth, holding back the squeak of a cry. She heard someone get up shortly after.

"My name is Captain Vicks Regar. Come with us. Is there anyone else in the home?" Vicks asked.

"No, no one else," Noren said.

Lira heard the rain begin to hammer down on the wooden roof of their home, echoing the pounding of her heart. Some water trickled through and dripped on the floor. *Why would he say no one?* She was hardly able-bodied. Lira wouldn't be able to carry herself in heavy armor, nor was she skilled in combat. They wouldn't take her, so why would it matter? She would only stay until they left. She heard the ruffle of bags, and the door closing. Lira rushed to the front door, and carefully opened it a crack.

Rain crashed upon the ground; the dirt and stone road was muddy and drenched. Twenty men carrying rucksacks followed a team of soldiers along the road. Noren hurried into line with who she assumed to be Vicks, at his back. Lira's lip curled in as she watched. Tears formed in her eyes from the feeling that she wouldn't see her brother ever again. She was overcome with emotion, and recklessly abandoned her brother's order.

Bolting outside, she yelled, "Noren!" She had to say goodbye.

Everyone turned to her, including Noren. He showed only unparalleled fear. "No," he mouthed to her.

"Well, well, what do we have here?" Vicks observed. "You're a beautiful little flower," he said as he sauntered up to Lira. He was as tall as her, nearly six feet, but with twice the broadness. He pulled the neckline of his thin leather jerkin and scratched his clean-shaven face. He gave a curious smile of mottled teeth, to which Lira responded with a visceral cringe. Vicks ran his gauntlet softly through her soaked black hair, slowly looking her body up and down.

Lira was paralyzed with fear. He suddenly grabbed her by the neck, tighter than a giant's grip. She coughed and struggled, trying to smack his hand away as she gasped for air.

"I don't like being lied to." Captain Vicks glared back at Noren. "You know, the Capital has been looking for soldiers the war, even women. A higher purpose than combat, they say. Gods only know why. They're useless, if you ask me. We do as King Drayfus commands."

A pause crept between them as the energy was drained from her. He said, "—and he follows the word of a god, which we can't dispute, either." He let her neck go. "Come on, girl, we'll bring you with us. Biggs, Wedge, keep the recruits going, don't just stand there." Vicks grabbed her by the arm and dragged her along.

As she resisted, Vicks somehow couldn't pull her with all his strength. "Let me go!" she screamed. She didn't know how she stood strong as he slid in the mud, but kept her stance.

"What in the hells? Do not resist, woman!" He pulled but could not move Lira from her stance. Two more guards tried pulling her, and once again, she wouldn't budge. "She's stronger than she looks!" After sliding in the mud, Vicks and the others let her go.

As she stumbled back, he swiped his steel gauntlet across her face, smashing her to the muddy ground. He pulled his long blade from a scabbard at his hip. "I've had it with you already, you little wench." As he raised his sword high, steel punctured through the left of his chest covered in blood.

Noren stood behind, staggering back with wide, panicked eyes, leaving the sword in the commander's torso.

The Captain dropped his blade, fell into the mud, and writhed in agony. "What? You!" He coughed up blood and cursed before he passed into the next life.

Noren embraced her tightly. "I couldn't, Lira. I couldn't stand there watching!" His grip loosened as the two other commanding soldiers tore him away.

Biggs shoved him against a tree and was about to slice a blade across his neck—until the other stopped him. "Take him with us. Arrest him. He can be used for the new jail. Vicks said things were being prepared for something important."

Wedge put a gag over her brother's mouth, and dragged him away with the other recruits, who looked upon him with despair.

"No!" Lira screeched from her hands and knees, hair covered in mud. She cried as strongly as the rain pounding the ground.

Biggs walked over with two others to pick up the dead Vicks. Lira scrambled to strike him but was struck with a gauntlet again, sending her into a daze. "Look at this." They mumbled a few words to each other, but she heard the word 'exempt.' "—and she won't be crossing anyone again anytime soon," Wedge said. She was driven to the ground again, only able to see the company walk down the road. She felt powerless. She was unable to do anything to save Noren; all she could do was stare helplessly at him being dragged away.

Before long, she rose again, and ran forward after them until and a hand grabbed her and pulled her back.

"Lira, stop!" Looking back, her childhood friend Calvin, stood with beady, concerned eyes staring into hers. "I'm sure he will be pardoned. It's best you aren't taken as well. Please, I don't want that."

Bawling, she shook her arm away from him, and collapsed to the ground. "You don't know that," she said quietly. He blinked twice and shook his head. It was an odd thing he always did, when he was stressed, or something was off. Seeing her brother and so many other friends taken, she wasn't surprised.

"The rumors aren't true. I promise. I couldn't handle both of you being taken. Maybe you could visit him?"

She nodded, and sniffed, barely able to handle the tears flowing from her eyes. "Okay," she blubbered. Walking away, she stormed back into her home and slammed the door on his face as he approached.

* * *

For days, she could only stare at the walls of her home. Her clothing went unfinished, and she didn't bother answering the door. *It could be them again. They could be back for me.* If she stayed inside, Noren wouldn't have been arrested. She felt suffocated by guilt, finding it hard to breathe. She could hear Noren, blaming her, in her mind. *If you did what you were told, I wouldn't be in jail. You wouldn't be in danger.*

How could you? she heard him say.

Another knock echoed from her door. "King's business," a voice said, this time, calmly.

Lira rose to her feet with shaky hands. *They've come for me.*

When she opened the door, a well-groomed soldier wearing intricately embroidered leather handed her a letter. "Lira Kaar?"

Lira clenched her fists, trying to calm her nerves. "Yes?" she accepted the letter.

"Your brother has been jailed in the Southwestern Loughran hold. As your father is part of the Orinde Monastery, he has given up his name. You are the next of kin, and this is your notification." The soldier bowed and walked away immediately after speaking.

She read it carefully with one thought etched into her mind. *I have to apologize. I must see him. I can't live with the guilt.*

The day after, Lira packed some of her things, and travelled a few days to the Southwestern Loughran hold with a supply caravan from Solmarsh. But when she arrived, the news was what she feared most. "He's been moved to another location."

"What? Where was he moved?" Lira asked. *Under orders from Drayfus' god, Lornak?* Lira wondered. He was the opposer of her goddess, but Lornak was said to be powerless. *But fated to return.*

"Isn't he 'missing' like the others?" another guard piped up, cocking a side smile.

The warden turned his scar-ridden scowl to his subordinate. "Shut your mouth, boy. I'll have you strung up for the crows with another comment like that." He turned his glare to Lira. "State business. Ask further, and I'll make sure you follow his footsteps, girl," the warden growled. "I could name you one of those savage Scions of Fire, and you'd be jailed for certain."

"But—"

"One more word, and I'm throwing you in and sending you with him. Understand?" The warden slammed his fist on the wooden desk, leaving a dent where his gauntlet hit it. "Get out of here. Best forget your traitor of a brother even lived. You're better off."

Lira drew back. *Forget him? How? And why? Is there no chance he'd ever be free?* she thought. *I want to find out where he went. Is he missing?* She had no idea how to go about it. Noren told her to stay safe in Solmarsh. *But how could I abandon him? With all that's going on, the rebellion, the war, and the rumors about prisoners never being released—or even executed—I can only imagine what horrors he could be put through.* On her trip with the caravan home, she wondered what she even *could* do. She was hardly a proficient fighter, or a traveler as a whole.

She holed herself up in her small home meant for two, worrying endlessly. She prayed to Shiada, for a means to save her brother. Some thought prayer and gods were worthless, but Lira knew their power was real. Before bed, she said one final prayer. She hoped in the morning she could muster the courage, or a means, to find him. *He could be killed, or something even worse.*

She couldn't stop the tears from welling in her eyes as she tried to sleep. Soldiers were everywhere in Loughran, the savage Scions of Fire scoured the lands, and thieves plundered vulnerable towns.

And I'd be searching aimlessly, alone, she thought, drifting off to sleep.

* * *

A gentle knock pattered at her door. It was softer than a state guard, or so she assumed. She inched toward the door, passing by the rays of morning sun gleaming through her windows. *The rule of three. Bad news comes in threes,* Lira thought.

The first visitor was the recruiter, leading to Noren's arrest.

The second brought his location, and Noren went missing.

She prayed for hope the night before; she wondered what came this time. As she cracked open the door, a bronze-skinned man stood half a foot below her eyes.

A subtle flame flickered over his messy black hair, and the shoddy boiled leather armor covered in cuts and frays contrasted the large blade encrusted with bright rubies upon his back. "Lira Kaar?" he said kindly.

"Yes?" Lira stuttered. It was strange for someone with a sword so large to speak kindly, let alone a Blazik, in Loughran.

"Sohgra, the owner of the inn here in Solmarsh and a friend of mine, sent me to you. May I come in?" he spoke gently.

She shook her head. "I'm sorry, I do not know you." Lira held the door tighter. She carefully leaned behind the door, and grabbed a dagger from the wall, holding it behind her left forearm.

"Indeed, my apologies. I am here on business, regarding your brother. I have heard of your situation, and I have a proposal you might find interesting."

Lira looked left and right. It had only been a few days, and almost thought her situation lost. "What proposal?"

The Blazik cleared his throat. "I can help you find him."

Lira's eyes widened. "Wh—what?"

"Please, I must speak with you in private," he said, glancing down the road.

She opened the door wider, keeping the dagger hidden.

He bowed his head, and carefully stepped into her home as she closed the door. "I don't believe I know your name," she said.

"I didn't give you my name." he kept a close eye on the door, waiting until the door *clicked* closed to continue. "I tend to keep it quiet until in private. I am Jirah Mirado."

Lira's eyes widened. "The—"

"—the leader of the Scions of Fire, yes." He sighed, looking out her window. "I'm here to offer a chance. An associate of mine gave you a shining recommendation, and from what I've heard, I could use a woman like you." He turned back to her and stared into her eyes. "I'm offering a chance to find your brother. All I ask in return is loyalty. You may leave at any time, but I ask you do not speak of us after you decide to leave."

Lira scratched the nape of her neck. *A woman like me.* "But what could I do?" she asked. *I've only heard stories of their savagery. But if I could find Noren...*

"Fighters aren't the only thing needed in a war. You can teach someone to fight. You can't teach a sense of loyalty and morality. I'm going to ask you once, and then I will be gone from here." He stepped forward, staring up into her eyes with his dark, almond-shaped ones. "Will you join us?" After seeing what could be best described as a child in awe and fear, he turned. "Take a moment to think."

Lira stared down at him. He was much shorter than she expected, but he had a strong presence. *I have only heard awful things,* Lira thought. *But if I don't go with him, I may never see Noren again.* She couldn't leave Noren to die.

If she joined she was a criminal—and could only imagine what would happen if she was caught. But most of all, she couldn't live in Solmarsh forever wondering what could have been. She stood for what seemed like minutes, and he simply waited, looking toward her window with a sharp eye.

Wondering what could have been, she thought again.

The pain of mystery.

She couldn't bear the thought. It was risking her life in order to avoid pain for a lifetime. She bolstered all nerves within herself, straightened her posture, and nodded. "I will."

"I'm glad." Jirah took a piece of parchment out from his bag and placed it on a small table by a lantern. "From here, it will be seven day's time before you reach this destination. Come to the camp and await further instructions. Follow this map and tell no one. Memorize the landmarks and burn it as soon as possible. I'll send a scout to inform them of your arrival." He gave his hand, and Lira shook it with the one not holding the dagger. "The land needs help. I'm glad you will be part of it. I won't be back there for a time, however. I have more business to attend to. I assure you, though, the officer present there is more than trustworthy."

As he bowed and turned to go, he turned with a smirk. "You would want a sharper dagger. Yours looks fairly dull." He gave a light chuckle before walking down the road with a cowl over his head.

Lira closed the door, pressed her back against it, and slid down to the ground. *With their help, I can find him.* She swallowed tightly, let out panicked breaths, and stifled her fear with a thought. *I'm coming, Noren. I promise. It's my turn to protect you.*

Chapter Two

The Unsullied

Lira Kaar

It was a peaceful night in the blackwood forests of Loughran, and Lira knew there was no going back. The moon's bloody red glow barely shone through the canopy above to illuminate her convoluted path. When she was a child, her father told her a blood moon was the sign of unity—but also of change. In recent days her life changed significantly. She became a criminal.

Hoo, hoo, hoo, hoo... the owls hooted around her. A blanket of shadow covered nearly all with accents of crimson from the moon; her dark copper skin was none but a shade of red. The branches around her scraped against one another, the leaves rustled in the howling wind, and the owls didn't let a moment go silent. *Hoo...*

Are you asking who I am? Lira thought. *I thought I knew. This isn't me at all. But without my brother, I feel I'm only half a person.* Noren went missing a fortnight ago from the jail he was kept in. She had to find him. If anything bad happened to Noren, it would be her fault. Not only that, but she would lose what little family she had left, save for her father. The twigs snapped beneath her feet, and she stumbled over a large tree root coiling out of the hard ground. She checked her bag to make sure everything was still there. She didn't bring much: only some food and water, her bow, a spellbook, and her brother's ring. She didn't want to forget him after the sacrifice he made for her. *I have to make sacrifices too. I'm not the only one hurt by the state.*

Conflict always made Lira anxious; armies, rebels, kings—she didn't want to get involved. But Noren's disappearance pushed her to make a change. Although, the dark forest wasn't making her feel any better about it.

Jirah offered her a chance to find her brother and help others. *And a chance to fight back, but I don't like fighting,* she thought. *I just want to help.* She wondered what kinds of unscrupulous characters she would meet in a rebel force—people she was nothing like, she was sure. Jirah told her she was welcome to join in the fight to stop all the terrible things the soldiers had done: the arrests, unlawful conscriptions, and murders. There had been a suspicious increase in arrests in the region, Lira heard, and they weren't being released, or even put on trial. Mistreatment of commoners and disregarding wounded soldiers was nothing surprising, but something seemed very strange about the capital's actions of late.

Lira stopped briefly and scratched her head. She came to a fork in the road, with paths curving into the darkness. She pulled out her map and tapped the end of her six-foot walking stick she had against her head to think. A bunch of scribbles on the parchment coiled through the forests north of Deurbin, but when it came to the fork, it stopped. *Which way?* Lira looked around, perking her ears hoping to hear something to guide her way. The owls stopped, the branches sat still, and the leaves fluttered gently in the wind. But then, the leaves above her rustled, a plop of leather on dirt echoed before her, and the glint of steel shone between her eyes.

"Who are you?" a raspy voice said harshly.

Lira jumped back. "Me?" she stuttered. She placed a hand to her chest, and her breath sped up to meet her pounding heart.

"Yes, you." The voice vibrated subtly, as did the arrowhead pointed at her. "Make it quick, or I'll let the arrow answer for you." The trees rustled and swayed, and the crimson moonlight showed a woman's face a foot below hers, with sharp features and a scowl decorated by a long, thick scar across her right eye.

When they locked eyes, Lira felt a strange painful sensation deep within her mind. The woman's pupils glowed a faint blue, and she winced as Lira did. At first it was a mere sting, but slowly grew to an unbearable burning that felt like an inferno. She clutched her head and dropped to one knee. She yelped in pain and prayed for it to end. Lira looked up to see the red light above flicker and wane, and the moon flashed to a subtle violet and back before she closed her eyes again.

"What the hell!" the woman yelled. She staggered back and gripped her head too, struggling to redraw her bow. "You better give your name quick, or I'm going to take this damn headache out on you! Is this your magic, witch?" She glared at Lira and bared her teeth. Her amber irises were decorated by the strange blue-lit pupils, brightly shining in the dark.

"Lira Kaar! I didn't do it, I swear!" Lira said. As they stared at each other, their breath slowed, but the pain only subsided a little. They stood up straight and basked in both the dark and the blood-colored light. "Who are you?"

The woman put away her bow. Her breath slowed, and her pupils faded to a deep black once more. She looked as if to curse or give a vicious retort but stopped in her tracks. "Kayden Ralta," she said, raising a curious brow. After a peculiar stare, she asked, "What's with your eyes?"

Lira didn't know what to say. She was more curious of Kayden's eyes. *Did it happen to me, too?* Lira looked up to the moon above, curious of what it meant.

After a long pause, the vicious woman, Kayden, sighed and rolled her eyes. "Whatever. Come on, you're late. I had to come out here to find you in case you got lost. You even *looked* lost. Do you even know how to read a map?" Kayden rubbed her head and started walking away. "Let's go."

Lira tried to stifle her loud, shallow breaths. It was finally starting to sink in. She was going to be a criminal. Pattering up beside the woman, she said, "Are you part of the Scions, too?"

"Shh," Kayden whispered. "Damn it, I can barely see out here. Quit talking about that so loud. Just follow me before you get lost again."

I was only a little lost. Lira tried to keep up, but Kayden walked rather quickly for someone so much shorter than her. "Where are we going?"

Kayden sighed, and didn't respond.

Lira rubbed her arms, looking around. All she could see was blackwood trees, and the dark silhouette of broad leaves on a backdrop of crimson moonlight. After a time, she could finally see the warm light of a campfire in the distance. It flickered and danced against the black trees, and as it grew, she saw more than a few individuals staring down the path at them.

Lira's breath barely slowed. She crossed her arms and stared at the ground, looking time and again at the growing flame. The flame revealed a flourish of color as they entered the clearing. Kayden's skin glowed a warm olive tone, and it revealed a thick, tangled mane of hair. The others in the clearing were a strange mix of individuals; some of forms she only saw in paintings and heard in stories.

TIDES OF FATE

Kayden passed the fire and those by it and leaned up against a tree. "Found it."

"Thank you, Miss Ralta. That was quite kind," a stone-skinned man said. He was a Terran, a human race touched with the power of earth. His voice was graveled, and without a hint of emotion.

Kayden shrugged. "I don't like it when I have to wait around for stragglers."

The slate-skinned man walked forward and extended his hand. "I am Gorkith Kildath. Sir Mirado is in another camp at the moment, and I have given them the task in his place. Please have a seat. Miggen will brief you." He motioned to a log by the fire, where another woman sat.

She had a similar long nose and soft jaw as Jirah did—and was a Blazik as well. She passed her dark obsidian-black hair over a bronze-skinned shoulder, the flame flitting off into the air around her.

The others seemed battle-hardened and more prepared than Lira ever could be. She glanced to the path whence she came. She shook her head. *No. This is what I must do.*

The woman shifted over and moved her gold-accented scythe to the other side, opening some space to sit. She patted the seat and gave Lira a warm smile. "I'm Domika. What's your name?"

Lira inched over to the log, and gently, *slowly* sat down, eyeing the others. "I'm, ah—" She lost her voice a moment, barely able to spit out her nerves. "Lira," she said quietly.

"Nice to meet you." Domika pointed to a heavily armored man with small horns protruding from his forehead, and a middle-aged man with a long grey beard intermingled with whites, wearing a loose, violet robe. "This is Magnus and Vesper." The young man gave a serious, blank nod, while the middle-aged man smiled brightly. Domika motioned to a third young man across from her.

"And this is Miggen. He's keeping an eye on us. We're all new aside from him, so don't feel like you're the only one here."

Kayden leaned aloof against a tree around the clearing edge, opening her hand mouthing 'blah, blah, blah,' before she rolled her eyes.

Miggen was a young man, barely sixteen she reckoned. While adjusting the scale mail and patting a spiked mace at his side, he stood up. With a subtle cough, he cleared his throat, and spoke. "The others already know where we're going, so I'll fill you in. The Lord of Koffer Forest to the west, Dolph Rogan, ordered a very large number of questionable arrests recently. We want to find out if this is Drayfus' doing. His castle is a day's walk out of the forest, but we have horses. We strike before night's end. Shouldn't be too hard. I've heard his guards are minimal. This is a reconnaissance mission, not an attack."

Drayfus. The previous royal advisor, and now the King after the late King, Bracchus Tirilin, fell ill a year prior. After his death, nobles claimed Bracchus's son was too young to rule at seventeen, and his brother was not a good choice due to a number of reasons. Unpredictability. Brutal. Unreasonable. Or so Lira heard.

Lira scratched the nape of her neck. "Will we have to fight anyone?" she said thinly.

"Not if I have something to say about it. If you do as I say, we should be in and out without a problem," Kayden spoke up.

"Shouldn't we let Miggen show the way?" Domika sneered. "You don't lead us."

"Actually Miss Mirado, I'm simply here to make sure things go to plan, and ensure our safety if things go south. As far as I've heard, she's the most qualified," Miggen cut in.

"Well, she certainly *looks* like a criminal," Domika said with a frown.

Jirah's sister, Lira thought. The pressure to not make any mistakes grew heavier. Lira looked over to Kayden, who scowled at her fiery accuser.

She had a plain face with a few thick scars across her eyes and cheeks, knotted mousy hair, and dirt accenting her olive skin. "I'll take that as a compliment. We're all criminals here," Kayden shot back.

"That's enough," Miggen said roughly. Stepping between their locked eyes, he said, "We're a team. We watch each other's backs. We don't exchange insults." He sighed. "Now, we might have to knock a couple out, but we aren't killing anyone. We need to find his study, or anything, to get evidence. These arrests are strange and suspicious. There are no trials, and there are rumors of them not being released." Miggen rose to his feet. "With the horses, we'll make good time—maybe a few hours. I'm sorry to leave so soon Lira, but as Kayden said, you were late. Pack your things. We're heading out." He pointed to Kayden and gave a commanding look toward Domika. "I gave her the map of the manor that we acquired recently."

Lira checked her things, got her rucksack on again, and started walking toward a horse. She didn't know how to ride one. Rubbing her throbbing head, she looked toward Kayden, which only made the pain worse. Especially when she turned with a sharp glare and eye roll as if reading Lira's skill level. Lira scratched her head, too embarrassed to say anything. She watched the others pick a horse that suited them. Kayden hopped up on a horse with one hand, with the other carrying a pack. She looked toward the opposing path she came from, wondering if she made a mistake.

Miggen tip-toed over. "Do you know how to ride a horse?" he whispered.

Lira looked to the dirt below and shook her head subtly.

He gave a soft smile and nodded. "I'll just say we can only take five. You can ride with me, all right?"

Lira nodded. "Thanks," she whispered. He helped her up onto his horse, and not too soon after, they took off.

They trotted alongside Magnus, whom Lira attempted to make conversation with. He was large, nearly half a foot taller than Lira at six-feet and four inches, but had a torso as thick as an old tree. His skin was pale, and eyes blood red. He was a half-Devil, a race of monstrous beings.

I've only heard terrible things about them, she thought nervously. They were a race of thieves and murderers—yet he seemed calm and kind. She probed him with a few questions as they traveled, but he didn't give much information up. She wondered what his, or rather, what *all* of their motives were.

Miggen spoke calmly as they went but kept one hand on the haft of his orange-sized mace. *Should I worry?* Lira wondered. He was a tanner before he joined Jirah's plight. Now he was a 'mace-wielding warrior of truth.' Lira giggled at his self-proclaimed title; he was an interesting fellow.

Most of the trip, the only sound among the clop of hooves was the sociable chatter of Domika with anyone who would listen, and mumbling from the older man, Vesper, who spoke whether he was listened to or not. His violet robe swayed in the wind as his horse trotted. He read from a large book named 'Focus of the Arcana,' constantly, barely looking ahead of him. His voice was vibrant, and he always tended to swish his finger in the air as he spoke to anyone who listened.

After a few hours, they stopped. Kayden motioned for them to hop off and tie up the horses. "We're almost there," Kayden said. She hopped off, and the rest followed. They walked together, along with Miggen, who was present to ensure the plan succeeded.

Clothier to a Scion of fire. Knowing Miggen was a modest tanner helped settle her nerves. The five companions around her walked with purpose, while she stumbled over root and thorn, trying not to make a fool of herself. It didn't help that her head still throbbed with pain; ever since she'd laid eyes on Kayden, her mind felt fit to explode.

Why won't this headache go away? she wondered. She glanced at Kayden, wondering if she felt it too.

Kayden looked back with a squint, shooing the others to move quicker. "Damn it, I can barely see with this blood moon." She walked at the head of the pack, quicker than the rest, despite her short stature. She hadn't bothered to learn any of their names, and instead gave each a nickname while they traveled. "Princess, keep up," Kayden said with a harsh tone.

Lira's nickname wasn't her favorite. She didn't mind it, but she didn't enjoy it much either. *I'm no princess,* she thought. *She's only making fun of me.* She tried to quicken her pace. "I'm trying. What if we get caught?" Lira asked. *I hope the allegations are wrong.* But most of all, she worried for her missing brother. She looked to her silver ring and spun it on her finger. It reminded her of why she'd joined. She didn't want others to lose family, and she didn't want to lose hers, either.

"We won't get caught, princess. How are they gonna know we're coming?" Kayden whispered. She rubbed the back of her head and grumbled, "Damn headache."

"Not to worry. I will be watching," Magnus said.

Lira could just barely see the small castle in the distance. A grey stone wall shielded it, and a mansion sat nestled within. "There it is! I can see it."

"Yeah, well, not all of us are blessed with the ability to see in the dark. How *can* you see? You're only human," Kayden spat.

Lira scratched the back of her neck. "I just can, I don't know." She always had good sight at night time; her and Noren would go out adventuring at night to view the stars, and she would have to lead him along.

"I can see it, too," Magnus said. Lira may have good vision, but Half-Devils could see in the dark as if they lived in it.

"Well, good for both of you. The old man and I can't, so keep an eye out."

Lira noticed that she didn't mention Domika, who walked behind her. Since they'd started off, Domika and Kayden hadn't gotten along. Blaziks were borne of fire, of which Lira always found fascinating. She hadn't seen more than a couple in her life, as they lived far across the continent of Renalia in the deserts, as well as past the southern seas in the land of Feyamin.

"Why are you at the head if you can't see?" Domika asked.

"Don't sass me," Kayden said with a growl. "Someone around here needs to take some initiative. Mace-boy isn't here to show us where to go. He's here to help only if we need it."

"Well, have it be Magnus or something. He can see perfectly out here," Domika said.

"Now, now my friends, let us be silent. Our first goal is to not get caught, yes? Miss Ralta has been perfectly capable of reading our path as of yet," Vesper said from behind.

Kayden waved a dismissive hand back toward them. "At least someone appreciates my work."

"All right, you five. Calm down. I may be an escort to make sure things go well, but don't think I won't step in if there's an argument," Miggen said. He kept quiet for the trip. "We should be at the castle soon. Keep in the shadows, and don't talk too much when we're there. Guards have been more vigilant in recent days. I actually helped on a mission a few cities over, and we stole all of the documents and orders from Drayfus. Arrests would come for petty crimes. We have no idea why, but it's concerning." Miggen's tone grew brittle. "Remember, what you do here is important. This isn't some practice mission. This could save lives—and ours are at risk."

Kayden looked back and nodded, then walked in silence.

Lira wondered how everything became so chaotic where she lived. After Bracchus' son pitted war against the advisor, Lord Drayfus, from the new nation of Orinas in the north, the realm worsened. To make matters even worse, the late King's brother brought war from the new nation of Zenato in the east, south of the neutral kingdom of Amirion. *Is it the war that caused issues? Or the new King himself?* Renalia was once one massive nation, but now was three.

Lira knew the rebellion started for a reason, and she saw it lay between the lines. They knew King Drayfus' reign was filled with corruption: from the extortion of tradesmen, to the mistreatment of injured soldiers, to the overtaxing of commoners. Not only that, but the arrests for petty crimes, or nothing at all. *And some are missing, like Noren. I hope I can find out what happened. I couldn't bear to lose him.* Lira wondered what they would find out tonight.

Part of her wanted to leave Loughran for one of the other nations, but she couldn't abandon her home.

The group came out of the thick, blackwood maple forest to see the manor. The gates basked in the dim light of adjacent torches and were accompanied by guards with spears and blades. Lira shuffled her feet. She wasn't comfortable with combat.

"We can probably grapple over the western wall, over there." Kayden pointed to a shadowed spot on the wall that was absent of guards. "I can get up there and fasten the rope better for heavier people. I'm light, so I don't need much to hook onto."

Lira walked forward and rubbed her arms. A cool breeze blew over them, and a chill ran down her spine.

Magnus' blood-red eyes fixed on Lira's, but it was a soft gaze. "Not to worry, my lady."

"Quiet." Kayden peered around the trees and closely analyzed the entrances and walls.

Magnus wore heavy, plated armor, and it made quite a bit of noise in the night. The crickets sang to the moon, the owls hooted together, and the wind soared through the forest to rustle branches and leaves. Lira hoped it was enough to cover the noise of their movement. She hoped the mission would go off without an issue, as it was their first. She didn't want her first experience to be a bad one—especially if her inexperience caused problems.

Kayden looked out, analyzing the walls closely, then turned back with narrowed eyes. "I spotted an opening." She swished a poignant finger at different parts of the keep. "We'll run along the forest line and hit the wall there. I'll grapple up and lead the rest of you in. We go down the wall and get into the mansion from there. Don't fall behind, or I'll leave you behind." Kayden pulled a rope decorated by a hooked metal claw at the end of it. "Let's move." She sprang forward, and Lira followed with the others.

As they made their way along the forest's edge, and a chill went down Lira's spine again. The walls were high, and there were a few guards far from where Kayden pointed.

As they approached the wall, Kayden swung the hook and threw it over with a quiet *tink* while the others looked out.

Lira worried the guards would hear, but she didn't hear any voices. By the time Lira looked back, Kayden was already up the wall. She disappeared for a couple of moments, then two ropes dropped over the side followed by her sly smirk. Miggen climbed deftly, as did Domika. Magnus seemed like he would tear the rope, but he managed. As Lira and Vesper climbed, she saw they were being pulled up. As she reached the top, Lira ducked down low as the others did.

Kayden motioned her hand low, and her eyes shot around to different parts of the wall, the yard below, and the towers around them. Her ears perked up, as if she could hear every sound in the area. Kayden pulled out the map and looked closely, tracing her fingers along the page. "Keep up," she whispered. She crawled over to the far side of the wall, looked over the edge, and dropped a rope she already deftly tied to a crenellation. She hopped off the side, waving with her.

Lira looked over the edge, seeing a large elaborate hedge garden beside the manor. By the time Lira hurled over the side, two armored men collapsed upon the ground. "Did you kill them?" she whispered in a brittle tone.

Kayden turned and fiercely put her forefinger to her lips, and then shook her head.

Lira's hands shook wildly at the beat of her pounding heart. *Calm down, calm down, you can do this...* Her breathing sped up, and heart sped faster than a horse's charge. A plate gauntlet rested on her shoulder. Lira jumped and nearly yelped, barely covering her mouth with a hand.

"Worry not," Magnus said in a deep whisper. He crept after Kayden, just below the hedge line. Lira tip-toed to the door where Kayden worked. Domika peeked around the corner and whirled her hand in a circle to hurry Kayden, who growled in response. The door opened with a *click* and Kayden slinked inside.

The others did their best to follow, as quiet as they could. Magnus's were surprisingly silent, even in his heavy plate. The halls were a pale grey stone, with a few paintings of men in satin rubes and silk doublets, many with the last name *Rogan*. Kayden checked her map every so often, only stopping to look frantically to each hallway, or pull out a small bamboo tube to blow a small dart into the neck of an unsuspecting soldier. They'd fall to the ground and that was that.

Lira felt a little embarrassed as she hadn't done anything yet. Kayden did all the work.

Kayden shifted her sharp gaze from one group member to the next, until she locked eyes with Lira, which made her freeze in her tracks.

Did I do something wrong? she thought.

After a brief pause, Kayden motioned in the door with a nod. "Princess, go in and find information, and I'll keep watch. Clunky, with me. You three, go with her," Kayden whispered. With a nod, Magnus stayed at her side.

Lira was surprised Kayden would pick her of all people, but didn't ask questions. She slipped into the office lined with ornate bookshelves. An intricately carved blackwood desk stood in the back with papers strewn across it. Lira ran over with Domika and Vesper. Miggen searched papers that were on the ground, and frequently peered out of the door to check on the others.

There were many notes on delegations to other advisors and high house citizens in the region, and some orders from the capital, but nothing out of the ordinary. Domika shuffled around the papers in a huff, stopped, and crossed her arms. Magnus stood back and scratched his head.

Kayden put her head through the door and whispered, "*hurry the hell up!*"

Domika just responded with "*There's nothing here.*"

Lira felt around under the desk. There had to be *something*. Inspecting the bottom of the drawer area, she noticed it was slightly larger than the drawer itself. She felt a depression in the wood and pressed it with a *click*. A drawer lowered, revealing a small stack of papers. "Here, I found some!" Lira said excitedly, almost doing a little dance. The others shushed her, but she felt useful. There were orders to arrest citizens for even small thefts, like food and other cheap goods. In Wyrwood to the southwest, laws were put in to arrest people for bumping into guards, claiming that it was 'assaulting a soldier of the state.'

Lira couldn't believe it. She covered her mouth when she read what was next. Prisoners were to be sent to a city in southern Loughran, Deurbin, for *torture*, each of them. They were to ask for information on the rebellion and—whether they knew anything or not—they were to be delivered to a designated location revealed soon for 'special treatment.'

Noren, no...

Two marks were set at the bottom of the letter—a violet lidless eye, and a scroll on a field of yellow and orange. She barely thought about it. She was more worried about the prisoners. *Why would they do this for such petty things? What do they mean by special treatment?* Lira wondered. It was her fault Noren was arrested, and then he was moved from the jail. Now she suspected he might be part of this movement for torture, or worse.

Domika's and Vesper's eyes were wide as dinner plates, mouth dropped open in shock. "It is true, I cannot believe it. Such a disgraceful King," Vesper said in a brittle tone. "What do we do?"

"Miggen, over here," Lira whispered.

Miggen crept over. "What did you find?"

She showed him while attempting to keep her composure. Her hands shook, not from nerves, but fear of what this could mean. She clenched her fists trying to stay calm. *I'll find him. I have to.*

Miggen's eyes broadened and he breathed loudly through his large nostrils. "This is concerning. Great work, all of you. Now, let's get out of here before something bad happens. This changes everything." Miggen grabbed the papers and shoved them into a satchel at his right hip. The others followed.

Kayden led them back to the door, and out along the hedges.

As Lira glanced up at the sky, the crimson light from the moon seemed to wane, and the color of the trees, hedges, and grass dulled to a pale grey. The sound around them muffled slightly, as if Lira was drifting off to sleep. The guards were still knocked out; Lira was glad. *Both for us, and for them.* They climbed back over the wall in the shadow of a tower, slinked over and dropped down once more successfully.

Slowly, the grey of the grass and trees seemed to fade as well, and it became hard for Lira to see. She glanced around as they waited for Magnus and Vesper to descend, and the sounds of the forest and manor grew eerily silent. There was no hooting of owls, rustling of trees, or even a breeze of wind.

As the forest wall froze, a throng of soldiers emerged from the shadows of the canopy, including a knight in deep black plated armor, with a helmet that looked like it was topped with a crown.

"*Soldiers!*" Lira whispered and pointed at them. They seemed almost translucent in appearance.

Kayden turned around and stared, as did the rest. "What are you talking about? I don't see anything."

"I don't either. Are you sure you aren't just seeing things?" Domika inquired.

"No, they're there! Don't you see them?" Lira said in a panic. Tension rose like a tidal wave.

Magnus drew one of the blades at his hip. "They come."

"I don't—" Kayden walked forward, and her eyes widened as the soldiers became fully opaque. "*What?*" She drew two blades and lowered her stance. "What is this, a setup?"

"Interesting—usually no one sees us coming." Asheron let out with a deep, hollowed cackle. He was surrounded by twelve other soldiers, each armed to the teeth. The knight drew his darksteel long blade, encrusted with black diamonds, and pointed it at them. "Did you find what you were looking for? Surrender, and come with us."

"Go to hell," Kayden growled.

Miggen pulled out his mace with a tight grip. "Highwind."

Asheron Highwind. One of the high captains of the Loughran Military, known for his lack of kindness. He wasn't as evil as his brother, Malakai, but still vile all the same. "Ah, Miggen. What was it you said to me last, boy? You'd kill me if you ever saw me again?"

Miggen tightened the grip on his mace. "You killed my sister for housing young ones."

Asheron looked toward his other soldiers, and shook his head slowly. "Housing children who aided the Scions." He took a calm, calculated step toward them. "I cut her throat because she was a traitor." Looking back toward the wall, he said. "Now what does that make you, boy?"

"She was innocent. They were *all* innocent," Miggen snarled. A tear led down his left cheek. "I meant what I said."

"Speaking of matters you do not understand—just like that traitorous leader of yours." With a chuckle, he shook his head once more. "Let's see if you can follow through. I never turn down a challenge." Swinging the dark sword, he changed his stance into a side, proper form. "Do you have any last words?" He waited for a response.

A dread silence hung in the air. Lira shrank back. She didn't want to fight. She had the power of divine magic—to heal—but could barely fix a scratch. She could use a bow, but only against animals. She carefully took her bow out with a slight shake to her hand.

"I see. In that case, my name is Captain Asheron Highwind, and you are all under arrest—take them alive. Leave the boy to me." Asheron disappeared in a cloud of black mist, while the other twelve soldiers converged on the group.

Lira drew arrows and fired them at a few soldiers, hitting one in the leg causing him to topple. She backed off then and let the others take the forefront. Kayden spun, rolled, and sliced her blades across the necks of three, while Magnus rushed two and knocked them aside easily with his shield. Vesper froze against the wall, and Domika whirled and slashed at their legs with her scythe, and swirls of flame followed her deadly blade. Lira tried to fire at two others, hitting one in the sword arm, and missed the other.

Asheron appeared behind Miggen and sliced the dark steel blade across his neck. Blood splattered out from the visceral wound all over Lira's arms as Miggen hit the ground like a stone. Asheron disappeared and reappeared behind Kayden and cracked her across her face with his gauntlet, smashing her to the ground. He disappeared time and time again, only appearing to strike from the shadows.

Two soldiers broke through them and rushed at Lira. She backed away and attempted to shoot one with an arrow, only to have her bow knocked aside and a club strike her temple with a mighty blow. She toppled to the ground, barely seeing the others fighting for their lives as she slipped out of consciousness. As her vision faded to black, the scent of Miggen's blood filled her nostrils, and her headache disappeared into nothing.

Chapter Three

Blaze of Treason

Saul Bromaggus

It was days from Saul's graduation from the Chromata military training program, yet he still felt more uneasy than ever before. His father planned to challenge their ruler's laws, and treason was a burnable offense. He shook his head and ruffled his thick, short black hair, trying to remember his father's fate, to calm himself.

Saul was at the top of his class. No comrade could beat him. He was his father's son—strong, stubborn and respectful—though Saul was not quite as quick of wit. *Wit doesn't matter when blades clash,* he thought.

It was on a night soon to come that he would travel before the Oracles in Hero's Fall. They bestowed a fate from the gods unto the Broken and their kin. They appeared as markings upon the dominant arm of the initiate and determined their path. The markings came with the color of his warrior form, a race he would act upon, and a symbol resembling his fate within it—*victory or death*, Saul thought. Most importantly, the markings came with the mark of their god. The Oracles' predictions were determined by powers handed down from the gods themselves.

The symbols were imprinted onto the initiate's fighting arm in a specific color, one of three. Red, blue, or yellow—the slayer, the protector, or the mediator. Saul looked to his left arm, wondering what kind of markings he would soon receive. Every Broken had a burning desire for their fate. It showed them the path. Without it, they wandered aimlessly through life—broken, as their name implied. Saul wished to find his purpose. In his fate he would have it.

The highest mark on the shoulder was of their god. Saul knew his would be the one he prayed to: Gadora, the goddess of storms. Her mark was that of three encircling, clashing winds.

Just below the shoulder was the subject, the one he would protect, slay, or mediate with. The symbol of the gods represented any race—Human, Broken, even Dragon. The Dragon's mark hadn't been seen much in a millennium. *Many who bore the Dragonslayer mark died mysteriously in the blanket of night*, Saul recalled. The Dragon Obelreyon ruled over them with a mighty claw.

The final marking was the outcome, the fate. It resembled the blade or the drop of blood—*victory and death*. One either succeeded and lived through his path or died for it.

Saul rose from his hard bed and readied his gear for the trip to Hero's Fall. But first, he was to see his father address Obelreyon. Many unusual laws had been put into place as of late. The Dragon claimed that the god that he followed was the most powerful, and that his laws would be enforced. Some were still able to worship their own gods, as long as they followed the laws in place.

Saul was concerned about what his father would say. He would not challenge him, as were the ways of the clans. He could only watch as his father made his own fate. It was treason to reject your superior's orders—especially the dragon's. They were publicly executed to make an example. *My father is no traitor*. He felt for his father but did not waver. He was a proud Broken, strong and unyielding. His path was with the military in service of a god who favored battle, glory, and victory. The Broken worshipped the Glories, four gods associated with the elements, each with their own clan and city surrounding Chromata.

After strapping on his battered, scorched armor, Saul picked up his blade and shield from the table and walked out of his room. It was a small space, granted to him by the military, but it was all he needed.

He sauntered to the keep under the cover of the forests of the northern Vale. It was filled with a vast forest of blackwood maples, broad oaks, and strong, russet-brown pines, with roots as thick as a man's torso, and seas of leaves that changed color with the season. When the season of earth came, the leaves would turn from green to red, orange to yellow, before they fell for the season of air that came after. In the southern Vale, there were plentiful forests of elm and Sirilius trees, the forest floor filled with brush varying from thick, sharp brambles to poisonous frockwoods.

Saul looked to the canopies far overhead, and the sky could be seen well enough. Saul passed between various barracks and training yards. He heard the clash of steel and yelling of Captains for their men to keep up or gain more scars. *I have earned many in my training,* Saul thought cheekily.

Obelreyon's keep was a massive temple over a hundred feet high. It was rectangular beast, coming to a point at the top with a sculpture of an eye, called the God's Point. The temple was big enough to house the Dragon himself on the upper floor, where he sat on his observing perch in the council room.

The keep was surrounded by guard towers hung with banners of a lidless eye on a field of violet. Archers and magicians stood at the tips. Smaller Broken were fit to be archers and magicians; Saul resented them. The small were weak, resorting to magic for power. *They aren't brave enough to fight us with weapons.*

The front of the keep was covered with intricate carvings depicting various victories of gods and Dragons. One even showed Obelreyon's ancestors defeating the old lords of Kathynta. The damned Dragon was young for his race, yet ruled over them as if he knew all.

"Where do you think you're going?" one of the keep guards said. He wore the bronze armor of the Vale guard, scaled in some places and chained in others. Grikoth, one of Obelreyon's grunts, bore the color blue, in the form of a Broken and a blade. His hatred for Saul's father trickled down. Saul had no time for blundering or arguing.

"To my father's audience. Get out of the way before I break your skull. I know the law."

Grikoth coughed up a laugh. "If you come anywhere near my command, I'm putting you in hell, whelp," Grikoth shot back. The guard stood aside, seeing the other guard's sharp expression. They both believed in Urikar, another god thriving through battle on the seas.

Saul walked by and bumped into them. He didn't apologize, as they didn't deserve it. The halls were lined with paintings and carvings of gods, each in valiant poses or slaying enemies. Statues of ancient weapons, pieces of armor, and other relics on pedestals stood in the center of the halls. Saul felt bolstered in their presence.

Saul saw a powerful figure standing at the base of the center stairwell that led to the council chambers above. His stance was proper and wide, as always. His chin was broad with a slight grimace, skin a deep smoke grey as many of the Broken, with eyes dark and almond shaped. Blood ran strong. "Good day, Father."

"I appreciate that you have come to attend," his father said.

"Father, I would advise against what you're about to do."

"Straight to the point." His father chuckled but gave a stern gaze. "I will not sit idle while he abolishes our freedom."

"You'll be *killed*!" Saul gripped his father's right arm. It was less brawny in his age, and he spent less time in training and more at the council over the previous years. His arm bore yellow markings with three clashing winds, the mark of the Broken—a cross through a horizontal line—and the upturned blade. *He will live*, Saul thought. He couldn't bear the death of a second parent, but Saul took solace in his father's markings.

"I do my duty. I refuse to betray my beliefs. Neither should you." His father placed a hand on Saul's shoulder. "You will be granted your marking soon. Remember, you must follow your own path no matter the mark." His father smiled, and he *never* smiled. "Your mother always saw greatness in you. A strength many never receive. You follow your own beliefs—not his, not theirs—yours. Do you understand?"

Of course I do, Saul thought. "I will, Father." Since his mother passed in the wars ten years prior, his father became obsessed with the failings of fate, and whether they truly existed or not.

His father nodded, stood up straight, and walked up the council stairs. Before they arrived at the top, his father turned to say one thing. "It takes great strength to stand stoically while one watches their father address a Dragon. It takes more to run. Don't forget that."

As Saul ascended the stairs after him, he heard Obelreyon's guttural voice speaking in the Dragon's native tongue. All Broken knew it, as orders were given in it.

"Why have you come before me, Bromaggus? What is it you want?" the Dragon said. The light from the outside seemed to dim by Obelreyon's dark scales. Saul heard the Dragon could drain the strength of any enemy at will with just the touch of a claw. His eyes were darker than the deepest night; Saul felt that the souls he burned were trapped inside them. The number of traitors he killed gained him the name 'The Shatterer of Souls.' Even his scales could cut flesh, each as hard as the blade Saul carried. There was once a small uprising against the dastardly dragon; each blade and spear thrown and swung shattered against the might of the steely scales, and each Broken was burned by the dragon's breath or eviscerated by a single swing of a claw.

Saul's father stood tall, shoulders back, with his hands open to show confidence and respect for the one he spoke to. He saluted Obelreyon with a fist to his center and bowed. He returned to his open stance shortly after.

"Lord Obelreyon, I ask your reasons for changing our ways."

"You need not know my reasons for these laws, Bromaggus. It is not your place to question orders."

Whispers echoed from the other observers in the hall. There was unrest in the clans, and Saul's father wished to relieve it. It was his purpose.

The Council of Fangs stood around the outer rim of the room. Each were the head-of-clan, each worshipping a different god. The ceiling came to a large oval dome at the top, extending to a longer edge—the open air of Obelreyon's perch. There were venomstone stands on either side of the long room. The entire council was present: The leaders of the Kannakash, Urikar, and Yggranda clans, and the final attendee being his father, Greln Bromaggus, of the Gadora clan. Saul walked to the east side and sat atop the stone seats.

"My Lord, we all worship gods which proclaim glory in battle. We have not seen war in ten years, since our defeat. Why must we follow the words of a new god we have not yet seen?" Saul's father spoke in the guttural language of the Dragons, with rough sounds of the throat and deep, orotund turns of the tongue.

The Dragon's eyes narrowed, his lengthy neck pulling back slightly. "The new god is more powerful than we have ever known. He brings glory and victory though the defeat of the Renalian kingdoms. We work with them to achieve our goal. Do *not* question me."

The Dragon turned away, but Saul's father did not back down. "You wish for us to work with beings of chaos? They will not bring us victory. Their tactics will bring us defeat! We should take our forces to Renalia on our own wood and steel! Or to the Serpent's Plateau, or the Torch of Lathyria! I refuse to let us align with beings we cannot trust, let alone violate our ways and betray us!"

Saul steeled himself for what was to come. To show emotion during a moment of disgrace brought execution. *No, Father you will have victory, your fate was determined,* Saul reassured himself.

Obelreyon turned swiftly. His tail crashed into the side of the room and shook the walls, along with every resident of the hall. "Do not disobey me, wretch! I will burn you alive if you question me again. The god Lornak has promised us Renalia and more, if we bring our armies to him. We must make sacrifices of those who are unwilling, so that we may survive! That is what the war was for, and that is what you will do!"

"The war ten years past was a wasteful massacre. The tactics were foolish, and we must plan differently! This god, Lornak, demands that we challenge the Isles again? The west of Renalia may writhe in rebellion, but that does not make this any more foolish. We must focus on the Glories, not some other God who claims to ally with us now! I must protest!"

"Would you die for it and disgrace your name? Your *family's* name?" Obelreyon roared. "Soon will be our time to strike! When his harbinger breaks into this plane, we will take the war to the and strike against them from both sides without warning! Would you rather seek failure, or victory? What do you say, Councilor? *Does that satisfy your concerns?*"

Without a beat of a heart, Saul's father retorted. "Not in the slightest! We have been ruled for centuries by the Dragons, and we respect the laws. This new war—joining with a god we do not know—I cannot support it. Lornak has been known as a Lord of Chaos, the opposite of what we represent as a people!" Though Urikar and Kannakash dabbled in chaotic actions in combat, and that was respected—the other two clans did not share this action.

Obelreyon smashed his claw onto the keep's floor, cracking the stones beneath. "Stay your words, ingrate!" The Dragon let out a mighty roar which caused the hall itself to shudder. "You will follow my orders, and that of Lornak, else you commit treason. *Do you understand?*" Obelreyon yelled.

His father's face showed nothing. No surprise, no fear. "You choose for your survival. I choose ours. We should not worship this god of yours." He straightened his posture, and pounded his fist to his center once more, and kept it there.

"Then by your treason, you burn." Obelreyon inhaled sharply and blew a column of black fire down the hall, between the stands. The inferno engulfed Greln's unmoving body. He did not scream or cry—but stood strong in his salute until his charred bones fell from the weight the air. Only silence followed.

Saul sat still. He did not know his fate. Fire and rage burned within him but refused to let it take claim of his body. He cared for his father—he raised Saul alone since the war ten years past and taught him nearly everything he knew. Now Saul was alone.

His different way of teaching young Broken in the Gadora clan caught him with criticism, but he remained stalwart. He was respected and loved by his people. Saul loved him as well, despite rarely saying the words. He wondered what would happen to him, as he was the son of a traitor, now. *Will I be accepted into the military, or executed?* His father was no traitor to his people, but a harbinger of things to come. *His marking showed victory, but this...*

Obelreyon turned his dark gaze to Saul. "What say you, boy?" he rumbled. "Are you prepared to die for your beliefs?" Every eye in the room turned to him.

A long silence followed as Saul struggled with the thought. To him, fate was everything. Now he saw fate fail before his eyes through his father—just as his mother's seemed false. *Are the fate the gods grant us false?* he wondered. *No, that's impossible.* His father mediated for so long between the clans, perhaps his fate was fulfilled. *But even then, he stood up to the Dragon in the name of his fate, and he burned before my eyes.*

Saul rose to his feet, staring into the dragon's dark, abyssal eyes. *My father made his choice. I told him not to commit treason. I must do what any Broken would do. I should fight and kill the Dragon if I could for what he did. But my father would curse me from the afterlife if I threw my life away.* "I graduate in four days from the academy by the word of the Oracles, my Lord," he said poignantly. "My fate lies with them, not with my father."

He denounced his father in front of the council. It was treason to say otherwise. *This is my only option.* It was, but he hated himself for it. Most of all, he hated the damned black-scaled beast who sentenced him.

The Dragon let out a guttural chuckle. "Well said." He turned away, looking over the barracks and the smoke of distant forges. "Your words are honorable. I will allow you to undergo the ritual. Following this, you will be exiled across the Fissure, no matter their prediction."

Saul flinched forward and barely restrained himself. He wanted to scream. Draw a blade and leap at the scaled abomination of a ruler.

My words meant nothing. I chose to disregard my father to follow the Dragon, and for what? To be exiled, the highest dishonor. A Broken found their greatest honor in combat and victory, or in death for that purpose. To be exiled was to be ejected from their ways, to be disgraced publicly. It was a vile Dragon's revenge on a man who now lay dead before them. Saul hated the Dragon's change of their traditions as many had, but all feared Obelreyon's power. The only way one could overthrow a leader was to defeat him in combat. Without another word, Saul stormed out of the council chamber with fire in his eyes.

Exiled across the fissure. Only death awaited him there.

Saul silently chose to accept his fate. He would not end his own life, as some Broken would. Saul was proud. He was proud of his father, proud of himself, and too proud to exit his current situation by his own sword like a coward. He nodded to his ruler and stormed out of the hall. As he descended the grand staircase, he heard Obelreyon yelling commands and threats to the council to trust in his orders, or they would suffer the same fate.

Saul worried for his comrades, as the new laws restricted their worship, tactics, and beliefs. In the Neck, religion was free, but some of the seven cities were lawless.

Despicable, Saul thought. *Exiled, I cannot believe it. I hope the Oracles will bestow some fate upon me that will guide me. My father lived for many years as a mediator, and his fate was true for a time, especially during the wars.* Saul even questioned the possibility of fates being false, seeing his father die.

The thought of the flame made him wince; the flame that took his closest friend, his father, away.

He was furious at the decision. His face showed no kindness any longer, only furrowed brow and bared teeth. He bumped into the guards on his way out, uncaring. It was not worth his effort, nor his time. He stormed back to the Vale barracks to gather his things. He packed a massive rucksack filled with rations, supplies, and other necessities for travel. In the military they learned survival skills.

An initiate was taken to the middle of the deep Vale and left there with none but their wits for a fortnight. They either survived, or they didn't.

"Damn it, damn it, *damn it*!" Saul yelled, pounding the stone wall with his maul, cracking and breaking the bricks. "You wretch, why did you have to go against him?" he cursed his father. Now that his father was dead, his bloodline ended when Saul did. He slammed at the wall again and didn't stop until his lungs were burning. *Do I go to learn my fate?*

Will it be false? He dropped the maul with a clatter of stone and wood, and heard movement in the next room.

"What's goin' on over there?" a gruff voice asked. Grenneth, his training partner, appeared at his door. Multiple scars shone in the flickering torchlight, showing the past, and their sparring. He was a hard bastard, but respectful as all hell. He had no markings from the Oracles yet.

"My father addressed Obelreyon, the bloody idiot. Challenged his ways, and was burned for it. Now, I'm getting exiled after my graduation." In the Vale, there were only Broken. His people. Across the fissure, there were a multitude of peoples. Past that laid the Serpent's Plateau—where the vicious, traitorous enemy of his people lived. The Hydris.

"Quit bein' a whelp about it. You want me to pity you?" Gren asked, stone-faced.

The Broken showed little emotion, especially those such as fear, despair, and sadness. If one revealed it, they were seen as weak. Saul's father rejected that view in recent years, and he was only met with contention.

"No, I do not. You asked. I told. Don't make assumptions, or I'll make those training sessions real," Saul growled. Grenneth was a damned good training partner, and a good ally to have in battle, but he was no friend.

Grenneth was taken aback. He relented. "Guess yer right."

Saul's mind was somewhere else, and his curiosity could not be tamed. "What do you know about this 'Lornak?'" Saul asked. The Dragon spoke of him, yet Saul knew nothing about the deity. He knew the Dragon would press Lornak's ways on them, and Saul refused to give up his own beliefs.

Grenneth grumbled and shrugged. "New god. People say he's from Renalia across the sea. Tried to take over for his own glory but failed."

Saul did not know anything about the Renalian gods. He preferred gods of the Vale, who favored fair combat. *Why did Obelreyon go to such great lengths to gain his favor?* He did not know what Obelreyon's plans were—and did not wish to find out.

"His power was sealed away 'cross the sea, but the Dragon's sudden worship says different."

Power does not mean conquering, his father told him. *The greatest warriors protect rather than rule the weak.* His father was adamant that killing wasn't the only honorable deed. *I won't forget your wisdom, father. I won't.*

"Dunno what to think. Don't like it. The tribes don't like it, none of 'em. But they fear Dragons more. My clan'll fight to the end—our god and ways are our biggest assets."

"I'm not afraid of him," Saul boasted.

"*Should* be. He burned yer father alive." Grenneth's words were without honey.

Saul cringed at the comment. "Don't make me cut you down." *No one insults my father.*

Grenneth's dark almond eyes didn't shift, nor did his face. "If ya can't handle it, that's not my problem. Ready for the Oracles?"

"I am." Their word determined a broken's fate in battle. It gave Saul guidance and purpose, and the thought soothed him.

"What'd'you think they'll predict?" Grenneth asked.

Many felt their fate before they went to the Oracles. Saul knew what he wanted—the Dragon's head. He steeled himself for the audience. He knew his father was subject to fate, but he now felt the recent event determined his. He was still furious. In his anger, he thought, *I will be a slayer, and I will slay Obelreyon myself. Live to do it, or die trying.* "I don't know." He wished for the fate of a Dragon slayer, chosen for victory.

"Guess we'll find out. Gods be with ya," Gren said, saluting Saul.

"And with you." Saul returned the salute.

"I'm sure I'll see ya again, you stubborn wretch. If exile won't kill you, I might have to." Grenneth was a man of his word, and Saul wasn't sure how to take the comment. Gren was not the most humorous Broken around.

"You can dream. Remember, in training, I went easy." Saul chuckled in his face. He walked by him in his armor and a rucksack over his shoulder.

Grenneth laughed back, "So did I." He gave a sly grin.

Stay alive, Gren, Saul thought, as he headed to the stables to ride to Hero's Fall. Without his father, fate was all Saul felt he had left. Saul clenched his fists, thinking of his father overtaken by black flame once more. He wanted revenge. What he needed was a means to get it. *Perhaps the gods will give me guidance, or a way to bring vengeance.* He would get it no matter the cost.

He was ready to learn his fate.

Chapter Four

The Failed Hero

Lira Kaar

The putrid smell of rats and defecate caused Lira to cringe in disgust. Focusing her eyes, iron bars surrounded her, along with the vague small frame of Kayden and her mane of hair. "Ugh, what happened?" she said aloud. Her mind was foggy and throbbing with pain. She noticed her head was bandaged from wounds she gained during the one-sided battle they fought.

Kayden leaned against the bars, arms crossed, mouth drawn in displeasure. "About time you woke up, princess," she scoffed. "We got the shit kicked out of us, that's what happened."

Lira glanced around to the dark walls of surrounding her. *Is it a prison?* Looking around, she recognized the walls for some reason. They were blank, near-black stones, only lit by the dim torches at either end of the hall. Slow drops of water trickled down the walls, and the air sweeping through the chamber seemed to howl.

She touched her head, feeling it ache from the club still. She wondered how much time passed. It seemed like less than a day. "I had the strangest dream." Within moments the vision was gone;

she only remembered one thing: a figure with violet eyes saying one thing, over and over: forget your brother.

"Well good for you for having a nice dream. We've been here awhile. Must've used magic to keep us under for travel."

Lira frowned. "I happen to think dreams mean something."

Her rough-willed friend returned with her own sharp eye. "I don't know what you saw, but we were knocked out at Rogan's manor, and woke up here. As far as I'm concerned, dreams mean nothing." She crossed her arms and sighed.

"But a voice told me—"

"Do you have any proof?" Kayden said with a hint of disdain. She rubbed her thumb along her forefinger, asking for more than beliefs.

"No, but I—"

"Then stop worrying about it. We have bigger problems right now," Kayden cut Lira off.

Lira rubbed her head, feeling it fire with pain once more. *With the information we found, I can only wonder what we're in for.* "What's going to happen to us?" Vesper, Domika, and Magnus were nowhere to be found in the hall.

During the mission, it was almost as if Asheron waited for them to arrive. She thought they were dead for sure, but Asheron wanted them alive. "Where are the others?" she asked.

"Stop asking stupid questions. Do I look like I know?" she snapped. Her sharp amber eyes glared at Lira for a moment, then went back to scanning the hall.

After giving Lira a moment, with a softer glance, she said, "I've heard screams from upstairs. We're probably gonna get tortured," Kayden said. She blew her hair from her face, revealing olive skin streaked with bloodstains that shone in the torchlight. "Miggen's dead."

Lira gasped. She barely remembered the spray of blood from Miggen's neck. His dry blood still covered her arms. She wondered if he had family, or if it could have been avoided. Since the others weren't there, she wondered where they were, fearing the worst.

Having witnessed the death of her ally, Lira slightly regretted joining the rebellion. One mission and she was already in jail, and one of them died. She didn't know much about combat, and her healing was less than satisfactory. Kayden was battle-hardened and tough; Lira felt they had nothing in common at all.

She looked around to the plain, damp stones of the prison wall, missing the forests outside. She tried to forget the jail for a moment and thought of the peaceful chirping of birds, the calm winds, and the light rustling of leaves in her hometown of Ordana. It was hidden among the deep forest further north in the Loughran region.

She remembered spending her days with her brother, running about and playing swordsmen with sticks—although, she was never very good at it. As an adult, she moved to Solmarsh in the south with Noren, to live close to her dad living in Orinde Monastery. She missed her brother. *Gods, keep him safe.*

It had only been a little longer than a fortnight since he was arrested and moved from the jail. *I hope he isn't involved with what we discovered at the manor.*

She shook her head and ran her fingers along her hair, trying to keep her mood up. She thought of the places she wanted to travel. She had been sheltered for most of her life, unaware of what was outside of the forests. The northern lands were behind the border—frigid, but supposedly beautiful. Strong cities built with stone that were filled with orderly citizens.

The southern bonebound gate led to the eastern deserts of Zenato, an expanse of golden-white sands with cities filled with every kind of people one could imagine. There were so many places in the land Lira wished to see, but she was stuck in the prison of Loughran. She never felt alone, until her brother passed. Now, she felt truly alone. Kayden hadn't said much of anything since they met in Wolf Camp.

"Are you worried?" Lira asked.

Kayden didn't seem worried; her personality was adamant to begin with. "Stop badgering me. I don't know you, so stop asking me questions." Her eyes didn't stop flashing from place to place. The cell. The guard at the back. The stairwell. The door of their cell. Lira. The Lock.

Lira didn't know what to say. Usually, people were more open where she came from, and she was just trying to be polite. Kayden was a bit hurtful. Lira wasn't used to these kinds of situations; after all, this was her first mission as a Scion of Fire.

For a moment, a smirk perked at the edges of Kayden's lips. Then it vanished. "Damn it, we need to get the hell out of here. I don't like the dark, I don't like shitty stone floors, and I don't like being caged *up!*" She bashed her arms on the bars. The clattering bellowed through the halls. Her eyes looked toward the guard at the end, as if watching for a reaction.

"Hey! Will you shut up down there, or do I have to come and teach you how to?" the guard yelled from his desk by the spiral stairwell to the upper jails. It was a newly repurposed prison, it seemed. The walls were weak and cracked, and it almost felt like the ceiling was going to collapse.

"*Hmph*. Drake," Kayden mumbled.

Lira hadn't heard many use such a word where she came from, as it was a serious insult. Ever since the Draconia enslaved the realm over two millennia ago, to call someone a drake was to imply that they were a horrible being. Lira wouldn't dare use it.

"Why are you so angry? I was only trying to be polite." Lira pouted. Kayden just scowled back, arms still crossed. Lira was concerned for the others, but Kayden didn't seem to care. *How could she be so self-focused?* Lira pondered. *Doesn't she worry about the others, especially while they're being tortured?* Lira scowled at her this time, but quickly lost the look when Kayden's eyes met hers.

"Listen, princess, I have more to worry about than being in this jail. We have three missing, and someone set us up. It could have been *you*. Was it? Huh?" Kayden grabbed Lira by the neckline, and quickly let her fall to the floor as she stared back to the other cells.

She may be right, Lira thought. It was awfully coincidental that they knew where and when to strike. *Kayden couldn't possibly have thought it was me, could she?*

"It wasn't me, I swear! I wouldn't do such a thing!" Lira rose to her feet and leaned forward.

Kayden mocked her with a laugh. "Take it easy, princess. You're way too innocent to be a traitor. If you are, you're one damn good actor." She curtsied daintily.

Lira kept her mouth shut. She was trying to be nice, but Kayden only rejected her words. *How could she be so mean?* she wondered. Kayden came from the deserts of the east. Lira didn't know anything else of her past, but she knew people from there were a little less than well mannered.

The screams above stopped. Powerful, steeled footsteps and the dragging of cloth could be heard from the stairwell. Asheron emerged clad in his dark armor. She barely remembered the fight, but recalled him moving across the battlefield at a rapid pace, using the shadows as his aide. He would walk into darkness, disappear and reappear behind them, making swift strikes with the flat of his blade, while they all swung at nothing but air. The power of the shadows was surely with him. He came to them with three knights, who brought Lira's allies in tow. The knights dragged them into separate cells before returning to the stairs.

Asheron spoke to the guard before walking over. The guard asked him when they would finish fixing the jail floor, mentioning its renovation. Another armored individual emerged from the stairs—similar height and build to Asheron, but his armor was a bloody crimson.

Grandis Prison, she recalled. She'd caught word that an old, abandoned temple of Shiada was under renovations recently—to become Grandis prison. A temple she once visited.

Without answering, Asheron sauntered over to the cells, the crimson soldier close behind. "I see you're finally awake." His icy, resounding voice echoed throughout the hall. His armor was a pure black that seemed to suck the light from the room. His helmet fully covered his head crenellations all along the front, the only gaps for his eyes, which seemed like an abyss with no end.

"What do you want?" Kayden growled as she shook the bars, clenching her teeth.

"Aggressive," he began, chuckling.

The crimson knight spoke up from behind. "I'll have fun with you, little one. We'll see each other—soon." He let out a deep laugh before turning to leave. Asheron simply turned and walked away, his knights in tow.

"Wait," Lira rushed to the bars, and called out to Asheron. "Is this Grandis Prison?"

Asheron stopped as if time paused with him. Turning his head, he simply nodded. "I prefer to call it a 're-origination center.' To *convince* individuals to change their ways." Turning back, he and his soldiers passed up the stairs and out of sight, metal clattering on the stone.

The torchlight brightened once more, and Magnus's worriful eyes met Lira's.

Lira crept up to the bars. "What happened to you three?" Lira asked.

"A shakedown, my lady. Soon they may grow more severe," he said plainly. Stretching his arms, Magnus winced. His sharp grey nails were broken and bloody from the torture. Lira was scared to think she and Kayden were next.

Hopefully we can get out. The others seem afraid, but Kayden doesn't seem worried at all, Lira thought.

Vesper was in the fetal position. His thick, grey moustache and beard were askew. "I cannot take that again," he whimpered. "It was as if they were inside my head, using my own nightmares against me. Who do they think they are, using these tricks?"

Domika was huddled in a ball at the corner of her cell. Her shoulders shook as she quietly sobbed.

The group glanced at each other and exchanged shrugs, except Kayden, who scratched her shoulder and winced.

I can't sit here. I can't be caught like the other prisoners. I won't find my brother if I become one of them, Lira thought. She stood up, and nudged Kayden. "We have to get out of here. We're next, and who knows what else will happen to us." She tried to whisper it as confidently as possible, not to embarrass herself.

Kayden raised a brow, and a sly grin formed along with it. "And do you have a plan?" she whispered back.

Lira scratched her head. "I thought you might know how to get out, because—"

"I'm a criminal?" Kayden chuckled. She tapped her foot for a few seconds, looked at the guard, and sighed. "All right, let's get this over with. I've probably pissed the guard off enough. Stand back," she whispered. She repeatedly rattled the bars, clanking and clattering. The guard attempted to ignore it, but after a minute of constant shaking and general annoyance, he frustratingly rushed over.

"What? What *is* it?" he asked.

Kayden's gaze on him was softer than Lira had seen. It was strange, and a little frightening.

"I'm lonely," she pouted. Her tone was soft as silk, and she stuttered her words. "I get really anxious in the dark." She took her hands through the bars and fidgeted them nervously.

"Hey, get away," he pulled back cautiously. "You didn't seem like this before."

"I'm scared."

Even Lira knew better than that.

"I don't know how to handle these situations alone. Please, can you at least put me in the upper cells? I hear they have light up there. I'll tell them anything! *Please*!" She drew her lower lip in and bit it. A tear formed at the corner of her left eye as she stared the knight down.

Until then, Kayden had been anything *but* sad, frightened, or lonely.

The guard shook his head abruptly and turned around. "No. I can't do that, you little witch." The guard clenched his fists. "I don't like prisoners trying to mess with me, you little—"

Suddenly, Kayden leapt onto the bars and wrapped a thin, metallic string around the guard's neck she'd hidden beneath her mass of hair. The knight struggled for his blade, drew it, and swung back toward her head. She deftly dodged around it but took two small slices on her left forearm. He quickly passed out and slid to the ground.

"Damn it," Kayden growled, gripping her bloody arm. "Well, that was easy. What'd I say, princess?" She snorted a laugh as she wrapped a bit of her dirty linen clothes around her sliced arm. She quietly picked the keys off the guard and unlocked her cell, carefully snuck the door open, and unlocking the others.

"Oh thank you, thank you!" Domika exclaimed, jumping at Kayden with a hug.

"Get off of me, you idiot!" Kayden whispered, shoving her away. "Be quiet. They'll hear us."

Lira carefully tiptoed down the hallway and noticed a door beside the guard's desk. The spiral staircase to the upper floor sat across from it. She moved to open it but stopped short. *What if there are more guards?* she thought. Lira was cooperating with a jailbreak, something she thought she'd never do. Kayden walked right past her and opened the door carefully. "Kayden, wait! You shouldn't go in there."

"Hey, here's our stuff. What a bunch of morons for leaving it here," she whispered with a laugh. She began to rummage through the chest to find her things. Kayden didn't seem to have much care for caution sometimes. "What? I heard them talking about storage while you were napping."

Kayden quickly threw her outfit back on over her tattered clothes. It was sleek but loose fitting, a dark russet tunic and long pants, with an old, tattered teal wool scarf around her neck. She strapped on her deep black leather armor lined with dark silver studs, which ran from the top of her neck to her boots. She picked up her two light blades in a sheath and fastened them to her belt, along with her throwing knives.

Lira went in after Kayden and carefully picked up her light brown leather jerkin, then her bow, and held it close. It was given to her by her brother before he passed, along with her book of divine magic and silver ring. She turned to Magnus. "Please be careful, your armor is a bit—"

"Clunky," Kayden butted in. "Keep it down, or I'll slice you." She held her one of her blades at him.

He slowly ran his fingers through his thick hair and rubbed his rough-stubbled chin. He was a large man; broad in the shoulders, but not in intelligence, it seemed. He didn't talk much, and always looked like his thoughts concerned simple fare. Lira and Domika clumsily helped him assemble his steel armor, as Kayden took it upon herself to be the lookout. He grunted and winced as they helped him put it on. He was still weak from the torture he underwent at the hands of the knights. He had burns, bruises, and multiple cuts, at least on his hands. He'd clearly gotten the worst of it.

"Thank you." Magnus smiled weakly at Lira and Domika. He strapped two swords in scabbards to his left hip, and his heavy steel kite shield to his back. Domika threw on her golden yellow dress, flowing below a cover of chainmail, and picked up her scythe. She was dangerous but oddly beautiful on the battlefield, spinning, almost as if dancing while she sliced her enemies. Lira and Domika nodded at each other, then noticed that someone was missing.

Vesper was nowhere to be found.

"*Where is that idiot?*" Kayden whispered harshly.

He popped up from behind the chest wearing his long, pale violet robe. His beady blue eyes examined his belongings carefully. "My my, these people are so clumsy with my things. Do they not understand each material must be kept separate, and this could cause a problem with finding things in the future? Why would they—"

He glanced to the group to get their agreement, only to receive looks of irritation, bewilderment, and shushing motions.

Lira felt bad. Vesper seemed to be an orderly person, and he didn't understand that they had to be quiet. He didn't even seem affected by the torture anymore, and Lira found it *very* peculiar. He had a one-track mind, which may have needed a shake.

"What? What did I do to offend you? I was only speaking about the disorganization of these foolhardy knights. Do they not understand the importance of organization? How can they not comprehend these important ideas when all they do is sit in this prison and wait?"

Kayden quickly walked to him, grabbed him by the neckline to pull him in. "Shut *up*," she hissed, clenching her teeth. Panicked, his eyes shot around person to person, focused on Kayden again, and nodded feverishly. She let go of his robe as he gasped for breath. Kayden grabbed her left forearm, the cloth now laced with red.

Lira caught her letting out a brief whimper before returning to her steely demeanor. "Here, let me help," she said, reaching for Kayden's arm.

Kayden pulled her arm away. "Your magic doesn't work here, princess," she said.

Lira frowned. Tough or no, now Kayden was just being silly. "And you are going to continue bleeding. It will fester if you don't let me sew this up. Just because I heal with magic doesn't mean I don't know how to treat a wound. Since you haven't tried to yet, you probably don't know how to sew a cut with one hand." Lira was surprised with herself; she normally didn't stand up to people like her. She held out her hand and stared into Kayden's sharp amber eyes. "Arm."

Surprisingly, Kayden sighed, looked away, and held out her bloody arm. Lira pulled out her kit of herbs and tools and began working away.

Vesper, Domika, and Magnus organized what belongings they could find and looked around while they waited. Lira deftly sewed the wound and treated it with some natural remedies she had in her bag. "There, all done. How does that feel?" She smiled sweetly.

"Better," Kayden said coolly. She looked down at her arm. "Uh, thanks." She seemed reluctant to show gratitude, but Lira took that as a huge compliment and secretly congratulated herself.

Most would have found Kayden irritating and difficult to be around. Lira's limits were definitely being tested, but her father's words rang through her head. *'Everyone has a story, Lira,'* he would say. *'Some people may be evil, but some have simply had an arduous life. There is a difference.'* She missed her father, now a monk in the Orinde monastery. It was south of her home in Solmarsh, and he left after her mother Aya passed years ago—*'To live in peace and harmony.'* She went to visit when she could, since he didn't leave the monastery much. She still regretted being away when her mother passed.

Lira longed to see him again, since he was one of the few family she had left. Her parents moved to the Loughran forests from the Deserts before Lira and Noren were born, and it was only the four of them—or three, at least, for now.

Kayden smirked devilishly, ready to move. Each person looked at each other as if they'd just ran into battle without a plan or any gear. Lira contemplated the situation. She knew there were guards upon guards above. *A deathtrap, clearly*, she thought. *Sure, they're good at fighting, but we were all caught before.*

"Well, do you have a plan?" Domika snapped at Kayden.

"Shut it. I'm thinking." She eyed the stairs. "Could be a lot of guards up there—"

They sat below the surface in the lower dungeon of Grandis prison, a repurposed...

"*Temple*," Lira said aloud, astonished.

"Pardon, my lady?" Magnus asked. Everyone turned to her curiously.

"Temple," she said again. "Grandis is being renovated from a temple I worshipped at ages ago. There were pathways under the temple to a couple of nearby areas. They're changing it due to the higher volume of captives but sealing off the rest of the floor." She looked past the four to the stone wall behind them. She shoved the wall, and it didn't budge, but it just seemed out of place she could have sworn years ago, that the lower floors had a worship room…

"Lira, we shouldn't mess around," Domika whispered.

She didn't listen. With enough of a pull on one larger brick, she fell back to the stone floor, hurting her leg. The brick clattered to the ground, revealing darkness beyond.

Kayden crouched beside Lira, who watched the hole in awe. She slapped Lira's shoulder and shook her. "*Nice work*, princess. C'mon, let's move some bricks but be quiet."

Each of them removed large bricks until they could move through the wall. Lira was surprised that the roof itself didn't cave in, but the wall seemed recently worked on. A weathered hall lay before them.

"But my friend, what if there is no way out that way? What if they catch us? What if there is devious, dangerous magic in there?"

Lira shrugged. "There isn't, though It's been awhile so I may not know the pathways. It could be a dead end."

Everyone looked to her, then each other. Kayden held her chin high. "Well, I'm taking the chance. What do we have to lose?"

Chapter Five

Foreboding Visions

Jirah Mirado

The soft blaze of the large campfire in the center of Wolf Camp warmed Jirah's face as he gazed toward Gorkith Kildath with disdain. Gorkith's rough, stone-like skin did not move, emotionless as a Terran was. The shadow of the broad oaks and jilani trees surrounding them hooded the men like a cloak with their enormous leaves.

"I assure you, sir," Gorkith said in a gravelly, monotone voice. "I did what I was told. I gave the five of them the message from you, as you commanded." His face moved less than the mountains themselves; his character was bland, and his words were to the point. He was exactly what Jirah needed, for a grunt.

"Well then," Jirah began in a rough voice, "why don't you tell me why my five new recruits—" he bared his teeth, and his black hair burst with flames to match the campfire. "—Are *missing?*" he roared.

Gorkith showed no signs of guilt—or of anything else, for that matter.

The others nearby jumped back, gasping. Although they seemed afraid, Jirah knew it wasn't his size. He only stood at five feet and four inches. Then again, it may have been the curved, burning great blade upon his back that scared them, or the thick scar across his left brow. What he lacked in stature, he certainly made up in prowess. He paced around the fire. "They could be dead. What does that say about us? We're trying to give people hope, not take it away!" he yelled.

Only the blowing of humid winds, crackling of fire, and the crunch of leaves under his feet could be heard in response. Jirah chose this as a more forward camp, a few days' ride from the capital. There were several other camps: Bear, Mantis, Dragon, and more. Each camp housed about twenty or more at any one time, but some up to a hundred. He would always keep a few soldiers in the camp to be sure no one returned to an empty home. He kept the other camp locations secret from nearly everyone, ensuring that if there was a traitor in his ranks, only he and a select few knew the location of their specific camp.

Jirah was brash but intelligent, able to keep large numbers of names, places, and orders all in his mind, perfectly organized, and he prided himself on it. He was a man of lists. Direction.

Stephen Felkar stepped forward. "Um, sir?" He only gave an awkward smile that spelled anxiety. "Maybe they—aren't dead? They could be—uh—"

Jirah quickly snapped back to him, his pupils darkening. "What?" he growled. "Oh, you're right, Felkar. Maybe they're just being tortured." Without pause, he grabbed Stephen by the neck. "My sister is being *tortured!*" he yelled. The flame across his hair burned brighter with every harsh word. Jirah sighed and looked at the frightened members of his camp. His expression loosened, realizing what he had done. "I apologize. I don't like losing people.

Miss Kaar joined because her brother was taken. My sister was in that group as well." Jirah brooded over the situation.

He looked to the dense woods that surrounded the camp. The trees were as thick as two men, blackness on either side from impenetrable forest canopies. The moon shone bright upon the camp, and wolves howled frequently at its glow. His eyes returned to his allies in the camp, person-to-person, seeing the unsettled look in each pair of eyes.

"This doesn't make any sense. The mission was supposed to be simple." Gorkith remained still as a mountain. Jirah didn't believe it to be his fault. Gorkith was loyal, or so he suspected. Jirah had a great way with people, able to read their loyalties from the first meeting. "Gorkith, Felkar, Alexandra, Pali, fall in." Each member called lined up in front of him.

Jirah eyed each of them closely. "I want each of you to head to a different town near here. Gorkith, you scout near the capital. Felkar, you head to Wyrwood. Alex, to Solmarsh. Pali, to Deurbin. I want you to gather information on the five we lost. Find out what happened and where they went. If you can't find any information within one day, get back here as quickly as possible. As always, see if anyone needs our assistance."

"Yes, sir!" they said in unison before going off to gather their equipment.

The other members of the camp relaxed. It was as if he was back in the military again. *The grand old days*, he thought. He missed the times when things were simple, and Bracchus sat on the throne. He plopped back onto the ground and stared into the fire. The flames soothed him.

He prided himself on his ability to read people, assess their loyalties, and lead them. His many victories during the Dragon Obelreyon's attacks on Renalia proved as such. Times had changed now, and the good soldiers were forgotten. Now was a time for betrayers and cold-hearted warriors.

He himself felt betrayed by his kingdom. It all started with the sickness of the late king. Something never seemed right to him, about the way he fell ill at the young age of forty. It was unusual and said to be incurable. While Jirah gave little mind to the power of gods, he pondered what powers were at work. Only time would tell.

He considered this as he sat with the fire. It was his friend, his foe, and his guide. Seconds turned to minutes, minutes to hours. The cogs in his mind turned rapidly as he organized all the plans he spun. There were more than a few stings and rescue missions in play all across Loughran. The war stressed Jirah out even more.

Kieran, the late king's son, resided in the new northern nation of Orinas, and started a war to retake his throne. No argument with that. The heir to the throne was that of blood, and Kieran was the rightful one, despite his age. If anything, Bracchus' brother Rawling deserved it as well, but he separated from the others in the desert nation of Zenato. Jirah cringed whenever he thought of the deserts; he hadn't returned to that place since he left his mother and sister behind twelve years prior. Rawling, the lawless bastard, gave little care to the rights of the helpless. Now all three were in locked a war against one another, and the low-borns were caught in the middle of strife.

It was all a matter of age. In Loughran, most men and women were not married before eighteen. King Rawling the second, also called the Bloody, near three hundred years ago, was crowned at the age of sixteen. He ordered massacres of those that questioned him, executions for little more than a stolen loaf of bread, and war with any nation or people that did not worship him. After that, the Renalian King never took the throne until eighteen, which Kieran was one year off from. Many marriage customs followed; no man or woman would marry until then, at least, in the forests of Loughran where Jirah was now. The north and eastern provinces kept a younger age at times. Once they were grown they were married off—for politics, and sometimes in a rare case for love, man and woman both. A King or Queen would never marry until they were ready to rule, since more deviancy in history occurred in the royal family.

It was not unknown for a young King or Queen in history to bring others to their bed in the name of love—only to have the other woman or man executed by the church of Illadis in the name of the royal dignity. Marriage was sacred, and not to be trifled with. Jirah never married—even though he was pushed to. He never fancied a woman. He had felt something for another, but they hid it from everyone.

Jirah believed Kieran was ready to rule, as did most of the Northern provinces. However, Fillion Drayfus crowned himself Regent as did the other nobles in the west, and now he was King. It was all a ridiculous ploy. Kieran started a war with the nobles of the north at his back. The wars had only one benefit: while 'King' Drayfus raged a war against the other two, Jirah had an advantage. He took the chance and began this battle for his people. *But no matter what I do, innocents still get hurt. My newest recruits were imprisoned by my own folly,* Jirah thought.

But then, something strange came from the fire. It was an image of some kind. He saw five individuals standing before the late king, including Lira—*what sorcery is this? Am I hallucinating?* Bracchus Tirilin stood before them. *Is it a ghost?* Just as it appeared, the vision quickly faded.

"You may thank me at a later time, my friend," a thick voice announced. A large, dark-eyed man in a hooded cloak walked through the dark forest into the camp. His velvet cloak accentuated his powerful stature, and his hands sat behind his back. All members of the camp drew their blades and bows at the strange individual.

"What are you going to do, kill me? I am simply a messenger." He had solemn red eyes, a black scruffy beard, and an unsettlingly wide smile.

"To what do I owe this pleasure, Krogar?" Jirah waved for the others to calm themselves. Their blades lowered as Krogar Steeltooth approached the fire and gently sat down. "And what exactly was that all about?"

A sweetened smile touched Krogar's lips, and he raised an eyebrow devilishly. He was always one for tricks and behind-the-curtain ideas. "Oh, I just heard you needed a little help." He let out a hoarse chuckle as he warmed his hands on the fire, his pale white ring shining brightly from the flame. He never took it off, but Jirah knew he wasn't married to any woman or man. "You needed to know where they were, and I showed you." He took a tome out from his leather satchel and began to read quietly. The crackle of the fire soothed the tone.

"Find a partner to replace the imaginary one, Krogar?"

Krogar glanced up to the page with a raised brow.

Jirah pointed to his unity finger. "You never take it off."

With a plain face, Krogar said, "You never put your hair out."

Another game. "I can't," Jirah replied.

"Exactly." Krogar chuckled.

Jirah glanced around to the others, who looked confused and suspicious. Serafina shot him an especially worriful eye from her patrol by the forest path. Her smoky Rhaegan skin shone brightly from the fire, contrasting the black eyes. Jumpy people had their benefits in a rebellion.

Jirah glanced back to Krogar, never sure of what to expect from him. He was old member of the Renalian military, who too fought in the war against Obelreyon and his Broken armies. Jirah could never read him, which was incredibly irritating. He was an ally in some ways, and an enemy in others. His personality was unpredictable, a bane to Jirah, and he always seemed to do what was most fun.

"So you simply came to show me a vision? What exactly was going on there?" he asked.

"Oh, I'm not sure," his grin didn't fade. "I just thought I'd do you a favor." His rough hands carefully turned the fragile pages of his spell book as if they were handling a feather. "Come now my friend, I thought we were on the same side, here." He continued, "I do like the little forests here. The Sirilius trees smell of lavender and smooth sea salt. Don't you agree?"

Jirah frowned and ignored the attempt to change the subject. "How did you find us?"

Krogar let out a deep chuckle as the fire blew swiftly with the wind, giving his eye a sharp glint. "Knowledge is my trade, my friend." He smirked without looking up. "I love a soft campfire. The flickering of an inferno growing from kindling and embers, glittering off the blackwood maples and sifting in the air, helpless before the elements that oppose it. Yet all fear the power of fire, even shadows. Why do you think that is, my rebelling companion?"

"Because fires burn."

"Exactly. But what does a fire do when a water looms?" His eyes shone in the firelight, revealing nothing but curiosity.

It reminded Jirah of his friendship with Richard, a Frozelia— Humans touched with the power of water and ice. Rich was his first friend in the military, and the last he would want as an enemy. "Befriend the water," he replied.

Krogar smirked. "Oh, you are a wise man. It's funny, though, that you don't see two feet in front of you. That might cost you. Or will it benefit you? I'm not entirely sure." His smile gleamed from the fire. "A shift of balance is coming, my friend. Don't forget the obvious."

"Why don't you quit being so cryptic?" Sera yelped from the path, hands fidgeting as she paced. She jumped back as Jirah's gaze turned fierce toward her. "I mean—" she stuttered. She had a problem with her temper. She was easily flustered with ambiguity, and people she didn't know. She meant well, though.

"Now now, is that any way to treat someone who's helping?" Krogar looked to her with his devious grin, as the fire cracked loudly. "You're a cranky one," he chuckled again. He scratched his beard slowly and turned his gaze toward Jirah. "Well, my friend, it seems like my presence isn't wanted here." He rose, closed his book, and turned toward the forest. "You might want to send some people over my way in the marshes. Things might get a teensy bit hairy there. Perhaps those recruits of yours—I like them."

"Hey, wait a moment. What was this?"

"Why, a bit of charity, of course." Krogar's grin became bigger than ever. Even Jirah was growing uncomfortable. "Don't worry, my little friend. We have to make sure they don't shuffle off this mortal coil, right?" He let out a loud guffaw. "Well, some of them."

With that, he strolled and disappeared into the dark forests. A deafening silence settled throughout the camp. The crackle of the fire echoed through the forest, the wind swept through the trees, and throngs of bats flew through the night sky overhead.

"That guy is weird," Serafina said, finally breaking the silence. "I don't like him."

"Don't worry, Sera," Jirah began, still in bewilderment. He looked to the forest, first wondering what Krogar hid up his sleeve, and then what happened to the five recruits. *Some of them*, he had said. *Is there something important about them? Or is Krogar just playing one of his games?* It frustrated Jirah beyond belief. "He's on our side." If Krogar was a book, Jirah couldn't read a single word. "I think."

Chapter Six

Two-Faced Fate

Saul Bromaggus

Saul arrived in Hero's Fall. The massive peninsula ascended miles upon miles to mighty barren cliffs. It was the same as he remembered as a child, accompanying his father to see the grand temple of the Oracles.

At the cliff face sat the titanic temple, made with impenetrable venomstone preserved by the gods. Saul could feel the power emanating from the various halls and domes; they housed the very spirits of the gods. He could hardly believe he was to stand before the Oracles now, the thousand-year-old prophets who predicted the fate of those who were worthy. No one knew where they originated from. Some theorized that they came from the long-sunken isle of origin within Urikar's Berth to the east, hidden within the haze.

Saul stepped off his Ravager, and ran his hand along its dark mane, patting it's short, snoutless head. They were great beasts in war; a charge of Ravagers would be seen as a throng of bright green eyes. Few men lived to tell the tale. If they weren't fed properly, some Ravagers bit off the rider's hand. He set his beast in the stable with the others, offering it a large steak of bull's meat, which it swallowed whole.

Saul walked through the grand opening, into the temple. Statues of the Broken heroes he idolized surrounded the main forum. He saluted each as he passed. One was Icarus the Terrible, the one who conquered Renalia before the Age of Draconis. Next was Grawth the stalwart, the Broken who defended her castle alone against an army of one thousand Draconians, dying in glorious battle. Legend said she pierced the final enemy through the throat with her own hand in her last breath. Last was Aggaroth, the leader of northern Renalia, who dethroned the giants of old and ended their tyranny. They were the heroes of ages past, bringing victory and peace to the land through combat. Each one was seen by the Oracles, given their fate as Saul would be.

Maybe I will be a hero like them, he thought proudly. He wished his fate would be to conquer the enemies of his people in Renalia, reclaiming it for the Broken. They originated there, until they were forced into exile to Kathynta centuries ago. Soon he would know the truth. *But if my father's fate was false, what could that mean?* Not only that, but soon he was to be exiled across to the land of the enemies of all Broken—the Hydris.

The main forum was filled with various aqueducts leading along the walls, with statues of gods, goddesses, and their relics. Rough stone and smooth black marble pews filled the center, made for the visitors who wished to pray to their gods or seek the blessing of greatness from the Glories as a whole. Murals of many Broken heroes were painted on smooth stone surfaces, depicting their victories and valiant falls. Saul saluted them once more, before going to Gadora's worshipping room. It was custom to pay homage to one's god before seeing the Oracles. It was said that it gave the true blessing of fate.

He knelt before the towering, powerful form. She was tall, with the sandstone-like skin of a Terran. She came to the surface to spread her people's influence, only meeting villainy and chaos from the demonic beasts that scoured the land in the first age—the Dark Ones. She led her people well and conquered her foes. He admired the fabled weapon at the statues side, Gadora's edge—*the blade that carves the skies*—its black hilt came to a Dragon's head, the mouth open to reveal the orange steel.

It was said she slayed ten thousand of the Dark Ones, a hybrid monstrosity of a race from the abyss who ruled the land and corrupted the souls of all beings. Their leaders were a set of three creatures: Valikar the Eviscerator, Thalasesh the Titan, and worst of all, Khardan, the strongest of them all, deemed the Chaos itself. Together they were said to be unstoppable embodiments of chaos.

Gadora proved the legends false, slaying each with her mighty blade alongside Yggranda, the goddess of the earth. After ending the Dark Ones, she ascended to the realm of the gods and became the goddess of Storms, bestowing power unto those who fight chaos in the land. There were theories of what came of the blade, but none truly knew where it went. The statue's blade was a replica, of course. Regardless, the stories of her gave him strength.

Looking over his shoulder, he felt the eyes of a Broken or two. With a huff, he asked his goddess for guidance. Once Saul saw the Oracles, he was to return to the Vale—before exile. The day after, he would be taken to the Fissure, and escorted across it to be exiled. Saul hated the thought. *Exiled and disgraced. Is life worth such a cost? To live with the Venari, and gods know what else.*

He pondered what would come of his people now. Obelreyon did not respect their ways. The dragon forced them to believe in Lornak, or to abide by his laws and follow his orders so that they may have Renalia. *Fools, anyone who follows him will only meet death.* He was not the brightest mind but knew a suicide mission when he saw one. Renalia may be at war, but they were powerful still. Not to mention, the Isles were in their way, the place they suffered their heaviest losses ten years prior. The Skirmisher's Guild in the islands was a powerful enemy at sea. He only heard stories, and from them he knew there was a reason the Broken armies were pushed back.

The Torch of Lathyria stood silent for ten years. Nothing more than small trades came in and out of the north now. Their guards stood at the mountainous border still as statues, unwilling to join any cause the Broken presented. If Lornak would help Obelreyon conquer Renalia, what was to stop him from taking the Torch, the Neck, and the Plateau? *What does Lornak want in return?*

That remained to be seen.

Saul prayed to his goddess. *Gadora, goddess of storms, give me strength in times of chaos, make me the storm of your will so that I may wash away disgrace and bring order to the land at your will. My mind like thunder, my body the rain, my blade as lightning from the skies. I fight for truth.* He rose to his feet and saluted once more, admiring her strength.

"Bromaggus," a rough female voice said.

Finishing his words of worship, Saul turned to find the temple leader, and the Warmaster of the Vale. Her powerful stature cast a shadow over him. Her rough skin glowed in the torchlight, and a shadow loomed over her onyx almond eyes, accentuating the crow's feet surrounding both. One would be a fool to think her weak, as Mirakia Othellun was a fearsome warrior who crushed the disrespectful.

"Are you prepared?" she asked, face hard as stone.

"Yes."

In Hero's Fall, one never danced around the point. To veer or confound speech was to show disrespect to another.

"Come with me."

The Warmaster walked softly, floating like a ghost. She took him through the intricate, ornate passageway at the north end of the main forum. As they entered, Saul looked to her markings. She wore yellow, with the symbol of the three crashing winds, the arcing star of the Oracles, and the blade.

The low ceiling forced Saul to crouch. After a time, darkness took them. Nothing could pierce the shadow of the Oracles, except for their own flames. A flickering blue light beckoned him forward to the end of the tunnel, slowly growing as he approached.

"This is it. Enter. Do not lie, do not fear, and do not reject their prediction. They will tell you when you are free. Come to me when you complete your task. Do you understand?"

"Yes," Saul replied.

Othellun turned slowly, her cloak flipped past as she returned to the main forum behind him.

Saul listened to her footsteps dissipate into silence. All he felt was a faint wind and the scent of incense coming from the dimly-lit room at the end. Saul approached with caution. As he passed under the arch, he saw three hooded figures making up three parts of a depressed circle around the tri-flamed brazier centerpiece of the room, with one part remaining in front of him. Pine and incense danced through his nostrils with a hint of lime. Colors were hard to make out, as all was lit from the torches at each corner, each oracle with one of yellow, red, or blue. The symbols of every god were carved around the outside ring of the seating circle; he felt as if they watched him. Judged his worthiness.

Saul did not know the intricacies of the ritual. He understood that their symbols would be imprinted along his arm with the light of the color he was to be given. Each figure sat with long, crossed spider-like limbs, coming to feet with seven toes. Their arms rested on their skeletal knees, extending to long fingers twice the length of their palms open to the sky, dimly lit by the flames.

"Sit," they said in unison, in an elderly, ragged tone. Saul sat in the open space with his legs crossed as well as he could, placing a hand on each knee. "Who do you worship?" the Oracles asked. Their black bug-like eyes watched him closely, as if looking into his soul.

"Gadora."

"Why do you worship her?" their voices slithered like snakes in the air through their sharp teeth.

"She is a valiant warrior, striking against tyranny and chaos. I wish to do the same." The Oracles stayed silent for a time. Saul wondered what they thought. They had eyes that saw fate itself, foretelling the future, or so he was told. Some said they were once Broken, twisted by the isle of origin and its mysteries, transformed by the power of the gods.

"She sees you," the Oracles said, as the central flame grew more intense, and then split into two that circled one another. "But she is not the only one."

Not the only one? He wished to ask what they meant, but the Oracles were not to be addressed until they asked a question. If he did interrupt them, their predictions may fail, or he could be executed for disrupting the ritual.

"You will conquer," the left Oracle said. The torches burned bright red. Saul was taken aback, but didn't show it. *How does one conquer without an army?* he wondered. *How does one conquer in exile?*

"Yet your fate will bring death," the right Oracle said. A rush of wind swished around the room, causing the red flames to swirl faster. It sent a shiver up Saul's spine.

"And yet, that is not your only fate," the far Oracle finished. The wind calmed.

"What is your family's call?" they all chimed.

"One who would not die for honor, never lives," Saul replied calmly. *My father died for his beliefs.*

"Your name will be true," they said. "We shall reveal the fate." The Oracles held each other's hands, outstretching one from his left and right toward Saul.

Saul grasped the hands of the Oracles to complete the circle and initiate the ritual. Their skin was as rough as gravel.

"Close your eyes, Saul, son of Greln."

Saul closed his eyes as ordered. Behind his eyelids, he could see a red light flow further from the center, heat crossing where their hands connected, and circling around his back. Suddenly, his arms felt as though he shoved them into a flame, burning and crackling and flaring his nerves. He put all his control into not gripping the Oracles' hands too hard or revealing any hint of pain. He wanted to scream, but he didn't. *My father died standing strong in the face of black flames. I can do the same. This is but a touch of fire.*

He felt his left arm sear all the way up, as if encapsulated by a fire. He wished for it to end but did not voice it; his desire laid in having a purpose before he left the Vale. *I will not falter, I will make my family and clan proud, despite my exile.*

Both arms burned. He did not understand, thinking it was marking but one. However, no one revealed to him how the ritual proceeded. Perhaps it represented the circle of flame, the life that he now belonged to.

He heard the blaze behind him fly up to the ceiling, and he could feel heat and light all around. The light was so bright he could still see the colors shift from red to blue and back again with his eyes closed. He felt lines of agonizing pain draw on either arm, as if the gentlest touch came with the sharpness of a knife. He clenched his teeth, resisting the urge to let go or scream.

But as the carving reached his shoulder, the pain disappeared as if it never existed. *Is it over?* His hoarse, pained breathing was the only sound that remained, and the light reduced to nothing. The winds faded, leaving silence behind.

"Open your eyes, Saul Bromaggus," the Oracles whispered. He opened them finally. The flame was gone, and the room was pitch black.

"Go now. Seek your fate," they said in unison. "The gods will be watching."

Saul rose to his feet. He was told by his father to say nothing, to leave silently. Yet he disobeyed. "Thank you, Oracles."

A long silence followed as Saul turned his back, beginning to walk toward the main forum once more, barely ducking before the arch to exit the room. A light beckoned him back to whence he came.

Along the hall, he heard the voices of the Oracles whisper in his ear. "Do not thank us, we are but messengers. Your fate is up to you now. Your name runs true."

Saul dared not say another word. *What of my name?* He walked through the dark hall, leaving the spider-like Oracles behind him. He was given his fate, which he would only see when the others do, as he entered the light of the grand forum. As the light touched him, he heard gasps of awe from the onlookers of the forum.

"Two?" one said.

"*Two?*" another called.

Saul looked to his arms, and both had markings. This was unheard of. Never before did a Broken display the Mark of the Oracles on both arms. On his left was the color red, the slayer. The first mark was the three crashing winds, the second, the sharp-edged wing of the dragon, and third, the drop of blood.

Death.

He wished to slay the dragon in the name of justice, but this? He was a strong fighter, but no dragon slayer. Even if he desired it so. *Am I to die? My father was given victory, but died in vain. What fate awaits me?* He remembered the few Broken who bore the Dragon slayer markings in the past; each disappeared within a fortnight. Fear crept into his mind like a spider.

The whispers and comments continued. Some Broken backed out of the temple, others huddled together, whispering vicious tones while watching Saul closely.

The color of the protector laid on his right arm. The god's mark was of a six-pointed sun. He did not recognize the symbol whatsoever. *What god would choose me, if I do not know them?* The next, a simple circle, a race or species he did not recognize. Last, the drop of blood again. *What in the hells is this?* Saul felt his fate was all he had left, and it showed his death.

"What treachery is this?" an old priest yelled. "*Two* markings? Clearly, the Oracles made a mistake."

"Impossible!" another individual yelled. "The Oracles are *never* wrong! This is a sign!"

Mirakia Othellun stormed up to him, gripped his arms like a vice, and pulled each close to her eyes. She kept a close eye on the surrounding Broken that began crowding around them. "Do you understand what this means?" she whispered harshly. She seemed to harbor more emotion than before, with a drop of concern. Her pale white ring seemed to shine brightly in the dim light.

"I am not afraid of him." He was. He watched the one he cared for burn days ago and he now feared the same for himself. *Should I run? Or should I stay, and die for my fate?*

"Well you *should* be. If I were him, I'd kill you the second I heard. The last one who received the dragon slayer mark died mysteriously two days later."

"That was long ago. I will be exiled. Is that not sufficient?"

The Warmaster grew irritable. "If you make it that long." She eyed him up and down, then sighed. "Let me embark you with a bit of wisdom, Bromaggus." She ushered him to follow her to the front of the temple with a hand on his back, and he obliged. "I was a friend of your father; do you know why?" Her eyes darted around the hall, to each of the Broken standing nearby. Her other hand laid on a sword hilt at her side.

"No." The gasps continued as they walked. He heard curses and whispers, mentions of blasphemy and treason, and some of a blessing from above.

The Warmaster began to push Saul forward as she sped up. "It's because I believed in him. I don't like being ruled," she said poignantly. "Your father wasn't a fool. What he did, he did because he knew it would ignite a fire within the hearts of our people."

He died for nothing. Everyone lives in fear now, Saul thought. It was all trivial; his father sacrificed himself so that everyone would be pushed further under Obelreyon's rule. *I wish he was here to see me receive my fate. Two markings is a gift, despite both showing death. Although, I fear what it could mean for me in the days to come. Some may believe it is treason, and others, blasphemy.* Some would fear two fates and some would admire them. *The ones who fear them may be the most dangerous.* As they arrived at the stable she said a few last words of wisdom as Saul mounted his Ravager once more.

"Do not let the fire be extinguished." She backed away and drew two blades. "You would do well to cover your arms."

Several Broken ran out of the temple, armed to the teeth. "Get him! Get the heathen! His fate shows he will attempt treason!"

"Go, ingrate!" Warmaster Othellun smacked the Ravager's behind with the flat of a sword, causing it to run ahead. Saul grabbed on and rode as was commanded, looking back to see her slice through limb and throat with her slick dance of blades, roaring at them with a mighty battle cry.

Chapter Seven

The Meager Truth

Kayden Ralta

Kayden sauntered through the cracked stone temple hall. *When will this end?* she thought. Her pace gradually quickened in hopes that it would be over soon. The fact that it was pitch black, save her torchlight, didn't help either. *I am not afraid, I am not afraid,* she chanted as a mantra to herself. She heard hollowed wind through the hall in front, leather and plate footsteps, and Vesper nervously rambling to himself. He always rambled when he was nervous.

Why is there wind here? The air flowed with a subtle howl, as if beckoning them forward.

"Kayden, could you slow down a little?" Lira asked. "Magnus can't keep up. He isn't as quick as you are."

Kayden scoffed at the idea. *Who does Lira think she is?* She looked intensely into Lira's dark eyes. Her skin shone a dark copper and hair black as the shadow of the hall, both rare in the west, or so Kayden heard. It was more than common in the deserts in the east. She was a simple-looking Human, but not a 'runt.'

TIDES OF FATE

Sighing, she knew she shouldn't be so hard on the poor, cow-eyed girl. She *did* find the passage for them. And sewed her arm. "Listen, princess, I'll walk as fast as I want. I'm trying to get us out of here," Kayden said. Even though Lira towered over Kayden by a foot, her personality was soft as a feather.

"You're getting *you* out of here," Domika jabbed. "I want to get back to my brother as much as the next girl, but you should slow down a little before you hurt your pretty little head." Her words sliced sharply, almost as sharp as Kayden's—but to no avail.

"Don't test me, flame-breath," Kayden shot back. She was not Domika's biggest fan, and the feeling was mutual. It at least helped that the flame atop Domika's long black hair gave a bit of light.

"Now, now, I am able to keep pace. Do not worry," Magnus said.

He's so slow, Kayden thought. *Sure, he's wearing heavy plate, but his size should accommodate for that.* At the same time, her concern drove her further toward getting out before they were all caught. "Listen. I know I'm moving fast, but we either keep a fast pace, or we'll speedily go back to jail," she asserted herself. She didn't need other people to tell her what she should do, let alone what was best. If escaping jail was the task, she was best suited to handle it. If she was going to be in the dark, it wouldn't be for long.

"You're right, but you can't just go around barking orders like a bossy little wench—no one likes that. Try being a little nicer next time." Domika sneered at Kayden.

"What Domika might mean to say is that people respond well to kind direction, rather than being a little rough. That's all," Lira said.

At least Lira attempted to be nice. Domika, on the other hand, has a different idea in mind, Kayden thought.

"Yeah, that's *exactly* what I meant," Domika said snarkily.

Kayden swiftly turned and pointed a fierce finger in Domika's face. "You better back off. At least the princess here has some respect. You're just stirring the damned pot." Kayden knew Domika wouldn't respond well to this, but she hated seeing an attitude like hers get in the way of the task at hand. A howling wind came from the hall beyond, sending a chill up Kayden's spine. She turned and raised a brow.

Behind, Vesper swished his finger in an eccentric circle. "Now, now my comrades, why are we in such conflict? We are having a lovely stroll through a temple path, are we not? Can we not simply walk in silence? Can we not we walk with meaning? Maybe we will find treasure, or possibly a way out of this death trap. I feel like we should worry about these things rather than keeping blades at each other's vitals!" Vesper was exhaustingly long-winded.

He's right, Kayden thought. Not that she would ever admit it. She turned back to the group. "Come on, I think I see an end to this god-forsaken tunnel ahead." She continued walking again— this time, slightly slower.

The temple tunnel became more and more rough-walled, and parts of the ceiling had fallen and damaged the floor. She swore it could all fall on her at any time. *This had better not be a waste of my time.* "How's the speed?" she asked Magnus.

"Better. Thank you, my lady."

"Don't thank me, thank the princess," she diverted the comment to Lira. Kayden wasn't one to accept thanks, and rarely gave it.

"She has a name," Domika growled.

"It's all right, Domika, I kind of like believing I'm royalty." Lira said, attempting to soften the mood again. The others didn't reply.

Kayden just chuckled. Soon, a switch of light came over down the tunnel. "Look, an opening!" Kayden dashed to the end of the hall, and found an opening into a ruined temple forum. It was as unsafe as could be, evidenced by the small ceiling stones that dropped to the ground as they walked through it. She wondered if a larger stone could fall on Domika, chuckling to herself and secretly hoping a 'happy accident' would occur. Leader's sister or not, she was not Kayden's chosen type of companion.

There were no doors, no extra tunnels, nothing else in sight. There was just a massive hall, with an altar for worship at the end. A white marble statue of a woman stood behind the altar. *Well, we're in trouble.* She stood in full plate armor, kite shield on her left arm, and a winged-hilt longblade raised in her right, with long wavy hair flowing down her back. A symbol on her shield resembled a shining sun with six points, waving out from the rim to a point. An inscription in the common tongue was carved into the wall behind, *without meaning, we have no power.*

Kayden sauntered up to it. *You must be Shiada,* she thought. *What have you done for me?* She'd never paid much attention to military or religious figures. They never had any relevance in her life; the kindness of gods was absent in every aspect. She believed they either didn't exist, or they hated Humans and all other races.

Kayden's life had been a fight the whole way through. Her family was poor, forced to scrounge for food day by day in her hometown of Kwora, near capital of the sands, Zenato. She would steal a loaf of bread or an apple from the market and bring it home for her parents to share whenever she could. She was an only child, without a sibling to help. Her mom and dad raised her until she was barely eight years old.

But then the stench of rotting flesh and the light of searing flames flashed across her. The image of their bodies in the inn rafters shot into her mind. The day her spirit died. Sometimes she even smelled the flesh no matter how clear the air or how succulent the feast in her present circumstances.

Her brow furrowed, and fists clenched as she remembered the past. *Damned be the gods*, she thought. They gave her nothing except scars and took everything. She made her own fate. She mockingly growled at the statue and threw a stone at it.

Lira walked up behind her. "Kayden, don't." She held a hand to her chest as if she believed all the teachings. Kayden knew who the goddess was. She'd read all about her and the history that surrounded her. She had ages to read and spent most of her empty childhood studying whatever she could find. While she stayed in Orinas, she lived in the library, until she was sent to prison for a string of crimes.

Ridiculous, Kayden thought. Gods and religions were a bunch of crap.

"She's the goddess of protection, serving the people, the weak and the helpless. Protecting us from the god of shadow, Lornak," Lira continued.

Kayden almost laughed aloud over the ridiculous nature of it all. But she *was* a little curious. "Oh, who is that, exactly?" Kayden asked. She knew, but they didn't need to know that.

"The god of power, you wench," Domika snorted. She sleekly strolled onto the scene, but spoke her next words in a quiet tone. "One who promises power and strength to all who worship him— at a cost," she continued. Domika *loved* knowing more than her, it seemed.

Lira nodded. "But the bringer of darkness. He spread chaos through the land, so he was struck down by Shiada herself two millennia ago—that's how the story is told, anyways. His followers nearly conquered the land, but her heralds fought them back. They say they he still exists in the nightmares of men, corrupting their minds. But Shiada holds them back." Nodding, she said, "This was a temple of Shiada. That's how I knew of it."

Gods, goddesses, and demons were ghost stories intended to scare children. Her parents told her the story when she was young, but she knew now it was a bunch of ridiculous fluff to inspire and frighten.

"Ahem, excuse me, my comrades," Vesper confidently spoke up. "I believe we have a more serious situation at hand. We have nowhere to go, and nowhere to hide. Will we go back? What will we do with the guards if they find us?" he hammered her with questions yet again.

Kayden just got more and more flustered. He needed to *stop*. "All right, all right, let's all just shut it. We can drag the guard in here, seal the wall, and try to get out. They're gonna kill us if we get caught, and eventually, even if we stay. Damn it, we're stuck." She paced back and forth, frustrated. *If this torch goes out, I am going to lose it.* She wasn't afraid of the dark, exactly; it just unsettled her a little. Okay, maybe she was a little scared. The past scarred deep.

"Oh gods, I cannot and shall not go back." Vesper declared. He scratched his wire-haired head frantically.

Kayden ignored his input. She looked to Magnus, who seemed as if he wondered what color the sky was. *He's no help. He's slow, both in movement and thinking. It's a surprise he even survived a battle.* She dared not ask Domika, who gave her a dirty look. "Princess," Kayden called. *At least she will help and not be a drake about it.*

Silence. Hard to believe.

"Princess?" she turned around to find her kneeling before the statue, praying. "For the love of—Lira!" She swiftly paced over to Lira and tapped her on the shoulder. "Would you stop that? We need to figure out how to get the hell outta here!"

Lira carefully looked over to her. "I'm asking Shiada for help. You may not believe in higher powers, but I do." She returned to praying, which only angered Kayden more.

How could she be so thick? This isn't helping the situation at all. "Could you hurry up? This is useless!" she roared.

"I'm almost finished," Lira said solemnly. She muttered a few more words, finishing her prayer. With the last few words, Lira whispered a couple of divine incantations, and placed a hand on the rim of the statue's base and—

Click. With that, the base lit up, and the floor shook slightly as the wall behind the statue slid open. Kayden couldn't believe it. She was still irritated, but slightly amazed.

"Useless, huh?" Lira gave Kayden a sassy smirk.

Kayden laughed heartily, patted her on the back, and waved the others into the newly open door before them. "I'm going to pretend that never happened. I won't give you the satisfaction, princess!" She leapt over the altar and glanced suspiciously at the statue as she passed to the doorway beyond. Her torch led the way, ahead of the others once again. Another room was beyond, pitch black as could be. The wall shut behind them. Her right hand twitched nervously as she held the torch, feeling the darkness closing in on her. The wind howled stronger here than before.

"My lady, are you okay?" Magnus asked as he placed a gauntlet on her shoulder.

"I'm fine." She swatted his hand away, looking back to see Magnus's sullen eyes. "I hate being unable to see. It's unsettling," she said with a cold tone. *I can't stand it.*

"Well, looks like the tiger's a little pussycat." Domika jabbed her with another snarky comment.

Fury boiled over. Kayden shot a dagger up from her belt, but she tried hard to resist the temptation to slice the idiot's throat.

"What?" she growled. Turning at a blistering speed, she drew a blade to Domika's neck.

Clang.

Magnus's gauntlet held her blade back. Not only had she never seen him move that fast, but she didn't think it was even possible.

Domika sent Magnus a curious, sultry eye, gently placing a hand on his gauntlet, effectively lowering his hand and Kayden's blade. "Thank you."

Kayden's gaze never left Domika's. "I wasn't actually gonna do it." She sheathed her weapon once more and turned back to the room ahead with a huff. "I just don't like her."

"Please, my fair ladies, we must work together in this plight. We fight for a good cause, do you not agree?" Vesper piped up from the back. "We must move on, or we could surely get caught!" He chuckled with a subtle vibration in his tone.

"All right, let's keep moving. I don't want to have us all die down here because I got irritated." Kayden coughed up a laugh before entering the new open room. The ceiling was twenty feet high, and the walls were lined with floor-to-ceiling shelves of battered, broken wood and cracked stone. Several books remained along the cases, some on their side, opened and torn, others straight and proper.

Lira's mouth drew open, and eyes alight as if she'd found a treasure trove. "This is the King's private library!" She skipped over to the long stone table surrounded by stools and started looking through the books that were there. "I knew he had a private library in a temple, but I didn't know it was *this* one!"

"Princess, stop—" Kayden said, trying to stop her, but her words dropped to a grumble. "Do you think there's a way outta here?" After no response, she replied to herself. "It wouldn't make sense for a King to have one single way into his private library."

"I agree," Magnus said quietly.

Well, that's someone. "Check for doors. Might be one like the last room."

Domika sighed behind, and Magnus went to look at some of the shelves. Lira searched through some of the books on the table, and under the table.

Vesper put his hands on his head and spoke up. "My dear friends, doors or no, please do not touch the King's belongings! It is improper to disturb—"

With that, a subtle voice spoke a word that echoed through the room. *Leave...*

Kayden raised a brow and looked around. "Ves, was that you?" She glanced over to him, seeing his throat tight as could be, as if he choked on something. He shook his head violently with eyes buggy as could be.

As she touched one of the books on the shelf, a ghostly figure in full plate rushed from one side of the room, right toward her. "*Leave this place!*" Kayden drew a dagger in a flash and threw it before it arrived, but the *thud* of steel into wood echoed from the other wall. She yelped, pinned against the wall with an armored—and translucent—individual in front of her.

He stood at taller than all but Magnus, wearing grand plate armor lined with green accents and silver rings. His hair was a dirty blond with a large, bushy beard, a pointed nose, and icy blue eyes.

The man hissed his words through his ghostly teeth. "What are you doing in my library? None are allowed here."

Vesper coughed and cleared his throat, hand trembling. He slowly walked forward and knelt in front of the figure. "My liege," he said, "Why do you come to us, great king?"

Still pinned to the bookcase, Kayden raised a brow. "*This is the king? He sure looks younger than I remember,*" Kayden placed her hands on her hips, head tilted to the side in confusion. "I ain't kneeling, though." *Why should I?* It was ridiculous. Kayden didn't praise anyone without earning her respect first, especially if they were born into royalty. He was a good king, or so Kayden heard, but what did he do for her? She'd lived through hell, and only when he died did she come to a feeling of freedom.

Lira smirked at Kayden and stepped forward. "Why do you come before us, King Bracchus?"

"I study here," the King said. He backed away, and a book formed in his hands. "Begone, before I call the royal guard."

"Royal guard?" Kayden's head tilted further. "You're dead."

"*Kayden,*" Lira hissed.

She just shrugged in response.

"You," he looked toward Kayden with a vicious eye. "Are you here to kill me? Well, the Royal guard shall be here any minute, and there is no way out." Slamming the book in an obvious manner, she made out a hand-written scribbled title *Paths of the Past*. The ghost king's hand drew to his side as if feeling for a weapon he did not possess. "The blade—Where is my blade?" the spirit began to panic.

The rusted blade? Kayden wondered. *The blade that only those of the royal family could hold, at least, more than a few moments without burning a hand off.*

Bracchus' ghost glanced around the room, as if looking for it. "I must find it. I must get it to her before it's too late—" He backed away toward one of the bookcases, and shelved the ghostly book where none sat, and it vanished. He soared off in a panic toward the back wall and vanished into the stone.

"Wait!" Lira yelped. "I have so many questions," she said with a pout. As usual. The princess and her Questions.

The others stayed dead silent.

Kayden looked at each of them—they either stood frozen, open-mouthed, or confused. "Have none of you seen a spirit?" Kayden had one-too-many times. Far too many.

"His spirit is bound here," Lira said, hand clasped to her chest. "Who was he talking about?"

"Not important right now. We have to get out, first." With a shrug, Kayden said, "Being bound here isn't special or surprising. It's rumored that he was murdered, so it makes sense. Probably stuck here til he's put to rest." Kayden started looking around the broken bookcases, tapping a finger to her chin. "He was telling us something." She thought about the book he held. She only read it a few times, but it never had the title on the cover—only images of roads winding into the sky, no words. *But the book was only copied widely a few years ago.* The ghost seemed much older—or younger—than that.

She eyed where he placed the book, seeing a small, barely visible indent in the base of the case. "Everyone, look for a book with a cover with roads going to the sky. No title on the front."

Domika raised a brow. "Does the rat know how to read books? That's oddly specific."

"And you're oddly irritating. Just look." It didn't matter if she knew how to read or not.

The fire-headed idiot threw up her arms and walked toward another bookcase. "Fine."

Kayden threw herself up a few levels by jumping from shelf to shelf, to the top to check the books up there.

Nothing. Just a few measly novels about deities. Temple stuff. *The Finery of Illadis* was one, *Arias of Light* was another. Those were both pretty boring ones from what she remembered.

Lira shuffled the books on the tables, scratching her head. Vesper walked rubbing his hands in a shaky manner, and Domika seemed like she just didn't care. Magnus stood opposite to her, on his tip-toes, reaching to see books a few shelves up.

After checking the rest of the top shelves, she hopped back down to the ground. "Nothing up there. Just—" She stopped a moment, seeing Magnus with a hand outstretched, a tattered tome in his hand with winding roads leading toward clouds across the front. "Boring stuff," she finished, smirking at his dopey smile.

Nodding, she turned to the space the ghost placed the book and slid it into the case. With a push, it lit up in a flash, and at the back, the brick wall faded to a translucent light, and then vanished. Behind, laid a rusty set of plate armor—and a stone indentation into the enclave wall leading upward.

It was decrepit, covered in rust and breaks all over. It seemed worthless, aged, and broken from battle—seemingly irreparably. One thing was certain, it was the armor the ghost wore.

Magnus crouched before it, running a hand along the rusty metal. "I wish to wear it," he said, sporting a curious expression.

"Are you serious?" Domika exclaimed. "It's a load of junk! It doesn't even look like his armor, when he used to wear it. I say we leave it and, *you know*, get out of here?"

For the first time, Kayden agreed with Domika on something. *It's a crap heap. But then again, maybe it's suitable for his personality. It's almost endearing*, she thought. "Not worth it. We have to get outta here."

"We cannot leave this here! It was from the King!" Vesper exclaimed. He pointed his finger fiercely at Kayden and Domika. "It should be taken to his family!"

Henceforth, an argument began between Domika and Vesper.

Kayden participated briefly, but noticed Lira was helping Magnus out of his armor and into the old, cracked set as they quarreled. She soon gave up and went over to help.

"You have my thanks. It is a nice suit of armor. I cannot possibly leave it behind." Magnus seemed happy with his find.

"Don't mention it. Seriously, don't," Kayden laughed. "Plus, I can't stop you from doing it, so I might as well speed things along," she said in a steely voice. "There, how's it fit?" It fit *horridly*. The shoulders were too small, the leggings too long and loose fitting, and the helm looked all kinds of wrong. She swore he was going to get injured from the rust alone.

"It fits well," he said happily.

It was kind of cute—innocent, almost. She wondered if he knew what well-fitted armor actually felt like. At least they were finished, so they could all get the hell out. "Hey," Kayden said. Vesper and Domika still argued fiercely. Intelligence versus passion was a bad mix. "Hey! Morons!" she screamed. Dom and Vesper turned around, shocked to see that Magnus already switched armor, and the other three were at the ladder, ready to ascend. "In case you forgot, we're *escaping from prison*." The two arguers shot each other irritated looks, nodded, and hurried to the ladder.

Climbing up, a translucent stone wall was at the top. The instant she passed through it, the smell of old, rotten flesh charged into Kayden's nostrils. She covered her mouth when she could, wrapping her scarf around tighter. They found themselves in the Lingrat stronghold, a military base home to operations against the rebellion recently.

Now abandoned, following defeat by Jirah's forces, it had been ransacked by thieves and brigands. The wooden walls were black and dilapidated, burnt from fires of the rebellion. Once they rose out of the tunnel, the stone reformed, and the path vanished.

"How sad," Lira said, seeing the dead of both sides lay there still.

By the smell, they were weeks old. Kayden was disgusted by the smell alone, but she was much happier with the light streaming in from the broken openings and what windows remained.

"Sad, but necessary. This place was the center of operations to assassinate rebellion groups and coordinate strikes from the capital. They killed rebels. Also children of suspected members," Domika said.

What a know-it-all. Kayden brought them back to the point at hand. "That's all nice and well, but if the stronghold was south, then we need to head east for about five days toward Deurbin, and then north for two or three days to the camp. We can probably make it in seven if we're quick about it, so let's get moving. They probably already think we're dead." She paused, looking to the stronghold they just left. "I swear, that was almost too easy."

"That's because we had Lira to remember it was a temple," Domika said." Let's just go while we still can."

Lira simply shrugged as she was mentioned and smiled.

"Let us go, comrades!" Vesper called, nominating himself to lead the charge.

Kayden snatched the hood of his robe, stopping him from walking any further. "*Uh*, nitwit, that's west. Do you want to go to the capital?" Kayden growled. *What is with this guy? Is he trying to get us killed?* She disregarded her concern, and assumed Vesper was just weird, as he had been the whole time.

"Oh, *ah*, no, I suppose not. Lead the way, my dear!" Vesper let out a hearty laugh.

Chapter Eight

The Shadow of Choice

Jirah Mirado

Night fell as Jirah travelled between the rebel camps. There were many—fifteen, to be exact. If one was discovered, there were always more to take its place like a hydra's head. He rode by horse, galloping quickly from Dragon Camp on the east end of Lilac Lake, to Wolf on the south side.

The looming, rough-barked blackwood maples of the forest surrounded him, and it felt as though they crept closer with every strike of hoof upon the path. The wind buffeted his face strongly, and he felt the cold on his teeth. While darkness covered most tracks, Blaziks were easy to find in the dark, due to the fire-laden hair. They were not common in the forests of Loughran. He knew the capital guard would stop him, *if* they could.

The moon shone high in the sky like the crescent island. The crows cawed madly, crickets sung the song of night, and wolves howled at his presence in the blackwood. Stephen and Pali'ah returned to the camp, having found nothing of interest on their missions. No news came from the others, yet. He caught wind of Gorkith's return from a messenger, so he leapt onto his horse and rode back as quickly as possible. The other camp members warned him against it, but his mind was focused on his men. His own safety paled in comparison.

Jirah thought on the successes of his teams over the past months. Ordana was defended from the hunters from camps Dragon and Boar. Captured members of Snake had been liberated by Bull and Hawk. The Lingrat stronghold had been decimated, but only after he'd allowed the warriors who yielded to leave. The stubborn drakes that were left died quickly while cursing his troops. The stronghold still lay barren now, filled with decaying corpses. He mourned for their families. *I offered them freedom, I offered them forgiveness,* he reminded himself.

Jirah often convinced himself that he did the right thing. He wondered what Bracchus would say now.

You are an honorable man, Jirah. Be careful, as even the most honorable can be blind, the true King once said.

Jirah wondered if Bracchus thought of himself as blind. He grew sick over the course of a year—a sickness no cleric could heal. His lips grew a shade of deep blue then black, and in the end, all of his skin was as black as the night. Only a limited few were let in to see him as his sickness progressed, and Jirah was among them. So was Fillion. *You drake, what did you do to him?* he wondered.

An unsettling, quick gust of wind blew across the back of Jirah's neck. Light from his hair faded subtly. He rode faster, despite knowing what the eerie wind meant. The light of the moon shone dimly, and his path ahead faded before his eyes. Riding faster would do nothing, he knew. Not that it mattered in the end, because even the darkest shadow feared the light of flame. He saw the dirt turn black, and all color around him seeped from the area into the gloom of grey. He reined in his horse to a halt and hopped off quickly. The breeze whispered through the sounds of scraping branches and rustling leaves—the only sounds through the dark forests. Yet Jirah knew he was not alone.

"Show yourself!" Jirah yelled into the living shadows.

The ghostly figure of the Knight of Shadow—Asheron Highwind—walked out of the darkness. "Riding alone? That is bold, even for you, Mirado." He let out a deep, hollow cackle.

Twenty soldiers armed to the teeth in plate, shield, and blade emerged from the forest around Jirah. "Shall I have his head, m'lord?" one soldier wielding a greataxe asked, towering over Jirah by a foot. "I could crush his tiny skull." He clenched his fist tightly over Jirah's head. The circle of knights laughed mockingly.

Jirah growled quietly, and slowly reached for his blade. He did not like quips about his height, but usually let them go. However, these men and women were hunters. *Murderers.* If they were going to attack him, they'd regret every moment before their quick death. They murdered rebels, some innocent men and women. Even children were not let go. It disgusted him. It was abhorrent to even *think* he'd ever worked beside Asheron.

"Calm yourself, Mirado. I am here to—*talk*." He raised his hand slowly and waved for Jirah to relax. "And you," Asheron pointed to the axe-wielding soldier, "you do not obtain the skill to take his head, even if I wanted it, imbicile. Know your place. Do not let his stature fool you," he cackled. "Or maybe I should have him fight you alone—I know he would certainly not resist the challenge."

The soldier bowed his head and lowered his axe, receding back into the circle.

"Wise choice," Jirah said coolly, releasing his hand from his blade's hilt. "I say again," Jirah snarled, "what is it that you want?"

"I am here to give you a choice." Asheron slowly walked around Jirah in a circle. "I'm not a fool, Mirado. Your information networks will find out many things. Eventually, you are going to hear about individuals disappearing," Asheron gave a long pause. "And you are going to ignore it."

"Killing more innocents, are we, *wretch?*" Jirah growled.

Asheron hissed at him in response. Jirah was more livid with every word from Asheron's putrid mouth. The man lived with no morals, believing that orders were all that mattered. Jirah hated that day, the day he left the militia six months prior.

The soldiers converged on Jirah a second time, but Asheron once again waved them off. "Mirado." He slowly walked closer. His dark plate boots crunched the leaves and sticks of the forest path. It reminded Jirah of the innocent bones Asheron had broken. Each crack was but one of hundreds. "I follow orders," he said coldly, then halting. "You are a disgrace. You abandoned our cause to fight with animals. I maintain order. You breed chaos."

Each word from Asheron's mouth enraged him. His presence stole light from the moon, but the flame upon Jirah's head burned brighter as he angered. "What did you call my people?" Jirah yelled.

"Animals. Unsophisticated—" He took a step forward. "—barbaric—" Another step closer. "—animals." Before Jirah could yell once more, Asheron raised his hand to wait. "Ignore what you hear, or everyone in your little camps will die. With the number I'll bring, not even *you* can stop us, Mirado." Asheron cackled one last time. "I can't *imagine* what will happen to you."

The camps were all hidden. The only one that knew all the locations was himself. "You're bluffing."

Asheron looked to the soldiers that surrounded them. "Let me ask you this—do you truly wish to take that risk?"

Asheron was not one to play games. He was straightforward unlike his vile brother. He preferred his questions straight, his words succinct, and decisions without any form of ambiguity.

Asheron pushed with a list. "Death will come for them all. Your giant, your emotionless rock, and even your sister, Mirado." He took a step forward. "I know where your camps are."

"Where is my sister?" Jirah said. She wasn't in a camp. She was missing. *I lost my entire family for far too long. I can't deal with that again.* Ever since he ran from his home, he thought of them every day. He feared going back even more.

"Caught in a web—I can say that much." Asheron's tone lightened, as if to smile crookedly behind his dark visage. "Choose, Mirado. Your men, or the others?"

Jirah thought for more than a few moments. *I can't abandon my men—I promised I would keep them safe. I don't even know what others he speaks of,* he thought. Jirah didn't know what to do. There were many unknowns, and his victories had been vast. He thought of his sister, Pali, Felkar, Alex, Gorkith, Serafina, and innumerable others. "You cannot force my hand, pathetic worm."

"*Hmm.*" Asheron stopped in front of Jirah. He turned slowly as his cloak fluttered behind him like a ghost. One measured step at a time, he approached Jirah. Asheron came to stand over him, the pits of eyes looked down on him. "You must decide." His voice was guttural and vile. "Or your men will die with them. They disappear, your men die, or they both do." He moved his black helm in close. Jirah's flame flickered in the reflection of the dark steel. "This is a professional courtesy, Mirado. Choose."

Jirah stared him dead in the eyes. Jirah honored his pact with his troops. *I will not betray them. I will accept my responsibility, and the consequences,* he vowed. "My men."

"Good." As he spoke, Asheron backed into the dark with his soldier. "Worry not—I will ensure you know that I speak the truth." He vanished without a sound save for four final words: "I will be watching."

"*Asheron!*" Jirah yelled.

His voice echoed through the blackened hills and trees. All that followed was silence. *Damned wretch, he's gone.*

The moon above brightened once more, and Jirah looked to it for guidance. *Ignore what you hear,* Asheron had said. Jirah did not have a concern for gods, believing it was men and creatures that ultimately influenced the land. Yet now he found himself asking the Four Creators for aid.

"Gods," Jirah said aloud, "what am I supposed to do?"

Jirah was always a man of answers.

Now he looked to the sky with nothing but questions.

Chapter Nine

Aura of Naïveté

Zaedor Nethilus

Zaedor walked through the streets of Amirion after his daily teachings, on the way to his favorite tavern for dinner with an old friend. As he went, he helped the sick where he could, answered questions, provided insight to those who needed it, and enjoyed the cool breeze that passed through the city from the eastern seas.

The sun-bleached stone streets were scorched a bright white, heating his heavy plated boots as he walked. His armor was proudly pristine, shining brightly in the sun. He removed his steel helmet to cool his head, and his long blond hair flew out the back.

As he went, he admired the ornate architecture of the old kingdom, grandfathered from the times of the God's War. They remained a neutral state, which the late King Tirilin respected. Amirion's present ruler, King Faelin Caldrilla, gained great respect within his kingdom. They remained separate from the Renalian nation but lived as allies.

Things had been turbulent since Bracchus's death, however. The fresh, self-proclaimed rulers of each new state sought King Faelin's aid, but he stood strong against their requests. Each claimed the high throne for himself, with the exception of the leader of the Risen Isles, Raiya Firkann. Amirion stayed separate from the fray, as they had been their own entity since the banishment of the Broken clans by Bracchus the First, who wielded the rusted blade—a sword said to be passed down to the royal family by Shiada herself.

Banners of all colors flew on the homes of each family in the kingdom. The lengthy Grand Knight Road ran all the way through the hexagonal city, a wide, flat stone beast that moved through every district. Zaedor's strolls always began in his favorite place in the city, the temple district. It was the smallest, but also the most revered.

The temples of many gods lined the streets including his own, which possessed the largest clergy in Amirion, the Temple of Shiada. The temples were long, ornate stone structures surrounded by pillars and carved insignias of each deity. Shiada's was the six-point sun. It was similar to Amirion's sigil, the sun with the upturned blade. He felt they were one in the same, as if she was a citizen of Amirion herself.

The temple quarter was always clean, its pristine streets well kept by the city workers who maintained the streets both inside and outside of the city.

Zaedor came to the merchant's district, where merchants and permanent residents alike sat at tented booths as well as stone and mortar buildings. They hooted and hollered about their deals of the day and offered food and drink to priests and military leaders at no cost. The smell of salted fish, fresh fruits, and baker's bread filled his nostrils, which were coupled later with the searing forges. While offers were thrown his way as a member of the clergy, he tended not to take free gifts, as he wanted residents to gain the income they deserve for their work.

His favorite establishment made him hunger for a fresh meal. *Ah, Flourin's Cookery.* He briskly walked through the thin double doors, his belly roaring louder than the merchants outside. He chatted with the owner, Flourin, and sat down with Lothel, who awaited his arrival for their routine dinner.

Zaedor trained with Lothel in combat years ago. He was a strong proponent of peace, using blade and shield only to defend his teams during sparring skirmishes. He was an honorable man, Zaedor thought of him as a brother. He always strove to protect, rather than defeat. "How are the new squires and recruits?" Zaedor asked.

"You know how it is. They don't know the stances or the tricks, but I'll help them learn," Lothel said. He was the teacher in the barracks now. Countless citizens went through his training, then dispatched to the city walls or in the town patrols, along with all other citizens trained in combat. "Any news from the temple district? I hear more and more gather there daily due to the war outside the walls."

Zaedor nodded. "Yes, it is concerning. More and more hope for guidance and assurance, but we can only do so much." In the month prior, the number of attendants doubled in Shiada's temple alone.

Lounging back, Lothel drew his mouth out in displeasure. "The war is raging across the plains, brother. Rawling struck at the north in a surprise attack, and hit quite a few cities, pillaging and burning towns to make a statement. What are we supposed to do? Sit by?"

"We are neutral, Lothel. We cannot dance about interfering, endangering all we have worked for." It was a horrible thing, but their kingdom remained strong because they stayed separate, and would continue to.

Over the course of the meal, they spoke of fighting tactics, their teachings, and the adventures of the hunt from a couple of days before, as Lothel hunted in his free time. Zaedor, however, preferred rock carving. His home held many small stone figurines of horses, gargoyles, mountain lions, and more.

Zaedor would always carve a figurine for his wife, Eryndis, on her birthday. She was beautiful—tall, with bright green eyes and long, fiery red hair. They had been estranged for the past year and separated just recently. On her last birthday, he still carved her a small wolf made of white marble, flecked with a smokey grey. It was her favorite animal, yet she had a hint of sadness in her eyes as she accepted it. Zaedor did not know why. He still hoped he could reconcile with her one day.

When Zaedor was well fed and their banter came to an end, he left his graces and the copper for the meal, shook Flourin's hand, and went on his way. He shook Lothel's hand and patted his shoulder as they parted, and his friend walked to his home in the residential district.

Zaedor continued to the military district, the largest part of Amirion. There were buildings upon buildings of battle quarters laid in neat rows, and thousands of citizens in the kingdom were trained in combat. All physically able men and women were trained to fight. Even though Amirion was neutral, one could never be too careful. The ramparts surrounding the city went on for days, and archers stood at all angles. Their warriors were great, unstoppable in battle.

From any point in the city, the grand Blue Citadel, home to the royals, could be seen in the eastern end. The banner of Amirion was visible throughout the city. It was a bright yellow, eight-point sun, decorated with a gold and silver blade, nestled on a field of ocean blue. It resembled a peaceful kingdom that brought light to those who wished for it. The Citadel was a massive, rectangular behemoth. It featured a near-flat front, with towers protruding out at an angle to overlook the city below. It was two hundred feet high, with walls thick enough to withstand any bombardment.

Zaedor walked through his kingdom's streets and couldn't be happier to see it every day. His life was dedicated to this place—his god, his city, and his king. He needed nothing more. He was as satisfied as could be; he lived to serve.

"Excuse me!" a child's voice called out. "Excuse me, Captain Zaedor!" the voice called again. It belonged to a small boy he spotted during his teachings that day.

Zaedor turned and lowered himself to the child's level. "Hello, young man, what can I do for you?" he asked, warmly greeting him with a smile.

"Can I come to your classes on combat? Please?" the child begged and shook his gauntlet feverishly.

Zaedor was taken aback. Combat was only for those who reached adolescence at the age of twelve, and this boy was barely eight years old.

"I'm sorry, my friend, but combat classes aren't until you're bigger! My teachings of Shiada are important as well, you know. Where would we be without her protection?" The child looked disappointed. Zaedor knew he needed to help him with what he could. "What's your name, son?" he asked.

"Noah." The child said in a quiet voice, eyes fixed upon the stone road below.

"Listen, Noah," Zaedor brought his chin up to meet him eye-to-eye. "We may be a warrior kingdom, but all of our ways are important," he began. "Look above you, and all around you," He pointed up to the grand arches of the God's Gate, the entrance to Amirion, then to the massive Blue Citadel of the royalty. "We have learned that patience is crucial in daily life. Without it, we would not have the patience to build such grand structures. Each building has its own base and foundation. Each building block is necessary to complete the final structure." Noah raised an eyebrow and tilted his head to the side. Zaedor diverted from the issue at hand. "What I mean is, one must train his mind first," he pointed to Noah's forehead. "And we must also train our hearts," he slowly moved to Noah's chest, "so that we can wield our blades with respect. Each teaching is important. Without learning the basics, we cannot be strong individuals, soldiers, or a people."

Noah's expression brightened, but he didn't seem entirely convinced. He thought for a second, then decided to make a small exception for him. "I'll tell you what," Zaedor leaned in close, whispering lowly. "Next week, I can show you a few defense tactics after my teachings. No weapons allowed, though. And just this once. How does that sound?" he offered with a warm smile.

Noah's expression brightened, smiling as he jumped up and down. "Oh, thank you, thank you! I can't wait! I want to learn to protect my dad just like my mom does!" he ran off quickly.

"What a funny boy," Zaedor said to himself as he resumed his walk.

"Captain!" a man hollered with a light tone. It was Fildon Creadath, and his wife, Lilanda. A short, stout man with a long, grey beard, Fildon was a counselor for the King. His wife was tall and broad, with long, auburn hair, a priestess in the Temple of Shiada. He knew her well, as they often crossed paths at the temple.

"Greetings, Counselor Creadath. How may I help you?" he asked.

Fildon's smile faltered, glancing to his wife. "It's Rawling. He came back last week for an audience. He asked for our allegiance again. Kieran came last month, but left, respecting our king's will.

He proposed a steady peace—as long as Amirion maintained their neutrality. Rawling seemed more irritable this time. I swear on the gods, that man is unstable. It worries me." He glanced to his wife again and held her hand. "What should we do?"

His wife touched Zaedor on the shoulder. "You know the king better than I. Could you speak with him for us? At least ask him what he could do? During these turbulent times, who knows what the other rulers will do. It just concerns us. What if we're caught off guard? Our children—" her voice dropped off softly. "We don't know what to do."

"I have some time tonight. I will go to speak with him. You actually caught me on my post-teaching stroll through the town," he chuckled to himself, looking to the clear blue sky above. "But what about you, Counselor? Would the King not be more willing to listen to you?"

"I tried. He believes that Rawling trusts his judgment, and he respects the old ways. He sees no reason to think otherwise." His lip quivered in as he spoke. "Perhaps if more voices speak up, he will listen. Let me know what he says tomorrow, would you?"

"Yes Captain, please let us know. I'll see you in the temple tomorrow? Shiada be with you."

"And with you. I will see what I can do." He smiled happily. A visit with the King was always a joy, regardless of the purpose of his visit.

Zaedor took his leave and headed toward the Blue Citadel ahead. The fortress represented the strength of his people—and housed a king of much respect. Every member of the city was a proud resident, especially Zaedor. He lived for his kingdom and his god. He loved teaching residents about Shiada. She was the deity of protection, devoted to aiding the weak, and she rewarded those who promoted goodness.

She was said to have aided all races alike in the struggle against the sinister Draconia in the wars of old. Without her, victory would not have been possible.

Zaedor came to the gate of the Citadel, and the guards allowed him to pass freely. He was a Captain and one of the head clergymen, after all. The Citadel was as high as he could see, featuring bright walls lined with broad blue banners bearing the sign of Amirion. It was truly a symbol to his people's strength and fortitude. The grand halls were a maze, impossible to navigate if he hadn't already known the way. The sun shone through the large open windows. Knights stood at every door. Their white armor was as bright as the Grand Knight road, paired with lances and blades sharper than he had seen.

Climbing the stairs of the Citadel was a true trek; some say men have died attempting to ascend the whole structure in one morning. Luckily, the royal chambers were on the third floor. He waited some time while the guards went in to speak to the king, and then returned sometime later to wave Zaedor in. Night began to fall since he arrived.

Zaedor finally walked through the large doorway, into the grand hall. Stone pillars ran along the throne room on both sides, leading up to the Amirion throne where King Faelin sat leisurely, his wife, Tilandre by his side.

The King of Amirion greeted Zaedor with a warm smile. "Ah, Captain! To what do I owe this pleasure?"

"Thank you for seeing me, Your Grace. It's about the so-called King of Zenato."

The King let out a long, exhausted sigh. "Shiada save me. Zaedor, not this again." He waved a dismissive hand and rose from his throne. He sauntered toward the window. Staring out toward the city, the King said, "Rawling is not going to do any form of nefarious work, my friend. Doing so may provoke other nations now. He respects the old ways, I'm sure of it. I've already sent our most esteemed general to him to talk peace."

"Eryndis?" Zaedor said with a drawl.

"Yes. I know you two have gone your separate ways, but she is still my most trusted general. If Rawling respects any trait, it is strength, and Eryndis is stronger than any one of us. Except me of course!" He flexed briefly, before grabbing his lower back in pain.

King Faelin was once a mighty warrior whom wielded his great hammer in combat. He was said to be the strongest warrior of Amirion, crushing his competitors in training and the arena.

But those days were long passed. "Eh—it seems my age is getting to me." He laughed loudly before returning to his throne, taking on a more serious demeanor. "Trust me, Zaedor, our grand kingdom is safe. Tell whichever counselor sent you that we have nothing to worry about." He returned to a relaxed posture and smiled warmly once more. "Go and sleep on it. I'm sure you shall understand soon. Eryndis will return, and we will be at peace. Shiada be with you."

"And with you, Your Grace." Zaedor replied, taking his leave.

He knew the King was not strongly associated with the church, but Zaedor was happy that Faelin respected it. The King did seem very confident in his words.

Zaedor did not know whether he felt reassured but did know that he should not let his personal life make him unsettled. As he descended the Citadel once more, the dimly lit halls relaxed him marginally.

The calm flicker of torches reminded him that there was always light within the city, and it wouldn't be extinguished. In the final hall before he left there were no torches lit, except for one at the end—the lone Torch of Night. It was meant to soothe those who needed solace in the Citadel, and to symbolize the light that was Amirion, staying strong even in the darkest of times.

In the short walk to his home, there were few people in the streets. A couple men stumbled after some time in the tavern, while a few children chased dancing lights conjured by a street magician. The banners of families were still visible from the torchlight inside the house windows. Eventually, he reached his home in the temple district near Shiada's Temple. His family banner fluttered in the breeze above his door, a black wolf on a field of yellow and blue. Nearby, he heard a short exchange of whispers. Two individuals discussing business, it seemed.

"After, the work in Solmarsh should finish it. That's why it's being done there." One gravelly male voice said.

"That disgusting atrocity of a town? Why there?" a silvery female voice said.

"Quiet place, that's why. Plus, that fool can do the work for us down there. He practically begged for it to be there."

"I *suppose* you are correct. He *is* very peculiar and eccentric. Let us depart. There is much to do. The Cardinal awaits us."

The two sets of footsteps walked off into the night. *That's peculiar*, Zaedor thought. *Who is this Cardinal?* It was probably nothing, he figured. It was just the mutterings of common folk in the night. He shrugged his shoulders, entered his house, and lit a small fire in the stone fireplace. He quietly ate his late dinner while remembering the long day of teachings ahead, approaching quickly: his lessons of Shiada, combat training, and arithmetic.

Zaedor put out the fire after eating and lay in his rough spun, cloth bed, exhausted from his fulfilling day. "Rawling—" he said to himself. "Eryndis—"

Something didn't quite fit. He had a strange feeling, but he trusted the king. He put his trust in his god, Shiada, as well. She was a goddess with real evidence of power, such that protects her people. It was a happy belief to have. It helped him get through tougher times, as he and Eryndis separated due to their divergent beliefs a little less than a year ago. He missed her still, but Shiada's protection kept him resilient. Zaedor thought over lessons of the morrow before he passed into a deep, restful sleep.

Wake up.

Zaedor heard a female voice in his mind. It was soothing.

Zaedor, wake up. You have to live.

Why was this voice telling him to live? Was he dreaming it?

Zaedor! Wake up! There's no time!

His eyes flashed open. His senses flared from electrifying triggers in all directions: alarm bells, the heat of flames, the scent of smoke, and screams.

Chapter Ten

Mixed Motives

Lira Kaar

Lira stared longingly at the boar she hunted, slowly cooking above the campfire. She hadn't eaten in a day. Her stomach was now a rampaging Dragon, painful and relentless. She needed to distract herself, as the boar wouldn't be ready for at least another hour, so she brought out the small sewing needles and lemon-yellow yarn from her bag and went to work.

She saw Kayden's ratty teal scarf and she decided to knit another for her to switch out. Knitting soothed her when she was stressed. She made most of her own wardrobe, as well for many people in Solmarsh. She was one of the few clothiers there. It was always something she could go to for a fun project, and it was always something new. She brought a few cloth dresses with her, even though she might not be able to wear them. It reminded her of where she came from.

They chose a lovely spot to settle: the sun was tucking in for a night's rest in the east, with a sky of red, orange, and golden yellow surrounding it. Thin, smooth-barked sirilius trees loosely surrounded them with branches overhead, their long, threaded split leaves leaving cross-hatched shade below. The smell of the campfire overpowered the flowers and boar thus far, but Lira didn't mind. She liked the scent—it reminded her of fires with her family when she was young.

The group hadn't spoken much since they began their trip back. Vesper muttered to himself, Magnus and Domika strolled and sat side by side and whispered to each other, although she did most of the talking. She was fairly inquisitive, but he seemed quiet and dismissive—although that seemed in line with his nature. As long as Domika was apart from Kayden, she was in good spirits.

Kayden sat alone in the tall trees near the clearing, scouting the area. She seemed to prefer the life of a lone wolf; Lira did not know why, nor understood it, preferring close relationships. Since her brother was arrested, she lived a lonelier life than she liked. The fateful day one month prior—the day she lost him—was one that laced her nightmares.

It was all my fault. If I simply followed what he'd said, he might still be here, Lira thought. *Now he might be part of the moved prisoners. I have to find him.* She dropped her wool and needles, curled her knees in closer, and wrapped her arms around them. She feared the worst. Prisoners were sent for torture and 'special treatment.' Lira wished she knew what it meant, but at the same time, she didn't. But the dream told her to abandon him. *Souls are in the balance,* it told her. *You will suffer as well.*

The thought itself frightened her. She didn't know whether to continue, or to go home to Solmarsh, safe and sound. At the same time, her guilt dug at her like a blade in her side. *We know prisoners are being moved to Deurbin. I know we should go there, but who set us up? Who can be trusted?* Lira knew someone in the rebellion must have set them up for capture. *What if we get captured again?* They had been diligent in their watch, especially Kayden. She spent hours in the trees, silent and watchful, never even closing her eyes. Sometimes Lira felt she didn't sleep. Lira would lie awake, worrying for her brother, and Kayden would be there, watching the path.

"What's wrong, princess?" Kayden asked. While Lira was lost in thought, Kayden jumped down from her tree and walked over. She seemed much more relaxed than in the jail. Lira looked to the clearing, seeing Magnus on watch. Seems they switched while Lira was deep in thought. Domika stood beside him, attempting to distract him with conversation, but he gave little notice. "C'mon, you look like a lost puppy over here. Domika is talking with her silent guardian, Vesper is over there practicing being better than us, and you're sitting all alone." She sat down beside Lira.

She was right—Lira *was* on her own, and quite unhappy to boot. "I'm just thinking about my brother," Lira replied. "He was arrested, two fortnights ago today. He might be part of the arrests we discovered before Asheron caught us."

Kayden looked to her with concerned eyes. "Oh," she began. It was almost like she didn't know what to say. Of all people, she was the most surprising to see speechless. Kayden always had *something* to say. "I'm sorry," she croaked out finally, looking back to the fire in silence.

Lira glanced over to the strange pair, Domika and Magnus. He patiently listened as she talked his ear off like a young girl about the deserts, holding his arm at times when she seemed enamored by her own thoughts.

Vesper was a curious one. He sat beside a small pond, weaving his arms back and forth practicing his spells. They varied from fox-ears, to swirling small flames, to forming tiny icicles in his hands. He was extremely methodical. He was more cautious than any magician Lira saw before. *Then again, magicians always have to be careful. The Cull of Magic was a thousand years ago, and since then, strict laws have been put on the magic one can use.* The Cull still frightened Lira, when wizards were found and killed in the streets, boiling up to a devastating war between those that could use magic, and those that couldn't. In the end, magic lost. Each nation now had a Council of Magi, discerning who could use what spells, and an academy to teach proper use. Vesper created water from nothing and placed it in flagons, then moved them with his mind to a flat rock near the fire.

"Thank you, sir," Magnus called to him. He carefully grabbed a cup for everyone and passed them out. His hands twitched as he offered them; Lira remembered the torture he was put through. Domika winced as she grasped the cup as well. They had blades shoved underneath their fingernails while Lira and Kayden were left in the cells. Lira worried about them but was glad they were free.

Vesper smiled and nodded before turning back to his spell casting with a fierce concentration, muttering the command words so quietly that Lira couldn't hear.

Magic was a curious thing to Lira. It was a force of nature, one of the many foundations of the world. Just like water, fire, earth, and air, magic was a separate, natural element of the world. It allowed people to manipulate the other elements to their will. Only few were born with such gifts. Lira was, in a way; she was gifted by birth with an affinity for divine magic. Divine powers could only be granted by the gods. If one prayed and did the will of their deity, their powers could range from weak to extremely powerful. There were powers of healing, shielding, and light, but also darkness, pain, and destruction.

The difference between Shiada and Lornak, Lira thought, examining the brand of the six-pointed sun upon her hand. Lira never used hers for much because she couldn't ever go beyond healing small wounds. Regardless, she still prayed to Shiada. She believed deities had a plan, so she chose to follow rather than reject it as nonsense.

"Is that ring from him?" Kayden asked.

Lira noticed she spun the silver ring round and round on her finger as she thought about it. "Oh, yes. It's one of the few things I have from him." Lira stared at her ring. The tiny inscription read, *Devotion and Faith*—words her mother said were important. "It's really hard, but that's why I'm here." She gazed to the fire, taking a drink of water. "To find him—and help people." Lira paused for a moment, glancing at Kayden. She stared hundreds of yards ahead, as if each was a thought running through her mind all at once.

Lira hadn't talked to many people since she'd left Solmarsh. Domika talked a bit to her, but she kept to Magnus for the most part. She wanted to try to get to know the ones she traveled with. She wasn't sure if it was normal for rebels, but she wasn't an ordinary criminal. "Why did you join the Scions?" Lira asked.

She hadn't asked anyone yet, and Kayden was the most curious one. She seemed like she didn't want to be part of the team at all. They were forced into a team for the first mission, and it went terribly.

Kayden blinked owlishly and looked to Lira with a reserved expression. "I don't like tyrants." She looked down to Lira's yarn. "What are you working on?"

Lira paused for a moment at the odd change of topic—then noticed she'd picked up her needles subconsciously and begun knitting again. She was quite good at talking, thinking, and knitting all at once. She was too embarrassed to say she was already making something for Kayden. "I'm knitting a couple of things. If I'm in for a long trip, I should get ready for the season of Air, right?" She let out a nervous giggle.

Kayden chuckled. "Long time 'til then, but I like your tenacity. What kinds of things do you make?"

"Oh, lots of things. I made my robe, my gloves, my—well, pretty much everything. I was a clothier for the temple where I was taught my divine magic, so I took it up as my profession once I was—*ah*—old enough to practice on my own." She half-hid the fact that she wasn't accepted to pretty much all temples due to her lack of healing or magical ability as a whole.

"I wish I'd learned some of those skills. I just practice my fighting. Not much else." She seemed want to say more but didn't.

An awkward feeling filled the air around them. She decided to change the topic. "What kind of profession did you do before joining this?" Lira asked. She didn't know anything about Kayden's past, as she was fairly secretive. Then again, she worried the answer was going to be something nefarious.

"I wouldn't exactly say I have a typical past, princess." Kayden scratched her head roughly.

"What do you mean?" Lira inquired.

"I lived in many different places. I lived in the east, the north, the northeast, the southeast—the list goes on." Kayden picked at her short fingernails.

"Of Loughran?" she asked, thinking it was just this province.

Kayden let out a quick laugh. "No. Renalia."

Much bigger. Five times that. "Why so many places? I've only lived in two towns, despite us being the same age." Lira wondered about all the places Kayden had been. It all seemed so wondrous.

Kayden's face was a blank canvas. "It was my job." She looked at Lira with a curious eye.

Lira felt her lingering stare, and finally looked over. Kayden's narrowed amber eyes analyzed her as if reading her mind. Lira looked around, not knowing what to say. "Is everything okay?"

After a strange pause, Kayden sighed. "Yeah, everything's not too bad, actually." She looked back into the fire. "I worked for the Guild of Shades. Heists, collections, and smuggling—" her voice dropped off. She almost said another word, but held back.

"What made you leave?" Lira asked. She wasn't that surprised at Kayden's past, but didn't consider it a problem. She felt Kayden was a kind person at heart.

Kayden shook her head and narrowed her eyes once more. "You talk as if you aren't even fazed by it." With a sigh, she said, "I left for a stupid reason. Should have left long before. Sometimes you just don't see what's right in front of you. It's the best decision I ever made."

Lira nudged her. "Well I'm glad you did. If you hadn't, you wouldn't be here, and I might still be in jail."

"Yeah, I guess you owe me one," Kayden said bluntly. "But you're the one who got us out of the hall."

Lira just smiled and looked at the dirt beneath her feet, glad she contributed. "What's it like in the east? I hear the sands are beautiful," Lira asked. She dreamt of them sometimes in her childhood, seeing the streets of desert cities, jumping, running, and seeing all sorts of wondrous things.

"They can be. They can also be unforgiving," Kayden replied. "People don't care about the laws—the few there are. There's a lot more discrimination. There's some in the north, too. Here as well, from what I hear."

Lira was taken aback. She'd spent all of her life in the west, living only in her hometown of Ordana. She also recently lived in Solmarsh, since her father moved to the Orinde Monastery. She heard the sands in the east were almost white, gleaming with the sun's rays every day of the year. In the marshlands, it rained nonstop. Thunderstorms were plentiful, and the forests were full of beasts. She dreamed of the sands at times, imagining the beautiful sandstone cities of the desert. She pictured their cultures and festivals, all the wondrous colors of clothing and banners and all the fun events they had. To hear they were discriminatory was a bit of a shock. Lira decided to press further, as discrimination could mean many things. She knew of the discrimination against the Broken and their kin due to the wars ten years prior, and the savage past they had. *What else was there?* "What kinds of discrimination do you mean? Blaziks?" she asked.

"No." Kayden brushed her mane of hair with her fingers. "In the north and west, some aren't a fan of runts."

"Runts? What do you mean?" Lira normally heard the term associated with mixed bred wild dogs and other animals. *What's so bad about them?* she wondered.

Kayden sighed, "Damn, you really are sheltered." she rolled her eyes and brushed back her hair, revealing a brand—a line with a snake coiled around it behind her ear. "Low-borns."

"I'm sorry. I didn't know. I don't think—"

"I know, princess. I can tell you don't care who we are—since you're low-born too, I guess. They're treated much better in these parts." Kayden sported a stony expression. "Although your need to reassure everyone is a little irritating. That, and your incessant questions."

Lira took a sip of water during the silence. She wasn't sure of what to say. Some gave her a different look when she came to a noble region of cities, but she thought nothing of it. She had a few negative comments directed toward her in cities outside her own, but she didn't travel much. "What about the east?"

"Slaves," Kayden added. She stared blankly into the fire. Her scarred olive skin glowed in the light of the fire, nearly making the marks non-existent.

Lira barely held back a gasp. "Slaves? How?" Now Lira was more curious than ever, and slightly afraid. She noticed some travelers from the east coming with multiple workers, but thought they were simply paid help. *They were all so nice,* she thought.

Kayden shot her an unsettling look. "Slavery is common. It's not illegal, and some people take advantage of that if you let them. Sorry to give you a bad view of your world, princess, but that's reality." Kayden dismissed her, quickly getting up. "I'm gonna get back to my spot and keep watch. Part of me thinks Mags won't be able to concentrate much longer with that one talking his ear off." Before she left, she turned her head to look. "I'm sorry about your brother. You'll find him." She walked off quickly.

Lira found Kayden's reaction a little odd but was happy she finally saw a kinder side of her. It was refreshing after so much of her rough-edged, intimidating side. Lira drew her hand to her chin, wondering what she meant. Kayden was short, but her personality wasn't lacking in stature. Lira wouldn't dare pick a fight with her. She was also knowledgeable, while Domika believed otherwise. Lira still didn't know much about Kayden's past, but she wished to learn more.

She couldn't rid her mind of the companions that surrounded her. Every time she spoke with Kayden, Domika, Vesper or even the quiet Magnus, Lira felt more and more sheltered. *I couldn't help it. What's wrong with a quiet life?* she thought defensively. Lira felt like she wanted to return to Solmarsh or Ordana, or even go to a quieter land, like the Risen Isles.

Everyone on the team was special in some way. Kayden was quick and stealthy, Vesper was magically skilled, Domika was fierce and smart, and Magnus was strong as an ox. *I'm not like any of them— I don't know if I belong here.* Lira stared upward, watching the sky begin to darken. The tree branches hung low overhead, drooping low to the ground in places. The sound of crickets echoed from around her, and the smell of boar meat filled her nostrils. It only made her hungrier. Lira glanced back to Vesper, astonished by his resilience. She knew the magical arts were high-maintenance, practice and study being most important, but his practice seemed excessive.

Vesper's eyes never lost focus. He moved the water in the pond beside them about. He raised it, lowered it, turned it into a blade, a set of small orbs, and more. He muttered the commands of various spells, but Lira couldn't hear. For some, he didn't say a thing.

Lira no longer faced the fire but faced Vesper's display. She couldn't help but stare.

His hands moved gracefully, coddling balls of flame, swiping his hand with a blade of ice, and pressing the earth gently beneath him. As Lira watched quietly, Vesper moved with more and more ferocity. He almost seemed to be in a trance, as if nothing could stop him. The flames grew, he lifted water in greater quantities, and he seemed to beckon the earth effortlessly.

Lira shuffled a little closer, entranced by his show.

Vesper didn't seem to notice her presence. He swirled a snake of fire around him, and Lira found even the ones behind her grew silent. He swung his weight around gracefully, and the snake with it, growing larger and larger, until he threw his hands forward; the snake soared out from him, and the column of fire flew right at Lira.

Lira gasped, let out a yelp, and shot backward onto the dirt. Vesper noticed her presence finally, swirled his hands outward then in, and the snake disappeared right a moment before her face. Only subtle warmth was left behind, along with the beats of Lira's panicked heart.

Vesper stumbled toward her, with eyes wide and breaths shallow. "M—my dear, are you hurt?" His eyes shot behind her.

Lira looked back, seeing the others standing up, ready, each as shocked as the next. Lira slowly drew her eyes back to Vesper. "I'm—"

"I must apologize. I became lost in the act. I was being absent minded. It will not happen again. Forgive me, *please*," he pleaded. He shook her hands, with eyes that spoke a tale of fear.

Lira couldn't speak a word, still feeling the flame that vanished moments ago that could have killed her.

Kayden, however, stomped over in an instant and grabbed Vesper by the neckline to force them face-to-face. "Be careful with your magic! How could you be so reckless?" Kayden yelled. "You could have *hurt* her."

"I didn't mean to, I swear it!" Vesper yelped, waving his hands around.

Letting him go, Kayden snarled a few more words. "I don't want to see any more of that tonight. The last thing we need is another body on our hands." Kayden growled. She hopped back up to her tree, keeping a sharp eye on the violet-robed wizard.

Lira tried to calm her shallow breaths. Vesper only got up, whispering he was sorry once more, and sat on a rock by the water.

Domika came to check on her with a warm smile before heading back toward her stalwart listener.

The sun hid beneath the horizon as Vesper raised his hands to rub his head and take a breath. Lira knew magic drained one's mental energy. She heard stories of magicians passing out, some never waking again, and some even dying from their use of magic too powerful for them to handle. Lira grabbed one of the cups Vesper gave them and brought it over. She was frightened by magic, especially with the show she just witnessed, but was still so curious. She was a little glad there would be no more practicing tonight.

"Why thank you, my dear," he said with an exhaustive breath. "I seem to be getting a little up in years," he whispered. He looked out to the bay, as if longing for something.

She had so many questions. She knew so little about the non-divine forms of magic. "Vesper, why do you concentrate so much on each spell? I've seen some people practice before, but you seem almost as if you strain too much when casting. Why is that?" Her first question seemed overly silly to her.

"I concentrate because I must control my incantations. You viewed the consequences of my foolishness." He rubbed his knees with shaky hands. "With each movement, even the most miniscule vibration of a hand may alter the resulting spell. Absolute control is a necessity when using energies like this." He cautiously ruffled his beard, eyes closed in solemn thought. "I do not want to injure anyone with my abilities," he said plainly. His face turned stoic. It was a strange, emotionless expression, especially on a man who was usually so vibrant.

"I know everyone has a ceiling of power," Lira said quietly. She fumbled with her fingers. "Mine is disappointing. I can barely heal a scratch." Phyrin, *to mend,* was the command—but did nothing for her. There were so many other spells—*Fhor,* the force of light, *Bashira,* to send one back… A priest found out she could use the divine magic when she was young, but he refused to take her as a disciple as he couldn't help her power grow. "May I ask how high yours is?"

Vesper sighed, rubbing his forehead. "High enough. I do not tamper with my ceiling. I dislike using powerful spells."

Powerful spells. Ones she feared to even think of using. One above all being *Mortanai Shala*—the light that sears flesh. She never saw much reason to use such a spell. "I just haven't seen much of the world of magic," she replied. "What kinds of things can you do?" She wanted to learn more about magic, and this seemed like a good chance. "Sorry If I'm imposing," she whispered bashfully.

His eyes closed and brow tightened. "Oh no, my dear, you are not imposing, not at all. I can do many things. I can create icicles, move water to my will, create a blaze, as you saw." His hands moved whimsically as he spoke. He paused, shooting Lira a curious eye. "And hear the conversations of others from afar." His voice turned somber. "I'm sorry to hear about your brother, my dear," he nodded. "With this recent news, it is concerning."

She frowned at his decision to listen in, but decided arguing wasn't worth it. "Thanks."

"Everyone experiences loss," Vesper added. "Miss Ralta has lost many things—that is why she has so many walls built to defend herself—and why she threatened me with such intensity after the incident. She seems to trust you, however."

Lira took that as a compliment, as Kayden seemed a little less brash with her than others. She wondered why, but in the end was happy that Kayden trusted someone. "How can you tell?"

He shrugged and pointed a finger to his eyes. "You can see it in her eyes. The look she has when she thinks no one sees."

"She is fierce, but I saw a new side of her today," Lira said.

"Indeed, I noticed. She actually smiled without mockery. That is quite an interesting development. Perhaps it is because we kept her and Miss Mirado separate." Vesper chuckled. "As for Miss Mirado, I have not had the opportunity to talk to her as of yet. She does seem quite preoccupied with herself. Sir Magnus, however, is an interesting one."

In the distance, Magnus still listened to Domika's ranting. "Interesting? How do you mean?"

He looked towards them in the distance with a tilt to his head. "He does not seem intelligent, yet his words are proper. He does not seem fast or battle-ready, but his armor was battered and burnt." Vesper ruffled his beard, snapped his finger in the air, and swished it in a circle. "I believe he is hiding something."

Magnus' voice erupted from the clearing. "Why do you not leave it be? Never ask such a question of me again. It is not your place to ask!" His calm demeanor was broken. His red eyes burned with anger. He jutted his chin, clenched his fists, and stormed off into the open forest with stomps louder than a bull.

"What in the hells? Mags, wait!" Domika called, running after him. She stopped briefly in front of Lira and Vesper. "All I did was ask his about his family, a few—*several* times," she mumbled to them. Domika returned to a run to go after him. Lira could hear her call to Magnus, then her attempts to reassure him.

Lira saw Kayden up in her perch with a smirk. She chuckled before she returned her gaze to the nearby areas. *What is he hiding?* she wondered.

"Curious. Now why would he want to avoid his name being known, *hmm*? If he is the traitor, he is not hiding it well. I do not believe I am the only one with this in mind," Vesper said, hinting over to the perch, where Kayden glanced suspiciously into the forest where the two ran. "Why was he so adamant on acquiring the armor without stating his reason? I would gladly deliver the armor to it's appropriate place. But I stated my intention, as did Kayden and Domika," Vesper said eyes closed, deep in thought. "I suppose I feel it is slightly peculiar," he finished.

Lira pondered Vesper's words. *They're wise, but are they right?* Magnus seemed quite harmless, and kind. Why *did* he want the armor? Either way, he'd worn it ever since he received it, save when he slept. Even then, a hand was always on it. *Why does he not want people to know his name?* His behavior was certainly strange, but Lira grew tired of wracking her brain over it. Her stomach turned again and again in hunger. She glanced to the boar on the fire. It began to form pools of succulent fat on the skin as it crackled. The meat was ready. Her mouth watered for her first meal in a day. "Food's ready!" she yelled.

Kayden jumped down from her perch in no time. Domika and Magnus emerged from the forest at full speed.

"Finally!" Domika yelled.

Everyone gathered around the fire and they split the meat evenly, along with the berries and nuts Kayden gathered. The pain of yesterday was forgotten, and the rebellion was in the back of their minds, for once. Everyone seemed in good spirits. As Lira dug into her dinner, she still wondered about what Vesper said, and what it could mean for their future.

Somewhere, Noren lies in pain, or dead. I can't forget why I joined. Lira looked to the others as she ate quietly, wondering what their motives were. Domika wanted to keep her brother safe, Lira wanted to find hers—but what about the others? Kayden seemed to dislike authority, Vesper seemed like he hardly belonged, and she wasn't sure what Magnus wanted at all.

Chapter Eleven

A Coward's Way

Saul Bromaggus

Saul returned at dusk to the Gadora clan on the southwestern end of the Vale. Each clan was a strong, venomstone-walled city. The houses were wooden and stone, depending on the status of the family. He walked past the guards and entered the city after they raised the portcullis. He passed rows of organized houses, mapped in a methodical manner. A few were being painted white, silver, and bronze by Broken. Every citizen possessed a second profession used to serve the society: cooks, builders, clothiers, and more.

Saul was a talented chef—or so he thought. He cooked boar and stag the most, roasting them in succulent duck fat alongside seasonings of the Vale. He heard the torch and the plateau had their own specially grown seasonings as well.

As much as he hated the thought of going away, there may be some benefits. He learned from his other comrades in training about their trades, like carpentry, stonework, and foraging. He didn't know all the details and intricacies, but every profession had its challenges. No matter the artisanship, each Broken was just as quick with a weapon, even if they made silk robes or picked herbs and fruits on the side.

Saul arrived at his home, a large venomstone building lined with gardens. One grizzly Broken in black-scaled armor exited the home. His eyes gazed at the ground, not noticing Saul's presence.

"Uncle, is that you?" Saul called.

The Broken looked up, and indeed it was. His face was paler than Saul remembered, with dry, cracked skin wrinkled around his eyes and throat. His shoulder-length white hair was scraggly and unkempt.

"Oh my. Saul, you've grown!" The tribe keeper said, who tended to business in homes of those gone if he hadn't delegated the task to another. He was also family, so it was not out of the blue.

Saul raised a brow as he walked over. "I have not grown since I was sixteen years of age, uncle."

His uncle patted Saul on both shoulders, gripped them tightly, and shook them. "Ah, but you've grown stronger, my boy."

Looking over uncle Grotar's shoulder toward the door, he raised a brow. "What were you doing in my family's home?"

He gave a shrug, as if being in the home of another without them present was nothing. "Oh, I was keeping the home while members of the tribe paid their homage to your father. Despite his 'treason,' there are those that supported his view." Grotar sighed while feverishly scratching his head. "I am sorry for your loss. It is hard when a Broken loses their parents."

Saul had not truly let it click until then. His mother died fighting in the war ten years prior, and now his father had been burned for treason.

His cousins and uncle lived, but his close family was all gone. It was not common for the Broken to have more than one child, and his family was no exception. Saul shuffled his feet, and grumbled to himself. *The Dragon took them from me.*

"Will you be staying with us? Your graduation is soon, is it not? The Oracles have given you the mark?" Grotar moved his eyes in close to his left arm. "Oh my. Your mark says interesting things."

"There are more."

"Eh?" Grotar pulled back with wide eyes, still gripping Saul's arms. He moved in close to the other, and his grip tightened. "Oh my, this is even *stranger*. What do you think it means?" He raised a brow, and his eyes examined Saul closely.

Saul thought about it, truly. *Am I to die by the Dragon's claw?* "The Oracles have shown me a path, and I do not know how it will turn or proceed." Saul knew he was beating around the bush.

"I hope this does not bode badly for you. Your cousins would see you, if you would like. They are in the north end of the tribe. Just find my home, if you remember it, and I will show you to them. They have not seen you in a year."

"Tomorrow I will be exiled, Uncle. After my father's death, the Dragon decreed me to go across the Fissure into the wastes," Saul said. *Damned dragon. I should fight him and fulfill the fate that chose me.*

His uncle leaned back, releasing his arms. His dark eyes widened, looking at his nephew, then behind, and around him. "I see," he scratched the back of his head. The moonlight shone overhead, causing his grey skin to tint a pale blue. "I'm sorry, I suppose I should not communicate with you then. An exile is—"

"A disgrace," Saul admitted, eyes at the dirt below them. Communication with him would cause others to see his uncle as a fool, and Saul wouldn't allow it. "I will miss you, Uncle. I thank everyone for their homage to my father."

"He was a great man."

"He *is* a great man. Death is only the beginning."

Grotar laughed. "I suppose you are right, boy." He sighed, backing away to go to his home. "Good luck, Saul. You may be an exile, but you will always be a Bromaggus." A flash of the moon crossed his eyes as he turned to walk.

Saul nodded, thanking him silently. An exile was seen as a disgrace to a family, and some would strip them of the name. His uncle gave him a great gift.

Saul turned to the door and entered his home. Each placement of his boot echoed through the stone walls. Still as dark as he remembered—a forest green and filled with black mortar. The size was large for a Broken, two bedrooms, an eating area and food preparation room, and a place for seating and conversation. Far too frivolous.

Various weapons and battle gear laid on tables around the home. Pieces of plate, mail, scale, and weapons of all kinds were placed on the main forum table by members of the clan out of respect for his father. He saw the marks of many family names—Kitarin, Grodagh, Bordanok, and many additional members of the Bromaggus name. He silently thanked them for their honors.

His eyes scanned across the bedroom he had not slept in for a year—ten years since he left it for his military training and education at the age of ten. The old and cramped cloth-covered bed in the corner beckoned him after a day of travel—but sat with a note set with wax in his family's seal upon the pillow beside his father's dark cloak. Saul didn't notice his father wasn't wearing it at the audience; a cloak was one piece that a parent passed to their children.

Feeling the felt of the cloak, a tear crept from his eye, realizing it was the first—and last—cloak he would receive. His mother's was lost across the sea. She was always confident—perhaps too confident.

Saul lit a flame in the lantern by his bed to read the note. Saul did not know many written words, but his father used those he knew in the letter.

My son, today you are a warrior. You are born to lead, your training masters say. Be strong. The greatest warriors protect rather than rule the weak. I will be training in the skies alongside the greatest warrior I ever knew.

Your father,

Greln Bromaggus XIV

Reading his father's words, he tethered the brown cloak to his armor and lay on his bed. His arms were uncovered; he refused to be ashamed of his marks. Quiet and careful—but not ashamed. He still had to come to terms with his fate. *Tomorrow, I am to be exiled. Banished to the Neck of the Seven. I'd rather be dead,* Saul thought.

He wondered what awaited him in the south, where idiocy was rampant, and order absent. Residents of the Vale hadn't been there since the wars of Cadrayda, the leader of Serpentarius then. Two hundred years past, she attempted to take over the Vale and eliminate the Broken from the land.

The great warrior, Lokthori—quick as the wind, and deadly as a lightning strike—brought forth the might of Yggranda, cutting the continent in two, leaving the great Fissure between the north containing the Vale and the Torch, and the south containing the Neck of the Seven and the Serpent's Plateau.

The only connection between the two was the tether, a small set of carts that carried up to four individuals at a time, across the two-mile wide Fissure along a rope. Made of threads of Vale trees and intertwined with steel of the plateau, it was nigh unbreakable. Attempts were made, but both sides—while hating one another—understood the importance of diplomacy and trade.

Two ends that hate one another. But why? Being exiled is sending me to my death. They would slay me for going further than the city of Alin. Alin was supposedly a stronghold for the Hydris, in case of war. Both sides were watched, so armies couldn't cross to mount an attack.

His father wrote that he was born to lead. "Peh," he scoffed. *A man exiled is a man with nothing—no honor, and no reason to live.* His father wrote it not knowing what his actions did to his son's fate. He was banished to a land he would be killed for existing in. Saul was too proud to finish his own life. Perhaps he would bring combat, fighting the soldiers of the south in a valiant death, like Grawth the Stalwart.

He could hear the sounds of glory in his mind. The sounds of clashing blades, roars of battle, and the slam of shields echoed loudly. It was as if he was part of it. He felt exile was the path of shame with no glory in it. He was stripped of his place in society, left to wander the south alone. He had no army, no comrades, and no woman to unify with. No woman wanted a disgraced Broken for a husband. The clashing rang loudly, and his imagination ran wild with where he would go and what he could do. *You are born to lead,* he reminded himself. *A ridiculous thought.* His father's hopes were too high.

Yet even when his thoughts faded, the clashing, yells, and sounds of war still continued. Saul exploded off his bed.

The sounds are real.

A rush of flame echoed from outside, and a deafening, guttural roar echoed from overhead. Saul ran out with weapons readied. His people were fighting for their lives as Broken armed to the teeth stormed into his clan. A sharp stream of violet-black serpentine scales flew over his home, like the shadow of death.

The Dragon landed on the elder's home, crushing it into the ground. "*Where is the heathen!*" he roared.

Saul stood strong and ran forward to the battle he would win, but was grabbed and pulled into an alleyway against the black pitch of night. A powerful plate gauntlet covered his mouth.

A smooth, resounding whisper came with it. *"Do not speak."*

Saul breathed heavily through his long nose, heart pounding like a thousand horse charge. He struggled, but the grip on him was too powerful. The figure brought him further back, slowly. *Is he going to kill me? No, if he wanted to, he would already, or maybe give me to the beast,* Saul reasoned. He writhed and struggled, wanting to fight for his people. He heard rushes of flame and the screams of dying men, along with the smell of ash.

The dragon's voice barreled through the clan streets. "Traitors of Gadora! Your council member committed treason, and his son seeks revenge! You stand guilty as a clan. Turn him in and be rewarded, or reject me and burn!" Obelreyon yelled.

Saul saw Red marks on the arms of others, the mark of Kannakash, Urikar, Yggranda, and even *Gadora*. They had fear in their eyes, buried deep, but Saul could see it from afar. It was fear for their lives that pushed them to betrayal. "Let—me—*go*!" Saul screamed under the gauntlet.

"No. You have to stop talking, and come with me," the voice said.

"Let me die in defense of my people!" Saul roared. "I will not die a disgraced fool!"

"They die because of you. Do you want to die with them, or live long enough to bring vengeance back?"

Saul stopped struggling, but his blood still charged through his veins.

"Look further than two feet in front of you," Saul felt a dagger on his neck. "They are going to die, whether you are there or not. You will save no one this way."

The blade left his neck, and he was promptly released. Saul slowly turned to see a man—Renalian, surely—with a pale, sharp-featured face lit by the devastating flame from outside the alley. His hair was greyed, woven with white stripes. His armor shone brightly in from the flames, decorated with silver studs and golden rings, icy steel layers, and an ice-blue cloak hung down to his ankles.

"Who are you?" Saul demanded.

"No one," he said with a smirk. "A friend has sent me here to retrieve you, but I do hate kidnapping. I prefer you come willingly." His bright green eyes shimmered in the flame behind. If you must know, it's Highwind."

Highwind. That name was whispered through the clans during the war ten years ago. "Why help a Broken?"

"A friend asked for my help, and I am here to give it. I am here because I was called."

Saul was bothered by his cryptic nature. *Say what you mean, fool.* Saul knew better than to challenge a seasoned warrior, though, if Mirakia was any example. "Why must I flee?" Saul growled.

Two Broken ran into the alley with a battle cry. "There he is!" one yelled.

Kain threw Saul to the wall and dashed forward with the dagger. He deflected a blade and an axe with the small weapon, and cut both their throats with ease. "Because, I am risking my life to help you. Don't be a coward and run to a worthless death. Do you choose to run, or do you choose to die?"

It is cowardly to run, Saul thought. He struggled with the choice. On one hand he could fight a battle to defend his people and die with the honor he sought. On the other, there was a man who challenges his ways to run into exile and cower from his enemy. It tested every part of his being not to stand tall and accept the consequences. His people screamed from outside the alleys as they were carved, cut down, and burned. *I should be with them, I brought this upon them.* His anger for the Dragon seethed further, eyes burning with revenge.

My fate chooses that I die, Saul remembered. But a choice stood before him in the form of a man laden with silver studs, plate, and a silver cloak cascading down his prominent figure. *I can live long enough to bring vengeance. My father chose his fate, and I will choose mine.* He would bring it, whether by his own power, or with an army he could muster. "I will go."

"Took you long enough, lad. On the horse. We ride for the Fissure. It will be a long journey," Highwind said.

They jumped atop his massive stallion, black hair intermingled with silvers and whites. It was a great beast, running at full speed with both men atop its back. They rode out of the camp through a region of the wall that had been broken and dismantled.

Through the Vale, Saul watched the blackwood trees pass by, then the far mountains—places he may never see again. The white thistlefogs blew in the wind, flowering only in the deep forest of Obelreyon's Vale. The moonlight shone above, full and true. It felt blood red, as the color of the ground in the Gadora tribe.

For two days they rode, during which Highwind kept fairly quiet. He answered some of Saul's questions, but didn't speak to the majority. Kain didn't know anything about his marks, about the gods, or about the Dragon's plans.

"Are you lying to me?" Saul wanted to know.

"I'm not one for predictions, son," Highwind replied.

Son. Who does he think he is, calling me that? Saul hated that he ran from the one who killed his father. He was young, nineteen years, definitely younger than the man who ushered him from his burning home. Saul thought to fall on his own blade, as it was less cowardly than to run from a fight he caused. *Why live, as my people burn? Obelreyon wouldn't dare cross the Fissure. I would be safe. But I'm a coward. That's all I am. I'm running from my fate.*

"Why are you taking me to exile?" Saul asked. It was strange enough to be taken away by a human of all things, let alone during the night he would be slain.

"I've told you many times, son," he said with a sigh. "I was called, and I answered."

Saul did not enjoy vagueness. "Who called you, then?"

"A friend. You will see soon enough."

Saul questioned further but received no information, which irritated him. They rode across the plains connecting the bottom of Lathyria, the Vale, and the Fissure. Saul dared not go to the Torch, as Broken were killed on sight, rumors said. Open fields rarely seen, filled with tall grass, trees with bristles, and leaves with several points, bushes of black with small white flowers emerging from all sides. He never saw these, never having left Obelreyon's Vale and the three knives.

Soon, the Vale was gone, and he would live where he had only heard stories. Some cities of the Neck were lawless; some were so strict they would kill a man for bumping into a guard. Individual cities not bound to a king, only by a city leader.

What was worse was the Hydris, a slithering, snake-like race with arms and legs, smooth and sometimes scaly skin varying from reds to blues to greens, and snake eyes. A vile set of beings said to have stabbed the Broken councilors and warmaster in the back centuries ago, forcing them to split the continent in two.

It was separated by the Fissure—a chasm so deep, the bottom could not be seen. The sea flowed through thousands of feet below the surface of the continent, with the rest of the Ocean.

"Where do you come from?" Saul asked him.

"A new nation, Ornias, in Renalia."

Highwind was no doubt a military figure. His armor was worn in places, but well-made and he was quick to kill even with a dagger. Saul did not dare confront him. *He pulled me from the maw of death, as well.* Saul was confused of how this man even came to travel here, and how long the journey to Kathynta was; Renalia was a quarter season's sail away from the Vale. "Is it true that war rages there?" Saul probed him with another question. Obelreyon wanted to conquer Renalia with the aid of Lornak, and Saul wondered if war across the sea would better the Dragon's chances. Saul wanted to bring his people there as well, but on their own terms, with the Glories at their back.

"There is. Don't think it is easily conquered, son."

"I am not your son," Saul growled. The flash of black flames entered his mind once more. He clenched his fists and gritted his teeth from the mere thought of the black-scaled Dragon. Now the tyrant not only burned his father, but part of his clan. *They burned because of me, and I ran. I abandoned them.* Saul wanted to return with vengeance, but he did not know how. He hoped his goddess would guide him, give him the means to free the Broken, so they may rule themselves.

His father's fate was false. Saul was skeptical of his own. He was chosen to die, but now he could live. He hoped in exile he could find his path. They camped briefly, and Saul finally decided to wear leather instead of his plate. *If he wanted to kill me, he would have.*

* * *

After several days, the grand chasm laid in the distance. It reached a seemingly infinite distance through a cloud of thick fog, cutting along the land from end to end. A battalion of Broken stood behind a barricade, and behind them stood the cart of the tether and Mirakia Othellun, Warmaster and temple leader for the Oracles, with arms crossed. The last time Saul saw her, she was carving Broken coming for him at the temple in Hero's Fall; Saul was surprised she came.

Highwind reined in his stallion, neighing loudly as it lifted its hooves off the ground. He hopped off and removed his right gauntlet.

Saul followed suit. Each member of the guard followed Saul with their eyes closely. "What is going on?" Saul commanded.

"You have my thanks, Kain." With a subtle smile, Warmaster Othellun shook Highwind's bare hand.

Saul noticed Highwind also wore a pale white ring—the same as the warmaster.

"A pleasure as always, my lady." Kain turned toward Saul, nodding. They mumbled a few more words to each other, but Saul couldn't hear. "I always repay favors owed."

The warmaster smiled at her supposed ally before furrowing her brow and sending a glare toward Saul. "Are you prepared?" Warmaster Othellun asked.

How could I be?

Being exiled was the biggest disgrace of his people. He was judged and given his sentence. He had to accept it. Yet, something was strange here. "Yes."

"Come with me, Bromaggus," she said, leading him to the cart as she carried a large sack. Saul followed, nodding to Highwind as he passed. He returned the nod.

They walked past the battalion through blades and shields and ballistas; those placed at the Fissure stopped all enemies that dared cross the fissure with malicious intent. He waited until they were out of earshot before he spoke up, coming to the dilapidated cart.

"*What is going on here?*" Saul whispered. He feared the back of her hand would swat him across his face for questioning, but he had to know.

"You are being exiled," she said. Then the warmaster leaned in close, whispering, "If he didn't pull you out, you'd be dead. You're so proud that you'd rather die than escape to live. You're lucky these Broken don't know you're *supposed* to be dead."

Saul knew it was true, but what of it? His face screwed into a frown, and he stared into her dark eyes.

She let out a long, drawn-out sigh. "The people who survived the war ten years ago are those that learned to retreat and cut their losses, rather than wasting their lives." She stood back again. "He burned our tribe. Not everyone, I might add. There are many that will live. All of this is because of a ridiculous fate."

Saul clenched his fists, bearing his teeth in response. Before he could open his mouth, the warmaster stopped him.

"Don't you say a word. They died because of Obelreyon's fear." She pulled him in by the neckline of his armor. "*Do you hear me?*" she whispered harshly. "He's afraid of *you*." She let him go and opened the door to the small cart. "Now give him something to fear." She handed him the large pack, filled with food, water, and other traveling goods.

Saul walked into the cart. It was covered in moss, slightly rotted, but well preserved. It stayed for two hundred years—Saul was surprised it still functioned. As he closed the small door, the wind blew south, pushing the cart across the chasm.

Kain and Mirakia watched him as he went. They held up their palms to say goodbye. Each added a salute, pounding their fists to their centers.

The fog took him and encased the cart, slowly blowing it across the vast chasm. He wondered how long it would take—and if it would get stuck. He sat quietly in the suspended, dilapidated cart, hoping he would reach the other end of the Fissure without fail. White fog was all he saw now—and would be the only thing for miles.

At the other end of the chasm lay only the enemy of his people, and perhaps, his fate.

Chapter Twelve

Gentle Souls, Broken dreams

Zaedor Nethilus

Screams of fear echoed from the city streets outside. Zaedor looked around his home. Cinders and ash fell freely from the flaming ceiling. He donned his armor as quickly as possible. It was disjointed and askew, but he had no time to care. He drew his great blade and ran out of his home ready to defend his people.

The once beautiful city he knew was disappearing before his very eyes. The fluttering banners of families were aflame with the wild blaze of deception.

Two battle-hardened men with mace and blade in-hand emerged from the sewers and ran at Zaedor without pause. He deflected two blows with his blade and struck back with a mighty sideways slash that almost carved one man in two, splashing blood upon Amirion's once white stone streets. He leapt up with blade overhead to strike at the other warrior.

The man attempted to guard the blow with one blade and strike with his mace, but Zaedor's mighty blade broke the man's weapon in two, slicing into his skull like a block of butter as the mace clattered at his elbow. With the men dead, Zaedor stopped to grip his elbow smacked with the mace. It hurt to the core, but he couldn't sit by while his city was under attack.

Zaedor looked at his surroundings, only to see the bodies of men, women, and children. The beautiful city was scarred with the bodies of innocents. *How is this possible? The impenetrable city of Amiron, sacked? How?* To the west and south, he saw a rain of rock and flame crashing into the city from catapults and trebuchets in the fields beyond the city's walls.

He had no time to stand around. One objective shot into his mind—*the King*. The King was the most likely target for the attacks, and Zaedor had to save the crown. *Eryndis will go, and we will be at peace,* he remembered the king say confidently. He couldn't dwell on her now, though.

With swift legs, he ran forth to the grand Blue Citadel. His weapon sliced through shield, blade, and flesh as he charged to his destination. The colors of the banners that flew on the houses were no longer recognizable, either charred by flame or torn apart. Zaedor ducked, dove, and dodged the stones of shattered buildings as they blew across his path.

The smell of burnt flesh filled his nostrils. The overpowering scent he feared more than anything.

He reached his temple along the path as he ran. The once elegant dome of the main hall had been smashed in by catapult fire. It was surrounded by the bloodied corpses of those gathered to pray for Shiada's protection in their time of need. Lilanda was splayed out from the rock, body crushed by the stones.

"Lilanda!" Zaedor called, rushing over. He threw off what rubble he could. Half her body was broken, bleeding from the concussive blows of the collapsed building.

"Zaedor," she squeaked out. "My husband is dead. You must stop them from killing the King. Our hope lies with him." She could barely muster the words. Tears filled her eyes. An expression of lost hope. "Has—has Shiada forsaken us?" she barely asked, before passing into the next life.

No, it can't be. I have prayed to her my whole life. She would not abandon us, Zaedor thought. He closed Lilanda's eyes and said a prayer to Shiada in desperate hope that she still listened.

"Zaedor!" Lothel yelled, running into the temple.

"Lothel, what is happening?"

"It's Rawling! His forces got in, but no one knows how. They came through the sewer system, the sea, everywhere!" Lothel said. "The whole city is sealed off. My entire brigade is dead. The drakes broke into the barracks silent as the night, killing everyone!"

Zaedor grabbed him by the neck of his plate. "We have to save the king! Come with me!" Zaedor ordered, dashing toward the Citadel. Lothel followed him without pause.

Enemy by enemy, they combated their way to the Citadel. There were warriors of all kinds: dual-wielding soldiers, powerful wizards, and shamans of the sand. It seemed as though Rawling employed mercenaries, able bodies to add to his already powerful desert army.

"Die, traitors!" the villains yelled as they thrust blade, spear, and javelin into innocent residents of Amirion.

Why would they say this? Zaedor thought. *How could they believe we are the enemy?* Zaedor was struck on the arm and chest, bludgeoning blows that knocked the wind right out of him. He pressed on and shook his arm. His elbow still throbbed with pain from the strike of the mace, but he pressed on.

The once strong, clean-cut stone buildings of the city were riddled with cracks, breaks, and scorch marks. The Temples that stood for centuries fell before the might of Rawling's armies. His soldiers struck swiftly and with great power. Bloodstains covered the flat stone street as they ran. Soldiers threw bottles of spirits paired with lit cloth upon wooden roofs to burn all they could as the duo ran.

A disembodied voice whispered and echoed throughout the city in a language Zaedor did not understand, with violent turns of the tongue and guttural growls of the throat. Zaedor and Lothel stopped, looking around them.

"What was *that*?" Zaedor asked.

The voice became fierce as a massive violet orb of smoke appeared above the city. White, mist-like spirits passed quickly around the orb at rapid speeds. They swooped down to the city, and then returned to the sky.

"What *is* that?" Lothel echoed.

But Zaedor had a suspicion. *Dark magic.* He looked to Lothel with fear. Suddenly, a black spirit swooped in before them, making contact with the bodies of soldiers they slew, and those of innocent citizens of Amirion. The bodies were shocked alive, screeching in agony. A white mist was then taken by the spirits, dragged up toward the violet orb above.

"Zaedor! What in the name of the gods is happening? Should we try and evacuate?"

Zaedor felt helpless. He was one man—*what was he to do?* His whole life had been committed to his god, his people, and his city. In one fell swoop, it was all being taken from him. He had just one hope remaining. "The king!" he yelled. "We must ensure his safety! Without the crown, we are certainly lost!"

Lothel nodded in agreement. "Let's go, Captain!"

The two warriors dashed for the citadel together. Countless bodies lined the streets. Screams could be heard all around them as the spirits came to take the souls of all who were broken and bloodied. Zaedor could do nothing for them now. Boulders and firebombs from the catapults crashed into the buildings around them as they ran, stone pouring over the streets. It seemed like an unending rain of fire upon their broken lives.

The Citadel's stone walls were broken and cracked from the mighty bombardment. The deep blue banners of Amirion were now burned to a crisp, the surrounding spire lights extinguished. In they ran, only meeting soldiers of Rawling, bearing his sigil of the iron fist on a field of bright yellow. The bodies of Citadel guards were already strewn across the halls.

The corridors were absent of light save the fires. Zaedor could barely see forty feet in front of him. He and Lothel panted heavily as they carried themselves up the stairs. They charged to the throne room doors hastily. Deep impact marks covered the dead guard's chests. Their necks were riddled with blackened bruises, and their heads were caved in. The strikes even broke through the steel helmets they wore. Zaedor looked to Lothel with false confidence.

He was tired, panting from running as they sliced through countless warriors, his left arm burned from magical flame. Lothel nodded, and the two of them kicked the throne room doors open.

One lone man in a wolf-pelt cowl stood before the throne, holding the King by his beard. The queen's lifeless body lay against the cracked stone wall at the side of the large hall.

"Sorry, yer grace, but orders be orders. Thanks for the info," he said mockingly.

"No, please. I—" Faelin struggled to get out.

The man's arm turned massive, hairy and clawed.

"*No!*" Zaedor yelled, running toward them. But it was too late, as the sounds of ripping flesh and Faelin's hoarse scream filled the empty, broken hall.

The man turned with the bloody, lifeless head of Faelin in his monstrous, clawed arm. Zaedor and Lothel dropped to their knees at the sight of the murderer's face before them. It was lined with vertical, violet tattoos which reached down his arms, hands, and fingers. His jaw was chiseled and broad with thick stubble and emotionless green eyes cold as a northern night.

"Well, hello. I ain't a fan of onlookers, but I ain't about to kill unless I got to. With some exceptions," his voice dropped off, and he tossed aside the King's head carelessly.

Is he a shapeshifter? Zaedor thought. "You," Zaedor recognized his voice from the previous night. "I heard you last night, on the street! What is going on? What is 'the work in Solmarsh?'"

The man didn't respond.

Lothel stepped in front and fiercely pointed at the man. "Who are you? What the hell is this!" he yelled.

"They call me Cloaker." With a low, graveled tone, he said, "You don't see me comin', and never know what I'll be."

His answer meant nothing to Zaedor. Each word only angered him more. "My king, my people, my home!" His rational thoughts ended there. Filled with bloodlust, Zaedor let out a primal roar as he raised his greatblade and charged. "You die *here*!" he yelled.

"I'm with you, brother!" Lothel charged alongside Zaedor.

Cloaker cackled in his gravely voice. Strange colors and waves shifted around his body to transform him into a massive bear, twice the size of a normal man. He swiped his mighty claw, slamming Zaedor and Lothel to the floor with ease. Cloaker roared and charged at Zaedor. Zaedor deftly dodged out of the way, causing Cloaker to ram the pillar behind him. The pillar toppled, ceiling above caving in after it to *slam* onto the ground.

Cloaker shook his head, unaffected, as if ready to charge once more.

Lothel jumped atop the bear's head to jam his blade into the beast's shoulder. Cloaker let out a rageful roar, and caught Lothel with his massive paw and threw him against the wall. Lothel fell to the ground and croaked out in pain.

Cloaker shifted again, true to his name. This time, he changed into a red-scaled dragon. He flew up and charged full speed at Zaedor. Zaedor deflected his steeled claws and barely caught the dragon-formed jaw by the sword before a deadly bite could take place. Cloaker slammed him to the ground and pinned him down within a moment of Cloaker's saw-like teeth. Ceiling stones fell upon Cloaker as he attacked, and Zaedor took advantage of the opening. He turned his blade to deliver a vital horizontal slash across the beast's face. Cloaker screeched in pain, flew back to take a deep, guttural breath, and let out a fury of flame from his maw.

"Zaedor! Catch!" Lothel tossed his shield to him.

Zaedor caught the shield and barely protected himself from the blaze in time. His arm burned, but he had to continue. Zaedor ran forward, threw the blackened shield aside, and leapt at the dragon with his blade overhead. His mighty slash cut through Cloaker's belly scales, striking the sensitive flesh beneath.

Cloaker screeched again, falling to the ground. Once more, a new form arose. Waves and colors flowed around Cloaker's body as he changed. He shifted into a massive, vine-laden mammoth of a plant—a stranglemaw.

He grew to twenty feet tall, with a large mouth at its front, lined with three rows of blade-like teeth. The multitude of vines twisted and surrounded both warriors, grabbing them by the feet and slamming them against the stone walls.

Zaedor's ears rang loudly, and he was barely able to focus. Blood poured from his nose and forehead. *Is this the end?* he thought, distraught.

Does it end like this for me? He struggled to slash at the vines that held him, and he fell to the ground. Gathering his strength, he scrambled to his feet, weakly raised his blade, and clumsily charged once more at the plant-form Cloaker took.

Cloaker's maw turned to Zaedor and breathed an acid-like mist upon him. He collapsed to the ground into a dazing sleep, out of his personal volition. The last image he saw, while hazy, was Cloaker, grabbing Lothel by each limb with his powerful vines and ripping them away from his torso. The massive maw overtook Lothel's screaming body, and tore it in two with severing teeth, covering the room in his friend's blood.

* * *

Zaedor roused to the acrid smells of smoke and dry blood. The ceiling collapsed in from the battle with the mysterious cowled man, and broken stone littered the room. His mind and body ached from the beating he'd received. *How am I still alive?* he questioned. *Why did Cloaker let me live? Why the hell did he let me live?*

As he rose, Zaedor looked upon his old friend's body. Six pieces remained—four torn limbs, and a torso bitten in two. *A brutal savage,* he thought bitterly. *How could someone care so little, even enemies?* Zaedor's gag reflex was unstoppable. He threw the contents of his stomach upon the bloodstained ground.

His friends were gone, his life utterly broken. *Am I alone?* Zaedor wondered. He looked next to see the decapitated corpse of his King, Faelin, and the broken body of the Queen. The once-brilliant throne of Amirion had been broken, as his city now was. He dropped to his knees in anguish.

"Shiada, why have you forsaken us? Why leave us?" he asked.

Zaedor stared to the abused ground, mind drained of all life. His tears flowed without relent upon the floor; the only sound left was the wind of the dead passing through the halls of the Citadel.

His whole life disappeared before his eyes. All he fought for, all he *lived* for was now dead before him. He slammed his gauntlet upon the ground in anger, the clang of metal echoing through the empty halls of the broken Blue Citadel. All that followed was his scream of a broken man. He raised himself to his feet, barely able to stand. His sorrow and agony dragged upon his body like the mightiest of weights as he descended. The battered bodies of guards surrounded him while he walked the dark halls, not a light to be seen. As he reached the bottom of the Citadel, he stared down the main hall to the end, only to see all hope gone.

The lone Torch of Night was extinguished.

Zaedor's walk through the city was agony incarnate. His sobbing was continuous; he wished to hold it back, but could not.

He saw only broken buildings and dead friends. *This can't be happening. It's all a dream. I'm dreaming—this is all a nightmare. It must be,* he thought desperately. All that remained now was the sound of crackling flame and howling wind. No footsteps, no voices, no screams. The violet orb had gone, the magic finished. Whatever the army came for, they'd found.

As he approached the entrance to Shiada's temple, he saw a body he recognized, breath still remaining. "Oh gods, Noah!"

He still had a small blade in hand. "I tried, Captain Zaedor." The child could barely croak a word. His mother lay beside him, slaughtered. The boy's body had been pierced with an arrow. He could barely hold on to what life he had left.

"I'm so sorry," Zaedor cried for the boy, and the city he loved. "I tried to protect you," he continued, sobbing.

"Don't worry, Captain. I couldn't even protect my parents," he whispered.

"I can heal you!" Zaedor scrambled to look for herbs for healing, but it was too late for the boy. The gods left him.

Noah barely choked up three words that would follow Zaedor forever. "Don't forget us."

The boy's breath escaped his body as his form turned lifeless. Zaedor closed his eyes tightly, wishing for it all to stop, and for the nightmare to end. His own soft cries were all he heard, echoing through the empty alleys of death.

Please, let this be a nightmare, he thought. *My city is great, my king strong, my people, stronger. They aren't dead, they can't be.*

When his eyes opened, the bodies lay there still. Zaedor limped back to his home, the roof burnt but still standing. He curled into his bed, hoping that when he awoke it would all be the way it should have been: the people running and laughing, the king alive, his old friend still training the warriors in the barracks.

Please, gods, bring me back to reality, he thought. With his eyes filled with tears, he eventually slept under the moonlight.

* * *

When he awoke, the sun rose to warm the streets once more. The calm wind passed through his home, and his roof was still open to the sky. With reluctance, Zaedor rose to his feet. He sauntered to the door of his home and heard the caws of crows and vultures, and smelled the flesh of dead men.

No, please, Shiada. Don't abandon me. I won't believe it.

Zaedor opened the door, and it was all the same.

Buildings left broken.

His people bloodied and slain.

Prayers lay unanswered.

I have been abandoned.

Through the temple quarter, his precious shrine broken and bodies crushed. Through the market quarter, his favorite places burned beyond all recognition. Hundreds of heroes were left slaughtered and covered in dried crimson stains.

He gathered a small set of supplies while considering his path. He had to know the truth, and his anger for vengeance overtook him. *I cannot let this go unpunished,* he thought. Zaedor took up some of the food and water abandoned in the streets for the journey he knew he must take.

As he walked through the city gate, he looked back at the kingdom that once was. The bright stones were destroyed, the banners of hope burned, and the Blue Citadel scorched and broken. The flame of hope he kept inside for this place was now extinguished.

He turned away, focusing instead on the vast plains before him and the Zenato desert beyond that. The land he knew was behind him, and all else a mystery before him. The sun sat high in the sky, intense heat warming his steel armor.

"Rawling," he growled. His hands shook with rage, teeth gritted in anger, and eyes burned with ferocity. There was no place for kindness left within him. Only one thought entered Zaedor's once-pious mind now.

"I will burn him alive."

Chapter Thirteen

Safety in Numbers

Jirah Mirado

Jirah listened carefully to Gorkith's news after he returned from the capital. Alexandra came from Solmarsh as well, but Jirah hardly paid attention. The campfire flickered weakly from the gentle rain, and the soaked stones, mud, and soggy leaves covered the ground. The thin smell of ash was dampened by the scent of the wet foliage. Jirah enjoyed the smell of nature during a rain, but he preferred the dry heat. The midday sun carefully peeked out from behind the clouds above.

"They're missing?" Jirah asked, confused. If the five went to any camp, it would be Wolf Camp, where they received their first mission. Jirah kept the other camps secret from most in case of capture. However, Asheron may have known the locations of others if his threat was true.

"Yes, sir," Gorkith said in his stale voice. "According to the capital, they were imprisoned nine days ago. Eight days ago they escaped, and—Miggen was killed."

"No—" Jirah's voice dropped off. *You drake, Asheron. You'll pay for this,* Jirah thought to himself. Miggen was a good man and a good soldier. He was trustworthy, and now Jirah had one less under his command. "How did they get out?" he asked. *They could be dead. It could be a ploy by that wretch Fillion to get my teams searching in the open.*

"They don't know. The jail floor had a weakened wall leading to another room, but it was a dead end." Gorkith almost seemed to laugh as if he had a sense of humor.

Jirah wasn't sure what to make of them. From what he heard they were not resourceful. He only met Lira, whom he found to be innocent and anxious more than anything.

He did not know his sister well as he hadn't seen her in twelve years. Jirah fled his home in the east to join the war in the west against the Broken clans, among other reasons. His service was appreciated and rewarded here, unlike his old life in the east. In the military, he proved his worth to himself. *I showed my potential to those who mocked me*, he thought triumphantly.

"I might send you out to scout for traces of them. I can't continue thinking that I got them killed." He paced back and forth, squishing the damp ground beneath his plate boots. "Alex, what news comes from Solmarsh?" Jirah called out.

Alexandra stood up, towering over her commander. She ran her fingers through her thick, red hair that draped down to her mid-back. Her pale skin was dirty from many long days of riding, accentuated by the multitude of freckles decorating it. "Nothing about five people. No guards." She looked confused. She wasn't the brightest star, but a good scout and loyal soldier. She was a long way from her home in the northwest mountains of Renalia, and lived a vastly different lifestyle from her training as a tanner.

She was the final scout to return to camp. Nothing strange had been reported by Felkar or Pali, who sat by the dwindling fire nearby. He feared her answer would echo Asheron's words. *Ignore what you hear*, he said. After a strange moment of silence, Jirah knew he had to probe. "Is something else wrong?"

Alexandra's eyes widened and she fumbled with her hammer haft. "People missing. Not much. Two, three."

Like Asheron foretold.

Alex bit her lip and shifted her large feet nervously. She didn't say much and was not well spoken, but had a good heart and spoke honest words. Jirah looked to the other camp members, unsure of what he should do. *All of the members of your little camps will die*, Asheron said to him. Each member of his army was as admirable as the next, all good men and women who fought for what they believed in. He didn't want to let them die because of him. Asheron was a monster, but he was true to his word.

"What do we do?" Alex pushed, looking for advice.

Jirah had to choose. *Damn it, this isn't good. I can't sacrifice my men and women for a possibly false alarm.* "Nothing. It's probably nothing. We don't have time for it," Jirah replied. His words could have possibly executed innocent lives. Either way, people would die.

Alex seemed concerned. "Okay," she replied uneasily before walking to a large log surrounding the fire and sat beside Gorkith, who gave her a supportive look.

Jirah could feel the doubt emanating from them both. Jirah would usually attack a problem at the source at first notice. This was the first time he did the opposite. The rebellion's movements made him nervous in recent days: his recruits were imprisoned, he'd lost contact with several scouts in the southern marshes, and the war wrought by the late king's son, Kieran, neared the wall. *Bracchus's son is a strong warrior and talented leader, but I don't know what he would do if he took Loughran for himself.* Word reached Jirah that the Orinas Militia already took Ildenheim and Lothran, and cut around the jagged claw.

His old friend Richard was a powerful ally, and he trusted his judgment on being wary of Kieran. *But when a war rages, there are always innocent casualties. I try my best to minimize them, but wars are indiscriminate.*

Part of him knew he should send for Richard's assistance. He considered an alliance with Orinas, but he knew the game would change when other nations got involved. He dared not ask Rawling, who half the time seemed to think politics all were just a silly game. At the same time, their wars benefitted Jirah greatly; when the armies fought on the front lines, he could save the innocents from behind the curtain. All that stood in his way were the hunters who thwarted him thus far: *Asheron and Malakai*. Jirah dreaded the choice he'd made. He only wished that he could save them all.

But in the end, someone always dies.

"To arms!" Serafina yelled from the treetop. The rebels drew their weapons, Jirah's curved blade lit aflame as it left the sheath. The sounds of several sets of footsteps, cracking twigs, and the squishing of wet leaves closed in on the camp.

"Greeted with weapons in my face—feels like home," a raspy female voice echoed from the path.

The rebels lowered their weapons curiously. Jirah sheathed his blade and ran to the five individuals that entered the camp. The head was a short, plain-faced woman with thick, messy hair and sharp amber eyes. Lira emerged from the path close behind, a hand on her neck.

Then came a massive man with blood-red eyes, horns, and pale skin, a fidgeting, mumbling old man, and a fiery, black-haired woman with bronze skin that he hadn't seen in many years, and couldn't believe grew so much. He knew it was Domika. Her fiery eyes told the tales of the past.

"You're alive! Thank the gods," Jirah said as he came to a halt.

"It's been a long time, brother." Domika said with a sweet smile. She meandered past him to the fire. Jirah was confused but not surprised, as he and Domika shared a complicated past. His mind shot back to that fateful time, forgetting that the others were even there. It was as if he was in the splintered wood home. Knife in-hand. Filled with hate. Fear. He freed his family. But it came with a cost. He had to run.

Jirah subtly wiped a tear from his eye before his gaze turned back to the group, eyeing each one carefully. He paced left and right in front of the remaining four.

"Are you going to talk to us and tell us what the hell happened, or just pace back and forth, forever lost in your own head?" the short, scar-faced woman hissed.

Jirah stopped dead before her. "You must be Miss Ralta." He leaned in close to her. She was shorter than he was, with narrowed amber eyes, mousey hair thick and knotted, and a definite attitude problem. She had several scars on her face from fights, he was sure.

"You were sent here, were you not?" She got the information from someone, and she came from the north.
It had to be Richard. But why her?

Kayden's face scrunched. "I wasn't sent here by anyone," she said irritably. Her eyes didn't show any falsehood. Either he was wrong, or she was a very talented liar.

Jirah decided to give up on Kayden for now—he knew why she was there. He walked forward to the tall, slender, dark-skinned woman with broad, tired brown eyes and a joyful smile. "Miss Kaar, I'm happy to see you made it. Are you all right?" He smiled sweetly up at her. She was an innocent woman, wishing to help those who needed it, ever since the disappearance of her brother. *And now, I might be responsible for him not being found.*

"Yes, we're all doing quite well. Even Kayden, despite her demeanor." Kayden shot her a dirty eye, and Lira returned a sly smile.

"Good," he said calmly, chuckling before moving on. He came to the huge half-Devil with a torso as broad as a tree and a chiseled broad jaw. Small horns emerged from his thick black hair. "I'm not sure I know your name. My name is Jirah, what would yours be?" Jirah asked politely.

"Magnus, sir," he said bluntly. Jirah sensed something in his tone, unsure of what exactly. Magnus looked down to him with little reaction.

"Is it?" Jirah started. He took a lengthy glance into Magnus' red eyes—as close as he could for a man of his stature. "*Hmm*," he murmured. "All right then, Magnus. Nice to meet you."

The others looked to both Jirah and Magnus curiously before he moved on to his final recruit. Vesper mumbled to himself awkwardly. His short grey hair was interwoven with bright whites, along with his thin beard.

"Ah, the magician!" Jirah began. "The famous Vesper, of the circus twelve—"

"Desist from mentioning that circus to me. I am no longer a part of it," Vesper replied harshly.

Jirah drew back, feeling slightly awkward. "My apologies. I was unaware that things changed so much." Jirah scratched his head. He wanted to pursue the subject further, but Vesper's eyes told him to avoid pressing at all costs.

"Thank you," Jirah finished. "That's all I need for now."

"That's it?" Domika asked from behind. She pointed furiously at Kayden, who left the line to a leisurely lean against a tree with a smug smirk. "We aren't going to talk about this?" She spoke in the Blazik tongue. "Someone could have betrayed us."

"*Someone could have betrayed us,*" Kayden cut in with a mocking retort. "You can't expect us all to not speak your language."

Vesper pointed a finger in the air and swished it in a circle. "While you may not agree with his methods, we have to trust his instincts at this juncture. Tell me this, Miss Domika, how are we to discover the identity of this traitor? There is no evidence, no forms of witness." He slowly moved his hands across his vision. "We must wait."

"Thank you, Vesper," Jirah said. He walked to the entrance of the camp and relaxed his shoulders. Not only did he have possible traitors in his force, but it already endangered a mission and almost killed his own sister.

He knew Asheron was clever and devious, and probably knew Asheron better than anyone. Worse yet, Asheron knew Jirah better than anyone.

The chance that he knew of one specific mission out of many was unlikely. But each member seemed honest and trustworthy, from his experience. Jirah glanced to the others in the camp. Alexandra and Gorkith sat under their overhang, talking quietly, while many others chatted by their steeds.

Serafina sat up in the jilani tree atop the flat, broad branches. She looked out over the nearby forest and picked at her fingernails. Her pale Rhaegan skin was barely visible in the night, accentuated by the outline of pale white hair. Her bright white eyes flashed back and forth, contrasting the pitch black of the rest of her people. That is, from what he'd heard. Rhaegans haven't been seen on the surface since the column collapsed. Felkar was passed out cold by his small fire, snoring as loud as a bear's roar. Pali'ah sat beside him, meditating.

Jirah had to return to the five's update. He sat down, crossed his arms, and patiently listened to them tell the tale. From the attack, to their time in jail, to the cryptic words of the late King, it was all very peculiar. The information they received from Rogan's manor was especially unsettling. They weren't disappearances, but prisoners transported to Duerbin in the south.

Are they connected? Jirah wondered. Asheron told him to ignore the disappearances. He would ignore Solmarsh for now. He had to. *Miss Kaar may be displeased, but my hands are tied.* The prisoners were moved somewhere else after Deurbin for 'special treatment.' The vagueness of it frustrated him.

"I'm sorry to hear you had to go through all of that," he said to Domika, Magnus, and Vesper. "We can't take back what they did to you, but we can ensure others don't have to suffer so." The three of them had been tortured in their minds, and physically.

Jirah looked to Magnus's armor, wondering how it could be conjured in such a way. It was battered and rust-covered, ill-fitting, and awkward. It not only didn't seem special, but appeared to be a downgrade from any armor he'd seen. If he sent Magnus to battle in it, he would essentially be giving him an order to die. He seemed strangely enamored with the shoddy suit of armor.

"We can't take back what happened, nor can we yet determine who set you up. The appearance of the King is strange, but it is not abnormal for a spirit to roam their old homes. Time will tell." Jirah attempted to be rational. He hardly believed in the power of deities, not ever giving them much regard.

Deeds and actions proved one's worth, and all deities who mattered regarded that as enough. What happened was not enough to determine anything definitive, and thus they had to continue on their current path.

"All right. Let's prepare some food and speak about some new mission options if you're still willing to stay." Jirah said, unsure of how they'd take it. "You'll be going as the same team."

Kayden frowned. "I'd rather work alone," she spat. "I don't need the others dragging me down."

"Well, around here we work on teams unless we're scouting. Can you handle that, Miss Ralta?" he responded sternly. "If you fall, it's your team who picks you up."

Kayden crossed her arms in a huff and rolled her eyes. "Fine. But I don't like working with others. They slow me down and mess it up. I don't need them. If they get me jailed again, I'm not coming back." She received a few irritated glances from the others before Jirah continued.

He wouldn't send them to Deurbin yet. It felt too involved in Asheron's plans. He needed to send a scout first before a strike party. If Asheron hadn't showed up, they would have had a perfect mission. He felt responsible for it going awry, especially Miggen Latrang's death. He was a good kid and, while young, he was brave, and helpful to any who needed it.

He gave the group a few options, and they picked a couple that caught their eyes. Lira kept quiet, and the others picked one in Wyrwood to gather information after being denied Deurbin.

In time I may have to send them to Deurbin. They would leave after a few days, taking time to rest. Vesper took his sandals off to rub his feet, which were somewhat blistered and calloused. Kayden took one of the logs and leaned it up against a thick tree, closing her eyes. Magnus sat quietly beside the fire with Domika, who leaned in close.

Jirah rubbed his forehead. He hadn't been this exhausted in years. Ever since they were set up, he attempted to give his soldiers orders personally. Gorkith traveled to some of the other camps, but only to delegate missions that were less critical.

Most of his forces were in the northern and eastern regions of Loughran, liberating towns from state soldiers.

Asheron gave him terms. He didn't even speak of the towns where Jirah's forces lay, but of disappearances—Deurbin simply had arrests, but for further transportation. He hoped they weren't connected, so that his pact may not be broken.

How dare Asheron call me an animal. He was always high and mighty on his orders, but Jirah never put orders before innocent lives. When citizens began resisting the conscriptions and the taxes, they were only met with force. He and Asheron were ordered to take the men, take their families, and imprison those who couldn't fight. Hundreds of them. Jirah followed orders for a time—but when he was ordered to burn a town, he left Asheron along with their force that day. Fillion never deserved the crown.

I would rather be a traitor than a murderer of innocents. If only he could have a chance at fighting Asheron himself—then he could right the wrongs of the past. *Some of them. I still chose my men over Lira's people—if that's what Asheron spoke of.*

Jirah looked over to the entrance to Wolf camp, where Lira sat alone on a rock, huddled in close. Jirah sauntered over to assess any concerns. "Is anything wrong, Miss Kaar?" He crouched down to her level.

"I'm okay, I suppose," she said weakly, eyes set on the path.

"I didn't want this to be your first impression of what we do. It must have been a difficult experience for you."

"It's not that—I knew there were dangers when I signed up. I may not be skilled in combat, but I understood the consequences. Just because I'm not adjusted to this doesn't mean I'm going to roll over and give up." She rubbed her crossed arms and curled her toes now free from a pair of soft wood sandals.

"What is bothering you then? Are you reconsidering?"

A tear streamed down her left cheek as a ray of sun peeked through the clouds, causing her dark copper-brown skin to glow.

"I'm staying. I'm going to help those in need, but—" Lira turned and looked into Jirah's eyes. "I know we chose to go to Wyrwood. But I don't want to," she said. "I need to find my brother."

Jirah knew what she wanted. Ashweon's warning loomed. "Wyrwood may yield more information." That may be true, but he wished to avoid direct interference.

"I want to go to Deurbin. The notes in Lord Rogan's office said that's where prisoners were going. I can't stand by and ignore that. I have to go," Lira said resolutely.

"Miss Kaar, I'm don't believe that's a good idea."

Turning her head slowly toward him, her soft gaze grew sharp. "Why? We need to figure out what's happening. That's why I joined. I must know."

Jirah crossed his arms and stood up. He tried to divert the topic. *Brother or no, my men's lives could be on the line.* "We need more information. I can't send you there without finding out more."

Bit by bit, Lira rose to her feet, towering over Jirah by over half a foot. "People could be *dying*." After a brief stare between them, she spoke in a quiet, but passionate tone. "Isn't that what we're doing? Trying to help people?"

The mouse challenged the cat, it seemed.

But the hound still loomed over him.

"Do not test me, Miss Kaar," Jirah commanded. "This is a sensitive operation." He glanced behind him, seeing the rest in the camp silent, staring at them.

She shook her head. "I'm not testing. I'm asking. Let me go."

He sensed she was not a dominant personality, but her goal was clear.

They're arrests, not disappearances. Jirah pondered the risk. *It could cause a rift with Asheron.* Preparations had to be made. Jirah felt the silence and the stares behind him, waiting for his answer. He felt going to Deurbin was a dangerous task. Not for them, but for him—and the other camps.

"You would go alone?" Jirah asked, knowing she couldn't.

After a nervous breath, she said, "If I had to, I would. I would take the others, too." Lira gazed over his shoulder to the others.

Jirah saw something in her eyes. It wasn't fear or worry—it was resolve.

"She's right. That's what the notes said." Kayden walked up beside them. She slapped a hand on Lira's bony shoulder, causing the much taller woman to flinch. "I got you, princess."

Lira responded to Kayden's support with a smile. Turning back to Jirah, she said, "We'll be careful. I promise."

Kayden cut in after. "We're going. We will make better time going straight there than waiting around looking for information somewhere weeks in another direction." She headed back to her bags and began to check her belongings.

The crunch of leaves echoed from the clearing. "Incoming!" Sera yelled in a panic, but not fast enough.

A smooth, yet lightly graveled voice called throughout the camp. "I'm simply here to report; not to worry."

From the path emerged one crimson-armored man with a black cloak that bore the scroll on the field of fiery orange.

With a deep, graceful bow, the Blood Knight, Malakai, entered the clearing. Alone.

The scape of steel echoed throughout the camp, followed by a silence riddled with tension that could break a mountain.

"I'd like to have a chat," the Blood Knight said.

"Is that all you idiots do? Talk?" Kayden snapped. "

Malakai was born to lie.

This—this was a lie. "His brother talks," Jirah said quietly. "He is far more vile."

With a chuckle, Malakai said, "So perceptive. Mirado, this is a reminder. I heard you enjoy a bluff here and there. Worry not, I'm only here for one of you."

Asheron wasn't bluffing.

The evidence stood before them in the form of a monster.

Chapter Fourteen

A Whisper of Blood

Kayden Ralta

The crimson-armored horror just looked at the rest in the camp, and pointedto one member at a time. "One—two—three, four, five. I see a-man who wants to die." He pointed a finger to each of those in the camp.

Kayden looked over toward Jirah with a look of *is this a joke?* Jirah only said aloud, "No."

"Six—seven—eight, nine, ten, don't worry, it'll only be—" His finger ended on Kayden. "Them." He gave a light shrug. "Not a man, but close enough."

Jirah drew his great blade, and it lit aflame. "Step away."

Malakai removed a serrated silver dagger from a sheath at his hip. "Oh Jirah, I do miss you at our little gatherings. You always made things more interesting." He took the dagger and dug it under his gauntlet. As he let out an exhale and a grunt, blood seeped out from it as he walked around the camp edge. He muttered a few things under his breath.

"Girl," the drake said, looking to Kayden. "Have you ever looked death in the eyes?" He waved his hand, and five individuals in emerged from the earth, skin pale as the moon, eyes and veins engorged with blood.

She did. A thousand times. More. "Wrong one to ask, drake." Kayden said, as she rushed toward him with swords ready.

"Entertain them!" Malakai called. He drew his blade encrusted with blood diamonds and came in with an overhead slash.

She rolled behind him and around the strike, but as she turned, he didn't strike. He stood with a hand out-stretched toward her.

And her breath left in an instant. She coughed and hacked as a crimson mist flowed from her skin into his hands, and a cackle filled the air.

She saw multiple pale-skinned bloody monsters fighting the others, who were overwhelmed by the raw number emerging from the pool of blood the knight spilled.

Her ears rang, and it became more and more difficult to breathe. To think. To move. As Malakai got to her, he snatched her up by the throat with his open hand and picked her up. "Be happy; you're the only one I chose to take today."

A vision of Jirah swinging left and right furiously caught her eye. It was all a blur, but the swirl of flame came behind him. Her vision turned grey…

A roar of agony. Kayden felt herself slam upon the ground, and she barely saw crimson armor stagger backward. *"Have it your way! You all die, Mirado!"*

He spoke guttural commands, and held his hand to the air where a violet orb appeared above him.

And then screaming. Felkar. Alexandra. Jirah. Ves. Mags. Lira. But he ignored Kayden a moment as he thought she was dead. They always did. Idiots.

Kayden struggled to her feet behind him, watching white mist travel from them into his hand as he whispered guttural words.

She took a shaky hand to draw a dagger from her side. "Have I looked death in the eyes?" she whispered. She jumped on his back and dug the blade deep into his neck. "I *am* death."

The Blood Knight let out a guttural croak and crumpled to one knee. He reached behind and shook her off with a powerful throw.

As the life of the camp began to return, Malakai's bloody, liquid-laced breaths echoed from his visage. He removed the dagger from his neck and staggered toward the path before any could get to their feet.

He wouldn't get far.

She staggered toward him but collapsed from weakness. It was like her blood was drained form her. Vile magic.

But with a clench of his fist, the blood he shed and stole traveled up his arm and into his neck—mending the visceral wound that should have spelled death.

"Let this be a warning." Malakai shook his head and turned—only to have a mended wound upon his back where a slash should have been. He took a red crystal stowed under his cloak and whispered a command. "I'll be sure to drain everyone next time." He crushed the crystal and vanished into the night. With their master gone, the minions dissolved into ash that blew with the wind.

And then there was silence.

Chapter Fifteen

Choice and Consequence

Jirah Mirado

Silence was the only thing in the camp for hours, it seemed, while they all regained their energy. Malakai's lasting effect. It was a threat. A consequence of their involvement. All because he accused Asheron of bluffing.

Kayden barely managed to stab the drake. She was probably the reason they lived. Jirah failed to protect them. Asheron worked with shadows, and he was at one of his word.

Malakai was a creature barely held back by chains.

Lira crept over to him. "Jirah—"

"Go to Deurbin." He cut in, with eyes locked on the path. "Discover what's happening to the prisoners and arrests, but no more. Report to me *immediately* after you finish there. I will give you a location to meet. Understand?" He had to send word to the other camps. He had to send word to Richard. He could only hope things were ready in time. If he wasn't, the Brothers would come.

"I understand. You won't regret this," Lira said.

Jirah nodded.

I will.

Chapter Sixteen

New Home, New Hope

Saul Bromaggus

The cool, misty air was getting to him. Saul saw nothing but said mist for hours. He began to think he would never see land again. The wind howled through the rickety cart, and it creaked and groaned in response.

"Ready your weapons!" a husky, hissing voice yelled.

Saul thought it was a mirage. He saw a rough rock cliff with a battalion of multiple races on the other end: Humans, Naurali, and most prominently, Hydris. *The enemy of my people.* Bows and blades drawn, they waited for Saul to arrive. The cart slowed to a creeping halt at the edge of land.

"Out. Now," a Hydris at the back commanded. He was clearly the commander, a Hydris with hunter green skin and several blue fin-like outcroppings receding from mid-nose, over his head, and down his back. He wore pine green chain mail with grey studs attaching his obsidian cloak. The others were dressed in various forms of leather and copper scale mail, weapons at the ready. He sauntered forward and drew a sword to Saul's neck.

"What is your business here, Human?"

"I am no Human." *I am a proud Broken,* Saul thought. Humans looked similar to the Broken, but there were defined differences that set them apart—amongst other things. *Humans are a traitorous race with no honor.* Saul's skin was paled and greyed, and Broken as a people were more broad-chested and stronger than Humans.

He felt the need to strike them down if he could, but blades were at his neck and he had none in hand. "Exile."

"Some of your people would rather fall on their own swords than be exiled," the slithering commander said.

He was right, Saul didn't deny that. He almost did it himself. Many Broken sentenced to exile died from their own blades before it could happen. "I am not them." Saul spoke the words Highwind told him. "I could either die then, or live long enough to bring vengeance," Saul said, stone-faced. There was a long pause as the Hydris just stared at him. Saul grew impatient. "Are you going to kill me? Or are you going to sit there with a blade to my neck until I die from hunger?" If he was going to die anyway, he would face it standing tall.

The commander dropped his blade. "Vengeance upon your own people? You must be mad," he laughed.

"A Dragon is *not* my people," Saul growled.

The commander coughed up a laugh. "I suppose not, little man. You seek to kill a Dragon? I'm starting to like you." His blade returned swiftly to Saul's neck. "But I do hate spies—and Broken usually are."

Saul didn't flinch, he had nothing to hide. He untied the leather straps on his left arm, revealing the mark of the Oracles. "This is why I'm here. You think the Dragon would make me a spy with this?"

He examined Saul's arm with an intrigued eye. "*Hmm,*" he mumbled. "That's exactly what a spy would say, or have," his gaze returned to Saul's eyes. "Now what is this?" The soldier lifted the clothing on Saul's right arm. "Now this, I haven't seen." He drew along Saul's arm with the broad side of his sword. "Interesting."

The man was being vague. *Just spit it out,* Saul thought impatiently. "Just kill me if that's what you're going to do. Stop wasting my time."

"So bold," the snake said. "I, Commander Silkhagi, will not kill you. I will release you. If I were you, I would go to Rhoba first. One of the seven cities of the neck. It's south of here, but far. I'm not going to give you a horse, but I will give you your life. Rhoba lies between the Tarrant Mountains in the east, and the Loundas monuments on the west."

Loundas was a grand city of Draconia long past, swallowed by the azure lake in the torrent, a gargantuan storm which swallowed it whole. Rhoba was the central town of the Neck, in between the strongholds of Alin and Kaedor. Saul did not know what to expect there. "Why should I go to Rhoba?" Saul asked.

"You'll know when you get there. I'm not telling you anything else, Broken boy. I am letting you live. Be thankful." As Saul passed him, he said one more thing. "Don't die in the wastes."

I know how to survive. Saul left them behind, and they sat at the the fissure with their small barracks and homes surrounding the Tether.

Beyond them, there was only barren wastes. The Grim Wastes went for more than a hundred miles, they told him. It was barren land filled with seas of gravel and rock, scaled earth drier than a desert, intermingled with the degraded bones of old beasts. He did not see trees, shrubs, or plants, only mountain, bone, and crystals of various tyrian and azure shades emerging from the land like daggers. The wastes smelled of sand with the slight stench of rotting flesh.

Flocks of mysterious birds flew overhead: black with broad wings of violet and bright pink eyes. Herds of beasts ran across the wastes, peculiar ones he'd never seen. They were five feet tall with large horns with four long, spider-like legs and teeth that could tear through flesh like sharpened steel. One ran up to him quickly, and Saul drew his blade in response. He backed away, and the beast sniffed with its long, protruding snout and returned to its herd. He was curious of what kinds of beasts, peoples, and environments were found in this new land. It was so different from the Vale, even in his first day of travel.

He had been met with contention, but was set free. *Why did they let me go? I am a Broken—their enemy. After seeing the mark, do I now live because he believes I am a dragonslayer?* Yet, it was only after Silkhagi saw the second marking that he cared at all.

Not even Saul knew his fate now. He was banished across the Fissure, and would be killed if he returned. His clan, with many murdered and burned, was left alone under the reign of Obelreyon. Saul worried for his people, as they may be sent against Renalia once more in a foolish venture without proper preparation.

Ten years prior, they had been sent to war by the Dragon on a suicide mission. While the Broken proudly fought to retake Renalia then, Saul suspected things went awry for nefarious reasons. *A violet orb was said to appear above the final battlefield causing the dead to scream—according to the ones who retreated and lived.*

They'd lost more warriors than ever before—and forced to retreat after making enemies of the northern realms. *Damned wretch. He betrays our ways—and yet they follow.*

Damn the ones who follow willingly.

The other mark he received confused him even more than his future. He did not know the god of the six-pointed sun. *Who would mark me when I don't even know their name?*

Saul marched quickly, only stopping to eat his rations and sleep for a few hours at a time. He didn't know the terrain, the ferocity of beasts, or the existence of possible brigands. A small pack of black-furred leopards attacked and gave him a few scratches, but nothing more as Saul's blade was quick and ready. He had wood for a fire to cook, but saved it for when it was truly needed. Using resources at unnecessary times could kill a Broken in the wild.

The sky was much clearer here than in the Vale. It would rain heavily at times there, but in the wastes, there were almost no clouds; the nights were cold, but nothing Saul couldn't handle. He passed through various isolated villages on his travels, and witnessed the peering eyes of Hydris and Naurali who scowled in his direction. None spoke to him, but denied him entrance to their inns and shops with dismissive waves. Some villages held primitive traditions with tented homes, some wooden and dilapidated, and other cities crafted structures of stone. Saul often smelled freshly cooked meat, soups on the ledges of cookeries, and interesting, citric vegetables that he hadn't seen before. He asked what they were, but once again, the villagers did not speak or acknowledge him. He pressed on alone.

Days passed, and Saul finally came to a mountain range in the west just before dusk. The cracked wastes gave way to slight grasslands, decorated with seas of dried plants and shrubs. Further west, around an azure lake, lay many monuments of the Draconia.

Saul stopped by the lake to view the statues. Each was as impressive as the next. He knew they were a dastardly race, sharing an ancestry with the Hydris. He hadn't seen the monuments before, or a Draconia in general, as they were long extinct. Their rough, scaly bodies and long, powerful tails made them a formidable enemy. It was said that they acquired a special crystal to make the strongest of blades, which defeated the Dark Ones—but no one knew where to find it. If it weren't for the Broken, the Hydris may have gone extinct themselves. *Then they betrayed us,* Saul thought bitterly.

The Draconia were conquered by the Broken and the Glories two thousand years ago, with their forging abilities dying with them. They were utterly destroyed, as no magical steel could save them from the power of the Broken ways. Now, the Draconian city of Loundas was far beneath the surface of the mighty lake Saul looked upon now. None laid eyes on it since the torrent, a brutal storm which rained upon the land for a season, swallowing the mighty city whole.

The lake could not be manipulated by magic, nor could one magically breathe within it. It was protected by the gods—Urikar's might surely dwelled within it. Saul wished he had been alive in the time when great victories reigned. In his life he saw battle, but much failure. Saul wished to change the tide for his people. He wanted to bring glory to a race now brought down by the crushing rule of a Dragon and a futile war.

To the south, Saul saw a thirty-foot high stone wall extending for miles surrounding what seemed to be buildings, which he saw poking up above it. According to what Silkhagi told him, this was it—the city of Rhoba. Saul did not know what awaited him. He wondered what culture and attitudes it held. He questioned if he was even welcome within it. If the other small villages were any indication, he wouldn't be. He pressed on to the entrance, guarded by what seemed to be—*Broken?* Saul was stunned; he stopped in his tracks. *Is it the hunger? The lack of sleep?*

He hadn't heard of any Broken living south of the Fissure. No one spoke of it or even thought it was possible. There were two guards posted at the gate, each in silvery, thick scale mail. Saul walked up, having nowhere to hide among the now-desolate grassland.

"Halt. Who are you?" one of the guards demanded.

"I am Saul Bromaggus, exile of Obelreyon's Vale. What is this place?"

"This is Rhoba, the Broken sanctuary for those who have left the Vale, either by choice or exile. You are welcome to enter, friend, if you please. Simply abide by our laws. There is no violence here, verbal or physical." The guards smiled sweetly and opened the gate.

Saul did not thank them, from which they were unaffected. He entered the large city and saw Broken walk through the streets in nothing more than linens and silks, young ones running and playing with toy swords and chasing each other about. Many kinds of buildings filled the city, some made of dark stone slabs with white mortar and strongly built curved, sharp-edged roofs, and others with wooden siding and straw roofs. In the Vale, Broken homes were bound to their clans: uniform within but they varied greatly between the four clans. But here they intermingled like old friends.

Saul slowly walked through the main square of the town, still in awe. He saw a large well in the center, with many residents waiting patiently for others to get water from the depths. A small stone structure sat beside it, with a small wooden door going in. It was strange, as it was only big enough for one Broken.

Around the edges of the square sat various merchants in wooden booths, boards atop displaying their names, selling multicolored fruit and juices, meats of black, red, and russet brown, and various goods for homes. Most peculiarly, there were no banners or the markings of gods. Some of the Broken had the colored markings, but most had none at all. *Curious.* No one had a weapon or wore armor. Warriors of the Vale lived in a society where all were armed, and all wore armor outside of their homes.

A peculiar-sounding whisper crept deep into his mind. It was unintelligible; but he looked around to find the source. None seemed to pay him much attention, but the sound continued. He felt he knew this town, and the whisper sounded so familiar that it drew him in—toward the small structure by the well. He moved without stepping, without thought, as if it caused him to float. He crept closer to the door, the sound around him drowning to a whisper, until he was within an inch of the door.

"Excuse me, sir," a Broken said, snapping him out of it. He was a short individual, dark, smoky skin that was cracked and dry. Saul noticed that he had no markings on either arm. "Are you new to town?" he asked meekly.

Why is he so afraid? Saul wondered. "Yes, why?"

The man shrunk back from Saul's bold tone. "You have no need for armor and weapons, not here. We live in peace, without war."

Saul left his sword in his sheath, and he only wore leather currently, for the sake of travel. "Why do you not arm yourselves?" Saul asked gruffly. He noticed more glances on them as the Broken looked around, seeming nervous.

"We live on good terms with the other cities and the plateau. We have no need for a blade, aside from a few guards, in quite a few years. My name is Gurin Togg, the assistant to the city leader. What is your name?"

No weapons or armor?

These people would be squashed by any city or clan north of the Fissure. He did not like the meek demeanor of Gurin, let alone the strange atmosphere of the city. "My name is Saul Bromaggus. I was of the Gadora clan, in the Vale."

"Welcome to Rhoba, Saul," he said calmly. "Will you come to meet our city leader? He would speak with you."

Saul saw no alternative. Besides, speaking with the mayor may give him more answers, as well. "I will go."

Saul followed through the crowds out of the marketplace, along the dusty stone walkways intermingled with short grass. Everyone around them wore linen and silk doublets and tunics, sandals, or thin leather shoes. Some kept stables for herds, ranging from cows, to bulls, to goats, and even some beasts he knew not the names of. He even spotted one of the spider-legged horned beasts that passed him in the wastes.

"What are those?" Saul asked.

"Craghorns," Gurin said. "They live near the wastes as well as mountains, feeding on the flesh of beasts of those regions. They have no interest in us, strangely—although, they'd tear a Hydris to pieces. They're good for carrying gear, but they are not safe around children, hence the cage," he explained, meandering at a slow pace.

Could he walk any slower? They passed tiny farms that sprouted plants of corn, potatoes, and various fruits he hadn't seen before. The smell of wine filled his nostrils as he saw a large barrel with several individuals stamping their feet, legs covered in deep purple liquid. Many Broken of the Vale drank wine and mead, but Saul did not partake much.

"How do you grow so many different things on your farms here?" Saul asked.

"Some Broken here are alchemists, enriching the soil with various potions to give us a variety of options. You'd be surprised at what people can accomplish when they do not focus on battle."

Gurin's words were like poison.

Saul felt insulted, as combat was his greatest skill. There were vast farms in the Vale, but those Broken preferred utility over quality, and time making alchemical salves for farming could be used for something more useful.

"Here we are," Gurin said as he led Saul to a large building. The wall stones were grey, with greens and blacks in various places, held together with white mortar, and featuring a thick, wooden slab roof with straw. He knocked on the door, which was promptly answered by a large white-bearded Broken with a long, black silk robe and a gnarled wooden cane.

His face was covered with scars along his eye, cheeks, and forehead. His demeanor didn't match his appearance, as he greeted Saul with a happy smile. "Oh! You must be the new resident of our town. Come in, Come in." He opened his door wide for Saul and Gurin.

Am I really that obvious? Saul wondered. The city leader's home had many paintings and drawings, tools for building, and many, many, *many* books. No weapons, no armor, and no deities or gods.

"Tell me, friend, why have you come here to Rhoba? Where are you from?" the leader asked, inviting Saul to a soft cushion chair across from his. Gurin sat in another chair, beside Saul.

"My name is Saul Bromaggus, and I am from the Gadora clan, of the Vale." Saul said, stone-faced. He was suspicious of the man. Any Broken without a weapon or armor was more than strange.

The leader's eyes widened, but he swiftly hid his surprise with a calm demeanor. "Ah, the Vale, of course. Tea?" The man asked, offering him a small ornate marble teacup with a delicate, steaming steel pot. He took a drink from his own cup.

"No," Saul replied. He was thirsty, but there were other things on his mind. "Why is everyone here so afraid of combat?"

"*Oof*, this tea is hot. What did you say, my son?" He got up from his seat and grabbed a new pot. "Ah, here we are. This tea is much cooler."

"I am not your son," Saul growled. "Why is no one armed here?" Saul hated delays in conversation, especially in matters he felt to be serious.

"Just like the Vale, Saul. Quick, to the point, and far too brash. Have some tea, and I'll tell you."

Saul's fists clenched. *How dare he analyze me,* he seethed, but knew he had to cooperate, as it was not wise to disrespect the leader of a city. Saul was so bewildered by the city itself. The Broken focused on combat, yet these individuals lived with an absence of it. It made no sense. He took the small cup and pot and poured himself some tea, to which the old one across from him smiled. It smelled like sweet grapes mixed with honey fruits. He took a sip, and it tasted good.

"Combat is needless, as violence breeds violence. Do you not see this?" The leader carefully placed his teacup on a delicately-carved wooden table beside him. "A sword is important to a point, yes." He folded his hands and steeled them in his lap. He glanced deep into Saul's eyes. "I was of the Vale once. Since you haven't asked, my name is Gorum Kaelidan."

Kaelidan. Where have I heard that name before? "I recognize your name." Saul took another sip, as Gorum did.

"It's not surprising that you would. I was a Council member of the Vale, once. The member representing the Gadora clan, coincidentally." His gaze never left Saul's.

Of course, how could I forget? He remembered him from when he was a young boy. Gorum proposed a loss of arms, and a changing of their ways. He promoted a society of peace, to stop the needless violence. He had been executed—or so Saul thought.

"I can see by your expression that you remember me," Gorum said calmly. "Yes, I was supposed to be executed, but escaped. I formed this city with those that have crossed the Fissure since, by either choice or exile." He sat back and let out a sigh. "I made this city to make our people happy. Look around town—everyone here is happy, don't you see?" His dark eyes shone in the lantern light, dancing and flickering to the resounding tone of his voice.

Gorum was right, the people *were* happy. The children, the merchants, the farmers, and everyone else were high in spirits. Saul was conflicted over the thought. *Am I to stay here? Or risk the south—and for what reason?* "It does seem nice here."

"Do you read, Saul?" Gorum asked.

"No." Saul knew how to read simple things, short notes and letters, but not well. His father ushered him to learn, but Saul rejected it. He learned instead by practice, through swordplay, tactics lessons with maps, and other demonstrations.

"That's too bad. There are many books that can teach you so many useful things. If you ever wish to learn, you can always inform me. I am always open, *especially* to a former clansman." Gorum spoke with a honeyed tone.

"I'm not much of a reader. But I could try." Saul felt relaxed, and willing to learn.

Gorum sighed. "Your manners could certainly do with some work, but that will come in time," he smiled widely again. "We have a few homes set up right by here, actually. You may enjoy staying here, if you would like to try it."

Saul wished to stay a little while. They all seemed nice enough, and he was weary from his journey. "I think I will stay," Saul said, finishing his tea. "This tea *is* pretty good."

"Yes, I brewed it myself. I am glad you enjoyed it. If you ever want more, I welcome company. The shop by those winemakers makes it as well." He chucked. "Would you like some more?"

"Yes, please," Saul said. "How do you deal with outsiders when they come here?"

"Outsiders do not like the Broken, so they do not come. We are a peaceful group, so the other cities leave us be," Gorum said solemnly. "We live a self-sustained life, where blade and shield are unnecessary. We find combat to be more hurtful than helpful, don't you agree?"

Saul couldn't help *but* agree. "Yes, you are right."

"I'm glad you think so. We are sort of—*selective*—about who we choose to let live here, as we wish to maintain a happy society. I'm feeling nostalgic. Perhaps it's a connection between us, due to our markings. May I see yours?" Kaelidan rolled up his robe from his right arm, revealing yellow markings: the three crashing winds, the drop, and the cross through a horizontal line. Saul loosened the plate on either arm and showed his. "Ah, there are two. How interesting. A great burden," he said with a raised brow. "I too had a fate—to die in the service of my people. I almost had, but fled. I believed I would be of greater service if I lived. Look around town. What do you see?"

"I see many Broken, happily living in peace."

"Exactly. I lived, and now I can be of service to my people in a much better way. Don't you see? These markings are not truth. They are inclinations, which we interpret as true, but we choose our own fate, in the end." His words were wise, and undeniably true. "This is what I have discovered. Those that wished to run from the Oracles before they are marked come here. There are those who run after, but sadly, they are few."

"How did they cross? Is the cart not guarded?" Saul asked.

"Oh, it is, but you can lie your way around it. There are also other ways across."

"Like how?" Saul wished to know, if he one day decided to return. However, now he wasn't sure if he ever wanted to leave this place. He was with his people, and they found new purpose.

He felt compelled to stay.

"I think that's enough tea for now." Gorum placed his teacup down beside him. "Maybe I can tell you another day, my friend? I am quite tired. Must be my old bones."

Saul couldn't help but agree, but something fought within him.

"My dear friend, will you stay with us? We are in need of strong farmers, and you fit the part, truly. You have no need for a blade now, and you can rest well here."

Saul wished to stay, he truly did. He enjoyed the chat, and he believed every word about purpose, about the markings, and about this new place. Yet something still dug at him. A feeling that was once a jagged knife, reminding him of his beliefs was now a mosquito's bite, but it still remained.

He felt a second guess, and a change of mind may be in order. "I must think about it. I am not entirely convinced. May I have some time to consider?"

Gorum's expression hardened, then turned to a smile once more. "I see. Yes, you may have some time." He struggled up from his well-cushioned chair. "Gurin, would you see him to the guest house? Our guest must rest—he's had a long trip." He moved toward the front door, opening it slowly. "Perhaps I will see you tomorrow when you have decided."

Saul bowed. "Thank you for your hospitality, my friend."

Gorum smirked. His dark eyes shone in the dim light outside. "Of course. Do have a good rest, Saul Bromaggus."

"I shall. Thank you, sir." Saul exited through the wooden door and followed Gurin. He felt relaxed. The voice of Gorum was soothing, and the tea was redolent. He meandered through the streets, walking by several Broken who glanced at him oddly. Saul thought nothing of it, as he was in too good a mood. They soon came to a modest venom-bricked house with bright white mortar.

"Here we are," Gurin said, opening the small wooden door.

Saul closed the door, looking around to see a modest set of ornate wooden furniture. He walked straight to the bed, finding that it was softer than he would have liked. He missed the hard beds of the barracks, the clash of steel, the roars of victory, and most of all, his father. He, alongside his Warmaster of a mother, taught Saul everything from lessons of respect, honor and tactics, to the beginnings of fighting before Saul even entered training. He was gone now, burned by the Dragon Obelreyon, the dastardly serpent who ruled his people. However, now his people were in Rhoba, as well; peaceful, happy, and with a complete lack of a need for conflict.

Saul's mind and body were tired from the long day. The tea he drank was seemingly somnolent, however, he marched for hours upon hours, for days. Saul's people lay far to the north, his clan damaged, and possibly desolate.

Am I a man of nothing? he wondered. Saul contemplated the question as he slowly drifted into a dream. He wondered if these were his new people, since he was an exile now. His mind felt more than tired, and he couldn't help but nod off. Before he slipped into a deep sleep, he thought, *maybe this is where I belong.*

But why do I feel so uneasy?

Chapter Seventeen

Revenge Served Hot

Zaedor Nethilus

Zaedor's armor seared with heat. His mouth was drier than the cracks of Krot'ahk's valley, muscles so weak from exhaustion he could collapse at any moment. Yet, he'd reached his destination. It was more than a fortnight that he wandered through the deserts.

Five days without food and two without water, Zaedor slept in nothing more than a tattered, ice blue cloak he found on a dead body in the sands. His armor and greatblade were heavier than ever. He smelled of stale sweat and death. The grand cliffs of Zenato extended high above him, ascending half a mile with a well-crafted stone stair spiral from the base to the tip. It was many miles wide, the cliff as straight as a perfectly chiseled stone. Men of Amirion who went to Zenato and returned said Rawling's favorite execution for those not deserving of a battlefield death were catapulted from the cliffs.

It was simple, effective, and despicable.

Zaedor looked to the outer city once and again, feeling as though he climbed either to his death, or his destiny. *I will have my revenge*, he thought bitterly. After a day, or so it seemed, he climbed the final steps to view the great sandstone gate of Zenato. Its pale, sandy color was lined with cultured jewels, and the skulls of large beasts.

The sand-covered city was the opposite of Amirion. Gambling was prevalent, and brothels were common. Laws were minimal, and the people liked it that way. Zaedor cringed at the concept. *A city of savages*, he viewed them to be. *Full of traitors bent on savage magic and destroying the innocent. They have no respect for anyone.*

The city was primarily made of tented homes, along with some mud, brick, and wood houses. The people were dirty, the streets were filled with sand and loose rock, and stray animals were everywhere. It was pitiful and disgusting—especially the smell.

In his weeks alone, Zaedor thought of nothing more than his destruction. His beliefs were destroyed when they were ignored. His city was decimated by the city he came to. His King was killed by their King. *Rawling may not have been there, but it was him who gave the order.* His fists tired from clenching them so tightly. The flames, the screams, and the dead silence after the battle haunted his nightmares.

He tried to keep faith. He tried to be resilient—but that was gone.

Now he came to the city that brought the terrors upon him. He felt like years passed, with how much changed within him.

Zaedor's thoughts didn't match the happy music being played nearby. A ridiculous song rang out from a mandolin. He hardly believed music was played in a place like this.

"Pitiful," Zaedor croaked. His throat was barren from dehydration, and he could barely speak. His strength was drained from walking for weeks on end. He dropped to his knees from exhaustion, and not even his drive for revenge could pick him up.

"My friend!" an elderly, hoarse voice called.

The music stopped, and a pair of sandaled, mottled-skinned feet appeared in his vision, with and long, gritty toenails. "What'd you say is pitiful?" the voice said again, from above him. A large, mottled hand held a waterskin before his eyes. Zaedor was enraged that this man would even *ask* him such a question, but couldn't resist his need for water. He ripped it from the hand and chugged every last drop of the incredible, satiating water.

"My, you're a thirsty one. My name is Nargosh, Nargosh Shagon. What's yours, my young friend?"

Zaedor looked to him with a fierce eye. Nargosh was short for man, probably five foot four, with crooked teeth spread widely on either side of his mouth decorated by a scraggly white beard. He wore tattered clothes, old, sweat-stained, and wretched smelling. The man looked at him with a sweetened smile and large, lemon-yellow eyes.

"Zaedor of Amirion," he said bluntly.

Nargosh helped Zaedor up. "Now why would you be walking through the desert all alone? That's a dangerous task, you know!" Nargosh said. "What would you say is pitiful, Mr. Zaedor?"

Zaedor was angered at the question alone. *How could he not know! Who is this fool?* "How could you even *say* that? Look at me! Where do you think I'm from?" Zaedor yelled. He was never this way, but cared for little now. Revenge was all he had left in his heart.

Nargosh seemed taken aback by Zaedor's comment. His eyes drooped. "I was just asking a question, old bean." Nargosh quickly turned away and began walking. As he went, he turned his head. "Trying to help a broken man. What goes around comes around, old bean."

Who cares what he thinks. It will come around to them, all right. Zaedor wanted to give this city what they deserved. It was filled with a bunch of rambunctious, gluttonous knaves who cared for nothing. His stomach roared like an Ogre's call.

He walked through the city, slowly dragging his feet through the sand. The wind blew through his bright blond hair. Gasps came as he passed through the streets. *What are they looking at? Haven't they seen a citizen of Amirion before?* he thought miserably. The townsfolk wore simple clothes, whether they were carpenters, clothiers, or scribes. There were seemingly no nobles among them. Everyone was dirty and wore tattered clothes, and there were minimal guards. *Due to the casualties of war, possibly.* He scowled at every person he saw. He wished to hit them where it hurt. Where *he* hurt. Their king.

He found a tavern at a crossroad in the slums. The building was broken and dilapidated, made with rotten wood and had a crooked door. The chains holding the sign clattered in the wind. It read, *Leena's Lagers.* Zaedor stumbled to the door and slammed it open. It was shockingly bustling, filled with unscrupulous thugs. The splintered oak wood bar extended from the stairs on the right all the way to the middle of the room, leading to a seating area filled with men and women drinking and feasting all around. He walked to the bar and slammed down into a stool.

"Food," Zaedor said bluntly. He didn't care what it was.

"Oh, *um*, okay," a high-pitched female voice said. He didn't look up to see who it was. "Would you like a drink?" she asked.

Zaedor didn't drink any form of spirit, not before. He thought it clouded the mind, but now his previous beliefs were moot. "Mead," he grumbled.

After a quick moment, a glass appeared in front of him, filled. He gulped it down, eyes never leaving the table. It burned his throat as it passed, but it felt strangely good. He asked for more, and received it promptly.

Zaedor thought about all the ways he could get through the guards and destroy the keep. He sliced through many of Rawling's warriors in Amirion. *How would this be any different?* he wondered. His battle would be a worthy sacrifice, to avenge his kingdom by killing the one who destroyed it. Rawling was the old champion of the arena, but he was also fifty years of age. The grand coliseum stood beside his castle, where the gladiator games were held every few years. Members of all walks of life and every sect joined to celebrate the glory of competition in combat. Amirion battled well in all sections, of course, but was no more.

Zaedor gripped his stein tightly and huffed a breath. A plate slid in front of him. It had various dried vegetables, desert fruits from the Mirage Lakes, and a small kettlebird leg.

"Um," the woman seemed to squeak out a whisper. She paused in front of him. "Are you okay?" the female voice asked. She only made Zaedor grip his glass tighter.

"I'm fine," Zaedor grumbled. He lifted his head to finally look her in the eye.

Her bright yellow eyes glistened in the sunlight streaming into the bar, along with her tattered necklace—with a medallion resembling a blue sun behind an upturned sword. "You." He paused, confused. *Is she from Amirion? That's impossible,* he thought. His eyes widened, and he leaned back from the bar.

"I, uh, what about me?" she squeaked.

"What is your name? Where do you come from?" He gave no honey in his tone.

"I—I'm Leena. I've lived here my whole life," she stuttered. "Might I ask who you are?"

Zaedor detached from the situation again, leaning back, unimpressed. "Zaedor, of Amirion," he said.

"You're from Amirion?" Leena said carefully.

"*Yes*," Zaedor said with a vicious grunt, slamming his gauntlet on the bar. The room went silent, and the eyes of all patrons turned toward him.

Leena looked around awkwardly. "I'm sorry, I just heard that there were no survivors," Leena said. "Sorry."

"Well, looks like you're wrong." Zaedor growled at her. The mead was getting to him already. "How can you people be so horrible?" More heads sent lingering stares over to Zaedor.

"I'm only curious—" Leena's voice dropped off.

"Hey, bub." A man's voice called out behind him. "Be nice to the little lady. She just served you food and drink without making you pay first—even though you are being rude. You should be more polite. She's a nice girl." He placed his hand on Zaedor's shoulder.

Who the hell is this guy? "Why don't you mind your own damn business?" He smacked the man's hand away and shoved him. The light barely showed the man's hairless face and scalp. He only wore simple, ratty clothes.

"It's okay, Rodrick. I can handle it just fine." She gave the ratty man a warm smile. "He's been through a lot. He's from Amirion," she said quietly.

Zaedor clenched his fists. His mind was foggy from the mead, and he saw only red.

The hairless man drew out his mouth in displeasure. "You're right, Leena. I'm sorry. He ain't worth the fight." The fool said it as if he had no cares in the world. He turned his back.

Zaedor had something else in mind. He wore a suit of armor, as citizens of Amirion did, and this man wore nothing but a cloth tunic and pants. *Who does he think he is, challenging me?* "What did you say? I'm not worth a *fight*?" Without pause, he charged at Rodrick with his fist raised.

The skin of rodrick's arms shifted from pale flesh to bright in the blink of an eye. He caught Zaedor's gauntlet with one hand and swung his other to crack it across Zaedor's chin. Without pause, Zaedor crumpled to the ground, and everything went black.

* * *

The commotion of commonfolk echoed around him as sandy wind blew softly across his face. He opened his eyes to see himself laid in a small, hard bed with his feet extending off the end. Zaedor rose from the bed, feeling a stab of pain in his back from the sleep. His head still pounded from the previous night. The walls and floors were old wood, but stable enough.

"Ugh, what happened?" Zaedor placed his hand on the spot Rodrick struck, and it was very painful to the touch. He was glad he wasn't in jail—or worse. He still had a job to do. Zaedor lurched to a stand, still in his weathered plate mail, smelling of old sweat.

He cracked the door open and heard talking from the stairs at end of the hall. *Am I in the tavern?* he wondered. He figured he would have been thrown to the street after picking a fight in a bar—even if he was provoked. Zaedor carefully crept to the end of the hall, passing closed, splintered wooden doors. He crept down the stairs, seeing the open hall of the tavern below. Leena organized kegs and glasses alone. No one else was at the bar at such an early hour.

Zaedor stood still, unsure if he should approach the bar or simply walk out before his anger overtook him again. *Everyone in this town is an animal*, he reminded himself. Before he could act, Leena's innocent yellow eyes locked with his.

"*U-um*, hello," Leena stuttered. "Rodrick carried you upstairs after giving you—*that*." She pointed to her forehead.

"He could have just hit me with his fist," Zaedor complained, rubbing his head.

Leena chuckled nervously. "Well, he did." After a moment, she said, "S—sorry. He's an Avatar. It's something his people do."

"Something they do?" Zaedor replied. He'd heard legends of the Avatars—shifters—but they were isolated far in the north, or so he thought. The image of King Faelin's lifeless head entered his mind. *Cloaker must have been one of them,* he thought. *A shifter. Now there are two of them.*

"Yes, they're from the ice forests of the northeast. All races there are born with the ability to shapeshift. It's really quite amazing," she said poignantly, with a tiny hop for emphasis.

Zaedor stomped down the stairs to the bar and slammed onto a stool once again. "I don't care how they do it. They're monsters. I saw one of them rip my King's head from his body," he growled.

Leena scratched the nape of her neck and rubbed her arms. "I'm so sorry," Leena squeaked. "I didn't know."

"They're beasts. All of them!" Zaedor roared. He hated them. He hated Cloaker *and* Rodrick, the murderous fools. Zaedor wanted their heads.

Leena drew back, frightened. "Rodrick is a good man," she said. Standing a little more firmly, she said, "You shouldn't judge others so quickly."

He got up then, finished with where he was. Leena did not understand. She was naive, blinded by innocence, probably sitting in a tavern her whole life. He walked to the door and stopped. "I don't have any money. I won't be back."

"That's okay," He was surprised to hear no complaints or resistance. "Rodrick paid your tab, and for your room."

He didn't want their pity. Zaedor had his mission.

"Why are you in Zenato, of all places?" she asked.

He saw no reason to tell her. She was weak, fragile, and didn't see the truth in front of her eyes. "I'm taking care of business," he said bluntly, hoping that would end it.

"Revenge isn't the answer," she said quietly. He only heard one last thing before he was out of earshot. "It only comes back."

Satiated and ready, Zaedor walked through the sandy streets to his final destination: the castle. It sat beside the grand coliseum. He never saw the arena, and never competed in the games. The few who fought there always spoke of how fantastic it was: the feeling of a victory, with thousands of cheers backing your blade. The core of the city had many temples of gods who focused on battle. None of which were Shiada, whose temple resided in the residential district. It may have been desecrated for all he knew. Zaedor refused to seek it—and disregarded her power entirely.

The coliseum was truly colossal. He could hear the cheers from outside its mighty walls. There were statues of combatants all along the many levels on the outside, some brandishing weapons, bare hands, or flowing flames. Surrounding the whole building was betting tables and booths for the fights, along with all forms of merchants.

Zaedor came to the fortress of Rawling himself. It was a miniscule, plain building in comparison, built with sandstone. The thin pillars surrounding the structure bathed in the bright desert sun almost constantly. Two soldiers guarded the door of the large, domed structure.

He stood outside not a hundred feet from the steps with fists clenched, thinking long and hard about his task: how to defeat each soldier, how to adjust for their weapons or if they wielded magic, and preparing against whatever form they would take. The biggest obstacle was Rawling. *He is weak without his guards*, he knew. *He is an old man, and a coward.*

Minutes went by, and his stance stayed ever resilient. Soon, hours passed, and he remained adamant. He grew hungry but did not falter. He grew thirsty and did not weaken. As night fell, the guards closed the doors and moved inside. People walked around him, and long stares and confused looks followed as he glared the castle door down. He ran through the scenario a thousand times in his head, working up to defeating every soldier in the damned kingdom and murdering their king. *Blood will have blood*, Zaedor swore. In his last standing moment, he could not think of any other way to live on. He chose to fight for justice. He stepped forward, toward the castle.

"Hey! Hey you!" a man yelled.

Zaedor looked around, confused. A small man shrouded in the darkness of night waved his hands wildly. He looked back to the castle's doors. *Not now,* he calmed himself. Revenge could wait a few moments. "What?" he called back.

"My house is being robbed! Help, please! Brigands! I need help! *Please!*" he yelled desperately. Zaedor looked around, seeing no one else in the distance. He couldn't turn an emergency such as this down, not even in his new state of mind. He dashed around the corner, meeting a powerful fist to his face. He staggered back, only to take two more strikes to the gaps in his armor. An arm came around his neck and restrained him, making it difficult to breathe.

"Haha! Rope 'im boys! I hear Amirionians like him are one-in-a-million now!"

Weakened from the blows, Zaedor couldn't stop them. His hands were bound, and he was soon blindfolded and gagged.

"You're gonna make us a fortune!" the man's voice echoed.

Chapter Eighteen

A Dream of Bloodlust

Saul Bromaggus

Saul opened his eyes and saw a vast land before him. He stood atop a circular stone platform, high above the clouds.

Am I dreaming? he thought. He peered over to see many formations of land on each side—forests, islands, lands covered with ice and sand—at a much further distance than any normal Broken could..

He looked over the edge to see the tower descend for miles, it seemed, built atop a mighty beast of rock at its base.

The platform was carved with various runes, each stone intricately placed and formed as part of the floor in an image of perfection with no match. The tower was lined with ten pointed stones, like a crown, each with a mark of a god—but two were shattered.

There were eleven in all. He recognized the three crashing winds of Gadora, the tri-pointed cracked earth of Yggranda, the five blazes of Kannakash, and the two waves of Urikar. Then there were many he did not know. A trident, a star, even the six-pointed sun he was marked with, among many others. Saul had no armor, weapon, or shield, simply a pair of beige linen pants and no shirt. A glow flickered along his arms—his red and blue markings.

"Where am I?" he said aloud. The crash of thunder and lightning echoed from behind him. He spun around to see a vision of unfathomable divinity.

A tall, granite-skinned woman with dark almond eyes, a bold-featured face and long, platinum-silver hair stood at the platform's center. "You are atop Eternum, Saul," a hard, female voice rang from behind. "In the center of Renalia." Stepping toward him, the subtle glimmer of silver ringmail shone in the light above, accentuated by the black cloth underneath gold rings sewn into it.

Deep down, Saul knew who she was, but couldn't believe it for a second. "Who are you?" he asked.

With a smirk, a subtle jolt of electricity traveled across the hilt at her side, coming to a blade's hilt shaped like a dragon's head. "I am Gadora. I know you see it," she said calmly, walking closer to him. "I took a form you understand."

Without a pause, he dropped to one knee with eyes at the stones below, a fist at his centre. Breathless. *Is this a dream?*

"Rise," she said strongly.

He hesitated. One bowed before elders. One knelt before royalty. One wasn't to look upon prophets.

But she was so much more.

Divine.

Infinity.

The being he would and always wish to represent.

He drew his eyes upward, seeing her dark eyes bore into him as if piercing his mind, body, and soul. "This is a dream," she said, smiling slyly. "I am here to give you a hand." To which she held hers out.

He froze.

This was far more than a being such as him deserved. He was forsaken. Exiled. Dishonored. She—she *was* honor.

But he held out a shaky hand, and she helped him rise to his feet—yet she still stood taller.

She strolled past him and stood at the edge of the platform. The rings lining her silver skirt that led from right hip to left knee made an angelic chime that echoed within his soul. "This place connects gods and men, even in dreams."

"But why help me?" Saul asked incredulously. He feared questioning his goddess—the most powerful warrior ever known. He questioned not knowing whether rushing her was a good idea or a foolish one. He was cynical that she even *was* Gadora, even if it was a dream. Saul rarely second guessed himself. Now, he second guessed every movement. Every thought. Every word.

Gadora glanced back at him. "Straight to the point. I like that." She chuckled. "The land is at an imbalance."

"How do you mean?" Saul inquired.

She shook her head, platinum hair blowing with the subtle wind. "The world is constantly in a balance between good and evil, order and chaos. Something set it off its tilt. Gods are constantly at war with each other, but we know full well that if you anger the balance, everyone dies. Balance is a silly thing, when calm and collected. Yet disturbing it has cataclysmic consequences."

But he was still an exile. A mortal. "What does this have to do with me?" Saul was still in sheer awe of being in her presence. He wanted to kneel and salute her again. His knees weakened by her very words, but he stood tall to show respect—uncertain if that was what he should even do.

She shrugged. "Potentially nothing. The imbalance is coming, whether or not we wish it so. Pieces of the game began moving the moment the blood moon sat high in the sky."

The blood moon. His father once told him a blood moon was a sign of unity, and of change. In past days, Saul's life had changed significantly. "What could I possibly do?" Undoubtedly, Saul was a strong warrior—but he was also an exile in a land of foes. He had no power or influence here. Or in Kathynta—but now, he was far from home.

His goddess looked to him with a furrowed brow. "Don't be a fool. What kind of person have you become?" She stepped toward him. Each step send a shock of fear through him. "You are of my clan in the Vale, and yet you question your existence?"

Saul knew not to apologize. He stood up straight, and said what was in his heart. "I wish to slay the Dragon. I want to spill his vile blood upon the land, and that of the traitors who follow him," Saul said confidently. "That is what I want. First, the Dragon. Then Renalia." *I will take that land back for my people.*

Silence. The Silence was unbearable. Her blank expression could have meant the end of him. Or greatness.

To Saul's surprise, his goddess smiled, then tilted her head as if enjoying her examination of the mortal before her. Then she let out a hearty laugh. "So bold. So honorable. Do you say that to yourself and the rising sun every morning?" She sighed and placed her hands on her hips. "I know," she said, looking over the land. "That old fool in Rhoba is right about many things, you know."

"Gorum?"

"Yes." Stepping toward him, she placed a stony finger upon his red marking of the three crashing winds. "What do you think these mean?"

Saul froze. He felt a jolt travel through him the moment she touched his flesh. "I," he stuttered. Looking into her dark eyes, it was as if she stared into his very soul. "I want to believe in my fate," he said plainly. "But I wish to choose." It was a choice to believe in a deity, in a leader, that made a follower the most loyal and valuable.

"Seems I believe you'll die, Saul." She looked at his arm a moment, and smirked. "Would you accept this fate that I have given you?"

Saul opened his mouth to speak, then stopped. He couldn't say those words. Doubt. He could be struck down. But looking into the eyes of the ultimate judge, he knew the truth was all he should give. "If you wished me to die for a reason I would not believe in," Saul said, eyes staring into hers, "then you would not be the goddess I believe in."

Silence and wind took them both. They stared into each other's eyes, and Saul felt his knees shake, and sweat collected everywhere. The way his father died. The way Saul escaped. Over the past weeks, he learned fate was fickle. "I wish to choose my own fate."

A proud smile grew across the face of his goddess. Glancing to his shield arm, she said, "I can see why she chose you as well, you stubborn fool." She laughed, meandering back to the center of the platform, where she entered. "I am glad we had a moment to speak." She gritted her teeth, and clenched her fists. "The Dragon murdered my people, you saw it. He deserves to burn in the Hells under Azoran's trident." With a smirk, she backed into a gateway of light that appeared behind her.

"Let me ask you one final question, Saul." She turned with strong posture, hands held behind her back. "If you had to choose between joining forces with an orderly and strong Hydrian society or a dishonorable, backstabbing Broken one, which would you choose?"

Saul had no response. To him, Hydris *were* traitors. They all betrayed the Broken. But if she believed them trustworthy…

"You do not have to answer that." She gave a sly smirk. "Do take time to consider it. The tides of fate carry us all out to a sea—it is there we accept our fate and drown, or we fight against it and survive."

Fight against it, Saul thought. *Am I fighting against my fate?* He stared out toward the sea beyond the Risen Isles, before looking back down to Renalia beneath.

"*Rai soli moria, gadoras faust,*" Gadora said from behind.

His goddess spoke in a strange tongue—one Saul never heard. He looked to her with a raised brow.

"It is the language of old. A Forgotten language. An important lesson. It means, 'Where warriors fall, heroes rise.'"

With that, she passed into the portal and disappeared.

He was left alone to contemplate the words of his goddess. *Where warriors fall, heroes rise.* His father fell before the Dragon, hoping others would be inspired by his bold sacrifice. *Maybe I will rise up a hero from my father's ashes.* His father told him the strongest warriors were protectors. He wished to be a slayer.

"Sometimes," Saul said, looking at his left arm bearing the mark of slayers, then to his right to see the mark of protectors. "We must be both."

The rumble of thunder came from above him. *Is this a sign from her, the goddess of storms?* The rain fell with a sudden might, building from clear skies to torrential downpour within moments. A *crack* of lightning came down to strike one of the crowned points on the tower, then another and another, in turn. They went around until each was struck, and a mighty rumble came from the black clouds above him.

Lightning streaked down from the sky and struck him with a continuous bolt, turning every vein within him ablaze. Saul writhed in agony and screamed for it to stop, but it did not. He shook as his skin burned until he could bear it no longer. Gadora's voice echoed though his bones: *Where warriors fall, heroes rise.*

* * *

As he closed his eyes he felt nothing, and smelled something very different: damp stone, decaying flesh, and shit. The putrid stench of the mix was disgusting, almost causing Saul to vomit.

He opened his eyes to see slimy green stone walls dimly lit by torches. His arms were held up, and rough iron grinded against the skin of his wrists.

Chained.

His armor and blade were gone, and his father's brown cloak hung on the wall. All he wore were the same beige linen pants from his dream. He saw two other Broken across from him, one marked with yellow, the other with red. He couldn't make out the marks. They seemed weak and lifeless, save for a slight bit of movement here and there.

"You," he said roughly, trying to call to them. "Broken!" Saul yelled. They didn't respond to his words.

A slow, dragging set of footsteps echoed from down the way. "Seems you have finally woken. You must have enjoyed the tea." Gorum's honeyed tone rang through the hall. He wandered into sight in his long robe, dark eyes shining in the torchlight. Eyes of a traitor.

"What the hell is this? Where am I?" Saul growled.

"Oh, a nice little place I keep beneath the town. I am quite the alchemist, you know. Khoria crystal, Ravager teeth, and a drop of god-blessed blood. In the right amounts with the right incantation, you can make a lovely little bloodstone. We have one keeping us happy and prosperous, sitting in the middle of town."

What the hell is a bloodstone? The middle of town—where he felt pulled toward it. The blood calling to him. Looking around the dungeon, he thought, *they were calling for help.* Saul wrenched forward and pulled at his manacles. The chains clattered as he tried to free himself. "Let me go! You said I was welcome here!"

"Oh my, yes, I did—yet you disregarded my invitation. I was so polite, and even my tea didn't convince you entirely. I must commend you, not many can resist its charm. I *am* a talented alchemist, after all." Gorum smiled slyly and stared deep into Saul's eyes. "The Vale is a corrupt society, and I have created a perfect one here. A man such as you would smash my lovely town and my people's lives for your gods, your honor, or whatever excuses you may make. I gave you a chance to join us, but you had to 'think about it,' which means you will leave. Instead, I have chosen to keep you for a more important purpose."

Pulling on the chains again, he beared his teeth in rage. "And what purpose would that be, you traitorous wretch?" Saul growled. "Something disgraceful."

"Well, you asked how we keep our people safe. I might as well tell you now, why not? I enjoy the reactions." Gorum chuckled. "We, as a people, have a shield that protects our town. Those with ill intent cannot pass it. One cannot see it, though." He slowly strolled to the wall, feeling the tattered cloak. "The markings you bear contain power, that much is true. If one feels passion for their gods and their purpose, it flows within them." Gorum slowly looked to Saul with a smile. "We use *your* blood to power the bloodstone. You are the reason we live, the reason we thrive in a happy society of free Broken. Is that not an honorable cause?"

"We are not slaves!" Saul yelled again, the sound of his chains clattering through the mysterious dungeon. "You will not get away with this. I will not allow it. I cannot!"

"You are not a slave, my boy, but a martyr! Your passion will be celebrated with the life of your people!"

"*My* people?" Saul snarled. "You are not one of us. What of the others, do they know about this?" Saul could hardly believe his ears. People like him, Broken, were using the life essence of their unwilling prisoners to live.

"Oh my, yes. Everyone in the town knows by adolescence—the farmers, the soldiers, the merchants. We keep you here so that we never have to see combat. It really does seem as though the pen is mightier than the sword—or at least, a gentle, polite hand is. Everyone here agrees with this practice. They know the brutal, horrid ways of the Vale, and also that their happiness functions on the power of alchemy. That, and blood magic, are the saviors of our people." Blood magic. Magic of the abyss.

Saul's fists clenched so tightly that his nails almost cut the flesh of his hands. He foamed at the mouth and became more and more enraged with every honeyed, vile word from Gorum's lips. "I will kill you. You—no, *everyone* in this town—are all a disgrace to our people. To *any* people."

"My friend, we are not a disgrace. We are the future! We build upon the ashes of the Vale to form a new society, one of peace. Do you not agree? Your blood is most valuable. Two sets of markings—my, that is rare. We may not need another soul for years. How could you be so selfish? You could provide a full city with health and safety for years on your own. There's only one way to find out. Let me first show you what will happen, and then it will be your turn. Did you not see the society above? There were happy people, running and laughing. Farmers tilling the land, winemakers squishing their grapes. This is all because of you, all of you, making this possible. Do you not want peace? Do you not want your people to be happy?"

"I want my people to be free." Saul growled at him again. "I want them to live freely, all of them! This is wrong, don't you see? This violates our very nature!"

The man Saul saw the previous night was not as he expected, not at all. His tone was sweet, his tea was somnolent, and his words true, but he'd said only half of what he meant.

Gorum's smile faded as he slowly walked back to the other end of the hall. He went to the enclave with the other two nearly lifeless Broken. He unsheathed a sharp, curved obsidian dagger from his robe, and stabbed it into the red god's marking on one man's shoulder, just beneath the skin. The man writhed in pain; his cries echoed though the dungeon. Saul saw crimson light seep from his mark into the dagger. Saul stood and watched, wishing he could do something to stop the wretch. The Broken became weaker and weaker until he fell limp, dead.

"Pity," Gorum said, strolling over to Saul. "He had been here quite some time—a year, almost. Luckily, we have *you*. Now, what do you say we see what those marks can do?" He gave a crooked smile as he lurched over to Saul.

He won't take me. He can't, Saul thought desperately.

The dagger shone with red light as he approached. "The gods won't help you now. They never have, and they never will, my friend. Your fate is here, with us."

Saul was frozen, unable to move as the dagger pierced his skin in the center of Gadora's mark. "I will not be *enslaved*!" Saul yelled. The dagger flew out from the wound and clattered on the ground. His marks glowed red and blue from his arms. Saul bared his teeth as his greyed skin darkened with his rage.

"What's this?" Gorum exclaimed as he fell to the ground.

"I cannot be stopped!" Saul's entire body tightened; the veins in his arms and body swelled, as if ready to burst. His chains clattered as he pulled them forward, growling fiercely like a beast. He dragged his arms forward with all his strength, his roar growing louder and louder, enough to match Obelreyon himself. His eyes bulged out as his scream reached its peak, and the sounds of shattering steel shot out from the slimy stone wall. Saul breathed heavily as his chains dangled to the floor. Fists still clenched, he ran at Gorum without pause. Saul grabbed his old frail arms, breaking each one with ease. As Gorum screamed in pain, Saul snatched up the obsidian dagger.

"No, my people! They depend on me!" Gorum pleaded, tears flowing from his eyes. "You can't do this, we are innocent!"

Saul grabbed him by the neckline of his robe, pulling him in. "*You* did this. You all did. You sat by, watching innocent people be drained of life so that you could live. You are despicable. Every single one will pay for this atrocity."

Saul took the dagger to Gorum's throat and sliced it with ease. His traitorous blood oozed from his neck and pooled upon the floor. Then he heard a yell coming from down the hall, and the clomping of leather boots.

"Hey, what's going on down here?" a guard yelled.

Saul shot up, his marks still bright. "The dishonorable must pay."

The guard came around the corner, meeting a swift hand and dagger. The man fell to the ground, bleeding from the neck and gasping for air as he clawed at Saul's leg.

Saul took up the sword the guard carried. Vengeance was at hand. He grabbed his father's cloak, tying it from his left ribs to right shoulder. He walked the halls, seeing Broken after Broken, marks of all three colors and various gods. Each one was drained and barely alive. *The townspeople will pay for this*, Saul vowed. The town above was armed, but no match for him. He trained for years for this, trained to fight against chaos, for honor, and for glory. Saul walked up the spiral staircase to the city above. He arrived in the south end, and recognized a few of the houses.

"A farmed one! A farmed one! It's free, it's free!" a man pointed, running into his home.

Many others ran from him into their homes, and quickly shut their doors. Four guards came to surround him, wearing nothing but leather and linen; Saul felt it was a joke. In plate, he fought normally. In no armor, he soared like Gadora's lightning.

He clashed blades with two, and swung his sword so hard that he easily disarmed one Broken and caused the other to stagger. He ran outside the circle, checking a strike from one Broken and slicing his elbow, then his back, and finally thrusting the blade through his shoulder. Then, while the first guard went to pick up his weapon, Saul parried blows from the two remaining men, slicing the wrist of one and the neck of the other. He stabbed the final guard through the chest as he dodged around his sword. Saul felt a great surge of energy flow through him, from mind to blade. He powered through the city from one Broken to the next, rarely contested by a guard.

Citizens of the city ran at him, winemaker, blacksmith, and merchant alike. They were disgraceful, but Saul didn't truly need to kill them all. But they came for him. "Kill the runner!" they yelled. "We need to keep ourselves safe!"

Each one knew what went on here, as all had been aware of Gorum's treachery. Saul spilled blood in slow motion, it seemed. Each enemy he faced had not picked up a blade in months or years, but Saul was born with a blade in hand. Where they moved slowly, Saul fought almost unseen. The glory of combat burned within his soul, and it was released upon the betrayers in a brilliant slaughter. The old, the sick, the healthy—all kinds of Broken who sat on their high horses of better purpose and false righteousness—came at him, attacking him. He spared all who did not come to kill him.

Saul slayed all those who attacked. Many escaped, but the wastes would take them soon enough. He left children alive, but if they came at him with a weapon, he gave them the death they asked for. Saul's rage was inexorable.

As the bodies piled, Saul slowly tired of swinging through flesh. He was beaten with clubs, slashed with pitchforks, and pounded by fists and tackles, but he would not relent.

A man, sliced up and near-death, croaked a plea. "Please, we only wanted to live in peace."

Saul stood over him and pointed his blade at the man's neck. "You lived in disgrace, not in peace. Now, you die for it." He sliced the man's neck without a pause to hear his next words.

It came time that no more chased Saul; inhabitants only ran from the city in fear of death for their crimes. He walked to the small stone structure at the center of town, by the well. He broke the lock and ripped it open, finding a large, blood-red well-cut crystal sitting atop an intricate golden setting. He picked it up and threw it to the dirt.

Saul raised his blade, and with all his might, he smashed the bloodstone to bits, causing an explosion that blew him back to the ground. Shaking his head, he looked to see the crimson pieces turned black. The people drained, he hoped, would now be free. The only innocent in this city of disgrace.

Saul returned to the dungeon, retrieved the keys from the wall at the end, and unlocked all the Broken imprisoned there. Their energy returned.

"Who are you, what happened?" a Broken asked. His marking was yellow with the sign of the Hydris, the rounded, four-point star. His skin was pale and rough as ash.

"You are free. The people of this city shall no longer live from your blood," Saul said.

There were twenty of them, all staring at Saul in wonderment. "What happened to the townsfolk?"

Saul turned to face the stairwell, then looked back to them. His heart beat wildly from the exhausting battle he just endured. His muscles burned like poison; he was in need of a rest, but there was no time for one. "Either dead, hiding, or retreating."

"How could you do that? All those people—"

"Are dishonorable cowards. Disgusting plagues, who leech life from the innocent, from *you*, without care. They died quickly. I don't torture." Saul was not a fool. Any man who tortured others without a just purpose was a coward.

Some of them seemed thankful, others confused, and the rest fearful. "Where will we go?"

Saul thought on where he wanted to go. He could not go to Alin or Kalidor, the Hydrian military bases. He had one option left: south. "You can build here, in hopes that none will attack."

"What about you? What is your name?" The yellow-marked Broken asked.

"My name is Saul Bromaggus, of the Gadora clan, in the Vale. I am going south. North is not an option. Maybe the plateau will bring more than death, as the Vale certainly would."

The small Broken walked forward. He had scars down his arms, where he had been bled much from the ritual. His yellow marks bore the waves of Urikar, the four-point star, and the blade. "I am Drofar Kollen. I wish to go with you."

Two more came forward with Drofar. "We, as well."

More and more joined the group, until they'd all agreed. Broken of red, blue, and yellow marks, crashing winds, stars, blades, and drops all came forward together.

Saul was shocked at his sudden following. "Why do you wish to come with me? What could my fate possibly offer you?"

"You freed us from this hell," Drof said. "Perhaps our fate lies with yours now."

Saul fought with the idea. He would be responsible for these people now. He freed them, but what if they died because of him? They sported proud looks and strong stances, each arisen from the ashes of death. *You are born to lead*, his father said. Saul felt the cloak tied around his torso, and knew he must bring them.

"We gather food and supplies," Saul commanded. "When the sun reaches midway from high noon to dusk, we ride from the south gate."

Each Broken struck their center in salute, Saul included. Then they separated, each moving from house to house. Some were flabbergasted at the bodies in the streets, others unaffected. Saul walked by the dead, seeing them as nothing more than a nuisance now. They gathered clothes and what weapons and armor they could find.

Saul recovered his plate mail from Gorum's home. When the time came, he took the lit lantern that still burned and threw it to the draperies. He exited, looking back at the burning house of a traitor, knowing it had to be done.

As the sun reached midway down the horizon, Saul came to the southern gate and met the others.

"Stop, fiend!" a meek voice called out.

Saul stopped and turned to see a small Broken boy, possibly ten years of age, with a longblade held clumsily in both hands. Saul raised his hand to calm the others, and walked closer. "Are you here for revenge?" he asked.

"You killed my father! I saw you. You killed my people!" he yelled.

Saul felt no remorse. The people deserved the death they received, whether they wanted it or not. "Your city drained the lives of innocent people. They all knew, and they died for it." He didn't fluff his words for the child's sake. "Do you wish to defend that?"

"I'll kill you! For my family!" the boy yelled.

Saul frowned. "What's your name, boy?"

The boy reminded Saul of himself, wanting vengeance for his father. The boy would come with them, die in the wastes, or fight right here.

"Gallin, Gallin Treydor!"

"Well, Gallin," Saul drew his blade, "you can walk away, you can come with us freely, or you can fight."

Gallin stood strong. "I will not go with you. I will fight for honor."

"Then fight, and the gods may see your valorous act."

Gallin charged with blade overhead. Saul dodged his awkward strikes, checking each with a parry. After a few more swings, Saul clashed with the boy's blade so hard, it flew twenty feet away. The next swing came back to slice the boy's head clean off.

"A child runs in fear," Saul wiped his blade, saluting the boy's corpse. "A warrior dies with honor."

Then Saul turned to see the others staring at him in awe. "We have a long road ahead."

Chapter Nineteen

Flower of the Night

Kayden Ralta

Kayden led the group of freedom fighters into Deurbin, a large town a few days trek to the south of camp and north of the marshlands. The sun began to set, leaving a sky of orange, yellow, and red spilling across the cobblestone street traversing the town.

Deurbin was lined with brick buildings and strangely showed little evidence of slums. It was especially known for its Flanbird stew and sweetened butter potatoes. Kayden could pass on the stew. It was so thick and grimy; she'd puke over the thought of the texture alone. She enjoyed potatoes but didn't commonly get any since she lived in both the desertlands and the northern snowhills, which were terrible areas for growing them.

Kayden wore a heavy black hood covering most of her face. She forced Lira to wear a hood—she did business in Deurbin before, so they needed to cover her up.

"Frozelian mead; I haven't had that in quite awhile. I recall it is quite the delight. I cannot wait!" Vesper proclaimed, swishing his finger in the air and eyes not leaving his book.

The brick houses were well made, and bold colors of mortar varied from one building to the next from ivory white to smokey grey to midnight black. Intricate, wood-carved signs declaring each vendor's household swung with the wind, the metal chains hanging them creaking and clattering.

Kayden kept an exceptional eye on the people passing by and standing around them. *Anyone could turn us in,* she reminded herself. A couple gave them a look or two, but nothing suspicious. Guards passed without a word, not even an eye. Some gave Magnus a glance, and she knew it was because he was a Half-Devil. They weren't all bad, she knew. Magnus was solemn and dull-witted, it seemed, but no rapist or murderer. She sensed no nefarity in him. *Domika was a different story.* Something about her bugged Kayden, not to mention, the drake was on her non-stop over everything.

Kayden looked at the well-kept gardens around the houses, attempting to forget Domika for a few moments. Flowers of all kinds grew outside in pots and holders: fluttering garlands with their long, bristle-laden violet petals, lilies with their bright day ivory color, and the black nightrain flowers which were closed tightly during the day, only to open at the moonlight. Kayden smiled as she passed those, as they were her favorite flower. They opened when least expected, the jewel of the night grew in almost any climate. Her mother always picked them for her when they lived in the deserts.

She wondered what to expect from this mission. Deurbin was a seemingly peaceful town but had a touch of corruption within it. Rebels were arrested or kidnapped, and then supposedly tortured for information, which they were sent to investigate. Some were minor offenders of the law, which concerned Kayden most. A punishment should fit the crime, and torture was no way to punish a thief. The noble in control of the marshes had information on the state's movements against the rebellion. *Those drakes.* They were oppressive scumbags. She couldn't stand the thought of them capturing innocent people—let alone torturing them.

She didn't know what the rest of the group had in mind, but Kayden swiftly made up hers. The word 'torture' alone freaked her out, and ever since she left the desert, she hadn't truly heard it. *It is for your own good,* Sheeran said to her, every time she did something wrong, or inappropriate. *Callidan will take care of it, and everything will be okay,* he said. She hoped to never see either of them again. She could still hear Callidan's giggle in her mind, and she could see his disgusting face when she closed her eyes. *It wasn't for the best. You lied to me. Now the marks won't let me forget it.* The names of the past. Ones she hoped to forget.

"Beast!" a man called to them.

Kayden was shocked back into reality. She stopped abruptly and turned to the voice. "Excuse me?"

"Not you, runt. *Him.*" The man pointed at Magnus, saddened by the comment. "What are you doing in this town, you horned monster?" the man snapped again. The eyes of onlookers began to draw toward them.

Fire burned in her veins, but she didn't want to create a huge scene. She put her hand on Magnus's arm, whispering, "Be calm. We don't need a problem." She turned back to the angry man. "Hey, bub, who the hell do you think you are? Why don't you leave him alone before something bad happens to you?" she hissed.

Oops.

"Someone like him violated my family, stole our belongings, and hurt my wife!"

A crowd began to form. Not good. She stormed up to the man, and stared up at him right in the eyes, whispering, "Oh, and that makes everyone of that race bad? He saved my life, and I'm a little girl. Is he going to hurt me, now? Are you here to *save* me?"

The man was shocked. He looked to Magnus with buggy eyes and glanced back to Kayden's intense glare. "N-No, I—"

"Exactly," she whispered, "You aren't going to say another hurtful thing. You are going to walk up to that nice man over there, and you're going to say sorry. Got it?" She bared her teeth as she finished. Then she backed off, smiled sweetly, and walked back to the group.

The man looked around awkwardly and stormed off in a huff. The crowd parted and moved on.

"Phew, that was close. Let's get moving," Kayden said, leading the group to continue again.

The group passed through the market district, and various merchants yelled of their wares of the day. "Fish for sale! Fresh fish off the south lakes!" some yelled. The smell of fish was quite strong, and unappealing to Kayden. She hated fish.

Magnus relaxed his shoulders and sighed hoarsely. "Thank you for your assistance," Magnus said. He smiled at her, but she didn't return it.

"Don't worry about it." Kayden did it for the mission, not him. "C'mon, let's get out of here."

Lira placed a comforting hand on Magnus' arm, and he simply smiled and nodded. "I am able to handle ridicule. I am older than you think," Magnus said.

Kayden never thought about how old Half-Devils were. Humans lived until fifty, maybe seventy years at the oldest, but Devils lived for centuries. She eyed him a moment, figuring he was of twenty-one years, twenty-two, maybe. Out of curiosity, she had to ask. "Well, don't keep us in suspense, Mags. How old are you?"

"*Hmm.*" He thought to himself, bringing his fist to his chin. "One hundred and twenty-six." He said it plainly, as if it wasn't surprising.

"*What?*" everyone said in unison.

"You barely even look twenty!" Domika exclaimed.

Kayden raised a brow. "I could've sworn Half-Devils aged half as fast as Humans." She moved some hair behind her ears. "I guess I was wrong." She let out a brief laugh.

Magnus had no response, just a stale look upon his face. *Well well, we finally learned a fact about him.* Kayden knew he was very private. It was peculiar, but everyone had their secrets—especially her. "We're finally here."

The tavern sign swung above their heads, battered and old, with two glasses cheering one another with a meat flank in the middle. Rubbed-out letters barely resembled, *Frozelian Mead and Meatery*.

Kayden walked in first, swishing the heavy tavern door open with a shove. The rest followed, entering as everyone in the room looked up to stare.

Two individuals sat behind the counter, one man and one woman each with pale, icy skin with hair seemingly made of ice. Their eyes widened, then narrowed shortly after. "Oh, h—how can we help you lot?" The man cleared his throat and spoke in a gruff voice. Jirah mentioned they were a Frozelian couple, Krag, and his wife, Dran.

Kayden leaned casually on the bar and spoke the words Jirah told them. "How blackened can you make your flanks? I'm looking for something that's essentially *on fire* when I get it."

The man's eyes popped out before he quickly shook his head and returned to a serious demeanor. "Oh, we can make that right away. Are you in need of a room or two?"

"Two for five total," Kayden said.

"May I show you to your rooms?" Dran said. "They're always ready here."

"I'd love that!" Domika seemed very excited to finally sleep in a bed. "But first, let's order our food." She grabbed a parchment with the food in a list and showed everyone so they could order as well. "Okay, now let's check out our rooms."

Lira and Magnus also nodded, while Vesper sat at a bar stool. "I'll stay. I'll have a glass of your finest mead. For the lady, too, I gather," Vesper said, giving Kayden a sly eye.

Kayden wanted a glass but wasn't fond of gifts. She took the glass, but before she could say she would pay for it, Vesper cut in.

"Here you are, my good sir," he said, swiftly tossing him four copper pieces. "Seems as though you are a little tardy on the coin purse, my dear." Before she could give a response, his wit was quicker than her mouth. "One must deal with the consequences." He gently ran his mottled fingers through his beard.

"Well, well, the old man has a tongue on him, it seems. Not just an odd ramble?" Kayden said. "Why buy *me* a drink, old man? Normally I just yell at you."

"You remind me of my daughter. Pardon me if I'm nostalgic," Vesper said. "She was the truth of our family's saying, 'Passion and power are tempered by compassion.' Although, passion was a light word for her type, I think."

Kayden hadn't heard him mention his family once. She was curious to hear more, especially if his daughter was like her. "Tell me about her." She sipped carefully as she wasn't exactly resistant to its effects.

Vesper's blue, buggy eyes flickered from the lantern light nearby. He closed them, smiling happily. "She was twenty, hair as beautiful as the sands, like my wife's, fair skin like mine, her nose, my eyes." He definitely seemed nostalgic. However, none of these traits were like Kayden. She noticed a subtle shake of a palm when his glass *clinked* quietly against his teeth as he took another sip.

Kayden sipped her mead, waiting for more, but he paused for more than a few seconds. "When is she going to sound like me?"

"She was tough," he said longingly. "Tough on herself, tough on her family." Vesper nodded. "She never showed weakness to anyone around her, but I knew it was there. I was her father, after all." That was the second time he used the word 'was.' Kayden became slightly concerned. He leaned in and looked into her eyes. "You may be mistrusting, but you clearly favor some of us." His voice had a hint of vibrato, yet a soothing, relaxed tone when he spoke to her.

Kayden wasn't sure what to make of his words. "Oh? And who do I favor, Lord Intelligent?" she sneered. She knew he was analytical, but he was also presumptuous. Kayden did not like assumptions; especially ones made about her.

"Sir Magnus, for one. Miss Kaar, of course," he nodded.

I don't favor them, she thought. She just saw them as slightly more trustworthy than the rest. Kayden grimaced at his words, leaving her glass on the bar.

"You can believe what you wish, Miss Ralta. As long as you do not trust the wrong individuals, you will be swell."

Kayden noticed that his name was not among the list. She wondered what happened to his family, and why he was with the Scions of Fire in the first place. Kayden certainly had her reasons. "I know who to trust." She knew many kinds of people in her time—some good, some bad, and some terrifying.

"I know you think me peculiar, of that I am very aware. I promise you, there is a method to my madness, as it were."

There was one bit of madness she was curious about. He was older than most, and he was not battle-hardened. "Why did you join us?" Kayden asked. "You concentrate so fiercely on certain things in silence, but sometimes you never stop talking, and you mumble to yourself almost constantly. It's unsettling." He shot her a sullen eye. "No offense," she added quickly. Yet even then, she trusted him. He was odd, but Kayden saw no wrong in his words or his actions.

Vesper chucked as he sipped his golden-colored mead. "None taken, my lady." He placed his mug down gently. "I have seen families torn apart before me. I live in the crossroads northeast of here, or, I did. I've seen fathers taken for war, mothers taken prisoner for trying to steal food, children taken for throwing a pebble at an insufferable soldier."

"Many people see families torn apart. They don't do anything. Why you?" Kayden asked

"Sir Mirado is correct, I was once the 'Mighty Vesper' of the Renalia Circus." He waved his hands in a majestic manner, before they dropped back to the bar with a slump. "I suppose maybe I joined because I have abilities that some do not, and I thought I would make a difference." Vesper's hands shook as he spoke. "I know what it is like to lose someone for a mistake. Miss Kaar lost her brother from a mistake; what mistake, I do not know." Vesper sighed. "I suppose I owe it to them."

"To your family?"

"Yes, I owe them my life. They saved me from a life I hated. I owe it to other families to make sure they are safe, and it is no longer safe in any town." His face tightened, and he got slightly teary-eyed. "My wife, Laura, Nala, and I were an act together—*The Great Magicians*. We each had our own part for the show. My wife used the winds, my daughter used water and ice, and I was fire.

"Then we would combine into earth, as part of the act, rising us on platforms into the air for the finale. It was a lovely show. The crowd always cheered and came to have our marks, invite us for meals, and be guests of nobles. It was fantastic for a time."

Kayden listened carefully to what he said. She felt she knew what was coming. While magic was fantastical and mythical, she was almost glad she was not born with the gift. Misuse had dire consequences. His eyelids vibrated subtly along with his pupils, and the lanternlight danced in them gently.

"I was always told how incredible I was. I let it go to my head, and my mind expanded to the size of Titan's Rock. One show, I tried something new without consulting the others. I made a dragon out of fire, and I wanted to breathe flames at my family, but stop it right before it hit them. Oh, what a show it would have made," his voice grew brittle and tremulous. "I moved my hands a little too far."

A tear formed at the corner of Kayden's eye. She quickly wiped it away, fearing someone would see. She felt his pain, a pain she had in her heart as well. She remembered the night he almost killed Lira with that fire snake of his. He seemed like he was in a strange trance, and he nearly made the mistake again.

"With my power, in my idiocy, I—" he could barely speak, hardly croaking out stuttered words. His head drooped, and tears spilled onto his knees. His cries were quiet but obvious, and his eyes began to gloss over. He tried to speak but couldn't.

Kayden looked around and perked her ears to hear any movement from the floor above. *No one better see this*, she thought. Luckily most had left the bar already after their dinners finished. She pulled Vesper into a lengthy hug, and his cries soon quieted.

"There, there," she said awkwardly. Kayden wasn't good at comforting, but at least she tried. He was an old mug, but now she understood why he concentrated so hard on his practices. She knew everyone had their limitations, as Lira especially did, but Vespers were much higher—or so he implied. He lost much, as she had, by his own hand. *Just like me. It's my fault. It's all my fault.* She tried her best to hold her emotions in. It was his time, not hers. Not to mention she didn't open up after only knowing someone a fortnight or two. Vesper seemed to readily open up, which was strange.

He returned the embrace as he slowly drew his emotions back in. He breathed deeply as he released the hug, looking to her. "I'm here so that no families are broken up any longer. I've seen it—families torn apart by the state. I cannot bear it." He chuckled slightly. "You really do remind me of my daughter. It is quite comforting. Thank you. You are kinder than you let on."

Kayden smirked at the thought, then spoke coolly. "Don't tell anyone." She looked back to the window by the back of the bar.

Clambering footsteps descended the old wooden stairs beside the bar. "Did we miss something?" Domika said. She groomed her long black hair into a ponytail, a subtle Blazik flame flickering along it down her back.

"No, Miss Mirado. We've been quietly sipping our mead. Do you really think Miss Ralta would wish to speak to me?" He meant to hide his emotions, but his expression still showed sorrow over anything else.

Domika could tell something was up but shrugged and sat down beside Vesper at the bar. "I guess I can't argue that."

Kayden knew he was saying that for her benefit, and she silently appreciated it. Her gaze didn't leave the window nearby.

"So, what's the plan, Kayden?" Domika asked. She scratched her head, hand in the small flame that flickered over her hair. The flame in Blazik hair wasn't truly real, Kayden knew, but still thought it was strange. It was warm, but not too hot, or painful to the touch.

Kayden was suspicious. *Why is she being so nice, let alone asking about my plans?* Kayden looked around the bar, seeing no one around. Even then she whispered to the others. "Sewers. Word is, the sewers lead under the noble's manor. They have guard towers

TIDES OF FATE

all around the place, as well as soldiers at every gate," Kayden whispered. *We really shouldn't be talking about this outside of our room, despite the bar being absolutely desolate*, she thought nervously.

"Ew, sewers! I *hate* the smell of those," Domika whimpered.

"Be quiet. Do you want people to hear us?" Kayden furrowed her thin brow.

Domika blinked owlishly and nodded quickly as her eyes shot left to right. She hadn't paid much attention. "Sorry." She smiled sweetly, looking to the kitchen door as Dran brought out goat flanks and potatoes for everyone, with a Flanbird stew for Magnus.

He likes that stuff? Everyone had preferences, she supposed. Flanbirds had brittle, translucent skin, yellow and white, with thick feathers. Their skin was filled with thick juices, which formed the base for the stew. It was goopy slop that curdled in the mouth. Gross.

Each of them dug into their meals. Vesper carefully cut his potato with fork and knife, as did Lira and Domika. Kayden grabbed her potato in hand, whole, and took a big bite. It tasted glorious. It was hot yet fluffy, not dry or pasty. "*Mmm*," she moaned. "Damn, that's good." She opened her eyes to see glances from the others, except Magnus, who silently sipped his flanbird soup. "What?" she asked.

Each of them held utensils. Domika raised a brow and gave an irritating smile, Vesper, a funny, sly grin, and Lira was altogether confused.

Kayden looked them right in the eye, turning her head to stare both ways as she took another giant bite of her potato. "*Mmmmm!*" she mumbled loudly. The rest laughed as she enjoyed her food. The potato was even all the way through, and it had been awhile since she ate a meal this well made. She finally used utensils for the flank, jamming a fork into it like an enemy she vowed revenge on.

She was shoveling pieces in as fast as she could. She felt as if she hadn't eaten in days.

Food was precious to Kayden, in a way. She went hungry many times in her life—in her youth, adolescence, and adulthood. When she joined the rebellion, she felt free. She felt the stares of her comrades at that moment but couldn't have cared less.

In her periphery, she saw that Magnus was the only one not staring, eating his meal quietly. He held his spoon like a feather between his middle and forefinger, clasped together with his large thumb. Eyes closed, he was sifting the spoon from the closest end to the farthest of the bowl to gather the soup, pouring it into his mouth without a slurp or even a sound.

The rest dug into their flank with a knife and fork, removing one piece at a time. The succulent meat juices poured out with each gentle draw of the knife. Kayden cut viciously, tearing off large pieces and eating them without pause.

"Someone's hungry," Domika said.

Kayden shot her a fierce eye with a mouth full of flank, swallowing her last bite. The last thing they needed was another fight. *Why did Jirah send us together, again? He knew there were problems before.* She just shrugged, attempting not to provoke an issue again. Domika actually turned away, deciding not to poke further, to her surprise. Kayden sat back, noticing that everyone was still eating. While she didn't mind the silence, she had a plan on her mind.

"Since I'm done, I'll explain what we should do," Kayden whispered. She looked around, seeing no one in the bar. She felt that Dran and Krag were trustworthy enough to overhear. "We go tomorrow night. Until then, we gather information about the manor and the situation, but don't provoke anyone." She sneered at Domika. "Then we move for the sewers and hope we can make it there. We don't have maps, so we're on our own."

Everyone paused their meals to listen, and they all nodded to her. *Well that was easy*, she thought. *At least everyone is being nice, today of all days.*

While they continued to eat, Kayden leaned on the bar and stared out the window. She knew what day it was, but clearly didn't mention it to anyone. It didn't really matter, anyway. Four seasons of the elements reigned over all lands—Water, the season of rain; Fire, the season of dry weather and heat; Earth, the season with minimal rain and the approach of the coldest season; Air, of cold winds and snow. She lived through the air in the north, barely. The season was as long as the others but killed many due to its severe cold. She liked the season of Water.

It was the fifty-seventh eve of water—her eighteenth day of birth. Kayden disliked birthdays. *Why does anyone need their own day? Why that day?* She didn't remember her birth, so it wasn't important. She hadn't celebrated a birthday since her parents' death. No one ever knew it except Jirah, who demanded the birthdays of all those who entered his command. The last gift she received for her birthday was the marking upon her back. She moved her arm to touch it, feeling the pain over again and wincing strongly. She asked Sheeran if she was to have a gift, and she certainly did when sent to Callidan. A shiver went up her spine and she shook subtly.

"Kayden, are you okay?" Lira asked. Her warm, brown eyes were wide and filled with concern. She moved her hand to place it on Kayden's back.

Kayden felt the claw of a dagger and shrank back with a yelp. Her eyes shot to Lira in an instant, and her breaths ran to a charge. Watching Lira pull her hand back to her mouth in a gasp, she—it took a moment to recover. Remembering. No knife this time. "I, *uh*, slept funny last night. Don't worry about me," she added.

"Okay," Lira said quietly. "Sorry, I didn't mean to impose."

"Don't worry about it, princess." She dropped into thought about the marks and what they meant to her—what they meant for her past and future.

"I must retreat upstairs, I have much reading to do," Vesper said. He glanced at Kayden, and she nodded in response. She would keep his secret.

Lira nodded. "I, the same. I have to improve my magic and do my nightly prayers if I'm going to be of any use!" she said. While she didn't have confidence in herself, she at least tried to help. "Do you want to come, Kayden?"

"No, I'm going to sit here a little while longer. I like time to myself." She spent long stretches alone, whether there were people near or far. Sheeran made her feel alone. She wanted to forget his existence entirely. For her, a day of birth was a day best spent alone.

Lira nodded and followed Vesper upstairs.

Domika grabbed Magnus's arm, leaning into him. "I *love* the moonlight at night. Magnus, would you walk with me? I promise I won't get us into trouble," she said longingly.

Magnus nodded slowly, finally finishing his flank and stew. "Of course, my lady. I will escort you."

Oh please, Kayden thought. Domika was nowhere near subtle. It was as if she found his quiet listening endearing. Kayden thought they were a decent pair since she talked and he listened. It was exhausting for Kayden to be within earshot; she had no idea how Magnus handled it all. She figured his age had something to do with it. She wondered how much experience he'd gained in the one hundred and twenty-six years he lived.

Magnus followed Domika out of the tavern and inn, leaving Kayden alone at the bar. He was calm and quiet, wearing his ridiculous, rusty, cracked armor and carrying two blades on his left hip, one inside a black sheath she hadn't seen as of yet. He always drew the brown one, which was a typical, steel long blade. He held the black sheath as he walked and kept it close while he slept.

She touched her teal scarf, wondering if it was something as important to him. He never spoke of it and ignored the questions about it—or was furious if anyone pushed the question. Kayden never inquired about it, as she felt his business was his business. *It's probably just a keepsake*, she reasoned.

The moonlight shone brightly through the windows. She loved the moon, her beacon of hope in darkness. She thought of the time she spent in darkness, wrought in fear of what her fate would be. '*I won't forget you, little lady,*' Sheeran would say, before leaving her for minutes, hours, days, or longer in the hole. It was always for her 'own good.' It unsettled her now, still.

The moon comforted her when she spent her nights alone traveling from Zenato to the crystalline forest of Kholrani, to Orinas, and finally to Loughran. She had been alone for a year, but it was the best year she lived since her parents' murder.

She had enough time thinking to herself. She wanted to dig her nose into a book or two—it had been too long. "Hey, do you have any books?" Kayden asked Dran, who was cleaning tables nearby.

"Oh, yes, m'dear. Just a couple. Would you like to see them?"

"Yes."

Dran brought out three books, one filled with cooking recipes, another about the history of the nobility, and one about species in the region.

Kayden didn't care for recipes much, and she already read the history book. "I'll take the one about the species. I'll put it behind the counter after I'm finished."

"You're very welcome, dear. Please let me know if you need anything else," Dran replied.

Kayden nodded, looking to her book. It detailed descriptions of various birds, wolves, and fish in the forestlands and marshes. Even some about the Treants in the north, living in the dead Forkal forest. *A bit of an ironic name if you ask me,* she thought. They would stand between six and twenty-five feet tall, but were peaceful as long as they were not provoked.

The Broken tribes in the north end of Loughran attempted to burn the forest to take over the region and not allow the Treants to interfere. Sadly for the Broken, they did not expect the Treants to be difficult to burn. They had to be carved down with weapons, which did not end well for the Broken. They were powerful warriors, but treants were over twenty feet tall.

Kayden sat at the bar in thought for over an hour it seemed, sipping at water while staring into space. She felt sleepy but resisted the urge to go upstairs. She did not know why, possibly because the others were still out. Her heart did not slow until the group was whole, whether hunting when at camp, or on a walk through the town. Whenever someone left her presence in the twilight saying they would return, her mind did not relax until they did. She knew if she attempted to sleep, it was wasted effort.

Another hour passed, her mind raced still. *Where are they?* she thought. *What if something happened? What if they were captured?* She tried to calm down but couldn't. After another half hour, her breathing became panicked. She looked around, only seeing Dran cleaning the empty tables by the other side of the bar. She smashed her fist on the bar, frustrated. *That's it, I'm going out there.*

Slam.

"Whoops!" Domika exclaimed, falling into the door as it swung open, laughing hysterically. She'd had a bit of the drink, clearly. She brought her forefinger to her mouth, "*Shhh,*" she said, giggling, her bronze skin glowing in the dim lanternlight. She lumbered to the stairs, tip-toeing as carefully as could be, otherwise known as loud and clambering.

Magnus strolled in after her with his hands casually behind his back. He glanced at Kayden, with a subtle smile. He meandered to the stool beside her, sitting down without a noise. "She requested a stop at an interesting establishment owned by Blaziks," Magnus explained. "We walked through the town. It is a delightful place at night."

"You shouldn't've been gone so long," she said, fists clenched. She was worried sick and anxious but wouldn't dare admit it.

"I apologize, my lady," Magnus replied.

"Just be careful next time," Kayden sighed. She wondered about his background. He'd been alive for over a century. *What has he seen? How much hate has he endured?* After a moment of silence, she added, "You can just call me Kayden, you know."

"I will, my lady." His comforting red eyes flickered with the light in the room.

Kayden sighed. "Well, it was worth a try. I'm no lady."

"And I am not a sir." He lifted his arm to feel the small black horns above his forehead protruding from his hair. "Who would knight a Hellspawn?"

She truly disliked when someone felt inferior due to what they were. His horns weren't bad—she liked them, actually. "I would. I don't care what someone looks like." She was a branded low-born; the only thing she wasn't was a bastard, but those weren't frowned upon in most regions as much as the others. Some of the royal Kings and Queens of the past were bastards, she knew. Even if one was born out of wedlock, the blood ran strong. "I just care if they're on my side or not. You're a sir to me, and clearly to Vesper and Jirah."

Magnus chuckled, "I am not knighted. Why name me a sir?"

"It's a term for a brave, honorable person to them. Titles don't mean anything. They name people knights for being high-borns, leaving low-borns to be farmers and other laborious professions. A knight can be a coward and a rapist. A rogue sell sword can be a brave man and a savior. You determine which one you are." There was a long silence after that, and Kayden's gaze didn't leave the wall. "How do you handle being called a monster for so long?"

Magnus paused, letting out a long sigh. "I know my people are monsters. I do what I can to change the tide." He drew his mouth to the side, "It never stops hurting, however."

"My people aren't monsters, either," Kayden said gruffly. She scratched her head and ruffled her long, knotted mane of hair.

"I know," he said, gazing at the brand behind her ear. "Some regions just need more guidance. If I'm not mistaken, the leader of the Archipelago is a branded low-born."

"She is?" Kayden blinked, wide-eyed. "I didn't know." *Maybe that will help. Maybe I could meet her—but doubtless, she wouldn't want to meet with me,* Kayden thought, dejected. They were silent for a time, sitting at the bar, leaving their silent words to the lanternlight and night beyond.

Magnus glanced at her as if he had something to say, one hand still behind his back. "Sir Mirado had a list in his bag of people's days."

Damn it, he better not know.

"Why did you not mention your day to the others?" Magnus asked. "I do enjoy days of birth. They remind me of my parents. Mine is on the fifth eve of Fire," he said with a light tone.

"I haven't celebrated a birthday since I was eight, Mags. No one's ever known it or given a damn," Kayden grumbled. "Who needs a special day for entering this world, anyway?"

"Everyone deserves to be appreciated," Magnus said.

I just don't like attention. Lira definitely loved a day of birth—Kayden already knew hers was on the thirteenth eve of Earth. *Did he tell anyone?* Before she could accuse him, he was ready.

"Do not worry, I did not mention it to anyone," he said. "I felt you would be displeased."

Not as dumb as he looks. She huffed and looked away, closing her eyes dismissively.

"I saw you smile at them when we entered town," he said quietly. "I thought you may like it."

She looked over, seeing a pristine, blooming black flower decorated with little starry-white specks and its quintessential veins of pale lavender—a nightrain flower—gently held between his large fingers. He held it out to her.

"That's really—" Overcome with emotion, she remembered her mother giving them to her on her birthday so long ago. She grew teary-eyed, and sniffed loudly, barely stuttering her words. "That's really sweet—" her voice trailed off as she held out a shaky hand. She carefully accepted the flower, in bloom from the evening sky. As violet-black as the universe above, its eye a white hue as beautiful as the stars. "It's my favorite flower." She sniffled and rubbed her nose as she held back her tears. "It's beautiful."

"It is beautiful," Magnus agreed with a light nod. "Do not forget that you are, as well."

"Th—thanks," she said in a quavering tone. "I haven't gotten a gift in ten years." She smiled, drowning in nostalgia. "You made my day."

Magnus smiled at her, getting up from his stool. "I am glad I could," he chuckled. "I will not mention you smiled, either."

She sniffled a laugh, still eyeing the flower between her fingers. "Your pretty ladyfriend is gonna be pissed to know you're giving other women flowers."

"It is not like that," Magnus said. "She enjoys talking. I listen. You learn a lot more from someone when you observe." He walked to the bottom of the stairs. "Good night, Kayden."

"Good night," she said, as he walked to the top of the stairs. *Suave idiot*, she chuckled to herself. He was observant. He was kind and strangely gentle, but seemingly very intimidating as a presence. She glanced around, realizing she was the only one on the bottom floor. The only light came from the moon and the ever-lit lantern behind the counter. She slowly twirled the nightrain flower in her hand. She smiled again. '*Don't forget that you are, too,*' he'd said.

"Thanks, Mags."

Chapter Twenty

Broken Consciousness

Zaedor Nethilus

Zaedor awoke to the smell of sweat, feces, and rotten food. His vision was hazy, the cloth he was gagged with clearly had some alchemical agent to sedate him. It was slightly cool in the echoed room he was in. He wondered where he was, and hardly believed he was still in the desert. Iron rubbed against his skin as he shifted—a metal cage. It was big enough for one man, but two would be too many—which there were.

"Where am I?" Zaedor asked the scruffy man. He was dirty, wearing a loincloth and a tattered wolf pelt around his shoulders. His shaggy, jet-black hair shone in the torchlight, and his scraggly beard glistened with sweat.

"You're in the pit," the man said. The man had a dead stare against the rock wall at the back of the cage. More cages lined the walls in the round cavern, each with one person, save the one next to them.

Zaedor took a better look around him. There were men and women, Blazik, Human, among others, sitting in their cages with the same look as the man beside him. It was a strange, dome-like cavern, with rough-hewn rock walls surrounding them, and guards at the single rusted iron door. "What *is* the pit?" Zaedor whispered.

The man's eyes widened. He exploded out of his rickety chair and rushed over. He grabbed Zaedor's arms with a powerful grip. "What is the pit?" the man said. He shook Zaedor, then let go and backed away slowly. "The pit is where we people fight," he said, eyes drooping. "We fight. We fight each other. If we aren't entertaining, we die. Either in the ring, or out of it."

Zaedor didn't know what to say. The man seemed like he'd lost all hope. "Can someone get out?" he asked.

"No one gets out."

Zaedor felt like he should change the subject. The talk about not escaping made his state of mind worse as it went. "What's your name?" Zaedor asked.

The man looked to him with owlish green eyes, as if he hadn't been asked his name in eons. He sat down carefully, leaning in. "Kindro. What's yours?"

"Zaedor, of Amirion," Zaedor replied with a sullen voice. *A place that no longer exists,* he thought.

Kindro sat up straight, ears perking up. "I have an uncle who lives in Amirion," Kindro said.

Zaedor looked to him with a regretful expression. *He's clueless. He has no idea that all of them are gone.*

"What, what's wrong?" he asked, sensing Zaedor's despair.

"Amirion was destroyed weeks ago by Rawling and his armies." Zaedor winced as he mentioned Rawling's name.

"Oh," His face grew sullen. "We don't get much information being imprisoned down here," Kindro said. Shaking his head, he slapped Zaedor's leg. "Look at the bright side: you're new here, so they probably won't have you fight for a few days." Kindro closed his eyes and nodded nervously. "It's about that time."

What time? Zaedor wondered.

The iron door to the room swung open, and a man in a red silk doublet and loose-fitted cloth pants strolled into the prison dome with flourish. He wore a strange, ocean blue wide brim hat with golden tassels, and had a curled silver mustache hooding a crooked smile. He went from cage to cage, eyeing each individual carefully.

"Fireback," he said first, pointing to a man with bronze skin and black hair with a flame atop it. "Lizard," he said next, pointing to a man with azure snake eyes and hunter green hair.

Zaedor didn't know what to make of that man. He never saw a race like his before. He only knew snakes were devious and vile.

The man stopped at Zaedor's cage. "You," He pointed at Zaedor. "It will be your first, won't it, Amirionian?" he guffawed. "We're going to have fun with you. Guards! Escort these prisoners and prepare them. The Amirionian first." His smile slithered like a vile snake across his face.

Zaedor backed away, shaking. *Prep me?* He didn't know what to expect, only fearing death after what Kindro said to him. The guards unlocked and threw the gate open. Both guards were taller and broader than Zaedor, with muscles bigger than his head. They gripped him with either arm while he struggled and resisted, and dragged him out of the room. Out of the rusted doorway laid a hallway with many doors and barred windows, each housing dome-like rooms with cages as well. Zaedor's thin clothes were drenched with sweat, dripping to the floor as they walked. He wondered if the guards even knew of the smell, that horrid stench—shit, sweat, and blood. It was so pungent it stung the eyes.

Zaedor was dragged into a room and thrown into a small wooden chair. There was nothing in the room except the chair, a table with long strings of cloth and leather, and a steel rod placed halfway into a corner fire. He attempted to run, but the guards shoved him back. Each one grabbed an arm, wrapping it in leather straps and cloth, intertwining it between his fingers as if to cushion his fists.

"What are you doing?" he asked in a tremulous tone.

"Making sure you don't break your hands, whelp," one said.

"They think you'll make a lot, so they need you to be useful," the other growled.

The man with the wide-brimmed hat entered the room with a stroll. With a crooked smile, he eyed Zaedor up and down. Zaedor pierced him with a glare, but he seemed to feel nothing from it. He sauntered to the flame in the corner, smoke rising to a ventilation tunnel above. He picked out a metal rod, revealing a white-hot searing end in the shape of an X made with spear tips and a fist at the center. He slowly turned to Zaedor, creeping closer. "You are mine now, Amirionian."

Zaedor was unable to move, still restrained by the powerful guards. "What do you want with me?" he yelled.

The man was unaffected, chuckling at Zaedor. "Everyone loves an underdog, boy. A lone survivor," he laughed maniacally. "And I, Maroia Fallad, will bring it to them!" He threw up his hands and looked to the ceiling, then back to Zaedor with the same crooked smile. The light from the corner fire flickered and danced in his maniacal eyes. He brought the branding tool to Zaedor's right arm and pressed it hard onto his skin.

Zaedor growled and roared in agony as the brander seared his flesh with the fist and crossed spearheads. As Maroia took it off, he sauntered to the flame to place it on the rock beside. Sweat soaked Zaedor's matted head of hair, and he panted from the agony he experienced. The brand laid on his arm as burned flesh, a scar to remain forever.

Maroia walked to the door. "Good luck, underdog," he said in a silvery tone. "You're going to need it." He walked through the sandy metal door and slammed it behind him.

"All right, Amirionian. Let's go," one of the guards said.

Zaedor feared what would come next. He felt like an animal. Caged, forced into a prison he could never escape, to be used up for someone else's benefit. *Yet more animals in the east, if that's even where I am.*

The guards threw him upward, pulled him through the door, and dragged him down to the end of the hall. He could hear chanting coming from the end, echoing all around him through the craggy cavern hall, dripping with moisture. Doors upon doors lined it, but they had no bars or windows. *Where do they lead?* he thought. The chanting grew louder and louder. A bellowing voice yelled from within.

"Ladies, gentlemen, and all others! Witness the fight of a lifetime!" the voice boomed.

What is this? Zaedor thought. *Fight of a lifetime?*

Before he could think further, the guards threw the door open and pushed him in. As he barely held his ground, he found himself in a massive, domed cavern, with stands built from rock blasted into seating. They were filled with people: poor and rich, wearing everything from dirty clothes to silk and satin dresses and doublets, all yelling for more. A large man stood at the opposite end, in clothes as dingy as Zaedor's were. His face was covered in thick stubble, surrounded by his mane of curly brown hair, and he was looking to Zaedor with murder in his eyes and a clench to his fists.

He doesn't seem so tough. He's surely no match for the might of a soldier of Amirion, Zaedor thought proudly.

A man in fancy linens and silk of many colors stood at the base of the stands, waving his arms dramatically. "Ladies and gentlemen and all others! I bring you a new fight for the ages!" he yelled, and the crowd went silent. "From the northern icelands, a man who fought bear, Troll, and Giant comes to you from the Kuralian company to destroy all in his path! Some say he killed a bear with his own bare hands, with no armor and no weapons at all. I bring you, Gorlin, *the Giant-slayer*!" his bellowing voice echoed throughout the arena, but the crowd's deafening cheer overtook him with ease.

The people's eyes, including the announcer, all turned to Zaedor. "And now, the treat of the night! Or possibly, the year!" he yelled proudly. "We now bring you, from the seawall of the northeast, a man who survived a horrid tragedy!" The man swirled his arms and spread them wide. "Amirion, devastated by the desert armies, left one alive! The man who survived an army's might, whose will is unbreakable, whose body is undefeatable! Fallad company now brings to you, the *lone survivor*!"

The crowd's deafening cheer echoed throughout the dome once again.

Zaedor walked closer, knowing what would come next. He truly wished to give up. He had nothing to live for, and there was no way out. Drawing it out had no appeal. *What do I do?*

There was no time left to think.

"*Begin*!" the announcer yelled.

Zaedor walked carefully toward Gorlin, raising his arms into a guarded stance. Citizens of Amirion were taught to fight with both blade and fist, after all. Gorlin exploded from his position, moving swiftly with long strides.

His fists were clenched but swung at his sides. *Why isn't he guarding?* Zaedor wondered. His arms were long and gangly, but incredibly muscular. They did not rise until they met. Gorlin was much bigger up close.

Gorlin raised his hands with immeasurable speed; his left threw Zaedor's block aside, and his right mauled him across the face. Zaedor staggered back from the blow, his nose riddled with blood. Zaedor grunted in anger while Gorlin approached again, and he was ready this time. *Just like my training.* Instead of guarding, he waited. Gorlin's fist came down again with a brutal swing. Zaedor deftly jumped to the side and gave him two jabs to his stomach, dodging a fist again to strike Gorlin across his chin. The crowd cheered, loving his retort. *I can do this.*

Gorlin shook his head, unfazed by the blows. Zaedor quickly backed off, but his enemy charged him without pause. Gorlin grabbed Zaedor before he could escape. Gorlin's strength was unfathomable. He threw Zaedor to the ground with ease. Zaedor tumbled and landed flat on his face.

The crowd cheered and laughed as he turned over, and Gorlin was already on him. Massive arms came down from the light above, bludgeoning his face and knocking his head into the rock floor. He felt each blow like a maul. Crack. Crack. Crack. Blow by blow, Zaedor's face was bloodied by the concussive strikes.

When the strikes stopped, Zaedor only heard the muffle of a crowd going wild. Zaedor barely heard the announcer calling the name of the winner as he bled out of consciousness.

"The state of Amirion once again lies in shambles! The Giant-slayer, Gorlin, wins again!" the announcer yelled, accompanied by Gorlin's guttural roar of victory.

* * *

The silvery hum of a song rang through Zaedor's ears—well-timed and beautiful. It was a woman's hum; it lulled him to a sleep that he wished never to end.

The hum abruptly stopped, and a deep sigh followed. "That was miserable," a female voice said.

Zaedor's head felt stabbed by a shiv. He felt the bandages tightly wrapped around it.

"Don't say that. It was his first fight," he heard Kindro say.

Everything sounded slightly muffled, and his vision was foggy. His jaw felt like it was broken, his nose misplaced and reset. It hurt terribly, and Zaedor had never had a break in his body before. It was his first real fistfight, since Amirion was a peaceful kingdom. He had only been through the battle training, never a true life or death situation. He also believed diplomacy came before brutality. In his naiveté, he believed that Amirion was an impenetrable kingdom, that their warriors were invincible, and that their wills were unbreakable. All he had been taught was defeated in less than a minute by a savage. He was dumbfounded, muddled, and confused beyond belief. His whole life, he saw his city as the strength of the continent. *Was it all a lie?*

He felt a hand lightly smack him again and again. "Zaedor, wake up!" Kindro chuckled. "You sure took a beating from that guy. How's your head? I heard he pounded you out."

The female voice guffawed loudly, "Can't say I'm surprised. Look at him." Her voice sounded as smooth as silk.

Zaedor's eyes focused to see Kindro's scraggly beard dangling above him.

"There he is," he said, picking Zaedor up off the ground. "Man, look at that welt!" He poked Zaedor's cheek. It felt like an electric shock running through his entire face.

"Ow!" Zaedor yelped, swatting his hands away.

The woman who spoke before laughed loudly again. "The others were right. You really are a sissy. To think, I actually warmed the crowd up for you."

"*Freya!*" Kindro growled.

Zaedor glanced to the next cage, which was previously empty. A tall woman in tattered, sweat-stained linen clothes leaned against the cage divider, arms hanging through.

"My apologies, mister sensitive." Freya sighed.

With skin as white as cream, eyes as bright emeralds, and distinctively long hair the color of blood, tied in a ponytail with multiple wraps descending below her lower back—Zaedor couldn't help but stare. was a sight to behold.

"You have something to say?" she said with a scowl.

"No," Zaedor stuttered.

After a lengthy stare, she sighed. "Where'd they pick you up?"

"Outside the Zenato palace." Zaedor was embarrassed. He was angry that he not only was unsuccessful, but that he was so naive to get caught. He tried to stretch his arms, feeling his body sear in pain. He was covered in bruises, and his joints ached with every movement. He couldn't imagine the condition of his face.

A smirk grew from the edge of Freya's lips. "Planning on an assassination, were we?" She sniffed curiously with her perky nose. "I can smell the anger on you."

How did she know? He looked to her with widened eyes, mouth drawn open. He winced, feeling his jaw *click* when he opened it wide.

"Calm down. Kindro told me about your city—I just guessed the rest." Freya sighed and smirked at him. "Sorry to hear about it. I knew some people there, too. I can tell that you aren't handling it well, and you certainly are bottling up the wrong feelings." She huffed lightly, standing up straight.

"Freya, you don't have to bring that up now. We can work on fighting later. They use Gorlin as a breaker for the new meat," Kindro explained. "Isn't as tough as the last one."

Freya coughed up a laugh. "Yeah, Quintaine almost punched your head off."

Kindro frowned, then chuckled. "Hey, that's hurtful. Y'know I heard he took his own cage door before they could notice."

They continued chatting, but Zaedor couldn't get Gorlin off his mind. *Gorlin was a beast, an animal.* He searched the room with his eyes. There were Blaziks, Half-Devils, and other savage races scattered about. Zaedor had a difficult time believing he belonged here. He looked to his hand, where his wedding band used to be. He had it when he got captured, but it was gone now.

"My ring," he said brittly. "It's gone."

Freya's gemmed eyes drew toward him with concern, rather than irritation. "I'm sorry," she said, touching her neckline. "They took the violet tether necklace my mother gave me," she pouted. "I'll never get something like that back ever again."

Kindro gave him a quick swat on the shoulder. "Don't worry, Zaedor. We'll help you. 'Round here, the more you fight, the better food you get." Kindro seemed more enthusiastic than before his fight. His fear was gone, his mood relaxed.

"You seem different," Zaedor commented positively. "You seemed quite shaken before my fight."

Kindro shot him a suspicious eye, turning his head quickly. "I'm no different."

Freya slapped the bars of her cage. "I knew it!!" With a growing smile, she said, "You were worried about me. Well well Kin, looks like you're a little scaredy-cat." With a laugh, she said, "I told you, Kin, you have nothing to worry about! They can't stop me." She flexed bodaciously. Her physique was very defined, with curves outlining her body around powerful muscles.

But he couldn't be distracted. His mind stayed on the pit. He hated the savagery of it. He was a man of clean living and sophisticated city life. Now, he sat disgraced by the gods, stuck in a pit of hell. He might as well have been in the realm of Azoran.

The people that put us here are monsters. "Beasts," he muttered.

"What did you say?" Freya quickly inquired with awestruck eyes.

"Zaedor, don't—" Kindro attempted to cut in.

"This place is filled with beasts. I don't belong here!" He shook the bars.

"Are you calling me a beast?" She shook the bars fiercely back.

"N-No, I didn't mean—" Zaedor stuttered. He meant the guards, but it was too late.

"Call me that again. I dare you." The bars rattled so hard, they almost broke. Her emerald eyes were filled with poison. She bared her teeth and clenched them tightly. Zaedor backed off to the other side of his cage.

"What's going on in here?" Maroia bellowed.

Freya closed her eyes and took several deep breaths. She backed off from the cage wall, glaring at Zaedor. "Nothing, we were just blowing off steam from the fight," she said calmly. "My apologies." The guards nodded suspiciously, and Maroia left once again.

Zaedor was shocked that a woman of such beauty could be so ferocious. *Like Eryndis,* he thought. He missed her, and feared he wouldn't live to see her again.

"Now you know, Zaedor. Never call her that," Kindro said. "She killed the last man who called her that in the ring." He turned to Freya, who was still attempting to slow her heart. "He didn't mean it," he looked furiously to Zaedor. "Right?"

Freya sighed, looking back to Zaedor finally. "We aren't animals, Zaedor. We've been kidnapped and brought here. Some of us come from nice places, too, as you did."

Zaedor wondered where she came from. He looked from cage to cage, only seeing broken spirits. *How long have they been here? Kindro said there was no way out.* He was proud of what he was but realized through several breaking points that he may be in need of some advice. He lightly toughed his face, feeling the result of Gorlin's violent strikes.

"Hey," Zaedor said. Freya and Kindro turned with raised eyebrow. "How do you two fight?" They glanced at each other extensively, nodded, and looked back to Zaedor.

"You fight properly, Mr. Noble, or that's what the guards mumbled about," Freya began. "You parry, you dodge, you jab." She shook her head dismissively. "There are no rules here. They don't pit someone your size against you. You can fight someone five feet, or seven feet tall. There are no cheap shots or rules, just one winner and one loser. People are going to kick your manhood and pull on your pretty hair."

Zaedor attempted to understand the meaning behind her words. *What is she getting at? Fighting using dodges and parries was the best way to fight*, he assumed. *What more was there?* He noticed her hair was full and pristine still, contrary to her comment.

"You were right about one thing, Zaedor. Sometimes, we are animals," she sighed, looking to Zaedor with disdain. "You have to discard your humanity." While Zaedor wasn't Human, he understood the meaning. "You have to become an animal. You don't fight to win. You fight to survive."

Zaedor thought hard about her words. *How did he become an animal? Why would she want to become a beast?* He cringed at his thoughts, knowing how Freya would react.

Freya's stare turned cold. "If you don't fight, you die. You only get to lose once to a breaker and live, and you lost already."

Chapter Twenty-one

The Manipulator

Lira Kaar

Lira and the others crept through the sewers; Lira almost threw up from the smell of mold and excrement. Kayden navigated at the helm, pointing them left, right, and forward toward the manor, or at least, where she thought the manor was. When they came to a ladder accompanied by a set of drain grates riddled with dry blood, they knew they arrived. They rushed up, storming the jail and the torture room, finding one lone man with a scourge in-hand with an emotionless white mask upon his face. Magnus threw him down and tied him quickly, while Kayden covered her mouth walking briskly out of the room.

"I'm going to scout ahead," Kayden barely said, gagging.

They questioned him briefly, to no avail. The brutal man sat tied against the pole of his 'temple,' as he put it. Lira shuffled her feet and looked around with a slight whimper. Domika and Vesper clearly detested being there, and Magnus seemed unaffected.

The sewer's putrid smell wasn't why Lira's stomach turned more than ever before. It was the nauseating, overpowering smell of blood. Dried bloodstains coated the walls, and vast stains on the ground left the memory of a river flowing out of the bodies of men and women. Lira scratched the nape of her neck while slowly scanning the room. She looked to all the devices, then the ceiling—anything to avoid his eyes. There were iron maidens, stretchers, and all forms of sharp, peculiar tools Lira never saw before. Poles stood at each corner, including where they had the man bound. Lira found it all extremely difficult to stomach; it was abhorrent to her sensibilities. She covered her mouth in shock but attempted to keep a steeled demeanor as Kayden taught her.

The man they detained was accused of torturing innocents, which was clear when she saw the slate grey room turned crimson. He wore an ivory mask with an emotionless face. Lira removed the mask and backed off quickly.

The man had sandy brown hair, patchy stubble, and hazel eyes. His face was plain and forgettable; Lira felt she wouldn't notice him in even the smallest of crowds. But his smile, the *smile*, was detestable even to look at. She could feel pure horror crawling from his skin.

"So, what are you going to do with me, *hmm*?" the man asked with a gravelly voice.

Lira wasn't sure. She figured she should ask him questions first. Kayden was usually the one doing the asking, but she was upstairs making sure they didn't get caught. *I have to try something.* Magnus stood with his arms crossed, and Domika and Vesper were leaning up against the nearby wall in a spot that wasn't covered in dry blood.

"What is your name?" Lira asked.

"Callidan Feywater. What's yours, little lady?" Callidan asked, eyeing each carefully. A creeping smirk uncoiled across his face.

"Lira Kaar," she responded. She felt responding might allow a bit more information to come her way.

"Don't tell him your *name*," Domika hissed.

Lira just shrugged her shoulders. She was just trying her best since the others did nothing. "Why did Lord Tammen hire you?"

"Oh, *he* didn't hire me," he said with a chuckle.

Lira twisted her face in response. "Well, who did, might I ask?" Lira heard Domika sigh. She knew she wasn't talented with interrogations, but she was at least trying. The others refused. Lira needed the information. It was her decision to come to town, after all.

"I think you know that answer," he said with a wide grin.

Lira thought of who it could be. If it wasn't the Lord Tammen of Deurbin, it must have been one other. "Lord Drayfus?"

Callidan laughed for a few moments before returning to a sly, wide grin, revealing crooked, mottled teeth. "Maybe. Oh, and it's King Drayfus now."

This was going nowhere. He was probably just waiting it out until they all got caught. Lira needed to try something more drastic. She didn't know how to use the tools but wanted to attempt a bluff. She didn't want to actually *use* them, as it was stooping to his level. Not to mention they were downright gross. Lira was squeamish. She looked to the sharp pokers, serrated knives with edges thinner than hair, and long, hooked scissors. She didn't know where to start.

"Where's the little girl who left? I like her."

Lira looked back to the other three, each responding with a tilted head and a shrug. Lira figured Kayden would injure him more than anyone else. "Why?"

"Oh, I don't know. She just seems cute." He laughed like a man deep into the drink.

Lira grimaced and looked away, unsure if she wanted Kayden there. She already seemed sick to her stomach when she bypassed the room itself—and that alone was strange. Of anyone, she thought Kayden would be adjusted to the scent of blood. "Maybe later." Lira picked up the tool with a sharp hook on the end. She examined it carefully, wondering what it did. *Does it go up the nose?* Lira cringed at the thought. The room was horrid and it frightened her, but she attempted to contain herself while speaking to Callidan. She dangled the tool near his eyes, then dragged it down the side of his face toward his nostrils. "How about you tell me why you hurt those innocent people?" she said in a quiet voice. "And maybe then I won't shove this up your nostrils."

Callidan chuckled as if he saw right through her. "Do it. I dare you," he said in a snarky tone. His breath smelled of rotten food and feces.

Lira held her breath so she didn't throw her stomach contents upon the floor. *I wish I was at home, back where I didn't know people like this existed.*

"I do it because I like it." His voice was like a creeping insect. The very sound made her stomach turn.

Lira sighed. "All right, that's all very interesting." She placed her hands on her hips as she stood back up. "How about you tell me what else is going on around here? Do you have information about other towns, or things King Drayfus planned?" Lira wasn't being convincing, but at least she got an answer from him.

"Oh, I might know a thing or two. I sent some of these people to a friend of mine," he said. "That is, if I don't have too much fun with them first. Sometimes I just use a tool or two. But other times, I get a little overzealous and use the saw." He motioned to a bloodstained, two-handled saw in the corner of the room. "But what are you going to do for me?" His grin stretched from end to end. "I hear nice ladies like you are pretentious, but *nasty* when the candles are out."

Lira cringed and nearly puked right then and there. She huffed and crossed her arms. "That's a little insulting." *Should we let him go if he tells us?* she mused. *No, that wouldn't be right. But how could I kill him afterward? He's unarmed, and helpless.*

"Getting answers out of me is going to be just as difficult as you dirty little rebels," Callidan said. "Luckily for me, I love my job so it's a little easier." His crooked smile grew larger. "Some of them talked, some of them didn't." He giggled like a little boy. "All of them have a true purpose now, I'm told, along with thousands of others coming from the east from that ridiculous neutral city." He giggled continuously as he spoke.

"The east? Where in the east? Where are they going?" Lira asked politely.

"I don't know. Although I might know more for a lovely kiss," Callidan responded.

Lira was resistant to even the thought of getting near him. *Where is Kayden when I need her?* She felt she could learn about getting information, but she wasn't ready for major interrogations just yet. "No, I don't think so."

"Well then, I guess I don't know anything."

"We might just have to kill you, then," Domika poked in.

Callidan ignored Domika's presence entirely. His gaze never left Lira. "Do it," he chuckled. "Kill me. Then what?" His smile didn't fade.

Lira heard the quick pattering of footsteps descending the nearby staircase to the castle courtyard.

"Say, you're a pretty little gem. Beautiful brown eyes, lovely dark skin, tall, slender, hair as black as night—I think we could have a good time together. I know how to treat a lady," Callidan said to Lira once more.

She almost vomited. All she spat up was, "No, I'd rather not."

The footsteps arrived. It was Kayden. "Hey guys, not too many guards up there. If we're good with timing and quick, we can handle it," she said as she walked into sight. "Who was describing the princess? It didn't sound like any of you—" She stopped dead in the doorway. Her stare grew as wide as dinner plates. Tears quickly formed at the corners of her eyes. "What the hell?" She fell to the ground and scrambled to get back against the rough stone wall. Her breathing was rapid and hoarse.

Callidan's chuckle rose to a guffaw. "Well, it's good to see you, too."

Kayden was frozen—unmoving. Lira motioned to Magnus to watch Callidan as she rushed over. "Kayden," Lira snapped her fingers in front of Kayden's face. No response. "Kayden!" she placed her hand on Kayden's cheek, moving to stand face-to-face. "What's wrong? Who is he?"

Kayden's breathing didn't slow. Her pupils darted between Callidan and Lira rapidly.

"Her and I are old friends," the torturer said in a smug voice. "Aren't we, little girl?"

Chapter Twenty-two

The Subservient

Kayden Ralta

"He—he—he—" Kayden repeated the word over and over again. "Torturer," she stuttered in a panic. Tears flowed down her face, with no signs of stopping.

"How's your back feeling?" Callidan called. "I bet you haven't forgotten that one, oh no."

Ice crawled across her entire body with the mention of it. She shuddered. Shivered. Remembering the blades across her back. Her nails lifted and dug under. Joints pulled. Her screaming so loud her throat stung and died for weeks. The laughter of Callidan. The eyes of Sheeran watching. Punishing. Then she felt jagged steel drag across her. She yelped out and tightened the grip on her shins.

She heared a muffle and saw blood spray to the side. Mags.

Mags swiped him across the face with his gauntlet, again and again. "Stop talking," he ordered in a rough voice.

"Kayden," she heard someone say. Sheeran's voice echoed with it in her mind. *My love*, she heard. *It's for your own good.*

Her own good. Her whole body seized. Frozen. Paralyzed. For a moment she thought she was dead.

Was she breathing? Couldn't tell. Her chest felt like a knife was buried into it. As if it burned. Her back felt steel again. Agony. She saw a hand near her. She shot away, flinched, waiting for pain. But none came. Didn't make sense...

"Kayden," a voice said again.

The torturer's voice called out to her. "You okay? C'mon let's have a little fun." That voice she knew. The laughing man, he was called. Callidan. Feywater. Monster.

Pain only followed that name. Every hair on her arm, leg, and everything stood on end just hearing it spoken. She just stared five thousand yards away trying to forget. Trying to ignore. Trying to pretend it would be over soon. Hoping she never felt anything.

"*Kayden,*" the name said again. It shattered her vision. Dark skin was in front of hers. Black hair. A woman. Didn't make sense. Who was she? Not Sheeran. Not Callidan. Not any of them.

"We're here. You aren't alone," the voice assured her.

She was alone. Always.

Kayden looked up, seeing warm, chestnut-brown eyes. Not the typical cold or stagnant blue or green. It was—she remembered a name, barely...

The face came into focus. "Lira?" Kayden whispered.

The woman smiled and gave a weak nod. She remembered. The weird girl that trusted everyone. Lira. Stupid, honestly. But endearing. Lira—she—she was the only one Kayden truly trusted. Dared not admit it.

Kayden kept glancing back to the vile Callidan. That's all she saw. Callidan. Memories. And Lira.

Lira's hand forced Kayden's face to hers. She flinched waiting for the pain. Confusion filled her each time her prediction failed.

"Look at *me*!" Lira yelled. Kayden's eyes met hers and stayed. The warm eyes melted her fear like flesh in a flame. Her breath slowed, barely. "You're okay. We're all here." But her eyes showed fear. Fear of the one behind her. Fear of the monster that sat there.

After minutes of slow, methodical breaths, Kayden fumbled to her feet. She gently touched her back and bit her lip. Her back. The scars. Brought by Callidan. Ordered by Sheeran.

The past was gone. But the past stood before her. With a deep breath, Kayden focused her mind where she could. To what she was. To ensure Lira never experienced this. To ensure no one did.

She sauntered toward Callidan and drew her blades.

"Kayden, what are you doing?" Lira asked.

Finishing it.

Kayden walked toward him blank-faced. Without thought. Without remorse. The Shadow of Death lived.

Callidan looked around Kayden, back at Lira. "Don't I get to talk to the tall one? She was pretty. Hey, Lira, come back! I thought we had a good deal going."

Kayden bared her clenched teeth, breath quickening once more. "Don't you dare talk to her," Kayden snarled. "Talk to me." Kayden picked up no tools. No need. "Did that drake Fillion hire you? Is Sheeran part of this?"

"Why don't you tell me?" Callidan said in a snarky tone.

Wrong answer. Kayden brought a sharpened blade to his chest and slashed it slowly across its width. It was vengeance. Fair play. Blood flowed from the wound like a river that spelled justice. Callidan screamed in agony as it dragged along his skin. It was odd seeing tables turn.

"Kayden, *no!*" Lira yelled. She ran to stop it, but Mags held her back. She was unable to match Magnus's strength. She slapped his arm and wrenched forward but gained no ground.

She needed to do this. Not for herself. But for the missing. For the ones he hurt. For the ones he *would* hurt. "I said who are you working for!" Kayden yelled, kicking his bloody wound. "Is *he* part of this?" With all she was, she hoped not.

"Fillion, *Fillion!*" Callidan cried with heavy guttural coughs. "He doesn't know. This isn't his work!"

A wave of relief came over her. First time in a long time. "Good," Kayden said coldly. "Why are you bringing people here? Where are they going?" Her face stayed as stone. Unlike his.

Callidan glared at her, clenching his teeth. His breaths hissed like a snake. "I'm not telling you, you little *whore*. He's after you, so I'm not helping you." She got to him. A bit. But mentioning he was after her… That was the worst answer he could give.

Lira tried to free herself from Mags' grasp, but to no avail.

Kayden kicked him into the pole and stuck her blade between his legs. "Last chance." Vesper and Domika were plastered to the wall in fear and struck silent.

"Fitting that you'd want to touch me, but I don't think *he'd* like that."

Another wrong answer. For a torturer, he was stupid.

The sound of steel cutting flesh and Callidan's screams echoed in the space as his manhood fell to the ground. He never touched her in that way. Never dared. But it was still satisfying. "*Answer me!*" Kayden screamed.

'Solmarsh! They're being taken there with the people who are disappearing! I don't know why! Stop, please!" Callidan pleaded, tears flowed from his eyes. His mocking demeanor broke like a bug under a boot.

Solmarsh. Lira's home. She felt the pain swell behind Magnus' grip. She could feel Lira's confusion. Fear. Shock. Sadness.

"What do they want with those people? I'm not giving you a warning this time—just like you didn't." He never gave warning. Sometimes she saw a nod from Sheeran, which he said was a kindness. A favor. But that meant nothing when a nod meant anything. A cut. A gouge. An evisceration.

"I. Don't. Know! I just—do what I'm told!" Callidan yelled through clenched teeth. "Malakai—he—came, with another. He—took a prisoner with him and—said things worked and could—proceed as planned. Had a—violet orb, said from—Amirion."

A far way away. Hadn't heard of Amirion since she was there a year ago. Kayden's expression stayed blank. Cold. Unsettling news, but she showed nothing. "Asheron's brother?"

"Yes—" Callidan wheezed. "The Blood Knight. Said Amirion was—a genocide. For their uses. The people here are to finish it."

"Kayden, stop this!" Lira pleaded. "Vesper, Domika, Magnus do something!" she yelled. Vesper was pasted to the wall, and he shook his head. Domika did the same. Lira wished to calm her, but Kayden's anger pushed her to continue. "Please Kayden, it isn't worth it!" she cried.

Her words shook Kayden.

Not worth it. He wasn't. He didn't deserve anything.

Kayden looked back to Lira with eyes filled with sadness and fear. She closed her eyes, nodding. "Fine, I believe you." She struck Callidan across the face again and again. Each one felt better and better like the past disappeared. Like she could forget it all.

His breathing was labored, eyes filled with tears. She stared right into his eyes. "You see? The last time we met, I was helpless. I was innocent." She grabbed a tangled mass of the drake's shoulder-length hair and ripped his head back. "And now—" She noticed his eyes drop. "Look at me." Kayden moved his chin up, but his eyes still focused on the ground. "*Look at me*," she growled. His eyes returned to hers. Her fierce voice turned eerily quiet. "Now, you are helpless, but not innocent. How does it feel?" She let his hair go.

Kayden stepped back. She shoved both blades slowly into Callidan's neck, staring into his eyes as she did it in silence. He choked as blood poured from his mouth and throat. "*Suffer*," she whispered. After his eyes turned lifeless, Kayden removed her blades and cleaned them on his clothing. She staggered backward and dropped to the floor, nose-to-knees with heavy breaths. Tears welled in her eyes as she stared at Callidan's mutilated body.

It was over. He was dead. Finally.

But it wasn't over. So many still lived. So many could come for her. And she was alone.

Magnus released Lira, and she ran to embrace Kayden on the ground. "I'm sorry," Lira squeaked. She didn't do anything wrong.

Magnus, still unaffected, sat beside her. Domika and Vesper were still frozen against the wall. They looked at each other, then approached with caution.

"My lady, are you okay?" Vesper inquired, outstretching his hand carefully.

She never would be. "No," Kayden whispered. "I'm not."

Lira didn't let go. Kayden pulled away, but she held on tight. In a visceral reaction, she returned the embrace with all her might, squeezing as hard as she could.

"I'm not the Grim, I'm not, I'm not—" Kayden whispered. "I'm sorry." She repeated it over and over. "She brought the past back. Her persona. The Shadow of Death. "I don't think he knew why they were taken."

"I don't think he was going to talk, even without doing that." Domika said carefully. "Don't worry Kayden, he—" she paused, seeming unsure if she would help or hurt. "He deserved it."

Her eyes shot to Domika. They always argued. Hated each other. But when she said this—it had understanding behind it.

Maybe she wasn't so bad.

Didn't trust her still.

"How could you three just stand there, letting her do it alone?" Lira snapped at the others. "How could you just watch?"

"Lira, stop," Domika whispered. "Don't you see she's upset? She did what she needed to do. We don't know what she's been through."

I did. She needed to kill him. She needed to make him suffer. Not for her, but for so many others.

Kayden's breathing quickened again. Her eyes were wide, not leaving Callidan's bloody corpse. Blood she spilled.

"Kayden," Lira said. Kayden's eyes glanced over to hers. "It's okay." It surprised her that Lira stayed resilient through the display. "He's hurt a lot of people. He deserved worse. You didn't do anything wrong." Kayden's gaze didn't change or move. "Do you understand?" Lira asked.

Kayden nodded quickly. She sniffled and smiled. "Yes."

Domika knelt down beside Kayden. "Hey," she said, bringing Kayden's attention to her. "It hurts," Domika nodded. "But we're in this together." She ended with a smile.

Kayden gave them a mystified look. Why would they lie?

I'm in this alone.

She gave a nod, which was a lie. She rose as Lira released her embrace. Kayden's breath slowed and her eyes narrowed, as per usual. She let out a large sigh and stared blankly at the mutilated body, and spit on it. *Enjoy hell.* Slowly, she turned and relaxed her shoulders. "I think we can continue now. I can take time after we're done. We have a job to do. We should probably head to the manor quickly. Luckily, this place is sound proof so our yelling didn't affect anything."

"What about those who were imprisoned here?" Lira asked. "We have to get them out!"

She pointed toward the other prisons she spotted while scouting. "Lira, Mags, you stay behind and get the prisoners out of here through the sewers. Dom, Vesper, you come with me. We have a noble to scare. Nothing violent, I promise."

"You sure you're okay?" Lira asked, lightly grasping Kayden's arm. "I'm worried."

Kayden gently shook Lira off of her. "I'm going to be okay. I'm not alone," she smiled sweetly. "I promise, I'm feeling better." Complete lie. Absolute bold-faced lie. Her past came back. She spent years in hell. She ran and was free for one. Now the past was back to claim her forever. Where there was Callidan, there were so many more. There was only one way out.

Kayden turned to walk toward the stairwell. "Don't worry Lira. We'll rendezvous back at the inn."

Once Lira said they were friends.

They weren't.

What friend would make their final parting words a lie?

Chapter Twenty-three

Down the Neck of Fools

Saul Bromaggus

The Broken came to the mighty tribal city of Sisla, and they feared what they would find within. The only other city of the Seven they experienced was Rhoba, and that was reason enough to be suspicious. The others grew restless; tensions rose between a few members of the group.

It didn't help that every night since Saul was imprisoned, his dream of Gadora became a nightmare. Every night he appeared atop the tower, and a storm of darkness struck him with lightning until he awoke from agony. But he pressed south. Searching.

Sisla was modestly built, but a vast city of many things: races of Hydris to Human to Blazik, beliefs in powers like voodoo and blood magic, and all sorts of foods and animals Saul never saw before. There were many witch doctors in booths and huts who wore the skins of animals upon their heads, from boars, to bears, to sabertooth tigers and even a Ravager's skull.

The people wore clothes made of beautifully colored cloth, metal rings, and feathers. The various traders Saul conversed with said many of their trades were made with the cities of Alin and

Shi'doba, and the Torch. Saul hadn't known that trade occurred over the Fissure, let alone out of the Torch of Lathyria in general. Stuck-up fools lived high atop the Torch's peninsula. However, the witch doctors that could actually speak the common tongue of Renalia said they were surprisingly helpful—at least if you had something they wanted. Saul didn't believe it for a second, but he saw more shocking things prior, such as the treachery in Rhoba.

Street musicians played on every corner, serenading passer-bys with all sorts of drums and percussion instruments, singing in high, vibrato tones and shrill shrieks to their gods. Saul didn't care for the act of song, but the people of Sisla believed that their songs brought them blessings. Gadora's singers were strong and orotund, Yggranda's were deep and hoarse, while Urikar's were shrill and ear-splitting, and Kannakash's were guttural. Saul respected those who paid homage to their deities, whether it be through battle, prayer, salute, or song.

Saul enjoyed the flourish of Sisla, but the merchants refused to let them stay. If they were to sleep, it was only allowed outside city walls. The townspeople knew of the curse of Rhoba, and now Saul understood why the small villages he visited closed their doors at first sight.

His mind turned to the crimson flow that now stained Rhoba's ground, knowing he did what was right. *It needed to be done. They were cowards who would kill the innocent for their own useless gain.* He avoided the shops of the Hydris; he didn't trust them. *They're my enemy, they might slay me where I stand, or I, them.*

They stayed in town during the day, inquiring at inns and to house builders, but they all said the same thing: "You are welcome to view our town, but you are not welcome to stay here." Saul attempted to convince them that they were not of Rhoba, but it was for naught.

TIDES OF FATE

* * *

They soon pressed south across the plains. When they reached Graline, they found it quite different from Sisla. It was a strong city, built with a vast stone wall surrounding the perimeter, with many engravings of names and warriors. There was a massive set of bronze statues at the center of town, towering over the city itself: two warriors, one in plate and the other leather, swinging blade and axe at one another. Saul saw many walking by and saluting it by crossing their arms in an X and bowing.

As he traversed the city, he noticed the people to be quite secular. The roads were barren of temples, markings of deities, as well, there were no witch doctors, priests, or even magicians. They were farmers and soldiers, trusting in a blade rather than a spell. Saul respected their ways and felt nostalgic. He enjoyed the feeling of the city, but despite his opinion and the others, the Gralinians respectfully turned Saul and the other Broken away, seeing them as very non-secular individuals. *Especially with our markings—that much is certain.*

The Broken respected their choice in turn. Being unwelcome in a city was not a life they wanted. Conquering was not an option, as the city was hundreds or thousands strong, and they were but twenty. The city had many races: Humans, Blaziks, Terrans, and even some traitorous Hydris. Saul did not know how these other races came to be in the Neck. He reasoned they were exiled from Renalia, the Plateau, or the Torch. Each city did not know much about the others, aside from their specialties and trades.

Graline was an expert in physical combat, but also farming. They were skilled in domesticating different varieties of corn, fruits, and other vegetables. Their seeds brought plentiful harvests, and other cities paid well for them. While Saul and the others did not find a home there, they did learn something very interesting regarding the state of the Serpent's Plateau: there was a civil war across their lands. The King wished to make peace with the Vale, while the Stormwardens, they were called, wished to annihilate them.

Both were foolish in their plights. The Broken discussed the war endlessly since, however. Whenever they rested by campfire, the topic returned. "Saul, what do you think we should do?" Drof asked, rubbing the side of his thin jaw. "The others are unsettled. None have had contact with the Hydris before, aside from the few at the fissure and the sparse villages."

"As with me. But it could be a trap," Saul said bluntly. "What would you expect me to do? Assist them?" Saul shook his head. "We have been raised to believe that all Hydris hate us. What if the citizens of Graline were dishonest? What if the Plateau is not at war, and they kill us on sight?" It had been drilled into Saul's head for years: the fear that the Hydris would kill them no matter what. "But it might be our only option if the others of the Neck reject us. Each city is highly isolated."

"What if we aid the capital?" a husky female voice asked from behind. The light of the campfire accentuated Fae Joran's powerful stature. Long, black dreadlocks spilled down her back like a thousand rivers, fitting her blue markings of a protector: the waves of Urikar, the four-pointed rounded star of the Hydris, and the blade of victory. She was a rough Broken but spoke her mind and hid nothing. She plopped on the ground beside Drof.

"But what if something goes wrong? We could just get caught in the middle," Drof said. His concerns were not misplaced. Each Broken came from the Vale, and each were exiled for his or her own reason. Drof was dubbed a coward, as he fled from orders of the Dragon. Saul fled execution; they were not so different.

Saul warned them all that betrayal would send them to the same fate as Rhoba. Drof had been reliable thus far. "He is correct. We may be caught between two armies," Saul began. "A war over the Broken. It is difficult to fathom. The rulers and commonfolk supposedly support uniting, while the others reject us and wish to conquer the Vale and slaughter our people." *Damn fools.* He knew they would walk to their death. The Broken society was strong, filled with well-trained warriors, *and* were led by the last Dragon of Kathynta, who had been alive since before the last true war raged two hundred years prior.

"If we're successful, we'll get respect. Maybe we can return to our land. Did you not mention wanting to return for vengeance?" Fae said. "Have you forgotten?"

Her words were strong, and she listened to Saul's ramblings. "I have not forgotten." While he wished for Vengeance, his journey had shaped his mind in ways he did not expect. That, and he had not found means for vengeance aside from foolish courage.

"I hear they worship the Glories as well. One of the witches in Sisla informed me." Fae pointed to Saul's crashing winds on his left shoulder.

Saul thought of the dagger that pierced it, leaving no scar after his marks lit up. *Remember your father's words*, Gadora said to him. It was just a dream, but of a place he never saw. His father's words didn't leave him, to protect the weak, rather than rule them. *The Hydris aren't weak, are they?* "For now we move to the jungles of Elaston and potentially farther to Shi'doba. Then we will decide our path," Saul said.

They could not confirm any rumors or trust anyone with referrals, as each of them fell for the trick in Rhoba. *Damn that Fissure guard, lying cur.* Like the night he left the Vale, he couldn't run to his death without proper thought.

Fae let out a scoffed at his words, "Sitting on the decision? I think we know who the coward is here." Saul saved their lives, and yet she was rough as a mountainside.

Saul retorted with a sharp tongue. "Speak to me in such a way once more, and I shall put you back in Rhoba's prison. Do not forget how you escaped." Saul had no time for challenges. "We may discover more information the further we travel. Time is a luxury, and we have no room to trust the word of anyone in the Neck. These are rumors about a war we know nothing about. We must tread lightly. Do you understand?" It surprised Saul to hear those ideals emerging from his own lips. Waiting. Patience.

Her prominent brow furrowed but surrendered. "I suppose. Just know that if we find more evidence of it being truth and you back away, I'll challenge you myself," she said, storming off. Not uncommon for an underling to challenge a leader.

"Noted," Saul called. He looked to Drof, who gave him a raised brow. A long silence followed, accompanied only by the songs of crickets and the crackles of flame, decorated by the smell of campfire's smoke and ash.

Fae turned to look at him and winced. "Look around you. You command and demand, but we don't want to sit around and find a home. We want to find a purpose." With a dark frown, she said, "Do you not? Don't act all high and mighty because you got us out of that place. You got yourself out and did what anyone would do. You haven't earned any respect because you broke a few chains." She walked to another campfire and sat down, crossing her arms.

Saul drew out his mouth in displeasure. "Why must she be so insistent? She's running in like a reckless fool," he said to Drof. He realized that was exactly what he would have done a season ago. Ever since his exile and Rhoba, he had been wary of running into battle—*or any situation, for that matter*—for the wrong reasons.

"Her markings, Saul. She was born to protect them. Didn't you notice?" Drof replied.

He noticed but paid it no attention. He thought the Broken of Rhoba disregarded fate now—but not all had. Fate drove the desires of many of his people, including himself. He still was not entirely sure of what to believe but followed his gut feeling. It told him to be cautious. "I suppose I hadn't. It seems we haven't all given up on fate."

Her marks showed victory.

But the mark of victory failed before.

He clenched his fists, remembering the day his father died. It represented how Obelreyon ruled. *Control. We have been controlled by Dragons for too long. Centuries, millennia, far too long. Yet so many feel it is right to be ruled by them. But why?*

"Have you? You bear two marks—the Dragon, and the mark of All." Drof said, pointing to both of Saul's arms.

Saul cringed at his words, but Drof was right. He looked to some of the other Broken, seeing other marks of the Hydris. One had the red of a slayer, one had the yellow of the mediator. He did not know his true fate. "I choose my own fate. As for the Hydrian capital of Serpentarius, I will think on it. Despite what you believe, they are still our enemy." He dismissed Drof, who stared into the fire with his golden eyes.

There may have been truth to the civil war, but if the rulers wished for unification, why not attempt to bring it to them? The Hydrian King was seeking peace with the Vale. But Saul knew Obelreyon wouldn't accept it. It was a fool's errand to make peace with the Dragon.

They were all rumors still, and they had little information to go on. Saul wanted to know why the King wished for unity and felt they would only know by entering the Plateau.

He looked to his left arm, seeing the sharp-winged mark of the Dragon. In his dream, Gadora told him theories of fate.

Gorum himself abandoned his. Saul did not know if he had to keep to his, but deep down he wanted to. He had to bring death upon the enslaver. Looking around the small camp, that was an eternity away. The Vale was filled with thousands of Broken. They were all too afraid to dethrone the tyrant.

Saul was now hundreds of miles from the Vale, halfway across the continent. He felt lost, wandering aimlessly for a purpose. He wanted revenge for his father's death, but he had no true means to accomplish his goal. He felt a pull to the Plateau but refused to answer it thus far.

The nightmares that plagued him were all too real—where he resided in Renalia. He wished to go there one day, to bring victory for his people on the field of battle. If the Broken were rid of the Dragon, they could return to Renalia and conquer it once again, like the legends of their past. To live in the home of the Broken.

Thinking about battle soothed Saul. He fought with fellow warriors in the core of the Vale, the main city of Chromata, where the council's temple stood. Through his markings, the exile, and the traitors of Rhoba, he felt separated from his mind. The clash of blades and flesh brought him back. The carving of traitors in Rhoba made him feel alive. It also made him question what his people truly meant. Rhoba was filled with Broken: his race, happy individuals, as well—but also the most horrid.

He dared not call them *his* people, yet they were Broken all the same. Saul didn't know what he belonged to anymore. He was part of a clan who lived for honor, yet it wasn't the race that made them. But he felt the other races weren't his people, either.

They wouldn't understand the life of a true Broken, as Saul was.

Drof shifted his legs, picking at his short fingernails. "Do you feel bad for killing all those people?" His peculiar eyes glowed in the fire's light.

Saul shook his head. "No. I do not feel shame for what I do. Even if I did, I would atone for it later. Regret slows one down," he replied. "Each was guilty as the last."

Drof went silent again, staring into the fire. He was a relatively quiet one, and always raised a question when Saul posed a belief. He called himself a 'balanced advocate,' someone who raises the other points to make sure one understands every viewpoint. Saul didn't like being challenged, but he knew Drof was simply keeping him aware. It was like a captain telling the general of an army where the weaknesses in his force were. It was no insult. It was necessary.

Saul unsheathed his blade and waved it from side to side in front of him. Thinking of his dream, he pondered the words of his goddess. *If you had to choose between joining forces with an orderly and strong Hydrian society or a dishonorable, backstabbing Broken one, which would you choose?*

He did not know. He experienced betrayal. But the Hydris…

It may have been a dream, but it felt real. The whispering winds, the smell of cold, thin air, the shock of lightning bolts—he felt it all. Her rough, granite skin, platinum hair, fierce eyes, and commanding tone filled his mind. *Did I meet the true goddess?* Saul wondered. He felt not, as it was simply his own mind bringing out what he thought she was, and a place that had only been described to him. The place he wished to see one day. It was a place where he felt he belonged—where his *people* belonged.

He stared at his markings, seeing fates that told of his death. "*Rai soli moria, gadoras faust,*" Saul whispered.

Where warriors fall, heroes rise.

Chapter Twenty-four

Alone in the Dark

Lira Kaar

Lira and Magnus waited and waited for the others to return to the inn. "Magnus, why were you so—*absent*, during that?" Lira inquired. "You seemed so calm while she—did what she did."

He shook his head. "I have seen much. I do not fear watching vengeance." He paused, realizing that Lira wasn't satisfied with his answer. "We needed information, and she needed vengeance. For what, I do not know. Perhaps in time she will tell us."

Lira sighed. "I suppose you're right." She wiped a small tear from her eye while she wondered what happened in Kayden's past. She preferred to be alone—and was closed off emotionally from what Lira saw.

She was as curious as ever, but knew probing was not the answer. She felt sheltered, knowing nothing of the world. Each member of their group had seen much, and Lira was the opposite.

She worried for the days ahead and danger creeping toward her—and her brother's soul.

Hours passed. The concern and anxiety set in. "It's been too long," Lira said. "I'm worried." Her stomach wrenching finally subsided; the scent of blood made her feel sick.

"I, as well. What would you suggest?" Magnus replied.

Lira shuffled her feet. *Kayden told us to wait. I don't want to go against her, but what if she's in danger?* There was something off—she could feel it. Not about the mission, but there was something she sensed. It was a hunch she couldn't shake.

The door to the room carefully opened. Domika poked her head in slowly. "Hey. Everything went well," she whispered.

The door swung open, and Vesper charged in with ecstatic arm-waving. "Correct! The plan went off without a hitch! With Miss Ralta's ideas, they won't even know it was us!"

Domika slapped Vesper's arm so hard he almost toppled over. "Shut up, idiot! You'll get us in trouble," she hissed.

Lira gave a few moments as the two glared at each other. She couldn't wait any longer. "Where's Kayden?" She rubbed her legs nervously.

Domika heaved her ringmail onto the floor with a *slump*. "She wanted to go for a walk to blow off some steam. She seemed pretty shaken up. I'm a little concerned. Should we go look for her?"

Lira bit her lip. "I'm going to go outside to look around."

"Would you like us to accompany you?" Vesper inquired.

Lira shook her head. "No, that's okay. I can handle it. I'm going to see if I can find her. With any luck, she'll be back soon, anyway." She got up and put up her hand for them to sit. If Kayden needed someone to talk to, it was best for only one to go alone. She didn't want Kayden thinking they were all ganging up on her.

Lira tip-toed down the stairs and slipped out the door. She listened in silence outside and heard nothing; it was the dead of night. She wandered toward the town gate, wondering where she would have gone.

She knew Kayden was a good climber, and that she enjoyed jumping from building to building during whatever tasks she had long ago. She liked the idea of escaping, or 'sticking it to the state' as she called it.

Lira strolled for a little longer and noticed a few particularly tall homes down toward the market. When she crept closer, she listened, and heard someone talking. She looked around, perking her ears up, trying to find the source. The tallest building stood with four levels reaching to the sky, with various steel ducts going from floor to floor. It was a tan home, with burnt orange, clay scaly tiles for the roof. Lira quietly stepped on a box and reached for the first level. She climbed up, barely. Then she jumped to the next one, clambering up awkwardly. She huffed and puffed, already exhausted. *How does she do all of this so easily*? Lira wondered. As she looked up, she saw the moon above, and then heard the sound of Kayden's heavy breath once more.

"It's just that easy. I could just do it, and I wouldn't have to worry anymore," Kayden said to the darkness.

The next two levels had small ramps and ladders, which made it easy. As Lira struggled to climb over the final ledge, she saw Kayden with a dagger to her own neck.

Her breathing was rapid and unstable. Tears dropped subtly from her cheeks.

"Kayden?" Lira blurted out.

Kayden turned around abruptly, with the blade still to her neck. "Lira? What are you doing here? How did you find me?" she said in an accusatory tone.

"You like tall buildings, and I have good hearing." She stepped forward.

"Go back to the inn, Lira!" Kayden commanded, waving her other arm away.

Lira flinched and almost stumbled off the roof. But she stood firm. "No."

Kayden's eyes widened. "I've had it, princess. I've—I've tried to run. For so long, I really thought I could get away from that bullshit. But I can't—you just saw it. I can't, and I never will. This is the only way I can forget about all of it!" she screamed. "You heard what Callidan said. He's still after me."

"But why? Why this? This isn't right, Kayden!" Lira's voice cracked, and tears began to sprout from her eyes. "I don't want you to die, I want you here!"

"Why do you give a shit about what happens to me? I've been a drake to you this entire time, and yet you're *nice* to me? What kind of idiotic goody-two-shoes are you?"

Lira stepped forward, and Kayden put her hand up and held the blade closer to her neck. Lira just pouted and said, "A goody-two-shoes who cares about her friends."

Kayden shook her head in disbelief and coughed up a laugh. "*Friends*? Is that what we are?" Kayden's eyes grew more fierce. "I flat-out lied to you when I said I'd come back. What kind of friend lies like that? I lie, and now you come for me?"

She only shook her head in response. "If you lied, maybe it was because you're afraid! I don't care about that. I care about *you*."

Kayden's expression turned to a sharp glare. "You don't understand what I've had to live through. No matter what I do, I can't get rid of the memories. I'm not worth the effort. Stop trying to help me!"

Giving in wasn't an option. Never would be.

Lira stepped closer and stood strong. "Stop making excuses! Why can't you just have a friend? Why do you have to be alone all the time? Think about what Domika said—we're in this together! You told me you wouldn't die because *no one* tells you what to do, and that you wouldn't give them the satisfaction!" Lip quivering, Lira's voice grew brittle as she begged the next few words.

Lira put out her hand. "Please, Kayden. Please, put it down. I—I don't know what I'd do—" Tears flowed from her eyes like an unending flood. "You don't have to be alone. *I* don't want to be alone."

Kayden wiped the tears from her cheeks with her free hand. "I've always been alone." Her eyes drew to the roof at her feet. "I always will be."

She stepped forward, and Kayden shook the blade at her own neck threateningly. Lira advanced again, and Kayden did nothing. "I don't want to lose my friend," Lira said weakly. "Please."

One more step, and her blade began to lower. As Lira stared into Kayden's eyes, they grew soft. The clattering of steel echoed around them, and Kayden stepped into Lira's chest. As Lira felt Kayden's emotions writhe in weak cries, she embraced tightly and wouldn't let go.

"We're in this together," Lira said, over and over, looking out into the night. "You aren't alone anymore."

Chapter Twenty-five

The Beast Within

Zaedor Nethilus

"It's been a fortnight since his fight with Gorlin," Kindro said. "Do you think they'll pick him again soon?"

"Definitely. They usually wait so they have a comeback after being broken for so long." Freya sighed.

"Do you think he's going to win?"

"No clue. He's got a good heart, and more anger than I've seen in anyone for a while. It could go either way. I have hope, but he could get beaten again. Poor guy."

"I'm awake, I'll have you know," Zaedor grumbled.

It was early in the morning, or so they were told. The guards kept time for them and attempted to allow decent sleep schedules. Fighters who slept well fought better. While those who imprisoned them were brutal, they weren't stupid. Zaedor's back ached from the awkward sleep, his nose ached from being broken, and his chin still had a strange click when it opened too wide. It wasn't enough to impair him. *'Your physical side is fine,'* Freya had said. *'You need the mind of a fighter, a man in the midst of a vital battle. You aren't sparring here.'* There was one question he hadn't asked, that frustrated him since day one. "Why are you helping me?" he finally inquired. Kindro coughed up a laugh, and Freya sighed loudly.

"Because, Mr. 'Zaedor of Amirion,' you have a good heart. Despite being a bit of a drake, you do deserve a mourning period," Freya said, rolling her eyes.

Kindro scratched his scraggly beard. "There's nothing to do around here, and helping you makes me feel like I'm not just here to die."

Zaedor chuckled. *What an interesting pair. A hairy, funny, scraggly man, and a beautiful, sweet, but fierce woman.* It had only been a week, and he felt like he knew them for years. Being locked up in a cage infuriated him; speaking with Kindro and Freya was the only thing *not* driving him mad. If it were not for them, he would have been dead already.

He lost his home, his leader, his friends, and his beliefs. Part of him wished he'd died in the ring a fortnight ago, but death refused to take him. *Why do you test me, Death?* Part of him wished to end it all right here. If he had a blade in hand, he probably would have done it already. He sprouted tears now and again, hoping Kindro and Freya didn't see.

"Listen, you can't be all frilly, happy-go-lucky in the ring. Use your hate and anger to your advantage. You seethe for revenge, and this is your chance. If we ever get out of here, maybe you'll get it for real. Just don't be a moron," Freya reminded him, playing with her long ponytail.

She was right, but Zaedor didn't know how to channel it. He only knew what made him angry—but what was he to target? His thoughts were clouded. He knew the event occurred, but he could only remember it in bits and pieces.

The door slammed open. Maroia entered, shooting a creepy grin to the room as he glanced from cage to cage. He didn't walk around the cages this time. He went directly for the one holding Zaedor and Kindro. The fire from the torches around the room danced in his eyes, and he had a skip to his step. "Your moment has come, Amirionian! Let's see if you can return from the hole Gorlin put you in."

Zaedor looked to Freya for one last piece of advice, and he felt a cold sweat drip down his forehead.

"Did anyone specific hurt you? Do you remember anyone that you truly hate from that night?" Freya whispered.

Zaedor closed his eyes and thought through everything. He remembered slaying a few brigands, who he'd fought with Lothel at his side. Then he remembered the drake that killed him—*Cloaker*, the disgusting shapeshifter. Zaedor saw his emotionless green eyes, sand-covered wolf cowl, and the voice that grinded his ears like a sharpening stone. His mind filled with rage, as if he was back in the Citadel again, witnessing his king's murder once more. He gritted his teeth, clenched his fists tightly, and screwed his face into an intense frown. He opened his eyes once more to her, nodding.

"Your opponent," Freya said, "is the one you hate."

Zaedor nodded fiercely. His desire sprung forward; he spoke without his mind even registering the thought. "Fallad! I have a request."

Maroia jumped back slightly, pausing as he approached the cage with his massive guards. "Oh?" he began, sporting a sly grin. "And what would that be?"

"I want Gorlin," Zaedor said. He didn't know why he said it. He saw Gorlin in his mind becoming Cloaker; they were one in the same. He wanted vengeance on both of those who defeated him.

"Zaedor, no! What are you doing?" Freya whispered harshly. "I've beaten him, but this?"

"Oh, how interesting!" Maroia hollered. "I do love a good comeback." He turned his back. "Now my friend, we don't usually do this," he pondered. "If you fail, which you most likely will, he might kill you this time. It's hard to keep people who lose twice in a row." He turned his head to Zaedor with a wide smile, showing all of his browning teeth. "Are you ready to accept that?"

Without pause, Zaedor knew his answer. "Definitely." He didn't bother looking at either Freya or Kindro. He sought blood. *Blood must have blood*, he thought. Zaedor shook the cage violently.

"My my, you're feisty today!" Maroia laughed like a hyena. "Don't let me down, now. And remember, you don't kill breakers." He turned, sauntering away. "Take him." The guards opened the cage and grabbed his arms. He did not resist and went willingly. He was being given what he desired, but that didn't stop the giants from bruising his arm with their grip.

Zaedor barely heard Maroia speak. Gorlin represented what he hated most: unyielding, brute force without mercy or attempt at diplomacy. An absence of sophistication.

It was the same as before, but different. They wrapped his arms with the cloth and leather to cushion his hands. *Cloth or not, I will break my hands if I have to.* Their grip tightened, forcing him against the back of the small wooden chair.

Maroia Fallad entered with a stern look. "Okay, Amirionian. You're getting what you want. I could have made a fortune off of you, and this could ruin my chances of that. However, Mr. Kuralia, the organizer you are pitted against, enjoys watching me lose, and had to take my larger bet on this fight," he said, glaring at Zaedor. "If you don't die in the ring, you won't live through the night." He gritted his teeth into a smile. "You look different. That's good."

Zaedor didn't say a word. He glared right back, bloodlust in his mind and heart. He didn't care if he disappointed anyone.

Maroia stood back. "Good luck, you insane fool. I'm hedging a lot on this. I do love a good gamble." He strolled out of the room and slammed the door. The sound of footsteps slowly dissipated down the hall.

The guards pulled him up and forced him down the execution hall, then threw him out the door to the pit. The crowd filled the stands from end to end. Gorlin walked out alone, willingly. *How long has he been here?*

"Ladies and Gentlemen! We bring a grand spectacle to you on this day! One week ago, we witnessed the *brutal* defeat of Amirion by our Giant-killer, Gorlin!" Gorlin's beard barely hid his smug smirk. His eyes mocked Zaedor, as if he saw a weakling before him. He towered over him by almost half a foot and had more reach. Although, it was like Freya said—*it's how you fight*. Zaedor had not seen her in a fight, but knew she defeated the 'Giant-killer' before.

"We bring you a story of atonement, a story of revenge! This special spectacle is a first time for all of us! The Amirionian has challenged Gorlin to a *rematch*!"

The crowd went wild. Their cheers were muffled, and Zaedor paid no attention. His eyes never left Gorlin's.

"Will Amirion fall again? Will they defeat the giant that has broken their walls? My friends, let us find out now—why wait? Kuralian company and Fallad company shall engage in combat once more, and there is no more time for talk! I bring you, *Gorlin, the Giant-killer*! Zaedor, *lone survivor of Amirion*!"

The announcer spread his arms wide. "Begin!"

Zaedor knew what to do. Agility was key, as was a lack of mercy. *Blood must have blood.* He saw the wolf cowl atop Gorlin's head.

Zaedor knew no fear, only anger. He dashed forward with no holds barred. He expected Gorlin's fist and dodged it. Zaedor swiftly grabbed the so-called giant-slayer's torso and struck the sensitive spot on his lower-mid back repeatedly, causing the beastly man to growl in agony.

He felt Gorlin's pull throw him to the ground. Zaedor kicked up in no time with the bounce, shaking it off. His stood tall as Gorlin dashed at him again. Zaedor evaded his charge, dropping quickly to slam his arm into the back of Gorlin's knee, causing him fall to his other. Gorlin swung for Zaedor's head, knocking him hard in the chin, but he latched onto the grisly man's arm; Gorlin couldn't shake him. Zaedor bit his arm with all his might, piercing flesh with his guillotine of a jaw. With another growl of pain, Gorlin gripped Zaedor's long, slick flow of hair and ripped it back, attempting to release his bite, and tore some hair out with the force. Zaedor released his arm, and both fell to the ground.

The crowd was in an uproar of applause, screaming for more. Both combatants rose and looked to each other with hatred and fire in their eyes. Gorlin released a clenched fist, dropping Zaedor's hair to the ground. He chuckled and circled around Zaedor slowly. Zaedor watched his every move: the vibration of his hands and muscles, the movement of his dark eyes, and the trickle of his sweat. Blood flowed down his forearm from the wound Zaedor gave him.

Dirty shifter! All he saw was Cloaker.

Gorlin dashed at him, but Zaedor was ready. He evaded the swings like Cloaker's vines, and his head-butt like the plant form's maw. Zaedor quickly dropped down, grabbed Gorlin's legs, and pulled them out from under him. Gorlin slammed onto his back. Zaedor jumped onto him and chopped his throat and shoved a fist, middle knuckle forward, under his ribs. Gorlin choked and gasped for air. Zaedor's fists came down immediately after and slammed Gorlin's head into the ground.

"Pay for what you've done to me! To my home, to my king!" Zaedor yelled. His teeth clenched like a vice. His fists pounded blood out of Gorlin's nose without mercy. Gorlin slammed the ground with his arm in surrender, but Zaedor didn't care. He didn't stop. He *couldn't* stop. His bloodlust had to be satiated. Gorlin attempted to block Zaedor's, blows but to no avail.

"We have a winner!" the announcer yelled. The crowd went wild. Zaedor did not stop. Soon, the crowd's cheers faded into silence. "Stop him, stop him now!"

With a final blow, Zaedor cracked Gorlin's chin to the side. His hands felt so brittle they seemed broken. The massive guards pulled him off of the corpse and dragged him away.

Zaedor's scalp was bloodied and his face was bruised. He stared at the body of Gorlin, also bloody with broken face. He lay motionless, eyes unmoving. It was Gorlin's body. Not Cloaker's. There was no cowl. There only lay Gorlin, dead and disfigured.

The announcer's voice grew tremulous. "Th—the victor—the lone survivor of Amirion!" The crowd stayed silent as the guards dragged him out. A thousand pairs of eyes watched Zaedor as he was taken away.

The guards quickly unwrapped his arms and moved him back to his cage with Kindro. Maroia stormed into the prison dome moments later. "What the hell was that, boy?" he roared. Many of the other prisoners grew alert. Zaedor looked slowly to Kindro and Freya.

What happened? Freya mouthed to him. She looked at his blood-covered fists.

"Are you trying to get me killed?" Maroia said with a steeled voice, pointing furiously at Zaedor. "Listen up, whelps. It looks like the traitor had a different idea in mind. You'll be lucky if Kuralian lets you fight against his own again, and you know what that means. If he says no for three weeks away from the ring—I'll let you wonder what happens then," he growled.

"Zaedor, did you *kill* him?" Freya cried, a tear forming at the corner of her eye.

Why is she sad, all of a sudden? She killed someone before. What's the difference? He stared back to Maroia. "You told me to fight, so I fought. You told me to win, so I won," Zaedor said bluntly, shaking the bars.

Maroia only showed a steeled, stone face, without a hint of humor. "You won me a lot of gold," he said, turning. "That's why I'm not going to kill you—yet."

"Then what do you want?"

"Just know you're hanging by a thread, just like your people." Maroia struck a nerve, knowing he would. "You killed a Breaker, even when you were told to stop. You're reckless, a loose cannon, and a danger to our organization. You pull something insane like that again, and I'll have you executed. Your friends, too. The hairy idiot, and the beast."

"What the hell did you just say?" Freya yelled, rattling her cage.

Fallad gave her a dismissive wave. "Calm down, woman. You fight like an animal—feral, pouncing as you fight. It's a nickname. You fight well, and the people like you. I would rather not have you die because of this endangered knave."

"I would die, so I killed in return. Perhaps you should be more specific." Zaedor shook the cage again, bearing his teeth.

The flamboyant slave-owner's face went stone cold. "Open his cage," he said. The Guards carefully opened the cage, and Zaedor stepped back as the door opened. Fallad quickly drew a metal rod and whipped Zaedor across his head with fierce might, causing him to topple. Maroia struck him again on the ground. Then he backed out, and the guards closed the cage. "Don't make me do that again. I should cut your manhood off, but I hear that kills one's ability to fight well," Fallad growled. "Now they have to choose a new Breaker, and I won't get anything from victories against them for months. You won me money tonight, but I will lose more over time, depending." He strolled away, slowly. "Do not disappoint me again," he said, before slamming the rusted prison door.

Zaedor shuddered at those words, the same ones Eryndis, his wife, used.

Freya turned to Zaedor quickly. "You killed him? What the hell is wrong with you?"

"What a way to go," Kindro said quietly, still huddled in the corner.

Zaedor knew what he had done. He killed a man who did nothing but his work, for the acts another man had perpetrated. He could have stopped and let Gorlin live. A man who lived as a slave died as one. Zaedor refused her criticism. *Who does she think she is? She's a murderer.* "What does it matter? You killed someone didn't you?" he snapped.

"Once. They were murderer before he came here. Serial killer. He did call me a beast, but he deserved to die for what he had done." She huffed and turned her head away.

"Oh? What was the 'Giant-killer' like then, Miss righteous? He looked at me with nothing but mockery and anger in the ring," Zaedor scoffed. "What could you possibly know?"

"A lot more than you, you idiot!" Tears streamed down her cheeks. "His name was Gorlin Taggard. He stayed in the cage beside mine before he became a Breaker," she paused. "He was kidnapped on an expedition for a new mine. He was a miner in Lothrad, a mining town east of Orinas. That's why he was a big guy." She bared her teeth. "He had a wife and three children,

Zaedor. Two daughters and a son. *You* just go around killing people without knowing what you're doing!" She crossed her arms and turned away. "Being a Breaker gives a chance of release. Think about that for a time, and don't speak to me until you have something intelligent to say, you sheltered ingrate."

She walked to a small, wooden chair in the back corner of her cage, sat down, and leaned up against the bars. She closed her eyes tightly.

Zaedor looked to Kindro, who simply shook his head in fear of them both, lowering his head to his knees.

Zaedor won a battle and shown his strength, he thought. Instead, he killed a man who may have seen his family again. Gorlin's wife, now a widow, cared for her children alone.

What kind of man have I become?

Chapter Twenty-six

Experience from Pain

Kayden Ralta

Kayden sat on the bed in the inn room the night after they returned from the manor. Her eyes still felt empty from the flood the previous night on the roof. The bed was soft—not what she was used to. It had a pink wool blanket, with bushy white feather pillows. There were a few candles and a lantern on the plain, rickety wood table beside the bed for lighting.

She felt relaxed, but not for long since it was more than her and Lira sleeping in the room. Of all people, she knew Lira was the most trustworthy, but Domika was with them too. Everyone was still downstairs having a slow dinner.

They pulled off the mission well. The prisoners were released, and the nobleman got the life scared out of him. They hid in the dark of his room, spoke from the shadows, and threw him the bloody torturer mask. She just hoped it worked in the end, and that things in town would lighten up. Callidan was dead—deservedly so—and the noble nearly pissed his pants; the main issue was solved, she hoped.

Old wounds were ripped open. They were wounds that drove her to the top of that building, drove the blade to her neck, but she was stopped in her tracks by Lira. Without her, the wounds would have bled her dry.

Part of her really wished to do it, wished Lira never found her, but something about Lira made her feel like she was home. Lira called her a friend; Kayden smiled subtly at the thought. She hadn't had a real friend in years. *Maybe I'm glad Lira stopped me. I can still make a difference. I just hope I can repay the favor one day.* A life debt she'd happily owe.

Kayden didn't deserve to be saved. In the past year alone, she killed over a hundred people in the dead of night—each one deserving of a painful death. But they had wives, husbands, and children.

She became what she hated most.

Fear flooded her mind at the very thought of what they'd think—of what they'd do with her if they knew what kind of person she really was. *The Shadow of Death.*

Kayden wished to take her mind off it all for at least a little while, if she could—and opened up her book, *Elemental Attunement*. It spoke of how wizards controlled the elements with magic, and how each individual channels their power differently. She was curious of Vesper's power; she hadn't seen him do much yet. *He's only a circus entertainer. What could he really do, after all? Then again, seeing the incident with the fire snake, I'm not sure.* Kayden felt for his loss, as she lost family as well. He had been more social with her recently, seeing something special in her. *I'm nothing like his daughter. I'm tough, but I'm not as redeeming as he thinks.* She carefully moved her hair behind her ears, barely containing it.

Kayden knew she wasn't magically inclined. Alas, she stared at her blades sheathed in the corner by her bed, knowing they were ultimately what protected her best. *I don't need magic,* she thought to herself. *I am strong enough to take care of me now. I don't need power like that.*

The pattering of footsteps shot up the stairs. Kayden closed her book in a hurry, placed it on the side table, and lay on her bed. Lira creaked the door open and slipped in.

"Sleeping in your armor?" she asked jokingly.

"Very funny," Kayden scoffed. "How was dinner?"

"It was great! Why didn't you join us?" She glanced over to the side table, spotting the big book. "Were you reading?"

"A little," Kayden replied casually. "I just felt like relaxing." She sat up and turned toward the window. The stars were out, and she needed time to cool off.

"Do you read often? I love reading. I used to read books all the time in—" she paused. "In Solmarsh. I learned in the temples when I was being taught divine magic."

Oh right, Kayden recalled. *That's her old town. That's concerning.* She remembered Callidan saying the tortured prisoners were being sent there. "I read a bit, when I can."

Kayden read more than a bit. She'd read every book in the old sandy library in Zenato. It was rarely populated, as most people in Zenato couldn't read or write. Kayden's parents taught her how to do both when she was young. While growing up alone, she found solace in reading. Even if she hated something, she read about it.

"Are you worried about your town?" Kayden asked. *Of course she is. But I can't just jump into it.*

Lira sat down on her bed, facing Kayden. She got a little teary-eyed. "Of course I am." She looked to the floor, curling her lower lip in. "I left because of my brother, and now the town is in danger. He's in danger too, and to make it worse, he might be there. What if I'd stayed? Something might be different. I could have found him. Now Asheron's brother is involved, maybe stealing their life with some form of blood magic." Divine magic had many forms—and blood magic was gifted from Baelogar, the Beast of the Abyss.

"Princess, come on. You can't help what's happened. Instead of being alone, you have a team now. We all can find out what's going on, all right?"

Lira's head didn't rise again. She didn't seem to hear a word. Kayden leapt off her bed, and lifted Lira's chin to look at her. "Chin up, princess. It'll be fine." Lira's sad, glistening eyes were identical to hers, years ago. It was a very different time, then. *I want to work alone, but I can't just leave her.* She said the same thing Lira told her the previous night. "We'll do it together."

Lira sniffled, coming back to reality. "Okay, thanks." Her dark copper skin shone in the lantern light as she smiled, finally. Kayden let her chin go, and Lira's expression changed to a curious one. "Can I ask you something?"

She better not ask about that drake in the manor, Kayden thought. She could only stand the thought of Callidan now that he was dead. She was a member of the guild for eight years, where she was controlled, punished, and alienated. She believed she couldn't do any better, worth nothing more than thievery. She knew different now. Kayden made her own fate. "It's about Callidan, isn't it?"

"Yes. It's okay if you don't want to talk about it—it must not be easy," Lira said quietly.

"No, it isn't," Kayden agreed. She felt like she could tell Lira, as she was honest, loyal, and kind. "Go ahead, ask."

"What did he do?" Lira asked quietly.

Kayden's eyes connected with Lira's dark ones, and she took a deep breath. "He worked for the Guild of Shades, like I did. When we messed up, we were taken to him." Kayden spoke in a quiet tone. "I didn't mess up, but others said I did. Many times."

Lira waited a moment, and scratched her neck. "Is that why you touched your back in the manor? Got upset when I—"

"Yes." Kayden got up.

"May I—May I see?" Lira spoke barely above a whisper, as if afraid of her own voice.

Am I ready for this? She hadn't shown anyone her scars, let alone her body as a whole, for a long time. She didn't like being touched, or even seen. Her skin crawled from the memories of her past. She carefully undid her armor, revealing her loose-fit, ocean blue linen shirt and matching pants beneath.

"You want to know why I hated him? This is one of the reasons," she explained. Kayden lifted her cloth shirt, revealing her back. Lira squeaked a gasp as Kayden displayed a massive, raised, three-inch wide scar, slashed from the upper left to lower right sides, encompassing over half the skin there. The rest was covered in scars as well, but they were just minor cuts and gashes. There were also malformed, pale red scars where smooth olive skin used to be. Kayden could still feel the blades dragging across her back, one by one, opening her flesh more and more.

"Without healing magic, I would have bled to death. Healing may be effective, but it doesn't hide scars." A rush of ice crawled up Kayden's spine. She felt sick from the thought of it, let alone revealing it to someone else. She quickly dropped her shirt, still faced away. She didn't hear a response. She turned her head to see Lira standing up, eyes hidden by the onyx black hair sweeping in front of her smooth-featured face.

Lira sniffled loudly and pulled Kayden into a hug.

Kayden yelped. This was the second hug she got from Lira in two days, and it was unsettling. Lira's brother was missing, Domika hadn't seen hers for over a decade, and Vesper lost his family. Kayden wasn't the only one who lost something. She wasn't sure about Mags, but she saw scars on his wrists, neck, and hands. He hadn't shown anything further than that, and he bathed in private. *We all have scars,* she thought. *It's the scarred ones who fight. But what are they fighting for?* she wondered. *What am I fighting for?*

Lira wasn't muscular at all but had a foot on Kayden in height. She held her tightly, quietly crying. "I'm sorry, I'm sorry." She kept repeating her apology, over and over again.

Sorry for what? Kayden thought. She dealt with it as best she could, and finally took her vengeance for it. "Don't worry, Lira. There's a reason I showed you. I can trust you, right?" *I also want to teach you a lesson.*

Lira relaxed, looking Kayden in the eye. "Of course, I won't tell a soul. Not a person, or a tree, rock, or anything." Lira went a bit overboard, but Kayden appreciated the effort. Lira released her, stepped back, and sat down again. Lira clearly wondered why she'd shown her the scar, but it was for a good reason.

Kayden had also been naive, self-conscious, and the opposite of confident, once upon a time. She made many mistakes, gained many scars, and watched her parents die. Lira watched her brother be taken, and he may have been dead already. It was only a matter of time before she blamed herself—if she hadn't already. "Lira, it isn't your fault."

Lira picked at her nails and rubbed her neck. "What isn't?"

"Your brother's arrest. It isn't your fault. I don't want you to blame yourself."

Lira dropped her head into her hands and cried quietly. "But it is—it *is*. If I had just stayed inside, he would still be safe, at least with the military." Her voice cracked and grew weak. "I had to go out. I just had to do it." Lira's hands shook as she tried to rub her knees. "And Malakai came here. He's—well, I'm sure you've heard stories."

She heard enough. Sadist. Blood mage. Brother of the bastard who put them in jail. And now, he was involved. They said he had a hundred lives because he would be injured in battle and heal himself using the life of his victims. She saw that first-hand. Surely there was a way around it…

"It's all my fault."

Kayden leapt over to the bed and shook Lira gently. "Look at me. As the authority in blaming oneself, I don't want you to."

"What do you mean?" Lira sniffled.

"I blame myself every day. I have to tell myself it's not my fault. I tell myself that I didn't send my parents out that door, and that I didn't deserve the years of hell I went through because of it." Kayden let a tear slip out, and quickly wiped it away. "Your brother would be proud of you. Look at where you are and what you can do. Think about what happened last night."

"I just wanted to help. I did what I could." Lira moved her hair from her face, blinking to resist the welling of more tears.

Kayden just gave a subtle brittle smile. "I remember when we got to Rogan's office, I told you to search the office. You looked at me like a deer in the night caught by torchlight."

Lira let out a weak chuckle. "I hadn't done anything at that point. You just looked at the experienced ones and then chose me. It—it made no sense."

"Give yourself worth," Kayden said, nudging her. "I didn't know Mags well enough. Vesper was weird, Domika I didn't trust, Miggen, couldn't tell what he wanted." Looking toward her friend, she said, "I trusted you. If someone like you was working for a rebel force—" She paused for a moment. "Then you would have the most drive to finish the job."

Glancing over with reddened eyes, Lira gave her an inquisitive look. "Someone like me?"

She felt bad saying it. "Unskilled for infiltration. Clumsy with a weapon. Too innocent to betray. Too kind to rebel simply due to raw frustration with the system." She just shrugged. "Someone like you would want to finish the job for your own reasons. You were there because it was personal. It was the look in your eyes. You were afraid." With a nod, she finished her words. "But you wanted to be there."

Lira stared at the ground, wiping her now-snotty nose. "You know, you're really wise for your age. We're both so close in age and I know so little compared to you."

"With pain comes experience, princess," Kayden said. *It came at a great cost. I don't know if it was worth it.* She'd seen more horrors than some old men and women.

"You seem like you want to hide it. I don't get it." Lira's eyes deviated toward the side table. "You read a lot, don't you?"

"Can't get anything past you, can I." Kayden glanced to her book on the side table. "I do. I didn't have anyone to confide in for a long time, so I turned to reading. Now, don't tell anyone I actually care to learn." She wrapped her arm around Lira and pulled her in. "If you want to talk about your brother, let me know. I'll understand either way." Kayden got up and walked back to her bed and plopped down. "I know what it's like." Kayden suffered alone for years.

"Thanks, Kayden. You're really sweet."

"Keep that to yourself."

They sat in silence for a moment, looking out the window to a line of homes and shops sleeping with the night. Seeing the stars, the roofs, the darkness… "I'm glad I found you there."

Kayden smiled, to her surprise. "So am I." She couldn't find the words to thank her enough.

A knock came from the door.

"Who is it?" Kayden called.

Vesper opened the door and poked his head in. "Is everything well in here? I heard sounds of harsh words and crying."

"We were acting out a murder in here—you know, for fun!" Lira stuttered.

Kayden slinked back with wide eyes. Lira laughed awkwardly, but no one else did.

"Oh, I guess that was a bad joke. Sorry."

"Oh yes, Miss, that was not the best humor," Vesper said.

Lira's expression drooped. "Oh."

He doesn't have a filter. Kayden thought. "We'll work on that." Probably extremely off-humor due to the serious topics they were discussing.

"I just came to inform you that the rest of us are tending to our bedrooms. Miss Mirado will be up shortly, I am sure." Vesper's eyes veered toward the table between the beds, and the book resting upon it. He squinted, examining it. "Oh my! *Elemental Attunement!*" he exclaimed, leaping into the room.

"Whoa there, old man. What are you doing walking into the women's bedroom?" Kayden asked. "Why don't you take a step back?" *He's fairly imposing. Does he ever know when to hold off?* He definitely broke up a serious moment, and with such vibrance that it was off-putting.

Vesper walked to the book without a word. "Who was reading it, if I may ask? Was it you, Miss Kaar?"

Lira blinked with cow-eyes, placing her hand to her chest. He looked at Kayden.

"Yeah, it was her," Kayden said. She didn't want the whole world knowing she found magic interesting.

While her words told one story, Vesper clearly trusted Lira's obvious body language more. "I didn't know you read, Miss Ralta, let alone about magic! I could tell you so many things, if you wish. While some are not born with the gift, there are many things one can do in self-defense," he said.

I pull out my book once, and everyone suddenly finds out, she thought, rolling her eyes. *Everyone is so nosy.* Kayden just wanted to sit alone and read her book without her whole team bugging her about it. "Nah, I'm good," she shrugged him off.

"Well, I shall tell you anyway. My daughter pushed me away, but I knew she truly wished to listen. Plus, I'm nowhere near a sense of fatigue yet!" he plopped down beside her and opened the large book.

Kayden crossed her arms and turned away. "I don't want to learn about that stuff. I can't do anything with it."

"Nonsense! Here, look at this." Vesper flipped to a portion of the book on charms and control spells. "What would you do if you were attacked by a muddling charm, or a control charm? What then, *hmm*? Miss Ralta, you must always be prepared," Vesper said poignantly.

Lira had a silly smirk on her face, indicating that she knew Vesper wouldn't be leaving anytime soon. Kayden wasn't too tired, so it was fine. She had to humor him.

"No one controls me," Kayden growled.

Vesper chuckled. "Yes, excellent. That is the proper attitude." His forefinger crept along the seasoned pages of the book, reading the lessons on resisting. "It is like a voice telling you what to do. You can either agree or disagree. A powerful magician can fill one's mind with so much information that it makes her own thoughts so convoluted that they cannot be handled. That, or they simply choose to follow the orders to end the madness." He glanced over to Kayden. "That' is why you remind me of my daughter. Yes, she was tough, but she also had a will of steel."

Kayden sat quietly as he read about different effects. He went through charms, telekinesis, illusions, sleeping curses, and many others. She enjoyed hearing about it but didn't say so.

Lira listened attentively as well, especially when he got to the divine magic. Belief was the biggest predictor of casting power, aside from the gods-given limits, but self-confidence was necessary.

Kayden knew Lira had problems with it, but maybe in time things would change. Aside from minor scratches and cuts, Lira couldn't heal much of anything. Lira had a lot of faith in Shiada, but no sense of self-reliance or fortitude.

How can she be so afraid of everything? Kayden thought. *Then again, so was I.* Lira was the same age, almost, but she was sheltered in small towns, unaware of the relentless nature that the land really had. Kayden lived in quite a few places in the deserts and the north: the Capitals, the gambling valley town of Jahar, Lothrad in the north, and she'd spent a year in the Kholrani ice forests in the northeast, as well.

As Kayden listened to Vesper's speeches about spells, her mind wandered to the task at hand. Prisoners were being sent to Lira's home, as well as others, for reasons unknown. They had to report to Jirah, but it was a waste of time. She didn't mind ignoring an order here or there but wondered how the others felt.

"I do not wish to bore you any longer. I am slightly fatigued now and shall retire to my room. Miss Mirado will be up shortly, I am sure." Vesper closed the book and placed it on the table once more. He slowly scratched his beard as he got up and walked to the door. Kayden went and opened it for him, tapping her foot.

Vesper strolled out the door but turned to her as he reached it. "Miss Ralta, would you like me to teach you a few tricks of the trade? With some actual experience, I mean."

Kayden thought about his offer. *Why not Lira?* she wondered. Maybe his nostalgia was talking again, like teaching his daughter magic before her. *Is it for my benefit, or his?*

Possibly both, Kayden reasoned. She knew Lira would want to learn, too, and didn't want her to be put out. Then again, if she learned well enough, she could teach Lira anyway. Kayden felt bad. She glanced at Lira, who was facing away. She couldn't do it, at least while Lira could hear. "No, I'm good."

"*Hmm.* I see," he said, turning away.

She almost closed the door but poked her head out as Vesper headed to the other room.

"*Hey*," she whispered. Vesper turned, tilting his head to the side. Kayden smiled and nodded feverishly.

Vesper smiled widely, nodded back, and did a small jig as he entered his room.

Chapter Twenty-seven

Justice from Hate

Zaedor Nethilus

Zaedor lay silent for days. Kindro attempted to make some conversation; he didn't feel the same as Freya. Zaedor did not oblige his efforts. He did not lay silent because of her words. No, he did not speak because of his own inner turmoil that he was struggling to reconcile.

Both neighbors went away to fight, returning with a bruise or two, but that was all. *Congratulations to you both*, Zaedor thought. He sat in his wooden chair, leaned against the back of his cage. Zaedor spent his time thinking about the world, and the differences between what he believed to be, and what was. *My kingdom was strong*, he thought. *Was it all a lie? It couldn't have been—but I saw Amirion burned to ash.*

The images of his home entered his mind often. Colorful banners, with all sorts of animals and objects on fields of vibrant colors, were burned to black and grey. Buildings of once strong brick were broken in an instant by bombardment. Innocent faces flew through his mind: Lilanda, Lothel, the King and Queen, and Noah. *I will not forget you, any of you,* Zaedor swore.

His fists clenched, but he calmed himself quickly. *I will not enrage like that again. I must remain fierce, but not reckless and destructive, lest I be as the enemy army was.* In the ring, he became what he hated most.

He carefully glanced to Freya, who hadn't smiled since the news of Gorlin's death. She was friends with Gorlin before he became a breaker. Kindro attempted to talk to her about it, but she didn't give much information up.

Although they didn't speak to him, Zaedor listened to their conversations. Freya spoke of life in the north, the different delicacies and traditions they had, and holidays Zaedor hadn't ever heard of before. They had the largest festival of Air, celebrating the end of the year. Much died over the season of Air, and much came to live again when the Water returned. They didn't see the Air as a deathly cold, but a rebirth of life. Every citizen would have a plan for something they wished to gain and pushed for change when the Season ended.

There were plays and other performances, large displays of magic that warmed the streets with many flames and torches through the streets by the Council of the Magi, and an exchange of gifts within families. Freya seemed to miss it, but spoke otherwise. Orinas was once a province of Renalia, but now a nation of its own. It was well-structured by laws, and the people preferred it that way. It reminded Zaedor of Amirion.

Kindro lived in the Risen Isles early in his life. He spoke of its prosperity and trading routes with the outlanders from Doderia to the far East. Their current leader, Raiya Firkann, was well respected across the islands, as well as in the deserts, or so he said. Kindro spoke well of their foods, traditions, and laws. Each island was a nation in itself. The region was ruled by a council with a single representative from each isle, with one chosen by the each to lead them. Zaedor involuntarily frowned whenever the Zenato was mentioned. *Rawling is still a traitor,* he thought. *The late King Bracchus Tirilin's own brother.* He could not forgive such heinous acts.

From what Zaedor could remember, strength was valued there more than anything, and it was proven in the coliseum. If one were stronger, they gained respect, riches, and exceptions to laws. *Pitiful. A man should be judged on his respect for others, his honor, and his contribution to society, not how dangerous he can be in combat.* The warriors of Amirion who attended the games said those who won in the arena were granted a wish from the Lord himself, if he could even be called that. Zaedor would never accept a gift from a monster like him.

Word in the pit was that there was more than just war between the nations themselves. A rebellion rose due to the injustice within Loughran. It was none of Zaedor's concern; injustice was rampant all over the land.

Zaedor looked around at all of the broken souls in the room. He knew more of their names now: Lirkosh the Hydris, Drena the Blazik, Lawrence the Broken, Rhogen the Human. He thought the other races were very peculiar. The Hydris intrigued him, a strange snake-like race that made his skin crawl.

Blaziks also seemed intimidating, being reminiscent of half-Devils, the vile fiends who lived as mercenaries, sent to pillage trading towns and set flame to farms, or so he'd heard.

Each person in captivity fought for their lives; they denied death every day with the hope that they may one day escape. Zaedor knew they weren't alone. He also felt this way since the night his city died. He was still furious at what happened and wanted revenge but felt helpless.

He wanted to make a difference, and knew vindication was the way to make it happen.

For the first time since the burning of his home, he truly looked inward. *What is my purpose?* he wondered. Before, he'd followed and represented Shiada's teachings, and furthered the prosperity of his kingdom and the happiness of those he interacted with. *Is my purpose to extend my hand, making those around me happy?* He certainly saw a lack of it where he sat in the prison dome.

He wished he could have saved his people, thinking over and over in his head wondering what he could have done. He was a useless fool. He couldn't save his friends, his king, or even a boy.

He needed to leave the past behind, but he couldn't. He wouldn't. *Don't forget us*, Noah had said. In his mind, he stood in the broken city once more, hearing the screams, watching the flames and broken structures. But there was one thing he forgot. *The orb*, he thought. *What was that orb?* It was a deep violet collection of mist high in the sky stealing souls on both sides of battle.

His mind was unable to shake the thought. Violet was the associative color with Lornak, the god of darkness, but he was dead for almost two thousand years. *Could he possibly return?* Zaedor wondered. The orb was possibly the work of another vile deity such as Azoran, Lord of the Hells, or Baelogar, the Beast of the Abyss. He wished he could find some sort of clue or indication of what it had been, so maybe he could seek justice for his people's ruination.

He wondered if he was the only survivor of the attack—though some may have escaped the city or been far from it when the army arrived. He hoped his wife Eryndis was still alive. He had to discover if she still lived. He still had love for her, despite their estrangement—and he found it difficult to believe a general of Amirion's army would vanish so silently. However, she visited the King of Zenato—the King that killed Zaedor's own—prior to the massacre.

He grabbed at feathers in the wind, attempting to find a way to stop the villains, or to help his people. There were nameless soldiers in his city that night, except—

Cloaker. *Murderous knave.* He jumped forward in his seat. He heard Cloaker's voice the night before the death of his home. "They're finishing it in Solmarsh," Zaedor whispered aloud. *Gods, why didn't I know to do something then—but how would I have known?* Zaedor did not know of Solmarsh. They'd mentioned it was a small town. Maybe if he went there, he would learn more. The only marshlands that he knew about were in the west. He had to take a chance.

Blood rushed through Zaedor's veins as he found a new purpose. *Bring justice, not revenge, for his people.* His purpose would drive him into a new era of man. *I can't sulk and hate. I've hurt so many already.* He glanced over to Freya, who stood leaning on the far end of her cage. *Her friend is dead because of me.*

Zaedor always defined himself by his god, his city, and his king. He saw these as part of himself—and he, a small part of them. *What does that make me now?* Shiada abandoned him, he knew. He spent his life putting faith in deities, while he should have had more faith in himself. He needed to carve his own path. *Gods don't make the man. The man makes himself.* His city was gone; he always was 'Zaedor of Amirion,' but it meant nothing now. *I am a man of good, of justice, of honor. Not of gods, cities, or kings. I will save those in need, and the people of Amirion need my help—perhaps in the marshes of the west.*

He had to make peace for what he did. He was been beaten, broken, and kidnapped, but that did not excuse what he did in return. He'd killed a man with a wife and three children. He couldn't take that back, but he could atone for what he did. *The man makes himself.*

"Kindro?"

Kindro jumped in his seat, probably surprised to hear Zaedor speak for the first time in days. He sauntered over with his chair and planted himself down. "Finally deciding to talk?"

"Yes. I apologize for what I did. I was wrong. I realize that now."

"We've all made mistakes. We're all stuck here."

Zaedor knew Kindro was a forgiving man, so he accepted that. He placed a hand on Kindro's muscular shoulder and nodded with a smile. Thankfully, Kindro returned it. Zaedor rose from his chair, toward the division of his and Freya's cage.

After a deep, anxiety-ridden breath, he spoke up to the one who hated him. "Freya?"

Freya looked to him with contempt. "What?"

He didn't dance around the point. "I'm sorry. I was a fool, and I know that now. He was your friend, and I murdered him in cold blood for my hate of someone else."

Freya's eyes widened. She turned and leaning against the divide. "I told you to become that way. I shouldn't have been so pushy about it—"

"No. You are not at fault. I was told to stop, but I continued my vengeful path." Zaedor looked to the hard floor. "I destroyed a family, and one day I must to atone for it."

Freya sighed, looking toward the rest of the room. "Funny, I have a hard time believing you're going to get the chance to do that." Her voice trailed off with a sigh. "You seem sincere. Fine, I accept your apology. You're still sheltered as all hell, though. One day you're going to talk to his wife yourself, if you can. I'll make sure of that."

Zaedor nodded. She was right, he needed a way out. They all did. *Does the plan have to be complex?* he thought. There were many doors in the long hall beyond their room, and only in some instances were the prisoners removed from their cages. He looked at Kindro, then the guards, the other prisoners, and finally, the hall. It suddenly all came together. It was reckless, it was stupid, but it could—no, it *must*—work. "I might get the chance. We all might."

Kindro and Freya looked to him, muddled.

"I have a plan," Zaedor claimed, tapping his forefinger to his chin, drawing his eyes to the guards, to the door, and finally, to his partner in the cage.

"I thought you were a law-abiding gentleman, Zaedor-of-Amirion," Freya said mockingly.

"Not when the law is slavery," Zaedor replied in a cold tone.

Chapter Twenty-eight

A Haven of Unseen Strength

Saul Bromaggus

Saul and the others failed once more in Elaston. The region was filled with forests. It reminded Saul of the Vale, with the exception that the trees were strange. They were more russet-brown, rather than the blackwood of the Vale. The forests were thick and humid, the leaves were broad and shiny, and lush moss covered every part of the forest's floors, it seemed. The wood burned brighter in their camps, the skies seemed clearer than Saul saw before.

Saul didn't mind the travel, as it reminded him of his training in the wilderness. The other Broken were restless, panicking more as they reached the Plateau border. Fae grew more reluctant to follow his rule, but chose to stay with the group until Shi'doba.

Elaston was a grand city, with smokey stone walls. They were very peculiar, more cowardly than Saul expected from a city in the Neck. *Then again, no one could be as bad as Rhoba. Spineless wretches.* He was right to cut each and every one of them down.

Elaston was afraid of outsiders. The guards questioned them endlessly about their intentions, about their goods, beliefs, combat ability, farming experience, racial preferences, thoughts on the Dragon of the Vale, and infinitely more. In the end, they still weren't allowed in. They saw only the guards: one Human, one Hydris, and no more. A pale-skinned, vibrato-voiced fool, and a slithering, shaking snake. Their voices were untrained. There was reluctance in their tongues and a severe lack of sophistication in their words. Something was off—Saul was sure of that—but there was no way they could get through the massive stone gate, or climb the wall, and thus, turned away.

With each passing day, Broken morale depleted. Each began questioning his or her purpose. Many asked why they couldn't make their own city in Rhoba, while the others said it was cursed land. Saul knew it was a place defiled by blood magic. They sought a new home, in one of the other seven cities, if they would have them.

Saul felt drawn to the Plateau, not knowing why. They were walking into a civil war and did not know what to expect. It was unknown who was winning, where the line was, or if the battle was simply comprised of secret meetings and small skirmishes. Fae and a few of the others wished to go to the capital to join the main force, while others stuck with Saul, wanting more information. *Rushing in could get them killed.*

He only knew that Hydris were cowards, a foolish race that used others. They and the Broken were once allies, but betrayed by the leader, Cadrayda Kashral, head of the Hydrian council, two hundred years past. The war raged slowly—and sometimes silently—for years above the Neck, until the Broken master of Earth, Lok'thori, split Kathynta in two. *Why did he not sink their land?* Saul wondered. *Possibly so that we may claim it for our own one day.* He did not wish to help the damned snakes. They betrayed his people. *But if there was a war over the Broken…*

Days upon days passed until the final city of the Neck rose on the horizon. Their Ravagers were exhausted. Although bred to ride for miles upon miles, they'd had no true rest in days. Saul's back and legs burned beyond belief. With the seven cities being isolated and withdrawn, especially Elaston, they worried about not finding a home. When the final city appeared, Saul wondered whether they would find hope there, or more disappointment.

Shi'doba was a smaller city than the others. It was encased within a series of large wooden pillars dug deep into the ground, with leather coatings extending from one to the next to form a weak wall. Saul saw many herds running through the plains as they exited the Elastonian Jungle, and they did not seem in short supply. As they approached closer, many of the buildings within were built with wood of the forests, a smooth russet-brown with straw roofs from the plains. In the distance around the city, he could see farms of corn, turnip, and potato, with many more in the distance.

Two Hydrian guards stood at the entrance, their narrowed eyes staring at the Broken who approached. *What in the hells are they looking at us like that for?* Saul thought. A couple more Hydris and many Humans passed by the entrance, making double-takes. Every one of them did.

The group came to a halt before the guards, each clad in azure scale mail but no cloaks, and battered leg plates. Saul spotted the insignia of a mountain on their shoulder plates.

"Is this Shi'doba?" Saul asked. He was suspicious of them. He looked to the others, who kept their hands on their weapon hilts and hafts.

"It is. What is your business here?" one guard demanded.

"We seek shelter, at least for the night." Saul gave the lightest touch he could, as this was the final city before the Plateau. He did *not* want to go further south just yet, even if he felt pulled there.

Nor did he wish to take shelter and gather food from the damned Hydris, but they had no choice. He needed time to decide and, with Fae's lack of patience, he didn't have long. With every day she grew more irritable, and the other Broken began to ignore commands. Some were cynical of the Vale teachings.

The guards exchanged curious glances. They shifted their eyes. "I'm not so sure," the same guard said in a hissing tone.

Saul eyed them carefully. "Is something wrong?"

"N—no, nothing's wrong." The guard's attention was off.

Saul glanced back toward the north, with jungles far unseen on the horizon. Food was plentiful there, but twenty Broken living in a damned forest was not a good life—and one with no purpose. Their choice was between seeking refuge in a city with some Hydris on the border of the Plateau or going into the Plateau itself.

"Oh, for gods sakes. Lyrshal, let them in. Hurry!" a modulated, silvery voice called out from between their shoulders in the Hydrian tongue. Saul was glad the Chromatan academy learned it; it was close to the language of the Dragons, and they needed to know the words of their enemies.

Here were enemies he actually sought refuge with—and this one weaved between strongly built guards with meticulous grace and no weapon—simply a small Hydrian woman with a finely-crafted magenta dress.

The guard, Lyrshal, growled a response to the small woman. "We can't, Lady Thalia. You saw what happened last time,"

What happened *what* time?" Fae growled from beside Saul. Always speaking out of turn.

The so-called Thalia waved a dismissive hand. "Nothing. We'll speak about it in time," she said in an innocent tone. "Come with me, all of you. We have plenty of room." Her azure, snake-like eyes bore into Saul's. "And you are—"

"Saul Bromaggus," he replied.

She smiled devilishly, looked across them, and eyed Saul up and down. "A pleasure; my name is Thalia. Come with me, and quickly. It's safe here. If you don't trust me, then you're free to leave."

Saul walked forward grudgingly. This Hydrian woman, Thalia, was more forward than those in Rhoba. This being the last city in the neck, Saul felt forced to enter by his own need to avoid the Plateau. The only places left for them to go were the Plateau itself, and the Blackcore Mountains where the Dark Terran Miners lay.

She walked with a commanding swagger, leading them with a flick of her finger. The guards sighed and moved aside. The Broken followed her, keeping their eyes on the surroundings. Her long, thick hunter green hair was decorated by silver and gold piercings along her rigid ears, and her braids shone brightly in the sunlight. She turned periodically to wave to and greet citizens, ocean-like azure eyes giving warm tidings. For a peculiar reason, she reminded him of the vale, hair as the dark canopy above, skin as the light ferns below.

It was fascinating to see such a small woman be regarded so well. She was a short and narrowly built, five feet and two inches, possibly—and likely unfit for any form of combat. She was half the size of Mirakia Othellun, his old Warmaster. Saul thought this new Hydris weak—hardly commanding in a Broken society. But with every smile she gave, they bowed. With every bow she graced them with, they bowed lower.

He watched each citizen they passed, seeing many double-take, or glance. They were a modest people, homes in the shape of cones made with large wooden pillars, leather, and cloth, leaving a smoke vent at the top. Others were built with wood from the forests, strongly made with sidings, and several gardens in behind for fruits and vegetables. Few were built with stone, only select ones made for people of a higher status, Saul assumed.

There was one distinguishable note of all houses in the city. All of them, without exception, were damaged in some way. The high-set cloth homes were covered in patchwork, the wooden homes broken and battered, wooden slats filling in the holes, fences were left dangling, and gardens were ripped up. The brick homes had breaks in the walls and makeshift mortar patched each one.

"What happened to the houses in this place?" Saul spoke up.

"We will talk about that when we get inside," Thalia said. "Be patient."

Saul could only feel impatient, and the situation reminded him of Rhoba. He had been led through that city, nicely and quietly, and then imprisoned. "I don't like being led to a mysterious place without knowing the purpose," Saul scoffed.

Thalia stopped abruptly and turned with a powerful step. Her silk, magenta robe swished along the earth below, revealing bare feet. The rest of the Broken jumped back, but Saul didn't flinch. She crossed her arms and eyed them carefully, particularly their arms. "Some of your allies have scars on their arms. Did you come from Rhoba?"

That took Saul aback. *She knew about the disgraces of that place and she took them in—and for what?*

"That's what I thought." She turned back. "Do not worry, this place is not like that." Her tone was modulated.

Saul felt he could trust her words, possibly. Gorum's tone was honeyed and discerning, while hers was bold and straightforward. He didn't sense a lie, but she was still a damned Hydris. Regardless, Saul wasn't planning on drinking any tea here. They passed a large stone building where Saul heard crashing of steel. He stopped abruptly. "There's a training area?" Saul asked, trying to contain his need for battle.

"Yes, but it's small. We try to keep it up, but there are some issues with that. We'll speak of that once we get to the homestead." She continued walking, waving for them to follow without looking back.

What is the homestead? He assumed it was a place to keep them for a time, since there were twenty Broken walking into their city. Saul was still suspicious, keeping his hand on his blade hilt. Thalia walked ahead with a strut, no weapon or anything visible on her. *How can she trust us? She's a Hydris. We are sworn enemies.*

His grip tightened on his blade as he eyed the townspeople around him. Each Hydris they passed looked to them with wide eyes but did not run or shrink back. They continued to till their small fields and gardens, hammer their nails, and tan their leathers. They seemed to be a simple people, but the repair of buildings, minimal plants in the farms, lack of leathers at the tanner's, and no blades hanging at the blacksmith was concerning.

As they walked, Saul looked down to her bare feet again. Walking upon such rough ground while wearing such fine silk was enough for him to speak up. "Why do you walk in bare feet? The ground is rough and stone-covered." Her habit confused him, and almost made him uncomfortable.

"I prefer the feeling of the ground. It's sort of soothing, don't you think?" She chuckled. With an abrupt stop, she waved her hand toward a long, stone building. "Here we are."

They came to a large stone building with a well-made, wood-planked roof. It was as large as the barracks in the Vale, which housed a hundred men. Its mortar was pale as the moon, and the stones were a smoky grey. She walked forward to the large oak door, which rushed open with a swish of her finger.

Saul raised his eyebrow, looking to the others. He reluctantly followed. Saul knew nothing of magic, and it was rare for a Broken to be versed in it, if any even were. Magic was seen as cowardly in some of the clans, as Wizards spent hours reading and little time in actual combat. The Hydris were not known for their magical abilities, either, but it was not unheard of to be so inclined. He kept his left hand on his hilt and cautiously approached the door. The others followed.

It was a large, open building with rough stone walls like the outside, and lined with beds. She led them to a seating room on one side with a long oak table, motioning for them to sit. There were twelve broad wooden chairs in all; some Broken sat, and the rest stood against the wall.

Thalia slid into the chair at the end, crossed her legs, and relaxed into a leisurely lean. "I'll be frank. The people of Shi'doba are Broken sympathizers."

"We don't need sympathy," Saul growled. He looked to the others, and they nodded in agreement.

Thalia waved her hand gracefully, but dismissively. "Oh, of course not. Why then are you wandering the Neck in search of a home?" Saul could hear grumbles from the others. "There's a civil war in the Plateau, did you know?"

"Yes, we're aware of it," Saul said plainly.

"Aware of it? You're *afraid* of it!" Fae slammed her fist across the table. Others yelled in agreement. Saul detested that they would even think that of him.

"I'm not afraid. Their business is not ours, and they are our sworn enemies!" Saul pointed to Thalia.

Thalia cleared her throat. "*Ahem*, I'm right here." Her voice was as smooth as silk. "Is that what you learn in the north? That I'm your enemy?"

"Your people. We've warred for centuries." But the words of his goddess crossed through his thoughts once more. *If you had to choose between joining forces with an orderly and strong Hydrian society or a dishonorable, backstabbing Broken one, which would you choose?*

He didn't know.

Thalia laughed. "The last true war was two hundred years ago. Do you know anything about that war?" she said, swishing her hand across the table.

"The Hydris provoked us. We defended ourselves, and the power of Lok'thori, who delivered the Vale from their treachery." Saul had been told that since he was young. Stories of the Hydris, who were once peaceful, but betrayed them and started a war that lasted years upon years.

Thalia gnashed her teeth. "Lok'thori saved both. The Broken were insulted by a peace treaty and attacked the Plateau. Do they tell you that up there?"

None of them had a response. *We attacked them? No, that's impossible,* Saul thought.

A smirk grew from the corner of Thalia's lips. "No, I didn't think so. That's what that Dragon tells you. That we're at war, and that we're the enemy. Is that right?"

"We have no reason to think otherwise." Saul said bluntly. "That's—"

"The reason your hand hasn't left your hilt yet?" Thalia cut in, eyes locked on Saul's.

She was clearly observant, and alert. Her ears were perkier than those of others, as if listening to every sound within a mile. Her slit of an iris scanned everyone at every moment, and made it seem effortless. "Now, enough of wars and enemies." The *clack* of her sharp, deep green nails upon the wooden table echoed through the room. "Tell me, how did you escape Rhoba? Rumors from the northern cities is that those drakes had a shield no one could get through. If you get in, you don't come out."

Each Broken turned his or her gaze to Saul.

Saul cleared his throat, feeling the gaze of the entire room. "I got out."

"He got *everyone* out. I saw him break the chains himself," Drof said. He tapped his fingers on the table as he stared downward. "Rhoba is destroyed. Everyone is gone, either they've run or died."

Thalia sat up straight and narrowed her eyes. "Everyone is—dead? You all killed them?"

"*He* killed all of them," Fae corrected her.

Thalia gave a sly smile. "And they deserved it," she said calmly, raising her chin. Saul leaned back, almost wanting to laugh. He didn't think she would condone it, not that he cared.

Thalia tapped an index finger to her chin. "Fascinating," her voice trailed off, eyeing Saul carefully.

"What's fascinating?" Saul said in a suspicious tone.

"Nothing," Thalia dismissed him with a wave, still giving him a side-eye. "Well, it's good you got out of there. Although they've given the rest of the Neck a bad view of your people, sorry to say." She sighed, face tightening slightly.

An air of awkwardness grew over the room as each Broken realized they relied on this new enemy for aid.

"Now, let's get back to the point. There is war across the Plateau, whether you like it or not, and it's over Broken. The civil force is small, but they're gaining support quickly due to the bastard who's leading them. They're called the 'Stormwardens' after Ithaca's self-proclaimed title the 'Soldier of Storms.'" She winced at the mention of it.

A couple Broken attempted to interject, but Thalia raised her hand and kept talking. "I'm sure you've wondered why several of our buildings are damaged. The civil forces especially seek out sympathizers and happens to cross into the Neck to come for us. All of our townspeople are trained in basic combat, but we're still just farmers and tanners. It's only a matter of time before they return." Her tone grew brittle.

"I fear they will move for the capital soon. Our ruler, Kovos, wishes to seek peace with the Broken, or at least wishes to extend his hand to show the wish for unity. The Blazik Lords of Feyamin are stirring, and the King wishes to unify so that war does not come from two fronts. He believes that if we do not unite, both perish."

"If only it were that simple," Saul said. "The dastardly Dragon commands them and teaches them to hate all others. How does this 'Kovos' plan to deal with him?"

"I didn't say unify with Obelreyon," Thalia said, slamming the table. "I said your *people*. Surely they don't enjoy his rule. A storm has gathered over the spire off the south cliffs recently. It's a sign, Kovos believes."

Saul looked to the others, who in turn looked left and right, to each one of them.

"Spire? What spire?"

"Surely you have seen a map before?" Thalia groaned.

"Don't insult me." Saul pulled out his map of Kathynta. The map detailed the Vale in the northwest with the Fangs, the Torch to the northwest, the Neck of the Seven, and the Plateau to the south, with the continent of Feyamin across the southern sea. Nothing off the coast.

Thalia eyed the map closely. Her long hair spilled over the map like a hunter green river. "Huh. Interesting." She chuckled. "Well, that's entertaining, especially with those marks of yours."

My marks? What about them? Saul scratched his head and raised a brow. Thalia smiled devilishly and pulled out her own map. It was similar, but with less detail of the Vale, and more on the Plateau. Many more towns and villages were highlighted, and a small, thin column emerged from the south coast of Serpentarius with three winds crashing into one another set over it.

"The Stormspire—" Saul's voice dropped off. "What is it?"

"It's Gadora's monument. Many worship her in the Plateau, though I favor Yggranda. Her monument is hidden in Feyamin."

Saul hadn't seen a worshipper of Gadora for some time. With the markings of Broken, it was easy to discern. With Hydris and other races, it was far more difficult. He trusted Thalia's strong words, spoken confidently and clearly.

Thalia sat back and slouched into her chair once more. "Either way, the monument is there. I know your people are a devoted bunch, but none can climb it. The storm is too dangerous." She sighed. "But that's beside the point. As for the civil war, those traitors kill those who don't agree with them. They especially hunt broken. They're a small force, but they fight like cowards."

Cowards. More of them fighting with disgrace. It's as Gadora told me in my dream. A storm is coming, Saul thought. *Magicians are cowards too, aren't they? How can I trust this slitherer of a woman?* Saul frowned as he shifted his eyes to Thalia and back to the map.

"Regardless, you are welcome to stay here. If they enter town, I recommend you don't engage them. They take supplies and kill those who resist. I think you can assume what they'll do with Broken such as yourselves. We don't provoke them because it's simply not a good idea."

"You just let them take advantage?" Fae growled. The other Broken were in an uproar. "*You're* a bunch of damned cowards! Running and hiding, while they hunt our people?"

Thalia stopped dead. Her azure eyes darkened as if a storm loomed over the ocean within. She rose slowly without a break of eye contact. "These people are farmers and tanners, little lady." The room grew dead silent, save for the subtle breeze beyond the window. "They haven't trained in combat for years, like you have." As one hand grew to a fist, it was as if her grip clenched the room itself. "We are not cowards—we are survivors."

Fae shot up out of her chair. "I can't stay in a city where you cowards shrink away. Some of us want to go to the capital to join with the others. It is my fate to protect the Hydris, especially those who fight with honor and with my people, not this mix with Humans. If we stay here, we'd become cowards like you—"

Thalia slammed her fist on the table, cracking the wood below, and throwing the room to a deafening silence once again. "Do not challenge me." She bared her teeth, revealing pointed fangs readied with venom. "Unless you would like to prove who the true coward is in this room," Thalia snarled.

"Fae, stop this now." Saul tried to silence the others before Thalia spoke further. "We must stay together!"

Thalia raised her chin high to Fae Joran. "Your people cower under the rule of a Dragon; you are no different. At least we have some respect. I thought you would be the same." Thalia said boldly. Her face was tight, brow furrowed. "If you do not wish to stay, you are welcome to leave."

Fae grumbled. "So be it. I am going to the capital whether you fools like it or not. I am no coward unlike these people. Whoever wants to go, come with me. Stay with these fools if you wish."

Saul was furious with Thalia's insult, but petty arguments were getting them nowhere. "Stop this!" he bellowed. "You cannot recklessly go into the Plateau not knowing where to go or who to trust! We must wait!" Saul could barely believe his own words. Mirakia Othellun told him to run, to survive, and he had. He wouldn't be as reckless as before.

Fae scoffed at his words. "*Pitiful.* You call yourself a Broken, and yet you speak to this tiny witch like she deserves respect from us. We followed, and now some of us are done with it. You freed us—that's all. You have our thanks, but we don't follow a Broken with no purpose, no destiny, and no self-respect."

The small Hydris, Thalia, tilted a head toward the towering Fae Joran. Clearing her throat, the room stopped to listen. "Miss—Fae, was it?" the only sound to break the silence was the clack of dagger-like nails on wood.

"Fae Joran," she snarled. "Have something wasteful to say?"

The storm born in Thalias eyes raged. Saul felt as if the walls pulled in, and like the roof and earth below shuddered with Thalia's glare. But her ferocity lifted, the room relaxed with her demeanor, and with a calm tone, she said, "Good luck on your journey."

Fae and several others got up and left the room. Saul heard the crash of the oak door upon the frame, grumbles and curses following after it. Saul looked around to see only eight remaining, Drof and himself included. They looked to him with wide eyes and curled-in lips. Saul wished to go after the others, but he knew there was no use. He didn't want to keep any who refused to stay.

With a long, drawn-out sigh, Thalia's posture relaxed, and she closed her eyes. "Well that didn't go as well as I expected." Thalia sighed and shook her head. "Your people can be a bit—*brash.*"

"They're proud. They don't like hiding, and neither do I."

"Understandable. However, you aren't hiding here, you're surviving. If you feel drawn to go, I won't argue. The people here are aligned with the capital of the Plateau. It's more of a diplomatic outpost to the Neck." She leaned back again and motioned to the door. "As I mentioned, the living quarters are in there. I hope you don't mind sleeping in the same room." She rose from her chair and meandered to the door. "Would you like to stay?"

The rest of the Broken nodded. Saul did so curiously, as she gazed lengthily at him.

"Well, like I said, there's a trapdoor below this table if you ever need to keep quiet. I know you aren't fond of hiding, but it's there if you require it. Welcome to Shi'doba," she said with a sweet smile. Without another word, she flashed a beaming, fanged smile, and passed through the front door.

Some slept peacefully and well that night, but Saul was restless. He fought with himself over the decision to stay or go, and he sensed that the others did the same. The recurring nightmare still raged in his mind; the lightning struck him until he awoke from the pain, and his screams woke the others each time.

The group would walk through the town intermittently, as Thalia provided them with some silver for a few nights. Over that time, Saul spoke to Thalia here and there, at least when she came to check on them. She was respectful, and helpful with their needs during their stay. But he still fought with the decision. *I feel as though I should go with the others. Like I should chase after them. They are in danger. Each abandoned us, yes, but who's to say they do not deserve an ally?* Saul paced back and forth in the main forum before the front door, fighting over the definitions of his people. His experience in Rhoba shook the very foundation on which he'd lived.

A powerful knock came from the door, causing him to jump. As he opened it, Thalia stood wearing a silk robe reminiscent of peaches from the vale and bearing a smug smile. The gleaming rays of sun caused her hair to glow bright green. "Saul, I would speak with you privately. Will you come with me?"

Saul glanced to the others sitting in the room, raising an eyebrow to her. "Yes, I will." He walked out briskly, following her out the front door. "Where are we going?" Saul asked, striding up beside her.

"My home. I have a couple of things I wish to speak with you about."

Saul didn't inquire further. She clearly wished to wait until they arrived. She led him through the marketplace, where there were displays of various potatoes, turnips, carrots, and other earthen vegetables grown in the area. There were butchers as well, as the fields surrounding the town were cultivated for raising cattle. The dust in the air made Saul cough; the constant steps of civilians tattered the grassy streets to dust and dirt.

"Are you the city leader?" Saul asked. "I did not ask before."

Thalia laughed. "Yes, I suppose you could say that. There are a few in town, so my presence isn't entirely necessary. I oversee new arrivals, and relations with the other cities. Except Rhoba, because that drake kept everyone out, and—well, you know the rest," She glanced over to him subtly, a hint of what seemed like concern in her eyes. "It must have been hard seeing that done to your people. Not the best impression of life south of the Fissure."

Saul nodded. "It was infuriating. The fact that people could betray their own to such a degree disgusts me." Saul remembered the smell of moist walls, rotten food, and shit. He was glad they were free, and that the traitors paid for their disgrace.

"Being part of a people means nothing," she said plainly.

"Being a part of my people is part of my being."

Thalia sighed, "Being part of *something* is important. You shouldn't restrict yourself to just a people, or else you'll end up like the ones you killed."

She didn't understand. *It was different.* In Saul's society, that's all there was: the clan, and the people.

"Before you go on a tangent about being part of your clan, and your people, and how important it is, remember this: people are important to you because you share values and customs."

Saul was so deep in thought that he almost tripped on a stone stair in front of him. He looked up to see a tall, thin wooden structure three floors high. The wood was pristine where it wasn't broken, and the door was colored a deep, fiery orange. Saul paused as he remembered what happened to him the last time he was led into a house by a seemingly kind leader.

Thalia walked a bit up the stairs and paused. "Is something the matter?" she asked.

"This is a bit familiar to the last city I was welcomed into," Saul said, narrowing his eyes.

Thalia let out a lengthy sigh and waved her hand dismissively. "I'm not going to give you anything to drink, and if I wanted to cast a charm on you to make you do what I want, I already would have. Satisfied?"

Saul was taken aback. She was brutally honest, and irritatingly bold. "I am not easily charmed," he growled, clenching his fists.

She seemed unaffected by his comment, laughing heartily, "Yes, Saul, and I'm not beautiful."

Saul tilted his head and raised a brow.

"I take it you don't understand humor, either," she chuckled. "Come now, I don't bite." She gnashed her teeth subtly, baring her sharp serpentine fangs, followed by a sarcastic side-smile. She unlocked the door with a key out of a small pocket at the side of her flowing robe, and sleekly pulled the door open.

Saul decided to follow, unsure of what to expect. While Gorum was sweet and solemn, Thalia was indeed kind, upfront, and bold. His hand still stayed on his blade's hilt, regardless. He wouldn't be caught unawares the second time around.

Upon entering, the building was indeed small. There was a set of bright yellow couches with a small table, and a modest kitchen with cutting boards, silver utensils, and several books scattered around the tables. Saul wondered what kinds of interesting spices and foods they had in Shi'doba and hoped that he could learn more from this land for his profession. But his survival came first.

She led him up a set of thin stairs, each step too small for his feet. He barely fit within the stairwell, forcing him to crouch and sidle. The next level of the home was lined with bookshelves filled to the brim, a small wooden chair and desk, and a larger, sky blue-cushioned chair with an intricate design of each of the elements embroidered onto it. The books were all sorts of sizes and colors, from a book the size of Saul's hand to one the size of Thalia's torso—which wasn't that large.

Saul could read somewhat, but not well. He understood some of the covers, but larger words escaped him. Many were about magic.

"Sit," Thalia said, pointing to the cushioned chair. He was glad to have that one, since he would surely break the smaller desk chair.

She led her forefinger along the bookcase, picking out a large red book, a small black one that was quite tattered and old, and another that was leather-bound and scratched beyond belief. She opened the leather-bound book and flipped through the pages, azure eyes rapidly scanning. "Do you have concerns with my spellcasting?" she asked.

He knew he should be more delicate, as she welcomed them to town, but he couldn't shake his attitude. "Magic is wrought with cowardice." Saul said bluntly. "Keeping your distance and avoiding your foes."

She continued to gander through the book with a tightened brow. "Oh really? What about a bow and arrow?"

"It can also be. If that is all the soldier is versed in, and then he runs from a melee. It is a natural ability to fight with bow, shield and blade, axe, or mace."

Thalia screwed her face into a frown, and then returned to a focused eye once more. "Being born with an affinity for the elements is natural. Just because one possesses the ability to use spells from a distance, doesn't mean we don't fight on the front lines. You shouldn't shame the natural abilities of others simply because you don't have them."

"I don't want them. I have what I need in my equipment," he said adamantly.

Thalia groaned and rolled her eyes. "That attitude is going to get you killed." With a plain and strangely unsettling gaze toward Saul, she said, "What happens when someone twenty feet away statches you by the throat and chokes you to death with magical energies?"

Saul didn't have an answer. He opened his mouth to speak, but nothing came out.

Her eyes went back to the book. "That's what I thought. Don't be so closed-minded, and don't shame me because of what I can do. Learn to gather friends, not enemies."

Saul detested her words. *I don't need magic, and I never will.* He crossed his arms in a huff. He hardly trusted the Hydris as a whole—having barely met any—and the stories of his past enforced this belief.

"Do you have any prophecies in your land?" Thalia asked, flipping through the tattered pages.

"Our markings decide our fate," Saul said bluntly, tapping his foot.

"*Hmm*," Thalia mumbled. "Do you trust your goddess?" she asked, examining both of his arms with her azure eyes. "Or should I say—*goddesses*?"

"I don't know this second god. I trust in Gadora, yes. She came to me in a dream before I was imprisoned in Rhoba."

"Fascinating," she said, carefully analyzing a specific page in the scratched leather-bound book. "What did she tell you?"

"She told me a storm was coming." Saul said. "After she left, I was struck by lightning. I dream of the same moment every night. I appear on a tower in the center of Renalia, and lightning strikes from above. I agonize until I awake. It sometimes lasts seconds, other times minutes, and sometimes longer."

"*Very* fascinating." Thalia drew out her words.

"What is?" Saul growled. "Are you going to tell me why you brought me to your home?" His voice grew harsh.

Thalia smirked and looked up from her book. "A magician trains her mind as much as a warrior trains his body. The same time is put in, and each has his or her own specialties on the battlefield. A small person with power over the elements should use it, just as a large warrior should use his brute strength." She brought out a map, and began drawing a line up, down, and around the Plateau. "Do you feel drawn to the south? The way you spoke to that insufferable Broken told me so."

"Yes," Saul replied.

Thalia grabbed a map out from her desk scribbled away on it. After a bit of silence, she handed him the map. "Here. This is a safe passage to the capital. If you expect to see your friends, take that route. The Terran Miners within the Blackcore Mountains shouldn't give you much trouble and will allow you to pass. If they try to cause problems, just mention my name."

Saul accepted the map and nodded. "Can you tell me about the Stormspire?" Saul wished to know more about Gadora's monument. He wondered what else they didn't tell him in the Vale. How much he needed to learn.

"It was raised from the sea shortly after her ascension, they say. The winds that surround it are quite strong, and anyone who attempted to climb it died. Either been blown off, or struck by lightning."

"I wish to see it," Saul determined.

"All the more reason to go. We will keep you and your people safe here, but if you wish to go, that is your prerogative." Thalia leaned back in her chair, looking to the ceiling. "Maybe there you will learn to discard the ideal of a people and raise one of ideals themselves instead."

"I can't simply abandon my people," Saul growled.

"You killed a multitude of them in Rhoba," Thalia said with a strong tone.

"They were *not* my people," Saul retorted. *How could she dare to call me that, after saying they deserved to die? What is she trying to prove?*

She shrugged her small shoulders. "What's the distinction? They were Broken, just like you. You killed them because they disgraced your ideals, not because of what they were. Tell me—if you were faced between joining forces with an orderly and strong Hydrian society or a dishonorable, backstabbing Broken one, which would you choose? Well?" She closed her book with a loud *clomp* and shot him a sharp glare.

Saul burst into a cough, barely able to catch his lost breath. He stared into her eyes with suspicion, shock, and disbelief.

Thalia looked around with a tilt to her head. "Did I—say something inappropriate?"

He shook his head slowly. She said the words. The question. The one his goddess asked. "I've heard that question before."

She just smirked, unknowing that she just spoke the words of a being of absolute power. "Good, that means I'm not the only rational being in the world. Do you have an answer?"

He halted as his mind sped up to meet his emotions, even now, Saul fought with the question. "I suppose I may—I—I don't know." Saul couldn't answer her. He was bound to his people still—and needed time to change what he was. He was a proud Broken, but he was also a Broken of honor and order.

Saul could hear loud voices barking of orders from outside. "I'll give you time to think about that." Thalia sighed. She got up from her chair, and rushed to the stairwell. "Stay here. *Don't move,*" she whispered. "There are too many of them."

Bang, bang, bang! A slamming knock came from the door. Saul heard Thalia's door swing open, and a Hydris with a commanding, hissing tone roared from outside.

"We have heard a small horde of Broken was sighted in the area. Have you seen them, woman?"

"I heard there were here, but they left two days ago, going to Elaston. How many were in the horde?" Thalia replied.

"Our scouts said twenty. You do realize what this means if you lie to us?" the man growled.

"I wasn't born yesterday," Thalia said. "Check the buildings and barracks—you won't find any. We've been cooperative."

Saul knew there was a trap door to the lower levels in the homestead, and he prayed that the others descended. Saul was furious. He wanted to slay the man where he stood, but he did not know how many soldiers were in town. He felt himself a coward, as he knew he could kill many of them alone.

"How about we break in your walls and make sure you are?" the other hissed.

"Not necessary. We've given many supplies, and stripped of most," Thalia said. Saul had seen the thinning supplies as they walked through town before.

"If it were up to me, we would take more. We know you're a little Broken-loving bitch just like your father. How about I bed you now and teach you a lesson?"

Saul shot to his feet and almost stormed down the stairs, but barely held himself before the stairs. Betraying her request would only anger her. He had to trust her. A Hydris. He held himself back, and sat back down…

A brief, frightening silence followed. But Thalia was the first to speak. "Try me," she said coldly. "Try it and I'll choke you to death." Another pause. "You know I can, and you know I will," Thalia said.

The door slammed loudly, and he heard no steps, no breath, nothing. *Stay up there*, Thalia had said.

Am I a coward? How could I stay here? I desire death of them. A man threatened to bed her—I should make him bleed to death for the threat, Saul thought. But something deep within him kept him still.

He heard plate footsteps outside, then running and yelling, but no clashing of blades, only arguments and commands. It went on for half an hour it seemed before the yelling dissipated, and the large door of Thalia's home opened once more. Quiet footsteps ascended the staircase, and Thalia appeared at the top.

Saul exploded from his chair. "What happened? What did that disgusting wretch—"

"Nothing, calm yourself." Thalia sighed. She touched a hand to her cheek, and gave a sarcastic, worriful expression. "Did you worry for me, Saul? My I must say I'm flattered." Thalia gnashed her teeth and chuckled. She placed a hand to her forehead and acted as if to faint. "Oh, my, I'm a damsel in distress, Saul help—oh—" She opened her eyes and gave a mocking grin.

Her jest faded, and she placed hands on her hips and walked to the window by the desk. "That ingrate always comes into town with his so-called knights, taking our supplies and harassing us. I had to keep an eye on them while they went through. Your friends weren't found. He wishes he could bed me, but I'd rather remove my own head before I let that thing touch me." Thalia shuddered in disgust and mouthed a *yuck*. "His threats are empty. Couldn't touch me if he tried. I'd disembowel him before he'd come within ten feet." She chuckled. "They're gone now. I'm surprised you stayed here."

"I wanted to leave," Saul grumbled. "I wanted to kill them all."

"Yet you probably couldn't kill fifty armored knights alone. Fifty civilians without fighting experience is one thing. Knights, another." She turned her head and gave a nod of approval. "It's good you stayed. They would have killed fifty citizens upon finding one broken here. You saved more lives than you would have avenged."

Now I live as a coward. "At great personal cost."

Thalia frowned. "A ridiculous cost. Don't be high and mighty, Saul. Would you feel so honorable if fifty died by your actions, when you could have saved them?"

"I don't live in fear. The blood is on their blades, not mine." She knew nothing of honor. She told Saul to cower while soldiers reaped the resources of her town. "Why don't you use your magic to save them?" Saul asked in a snarky tone.

"Don't sass me, Saul. Do not speak to me like I'm an idiot," Thalia scoffed. "It's not that simple. One person can't stop a hundred blades alone and save every innocent. It takes one death to fail. I save lives by helping them endure." She sat down in her small chair and slouched into it. "As for blood on blade, it's quite the contrary. If your action could save fifty, their blood is on both. Don't proclaim yourself innocent just because you did not cover your blade with their blood. Your hands would be just as stained as theirs would be. Negligence is dishonorable. Running out and killing a few soldiers, that provoke ten other soldiers to kill fifty civilians, is negligence. I'll let you make that connection."

Saul growled. He didn't like being corrected, let alone from a Hydris or a Sorceress. She was everything he saw as a coward—and yet, he was the coward now. She was right; many would die if he attacked alone. She was that which he couldn't stand, yet she had a strength of character that impressed him. For a small woman, she was very bold—in a way that was… No, he couldn't think that.

"You may be right." Saul admitted, very reluctantly. Not many could change his mind, and even he was surprised at the turn.

Thalia chuckled, "Good, it seems we're making progress. I believe we just had a moment." She grinned slyly.

Saul tilted his head. "What?"

Thalia sighed heartily. "Nothing." She began reading through the white-covered book on the desk. "Do you know what you plan to do?"

Saul knew. He felt drawn to the Plateau. He felt the Stormspire was what he needed to see. A monument to his god, a storm which could not be tamed. The very one that struck him every night. He needed to seek out Serpentarius, the Hydrian capital. He took a deep breath and stared out the window to the setting sun. The sky gleamed of red, orange, and a hint of violet. "I will seek the capital. We will stay the night and move in the morning."

"I thought so. I do enjoy prophecies."

Saul raised a brow. "What prophecy?"

"Ah, I spoke out loud. Just predictions and fates, like the blue one on your right arm."

Saul looked to the six-pointed sun. Fates. His goddess spoke to him about them. He did not know the origin of this second marking. He glanced to her as she looked into his eyes. "Will you join us?" Even Saul didn't expect that to come out of his mouth. Her demeanor was bold yet graceful, and her words tactful. She was a formidable ally, despite her shortcomings.

"No, I don't believe so. You're on your own. Although it is endearing that you'd have me join you," she said in a smokey voice.

"Don't take it to heart, I do not trust Sorceresses. A voice of their race might help, that's all," Saul said. *Her* voice, especially. She had a commanding way about her, one appropriate for handling the affairs of an entire city.

Thalia nodded slowly, closing her eyes. "I see," she chuckled. "Magic can come in handy, you know. Maybe one day you'll see."

She rose from her chair once more, walked down the stairs, and waved for him to follow. Saul obliged.

"Well, Saul Bromaggus, we will prepare some supplies for you and your band of warriors. Take the map." She gently touched his left marking, eyeing it carefully. "Be careful out there. As you said, a storm is coming," Thalia giggled, eyeing him closely as he left. With a subtle smile, she said, "Perhaps we'll see each other again?"

I would like that, Saul thought. But he couldn't bear to say those words to someone he only just met. He simply gave a subtle nod, and her smile grew.

Saul exited her home. He glanced back to look at her as he walked, and she waved. He looked back to the map, wary of his journey ahead.

Chapter Twenty-nine

Chaos of Freedom

Zaedor Nethilus

It had been another week since they initially thought of the plan. No one else had been told. Some may have overheard, but Zaedor was thankful that none told the guards. Zaedor wished he could have more information to go on. They kept the prisoners locked away, only letting them out to fight. They brought them past the other prison rooms, the first three doors, to the prep room, fourth door on the right, past the three rows of doors without windows, to the final door at the end, the pit.

I have to try. I can't give up this time. I have to fight like a monster but remain resilient and self-aware. I must escape, he thought resolutely.

Then he remembered that he shouldn't be so selfish. Since the destruction of his city, he only thought for himself. He was beaten, kidnapped, and broken at every instant as he thought without care for others. *No, we must escape together. All of us. I won't leave them behind.* Zaedor frowned and crossed his arms on his chest. *What if the guards get away? What about the knave, Fallad?* He had to do something about him. There were many unknowns to consider.

I must be ready.

"Hey, if you ever get out of here, what would you do?" Zaedor asked. He knew that would be a common question among the prisoners, so he paid no worry to the guards.

Kindro pondered to himself with a furrowed brow, while Freya played with her hair. "I dunno, probably head north. See if I can get work in a mine or something. My family lives there now, my mom and dad. My brother lives away from home, though. I don't have a wife or kids."

Freya paid the conversation no mind, not mentioning her plans. She winced from a comment about parents, especially the mention of a mother. "I don't know," Freya finally said. "I would rather not go home. I might go with bear-boy over here." She motioned to Kindro, with his overly hairy body and lengthy beard.

"Words can hurt, you know," Kindro said sullenly.

"Don't get me started on that brain of yours, it's a little lacking," she replied with a smirk.

"Just 'cause I'm not a high-born like you—don't know how to read or write or anything doesn't mean—well, okay, maybe it does," he scratched his jet-black haired head, drawing his large mouth out in displeasure. Kindro had a knack for laughing at himself, knowing what he lacked and where his strengths were. Freya was able to make fun of him, but Zaedor didn't feel the need to gang up, even if it was a joke.

Zaedor hadn't been there long, but it felt like he knew them both since birth. *Being right beside each other all day, every day can do that,* he thought with a smirk. After he got out, Zaedor knew his path. He wanted to go to Solmarsh. He did not want to part ways with his friends, but he felt he had to go.

"Why don't you come with me, to the west?" Zaedor asked.

They both looked at him with awe. "There's a war raging in that area. I don't want to get involved in that," Freya said.

"I just want a quiet life. I've fought here for too long. I don't like being chained up, and a war will get me just that," Kindro added.

He knew that would be their answer, but they were his first friends since the catastrophic event.

"Don't worry, Blondie," Freya said. "I'll be in the north. I'm sure if you come up there, you'll find us somewhere."

Maybe I will, he thought. He had his goal, but how long would it last? Would it be quick, or ongoing? So many uncertainties came with it, but Zaedor knew it was where he wanted to be, not where he had to be.

He wondered what the forests were like. He had never been there, only having seen pictures and heard stories. It rained more there than anywhere else in the land, giving life to many different kinds of animals and other creatures. He also wished to see the capital of Orinas, built with icestone streets, and walls stronger than any city in the realm. The stories reminded Zaedor of home, and he was nostalgic. *I will see you again.*

Zaedor saw the pillar of light slowly shifting, coming from the air vent in the roof of the dome. It slowly approached the spot, telling them the fighter's choice was coming. Zaedor watched it carefully, readying himself once more. He looked to Kindro, who nodded. They had a plan. *Quick as the wind, tough as a mountain, silent as the night.*

The moment the light hit, Maroia swung open the prison door and sauntered in. He walked directly to Zaedor's cage. "Well Amirionian, looks like it's your time again. Don't do anything stupid this time, or you're dead." His face scrunched, and his long mustache twitched with each sharp word.

Zaedor's mind raced, heart rate speeding to an incredible rate. *What do I do, what do I do, what do I do?* he repeated over and over in his head. He thought he prepared for this moment, but he began to doubt himself.

Fallad backed off. "Take him," he said. "Have him put out in five minutes."

Zaedor spat up the first thing that came to his mind. "Can I piss first?" He heard Freya cough up a laugh, quickly stifling it. "I really have to go. It might affect my fight."

The flamboyant fool laughed heartily. "Fine, let him piss. Make it fast. You have seven minutes to be out there. I'll try to calm the crowd. They want to see you fight again. Even though you killed a breaker, which I remind you, is the one fighter you *aren't allowed to kill*, it made you a fan favorite," he said, twisting his oily moustache. "Let him finish, and then get him ready." He walked to the door, closing it.

Foolish idiot, Zaedor thought.

"Piss. Now," one guard commanded.

Zaedor turned to look at Kindro, then walked toward the bucket. He went slowly, preparing himself for what was to come. He breathed deeply. *Calm as a summer breeze,* he thought. His lessons from Amirion helped; they told him that remaining calm helped one accomplish a goal that required careful execution. He knew what to do first. He couldn't have them yelling, after all. He slowly turned after finishing and walked methodically toward the guards who were now in the cage with them.

The cheers of the pit rang in the distance, yelling and chanting for the fight they hungered for; they were ready. *That'll cover the sound.* With a vicious flash, Zaedor jabbed the smaller guard in the throat, causing him to lurch forward, gasping for air.

Kindro did the same to the taller one, except he grabbed the guard by the back of the neck, throwing him further down to force his knee into the guard's throat again. He coughed in pain, but

Kindro was as large as they were, and faster. Neither guard could even croak a cry.

Zaedor kicked the back of the smaller guard's knee, dropping him to the ground. The guard grabbed Zaedor's arm in response and smashed his face with his fist. Blood spurted from Zaedor's nose, most likely broken *again*. Gasps echoed from the surrounding cages; the seven pairs of eyes watched the action carefully. Zaedor threw his guard to the ground and choked him with all his might. The guard frantically swung at him, smashing his eyes and nose, but Zaedor's grip didn't loosen. Nothing dimmed his glimpse at freedom.

Kindro continued kicking the taller guard's throat and head until they fell to the ground, unconscious. The taller guard's jaw, nose, and arm were certainly broken; Zaedor was astounded at Kindro's raw strength.

After the guards were both out, Zaedor quickly grabbed the two sets of keys and began unlocking the cages. All the cages in the room corresponded to their own room lock—except that there were 16 keys on the ring, and some with symbols instead of numbers. He scrambled to find the number seven key as their room was numbered. He rushed to Lirkosh's cage, and the key worked.

"What's your plan?" he hissed, backing away.

"Free everyone. Two can unlock. The more guards we take, the more keys we get. The more captives we free, the faster we *all* leave," he said quickly. "We take two rooms at a time," Zaedor whispered. Each guard carried blades on them. So he mouthed, *be careful*. "We can't get out alone! We need the others, but we must get free! They can no longer hold us captive. We fought for them, now we fight for ourselves!" he whispered fiercely with a raised fist, and the others nodded in agreement.

They split into two teams to make their escape. First there was Zaedor and the ones he freed, second was Freya and Kindro. They opened the doors creeping in quietly, taking the guards with ease, four on two. They unlocked the cages as fast as they could. Their pace accelerated. The next four rooms were taken at once, with the multitude of prisoners growing in strength. More guards arrived from the noise, but were taken with a few beatings by two of their men.

The prisoners banded to Zaedor, following his confidence without question. He showed no fear, knowing that this was their victory for the taking. They ran to unlock the final six doors, each leading to new halls. They split up, each team moving to check the halls. The crowd's cheers roared from the pit. They were clueless as to what was happening with the captives. Zaedor ran down the first hall, leading around in a curve to the other side of the pit, and the second set of prisons. Lirkosh went back to alert the other teams.

Teams three and four returned, claiming a dead end, other routes to the pit, and food and storage rooms. They joined forces and freed the next four rooms of prisoners there. Zaedor heard yelling coming from all angles. The jig was up, but there were too many prisoners set free now. *They can't stop us all*, Zaedor thought.

The halls were endless. Zaedor ran to a strangely ornate door that seemed out of place, with a granite tablet reading, *Maroia Fallad* beside it. Zaedor sent his team down the hall, having business to take care of. Zaedor kicked the door down. Fallad was readying himself to go to the pit for the fight.

"What in the hells?" he drew a small blade quickly, slashing at Zaedor as he approached. Zaedor deftly dodged it as he would fists in the pit, *calm as a breeze*. He knew Fallad was weak. Zaedor grabbed the knave's hand, striking him across the face, again and again. He clobbered him to the ground, striking more and more out of rage, rather than necessity. Not only for him, but for every man and woman imprisoned there.

Maroia was broken and bruised, spitting up blood. "Wh—what do you—what do you want?" he croaked.

Zaedor glared into his beady eyes, teeth clenched. He grabbed the small blade from the ground.

"Justice."

He stuck the pathetic man with his own sword, through his silk doublets and into his heart. His eyes quickly gave way to death. Zaedor rose, victorious.

I'm not out yet, he remembered. He looked around the office, seeing a small chest at the back against the rough rock wall. It wasn't locked, so he opened it. It contained various trinkets: bracelets, necklaces, clothing, and rings—*his* ring. Zaedor placed his ring of Amirion back on his hand. *Don't forget us,* Noah had said.

Zaedor found one other thing he recognized in particular, a velvet tether necklace interlaced with silver rings and rubies. He grabbed it and placed it in a satchel that he found beside Maroia's desk. He picked up the chest and brought it with him.

"Zaedor!" Kindro yelled. "Everyone's out, they found the exit! Everyone, even the guards and spectators, is running! Let's get the hell out of here!"

He looked back to Maroia's office with contempt. "Let's go."

Through winding hallways, he passed the corpses of guards, slashed in pools of crimson. *I'm sorry,* he thought. Zaedor felt responsible for their deaths. But they'd imprisoned innocent men and women, and it had to be done.

A light echoed from a tunnel heading upward, growing the closer and closer he came. He felt the warm breeze, and smelled moisture and plants and sand enter his nostrils.

Freedom.

He looked to see a hundred prisoners all around him. Each cheered for victory, survival, and freedom. Many horses, camels, and carriages rode off in all directions, fleeing the scene of the pit.

"To Zaedor! The man with no plan!" Lirkosh yelled.

The rest cheered, fists raised in the air. They were surrounded by palm trees, sun-scorched sand, and a large lake. *Where are we?* he wondered.

"It's the Scorpion's Oasis. A day's walk South of Zenato," Freya said, as if reading his mind. Zaedor raised a brow. "What? You looked around like a newborn animal."

The cheers slowly settled. Zaedor placed the chest down, allowing everyone to find their personal belongings. A couple of fights had to be broken up, but no man cared for materials now, just the fresh air in their lungs.

"Zenato is north of here. To those who are coming with, follow us!" Freya yelled, dragging Zaedor and Kindro behind her. Some followed, some went east, and others went south. Each man and woman thanked the others. Wherever they went, they knew they were now free.

The Hydris from the pits held out a scaly hand. "You have my thanks, Amirionian. I'll see you again—potentially," Lirkosh said.

Zaedor shook his hand, which suddenly burned white hot. He released it quickly and waved away the heat.

"Ah, apologies about that," Lirkosh chuckled. "My blood runs hot out here." He smiled, walking south.

The sun was scorching, but welcomed. Zaedor remembered his trek to Zenato the first time. If he didn't have the waterskins and rations he found as he left Amirion, he'd be dead. He wouldn't have been able hatch a plan to save the prisoners of the pit if he hadn't been captured. He was proud that he made a difference.

He didn't need a god, a city, or a king—he did it as Zaedor, with the help of his comrades. He stood tall, shoulders back, and walked with a slight strut.

"Looks like someone is feeling good about himself," Kindro said. "Looks like the victory went to his head. Better hope we don't get kidnapped again." His oily black hair was lighter in the free sun, and he seemed even more hairy. He slapped Zaedor on the back, who almost coughed from the pain.

"I couldn't have done it without you," Zaedor said.

"So humble." Freya laughed. "All it took was a bit of yelling." Her fair skin glistened in the desert sun. It reminded him of his wife, Eryndis. He missed her fiery orange hair, pale green eyes, and strong personality. He didn't know where she was, whether she was alive or dead; he simply knew his path was west, in Solmarsh.

* * *

A day passed, and they arrived to Zenato just after dark.

Exhausted, thirsty, and starving, they knew they needed somewhere to stay. Many went their own ways, shaking hands and exchanging thanks and goodbyes. Eventually, it was just Kindro, Freya, and Zaedor left. A few guards questioned them, but they didn't have manacles on. Zaedor just said they were poor and homeless and, since there were so may others living on the street, the guards let it go. "We need somewhere to sleep. I know just the place."

"Isn't this the way to the slums? You better not be pulling a fast one on us, Blondie."

"Maybe he's in withdrawal from a lack of fights," Kindro said.

Zaedor hoped he would be accepted there. Sand blew softly through the streets over the cobblestones, and people gasped and giggled at their appearances. They wore nothing but dirty clothes, barely covering their unmentionables. Zaedor doubted anyone would mug them, considering how they looked, and doubted anyone would be able to even if they tried. They came to the old tavern and inn, *Leena's Lagers*.

Leena washed the bar, cleaning up after a day of work. She glanced to the door, seeing the three sandy, dirty, sweat-covered individuals. She froze for a moment, speechless. After a pregnant pause, she piped up. "Oh my, Zaedor what happened? It's been weeks!" she squeaked in a panic. All patrons of the bar looked to stare from their stools and stables.

"It's a long story," Zaedor said, looking to the others. Rubbing his matted hair, he let out an exhaustive sigh. "Although, we may require a bit of help." He carefully sat down. "We need three meals, anything you have, and three beds," Zaedor pulled the ring from his finger, eyeing it closely. *Do I give this up now? I'm sorry, Eryndis, maybe I should let you go, too.*

"I—*we* don't have any money. I can give you this, however," he said unevenly. He held out the ring to her.

Leena's eyes widened. "Oh no, I can't accept that! That's your ring! It has Amirion's symbol on it, doesn't it?" she gasped, holding her hand to her mouth.

"Yes, but I cannot walk in here and ask for something for nothing." Zaedor smirked as he spun the ring in his hand. "I don't need it anymore." He outstretched his hand, ring in the center of his palm. "It's made with silver."

Leena reached out and closed his hand. "No, you've been through a lot," she smiled sweetly, her ivory skin shining in the torchlight, accentuating sparse freckles. "Everything is on the house. You can have rooms four and five. They're open."

Zaedor couldn't believe it.

He didn't deserve such generosity. He may have helped his comrades escape, but she had no part in that. Not to mention, Leena's inn was not the most well off. "I can't accept that. I don't want to be a burden. I want to help," Zaedor said.

"Don't worry, I can cover it. The hairy one can stay in my room," a gruff voice said from the tables. Footsteps approached; it was Rodrick. He placed a set of copper coins on the table.

Zaedor flinched as the hairless Rodrick stepped toward him, and stumbled on a bar stool, expecting a steel fist across the face as their last encounter.

But the peculiar small man began to tear up with a thousand-yard stare—no, he was simply looking past Zaedor to—

"Brother—" Rodrick said quietly. "I've been searching for weeks." His eyes were locked with Kindro's as they approached each other. They tightly embraced in a hug. "I thought you were dead."

"I'm alive, brother. I'm okay." They released, and Kindro looked to Zaedor. "We were caught in an illegal fighting ring in the south. People are kidnapped and forced to fight," he explained, looking back to Rodrick's eyes. "Zaedor finally hatched a plan to get everyone out," he smiled with a sigh. "If you could call it that. Simple, but effective."

Rodrick analyzed Zaedor's eyes closely, as if staring into his soul. After a moment, he gave a subtle, warm smile. "You look different," he said to Zaedor, holding out his hand.

He's still a shapeshifter, but Rodrick couldn't be that bad, could he? He refused to believe that a brother of his friend could be evil. His mind was clearer now. He held resentment for a single person, not a whole people. He remembered the knock to his head with the steeled fist. Zaedor knew he provoked the fight. He charged a man who seemed to be unarmed. Zaedor struggled with his resentment.

Rodrick didn't hurt your people. He gave you what you deserved and instead paid for your bed and food, he thought to himself. *Shake his hand, you know it's the right thing to do.*

"I suppose I have a broken nose, an askew jaw, and a few extra bruises." Zaedor took Rodrick's hand, and shook it strongly. "I apologize for provoking you, and thank you for paying for my room and board."

Rodrick smiled, and his droopy brown eyes seemed to shine brightly from the return of his brother. "You were mourning," Rodrick began, nodding. "A man needs his time to mourn before he can live again. It seems you've made it."

Leena sat at the bar, murmuring to Freya, both looking at the two brothers curiously. "Hey gents, I hate to interrupt your romantic moment," Freya piped in. "But why is one of you as hairy as a dire bear, but the other is hairless?"

Rodrick let out a chuckle. "Kin here never let me live it down. Commonly, shapeshifters have typical forms they take, and borrow traits from them. I form into Golems, and they are absent of hair." His laugh stifled, turning to a sarcastic smile. "Although, being hairless up in the ice forests of Kholrani doesn't help me much."

Zaedor thought of Cloaker. *A man in a wolf cowl, thickest stubble I've seen, forming into a bear, but he had so many other forms.* He screwed his face into a frown.

"Something wrong?" Kindro asked.

"I just remembered something." Zaedor said bluntly, sitting on a bar stool, still in thought. He noticed that everyone was staring. "Rodrick, do you know the name 'Cloaker?'" Zaedor asked. He did not know the size of the shapeshifter clan, or what kind of people they truly were.

Rodrick's expression darkened. "Yes, I know of him. His real name is Roker, mind you. What of it?"

Why is he so resistant? Zaedor wondered. He hoped they weren't in league with each other. "He's the one who killed the king and a good friend of mine, in Amirion." Zaedor said.

Rodrick turned away, closing his eyes. "He was the head of the tribe," his voice turned as hoarse as a dying beast. "He betrayed the council, killed two members, and fled, joining some religion we care nothing for. We haven't seen him since."

A religion? This followed his theory from before. "Which?"

"Lornak."

Zaedor shot off his stool. "*Lornak?*" he exclaimed. Everyone jumped back. He steeled himself again. *The orb must have been him. But what did it do?* "Lornak is powerless, isn't he?" Zaedor asked. In his teachings, it was said Lornak was fated to be released…

"I don't know anything about that. Roker seemed pretty sure of the opposite. He tried to convince us to join him, and—well, you can guess the rest when everyone refused."

"I'm sorry that he damaged your society, as well."

Kindro placed his hands on both his brother's and Zaedor's shoulders. "All right, let's cheer up. Tonight is a night to celebrate! Drinks are on my brother, here!" he boomed.

Leena's cooks brought out food of all kinds that were exports from the region: luscious fruits and vegetables that came from the oasis, meat from desert boars and pigs raised and bred in Zenato, and different insect ichors that were sweet and salty and crunchy and *gross,* but Zaedor even forced himself to eat those.

The mead was passed around countless times, along with stories of travels, societies, and moments in the pit. The fights, the regrets—but most of all, the joys of freedom were told. Zaedor's head grew fuzzy from mead, but he had no rage to fathom.

Rodrick told stories of his land, the frozen forests of the northeast—*Kholrani,* as he put it. They lived near Shiada's tomb in a secret location, first there to protect it, but lost their belief in it centuries prior. They remained due to tradition. It was their home, and they would die to protect their camps and tribes. The shifters were a simple people living in small camps and huts. They lived day-to-day hunting dire bears and other animals. They only took what they required and lived in equilibrium with the land around them.

Zaedor found it all fascinating; some in Renalia were born with the ability to shift, and some of whom could choose to live in the ice forests with them. *There are probably many shifters no one knows about, or even that they know of themselves*, Zaedor thought.

Kindro listened and laughed loudly at Rodrick's terrible jokes, painfully slapping him on the shoulder. Rodrick was much shorter than his brother, but the brother had hands of transformative iron.

Freya went on a long tangent about nobility in the north, and the level of hypocrisy that thrived there. Nobles followed the law and promoted family values, but she told that it was far from promoted in their homes. She did not go into detail, and none dared to ask what she meant.

Zaedor wished to see her fight but would not want to see her angry. He saw it once, and to his luck, there was a cage wall between them. She had a sweet and lovely personality, usually. Zaedor had her to thank for pulling him from the pit of his own sorrow with her harsh treatments. He wondered what kind of family she had, and why she was in the deserts, of all places. *Did she run from something? If so, what from?*

As the night grew late, Kindro and Rodrick retired to their room, laughing, hooting, and hollering from upstairs. The bar cleared for the most part, except for Leena, who cleaned the tables, and Zaedor and Freya, who sat at the bar quietly, drinking together. She placed a hand on her collarbone, running her fingers along it.

"Freya, why haven't you mentioned your family?" Zaedor asked. He lost a bit of his filter due to the libations. *Not like it matters. What's she gonna do, hit me?*

"It's personal. I have my reasons, Blondie."

"You can't run forever. I ran from my problems and look what happened to me." Zaedor chuckled and pointed to his nose. *Damn, it still really hurts*, he thought. It shot with pain when he poked it clumsily. "You helped me realize that I was being juvenile, pushing my problems onto others in my anger." He nodded and looked to her with a hopeful eye. "Practice what you preach."

Freya laughed. "Damn it, don't tell me that now. Looks like the learner is the master, is he?" She shot in close and stared between his eyes. "Gimmie your head." She grabbed his face and placed a thumb on either side of his nose.

"Hey, what are you—"

"Sit still, damn it. What's your favorite animal?" Freya asked. *Why does she want to know that?* "I don't know, a wolf?"

"*Wolf!*" she yelled. With a *crack*, a rush of sharp pain shot through his nose as she shoved it back into place.

"*Ow!* What in the hells!" Zaedor yelped, flying back as he gripped his whole face.

"I put it back into place. Don't be a baby. You like wolves, huh? Funny, since you aren't from the forests or the north."

"I always thought they were interesting, and it's my sigil, after all. Some travelers would bring them to the city. They're kind of a rarity in those parts. They would kill with such precision, but not more than they needed, with guile and skill rather than brute force while being fierce as all hell." *It was Eryndis's favorite*, Zaedor thought.

"I never liked wolves. They prey on the weak," Freya said.

"Vultures prey on the weak. Wolves prey on the ill-prepared."

"I guess you're right. You win again, Blondie." She fiddled with her long ponytail. She swished it about in front of her eyes. "I got my hair color from my mom. I miss her," she said. Her thick, straight crimson hair was a sight, as he hadn't seen a natural color like that before.

"What happened to her, if I may be so bold?" Zaedor asked.

Freya chuckled. "You're a lot more polite than I expected—when you aren't being a resentful child."

She didn't answer the question at first. Zaedor could see pain in her eyes, and a reluctance to open. The wound was fresh.

She looked quickly to him. A tear formed in her left eye. "My father killed her. He called her a traitor, and a liar."

"Why would he do such a thing?"

"She kept something from him. He is not a kind man—a horrid man, to say the least. He came for me, and my mother tried to stop him. He murdered her, so I ran away."

Zaedor's fists clenched at the thought. *How could a man be so horrible? What could she have kept secret that would drive him to kill?* he thought.

"He's the 'Red Dragon.' One of the Orinas generals," she said.

A General? Pathetic and hypocritical. A military leader was to be an example for their people, not a man of low morals. Zaedor listened quietly. He dared not interrupt her at such as sensitive moment. *Or should I?* "He sounds like a wretch."

Freya shot him a grimace before returning to her drink. "I prayed to the gods. Shiada, mostly. She didn't answer my prayers, only put me in that pit beneath the sands."

Freya glared at Zaedor as he stifled a laugh. "Sorry. I was just thinking that maybe she has a plan for both of us, if she cares at all." He paused, turning stone-faced. "I'm sorry for your loss. It's difficult losing a parent."

Freya nodded and sniffed loudly. "Maybe you're right," her voice turned brittle. "All I had from my mom was my violet necklace. They took it when I was kidnapped." She placed her hand where her necklace would have been.

How did I forget? The necklace! Zaedor smirked at her. "Turn around and close your eyes."

"What? Okay," she said, confused. She turned around on her stool, away from him.

Zaedor carefully got the necklace out of the satchel he carried, placed it around her neck, and attached the clasp securely. "Okay, open them." He turned her back toward him.

Freya opened her eyes and saw the necklace around her neck, violet tethers intertwined with steel rings and small rubies. She was breathless, then jumped at Zaedor with a hug. She held him so tightly it hurt more than a grapple from Gorlin. His arms would certainly bruise from the embrace, but he returned the hug, as she needed it. "I—I—I—" she stuttered. "Wh—where did you find it?" she asked, catching her breath. She looked into his eyes.

"It was in the chest in Maroia's office. It was as you described it, so I kept it safe." Zaedor smiled.

"Thank you," she said quietly. "Wait, why didn't you tell me?"

"I kind of forgot," he replied. She punched him in the arm with a smile in kind. He knew it was precious to her, the way she talked about it in the prison dome.

"You jerk, I thought it was gone. I was worried I'd forget her."

"You'll never forget her." He looked into her large eyes. "She's in here." He pointed to his heart, then his mind.

Freya smiled, nodding and sniffling. "Yeah, you're right," she moved in closer as she spoke. "Your city may be gone, but they live on through you." She batted her lashes, her gaze never leaving his. She moved in for an embrace, and he felt the bruises upon his back swell, but it was countered by the feeling of lips touch against his cheek. Her touch was dry from the desert, but passionate and welcomed as his heart surged forth.

Zaedor felt her words deeply and thanked her with a subtle nod. She was awfully close, and he hadn't been as close with a woman since Eryndis and him were estranged. Now she was gone. He cared for Freya, and he felt something he forgot for some time. The closeness over their time in the pit, the intense experience of the escape, and the journey to *Leena's Lagers*, all brought them closer. The sounds of wooden chairs scraping the ground and the lantern's flickering flame suddenly filled his ears.

Zaedor's eyes met the ground, then raised them to see Freya's again. He moved closer until there was barely a moment between them. "I've never seen a woman as beautiful as you."

But when he expected passion, there was a sigh instead.

Freya backed off, and expression changed from a relaxed, soothing warmth, to a subtle eye roll. "Uh-huh, that's what they tell me." There was a long pause to follow, and Freya drew her mouth to the side. "Well, we've had an intense day. We should get to bed." She got up and walked toward the stairs.

Zaedor followed her, walking to the second room they were given. "I'm sorry. Did I hurt you?"

Freya smirked. "No. Quite the opposite, actually. I care about you. Maybe not in *that* way, but—I hope you find your wife again."

"I do as well." Zaedor surmised, looking down. "We separated some time ago, differing in quite a few beliefs." He still cared for Eryndis, he knew that.

He worried that they may never be one again.

"Tomorrow, we take different paths. I'm going to find this 'Solmarsh' in the west, and you have your own way. But I promise I will see you again."

She simply nodded and closed her door softly.

Perhaps it was the moment; the candlelight, the days in the cages, but—she was right. It was all misplaced. A flash of emerald green eyes and fiery orange hair filled his mind; Eryndis. His passion felt for the one before him wavered...

Thoughts of his love were all that remained. He only wished he could see her once more.

Zaedor headed into his room, and put on the set of clothes Leena placed on his bed with a note on top.

These are for you. Good luck. Remember, good things bring more good in the world.

Leena

He smiled at her kind gesture. He lay down on the bed as he put out the lantern to sleep.

* * *

The next morning, he awoke to calls of his name. He got up and clambered down the old wooden stairs, in search of the voices, and met Leena at the bar..

"Zaedor, here, they're all waiting. I packed some bread and fruit, waterskins, and some other things. Have a good trip!" she exclaimed.

What? I don't even know where I'm going. "How do you know where I'm headed?"

"Ask them outside. They're all ready, and said they had someone to go with you. A nice musical gentleman is waiting with them," she said with a smile.

Zaedor raised an eyebrow, walked outside, and accepted her pack with thanks. "I won't forget this!" he smiled, running out the door.

"About time!" Freya said, tapping her foot. Freya, Kindro, Rodrick, and the old gentleman he ran into when he first entered the town stood outside the door. Freya was wearing chain link armor and carried a spear. Rodrick and Kindro wore no armor or weapons, and the old, ragged man wore the same tattered clothes and carried his weathered mandolin.

Nargosh Shagon, the musician, spread his arms wide in welcome. "Ah, Mr. Zaedor! I believe I'll be accompanying you to your destination."

As Zaedor was about to apologize for his previous actions, Nargosh raised his hand. "No need to apologize, I understand you were in mourning. It's all right, old bean. Your friends here mentioned you may be going to Solmarsh. I've been in that region and happen to be going that way! I do love the place. Best fish in the mainland! What do you say?"

The other three looked to Zaedor with a sly grin. "Well, Mr. Nargosh, I believe I'd be happy to go with you. However, I am without gear and supplies," Zaedor said.

"Here, we bought these in the bazaar this morning." Rodrick walked up, holding out a great blade, a long blade, a small shield, and scale mail. "It's not plate, but it's all we can find in your size."

Zaedor was overwhelmed with all of the kindness. He slept in, and now awoke to nothing but gifts. "I don't know what to say."

"Just say thanks, idiot." Freya punched him in the arm.

Zaedor rubbed his arm and bowed. "Thank you, I do not know if I deserve—"

Kindro laughed and patted him on the back. "You take yourself too seriously."

Zaedor shook hands with the brothers. They turned to walk toward the north gate. Freya shuffled her feet before approaching him.

"Don't forget, you promised," she said, giving him a strong hug. *I promise, I will see you again,* he remembered. She turned, glancing back to him with a smile before running to join the brothers.

"Do you care for her, Old bean?" Nargosh asked. His lemon-yellow eyes glowed in the bright morning sun.

"Yes, I do," Zaedor said confidently. *Maybe not as I do Eryndis, but she is a good friend.*

"Well, we'd best keep you fighting, then. Can't have anyone breaking promises, can we?" The old Nargosh let out a bellowing guffaw. "Shall we go? I can play us some travel music!"

Zaedor chuckled to himself. "Certainly, but you'd better hope I don't get annoyed with it." He laughed. "But will we be walking there?" Zaedor asked a moment later, worried. Loughran was a much farther walk than his last. He worried about their pace, as the west was not entirely far, and he wished to get there as soon as possible.

"Oh my, no. My old bones can't take that sort of weathering. I have a friend that owes me a favor. He's a traveling merchant and has a carriage that isn't carrying much—and happens to be on his way to northern Loughran, so we're on the way. He'll be at the western elevation gate, waiting for our arrival."

Zaedor was relieved. "Let us go find your friend." He walked toward the western gate of Zenato city with his new travelling companion, Nargosh.

Chapter Thirty

Disobeying Orders

Kayden Ralta

Kayden focused her mind as best she could. Whenever the stream of mist passed from Vespers fingers into her eyes, it was impossible *not* to do whatever he said. The clearing was covered in lush flora and surrounded by blackwood trees still drenched by the rain from the night before. They were half a day outside Deurbin, on their way to inform Jirah of what they found. Vesper started 'training' her immediately.

Vesper swished his hands over his eyes, then flung them forward. The mist traveled quickly and gracefully toward her; Kayden was ready for another try.

It seeped into her eyes without a hint of pain, but then the commands began. *Hop on one foot, do it, jump! Wave your arms around! Jump! Hop! One foot, one foot! Now! Now! Now!*

"I won't do it!" Kayden yelled. Her mind seared in pain as the commands continued. *Lift your leg, do it! Do it and it will all end! Don't be a fool, doesn't it hurt? Isn't it agonizing? Do it, do it!* the voice yelled. She tried to force her arms to stay still and attempted to plant her feet. But then her limbs began to burn. She hopped up on one foot, waved her arms in the air like a moron, and only found herself yelling at Vesper. "Stop it, damn it! Stop doing that!"

Vesper shot her a sharp eye. "Make me."

"You're *making* me look like an idiot. Can't you have me do something normal?"

"Whenever most take control, they make you do the things you don't want. Some make you do awful things—terrible things. Would you rather me use one of the harsher ones?"

Kayden rubbed the side of her neck. "No."

"Come, let's go again." Vesper swished his hands toward her again, whispering the command of control. "*Thrahal.*" The mist went in again, and the commands were the same. Kayden tried to resist, again and again, but each damn time, she hopped on one foot, waved her arms, and jumped up and down—until he let her go.

Kayden threw her arms up in a huff. "This is going *nowhere.*"

Vesper swished his finger in a circle. "Focus on commands. Listen to them, but don't listen to them. Hear them, but don't hear them. Obey them, but don't obey them."

All he's doing is contradicting himself. "Ves, that doesn't make any sense," Kayden complained. "Are you going to make sense?"

"Perhaps we should take a break." Vesper rubbed his head, scratched his bulbous nose, and sat on a large rock near the edge of the clearing. He patted the empty spot beside him.

Kayden sighed, and walked over. She didn't sit down, though. The breeze blew softly through her thick, mousey hair, and she could hear the faint voices of the others in the distance. Kayden preferred more privacy, especially with what Vesper had her doing. She was sure someone spied a time or two.

"My dear, the purpose of the spell is to force someone's mind. It has nothing to do with the body. You try to keep your feet on the ground, but that is the point—you are the one picking your legs up and hopping."

"I'm trying to resist it, but I don't know what to do. It hurts, and all the confusion from the commands overwhelms me."

"Miss Ralta, you shouldn't resist. That's what makes the spell so powerful. Resisting only gives the master more power. You have to twist the commands. Alter them to your own benefit. Think of it like a contract. You're looking for a way to get around the rules and regulations."

Using the gaps in laws to your advantage. The Guild of Shades was infamous for skewing the laws to avoid arrests. While low-born and not well-learned, they knew how to twist laws and commands to the way they preferred. Kayden learned that well enough. She thought of her past experiences, seeing how she could work around the commands.

One time a man begged for his life when Kayden went to collect a debt. She stood over him, listening to him pray to his gods for mercy. He shoved the money at her and asked for his life. Kayden couldn't kill him—it was implied in her contract that she should, but it wasn't blatantly written. When she returned to the Guild and Sheeran asked her why didn't cut the man's throat, she just responded 'The contract didn't say kill him. It said get the money back.' Sheeran didn't get mad at her, *that* time. "Let's try it again," she said strongly.

Take the money, but don't kill the man. Hop on one foot, but jump and attack, Kayden thought.

"Good, let us see what you can do." Vesper rose and brushed off his robes.

"Don't use the waving one this time," Kayden grumbled.

He only chuckled in response. "Make me." He pulled his hands across his eyes and threw them toward her. "Thrahal."

As the mist came, the commands followed. *Lift your leg. Do it! Hop! Jump off on your leg, do it, do it, do it!* Kayden grunted in pain, feeling her mind aflame. She didn't bother with her body, but focused on the commands. *Lift your leg! Move your arms around! Do it! You have to, or else it will never end!* The words ran together and contrived in a mess, but Kayden focused on a few. *Lift your leg! Jump off the ground! Move your arms around!* Kayden agreed. She lifted one leg, hopped off the ground forward with all her strength, fell to the ground and rolled. She popped back up, drew her blades and swirled them in a circle wildly, stopping straight at Vesper's neck. Kayden coughed and breathed heavily, feeling the commands disappear. Her chest felt tight; she worried for Vesper, as she could have killed him. But the look in Vesper's eyes wasn't fear, it was pride.

Vesper sported a sly grin. "Fantastic." After a long pause, he said, "Ah, would you put those away Miss Ralta? A moment is acceptable, but more than that is unsettling."

Kayden jumped back and dropped her blades on the grass. "Oh, sorry." Kayden stuck up her hands. "I did it!" She was proud of herself. After all those attempts, she finally beat him—once.

Noticing Vesper chuckle, she dropped her hands. She was surprised to even smile, remembering who she saw recently.

"What is the matter? That was a quite an accomplishment. Beating me, oh, that is an impressive feat." He rubbed his head again and sat back down. With a swish of his hand, rainwater from the leaves nearby formed into an orb of water above his hand. He took out a flagon from his pack, flicked the orb into it, and had a sip. He offered her a drink, but Kayden declined it.

"Everything that's been going on. All the prisoners that were moved—to Lira's home, no less—for some reason we don't even know yet. Lira didn't sleep last night. We need to hurry. It concerns me, and we're wandering back to Jirah which will take who knows how long." Kayden ruffled her knotted hair. Then she clued into what Vesper said. *Beating him is impressive?* "Wait, hold on. Why is beating you a big accomplishment?"

"I just haven't met many that could," Vesper replied bluntly, making no eye contact.

Kayden slowly narrowed her eyes at him. "Did you do this often? Control people?"

"Absolutely not. I was making a comment. Each individual has a place they learn their craft. Some would rather not talk about it."

Vesper was about to get up, but Kayden stopped him. "Hey, hold on. Where did you learn all of it? Where were you before the circus? Why don't you tell anyone?"

Vesper sighed. "I learned my craft from the School of the Magi in Orinas, my dear. Sometimes people run from something, and they don't talk about it." He scratched his beard feverishly, and glanced at her. His voice vibrated slightly when he spoke.

I would know. I've been running for a long time. "I know what it's like. That's why I'm here." He seemed to be very resistant to admit anything from his past. *The same for me.* She thought maybe talking about hers might help. *Help him, and me, too.*

Vesper raised a brow. "Pardon?"

"I'm running," Kayden admitted. She hadn't truly said it to herself, yet. "I ran from the Guild of Shades in Zenato. I ran after I was imprisoned in Orinas. I'm running so I can't be caught." Kayden rubbed her knees, and looked up to the cloudy sky. Water dripped all around them from the trees still drenched from the rain. She tried to ignore her feelings, her fears, but with seeing Callidan again, it flared into fruition once more. "I'm afraid." If the Guild found her, she could be killed, or worse, she'd be brought straight to Sheeran. He was the one who scared her the most. For years she was used, in the name of 'love.' She never wanted to return.

"You are skilled at hiding it. I am quite awful with it," Vesper said sullenly. "I am no stranger to fear. It must have been difficult for you. Very difficult."

"It was. I'm surprised I'm even alive. I should have died so many times—it's a mystery to me." Healing magic. *Sheeran kept me alive. But everything else I was died.*

"I am glad you are here, Miss Ralta. You remind me of my escape, the circus—the first time I was truly happy in a long time."

His daughter. "The circus was an escape?" Kayden asked.

"It was fun." He seemed to let out a weak chuckle before continuing. "People appreciated my skills, and I could make people smile, laugh, and escape from their lives, for at least a moment. I joined with my wife and daughter, as I mentioned, ten years ago."

Kayden chose a different path. When she ran, she didn't make people happy. She made them suffer. "You did something good. But why did you run?"

"The war against the Broken hordes. The late King Bracchus' Generals wanted me to fight for them; I was Lord Chora's 'star pupil.' He was an elderly man then and could hardly fight in battle. He ushered me to do it, but I refused. I ran. The war was still won. Lord Chora died a few years past, I hear. I hadn't spoken to him since I ran." Vesper rubbed his face. "He must have been so disappointed."

"There's nothing wrong with running." Kayden heard of Lord Chora before. *He was the Lord of the Magister's Tower in Orinas, the head Magi.* Vesper's words were reminiscent of her own. She rubbed her arms, barely spitting the past out; she hadn't talked about her past with anyone other than with Lira. "I ran because I was being used by the leader of the Guild. I was sent on missions time and again, and many times others lied to get me punished. 'She steered the ship into the docks and lost everything,' they would say. 'She killed the traitor before we could find out where he hid the money.' They were all lies to get to me. I was his best, in his eyes, but even the best would be sent for torture, isolation, or worse. I couldn't leave, else I would be killed. All I could do was survive. I had to survive. I don't know why, but something in me didn't let them win."

"The Fighter," Vesper nodded. "Admirable."

Kayden tilted her head to the side. "The Fighter?"

"My master once told me that there are three people in all of us. The Lover, the Fighter, and the Leader. The Lover does what they wish. They search for love, they run from their responsibility, or they simply engage in a hobby. They act without taking into account the needs of others. When I ran from my responsibility, I was the Lover. I loved my wife, I loved my daughter, and I was afraid of death."

Vesper took a deep breath, and continued with a poignant wag of his finger. "When you survived in the East, my dear, you were the Fighter. You did what you must to survive. Men eat bugs in the wild, they kill friends to save a hundred, or simply endure horror so they can live on. To serve justice at a later time."

"Finally, there is the Leader. They do all they can in their power to protect others. They act without regard for their own needs. They sacrifice. Sir Mirado sacrifices his sleep and his own personal needs so that his soldiers are safe. He abandoned the military, sacrificing his rank and his life for the innocent of the realm. At times, there is a moment in someone's life when they must choose between what they love and what they must do. It is one of the most difficult things in life. Choosing many lives over the life of someone important to them. Choosing duty over love. Choosing to kill rather than maintain life."

After a brief pause, he said, "The lover plays and enjoys, the fighter survives, and the leader sacrifices," he finished. "Which do you think you are?"

I don't know who I am, anymore. "I don't know," Kayden said.

He pointed a finger to the sky and swished it in a circle. "The happiest individual has a balance of all three. One who sacrifices all cannot truly be happy. One who only does what they can to survive isn't either. The lover is simply not a good person, as they never care for others."

Kayden glanced back to the others in the distance, wondering what balances they had. She suspected Domika was the lover, Lira was the leader despite her lack of confidence, and Mags was the fighter. With that, none of them would be happy. She felt it. *What does that make me?* Kayden stared to the grey sky above, feeling that's what her life was: shades of grey in a sea of morality. She stole, she lied, and she killed—even when she didn't need to. Good people didn't do those things.

She was running; that much was true. Maybe she wanted to redeem herself, too. "You still haven't told me why you never told us about your past."

"I learned at the School of the Magi, yes, and I have a high ceiling of power, but I don't want to use it. I've hurt people. I can't have that happen again. I won't let it happen again. I also do not want people taking advantage of what I can do." Shaking his head nervously, he looked into Kayden's eyes with his buggy ones. "I am quite afraid of it. It is like a reason similar to why you haven't told anyone about yours." With a quick number of nods, he drew his eyes toward the sky. "I am afraid of my past catching up with me."

Kayden nodded. "Part of me never wants to think about my past ever again. But it keeps coming back."

"It can be impossible to run from the past forever, Miss Ralta. I have run for some time, but it is not easy. When the past returns, it is your allies who pick you back up. My family was always there for me. It is too late for me—but you are still young."

Kayden remembered the night she stood with a dagger to her neck in Deurbin. Somehow Lira found her there. Kayden came so close to slicing across her neck to finally escape her past. But Lira brought her back. Looking back through the forest clearing, she saw Lira in the distance playing a game with Mags, clapping in a particular pattern, giggling as he couldn't quite get it. Innocence.

"Running is difficult. We've both been runners, Miss Ralta. You have lost much, but here, things are different for all of us. You fit well here. You've done well keeping an eye over us. Some of us need the comfort of another to watch over our safety. It helps me feel at ease—I haven't felt at ease for far too long." He seemed to smile weakly, as if to mask a sea of sorrows. He glanced back to Lira, still laughing at Mags' innocent look. "The strength of our allies is what keeps us standing." Placing a hand on Kayden's knee, he nodded once more. "I think it is best to end our lesson for today. I believe we would both like to end on a celebratory note, do you agree?" Vesper picked up his pack.

"Hey, wait," Kayden said, grabbing his arm before he could walk off. "Thanks for teaching me. It's been awhile since anyone's taught me something without wanting more in return."

Vesper nodded. "It is my pleasure, Miss Ralta. I shouldn't say it was not without benefit to me—it has been long time since I've been able to teach anyone something and have them appreciate me for it. There is so much more I could teach you, if you would have me." He started walking toward where the others were camped.

"I'd like that, actually. I'm enjoying it—though I could do without the hopping." Kayden walked close to him. Vesper always had such a peculiar, whimsical walk. He hadn't stammered much lately, which was strange. Maybe he was feeling less anxious.

He shrugged and a sly smile perked at the corners of his cracked lips. "If you do not wish to hop and dance, then you must end the spell on your own abilities. Come, we will need our rest if we are to return to Sir Mirado soon."

Returning.

It felt like a bad idea. A waste of time. She knew Lira grew far more anxious since they discovered the prisoners were sent to Solmarsh. Kayden worried about the time it would take to even get there. They were days from Wolf Camp, and it could have been days, or even weeks until Jirah would even arrive. He had so many other camps that the others didn't know about, and it was terribly inefficient. *Wouldn't he just send us to Solmarsh after anyways? Then again, he told us to return to report.*

As they meandered closer to the camp, Kayden could hear the swishing winds, the dripping of water on the dirt, and a tense, fiery argument between the others.

Down at the camp, the game ended. Instead, a war of words erupted in its place. "I don't think that's a good idea, Lira. That's disobeying a direct order!" she heard Domika say.

"But it could be *weeks* before we get there. We have to act now!" Lira shot back.

Kayden ran faster, her boots squishing on the mud. Vesper followed, but he wasn't a fast runner.

"I do not believe that is the best choice. Sir Mirado gave us a direct order," Mags said.

"I know, but this is serious. Things are getting worse, and who knows how many people have been sent there, let alone where they're being kept. We don't have time to tell Jirah what we're doing," Lira pleaded.

As Kayden entered the clearing, all three of the others stood beside the dwindling fire, leaning into their stances with intense glares. "What's going on here?" Kayden commanded.

Domika flicked a judging hand toward Lira. "She wants to go home and disobey orders. My brother told us to come back. He might have a better idea of what to do. We shouldn't go in blind."

Spreading her arms, Lira scoffed at her words. "We're going together. I know Solmarsh better than the rest of you. If something nefarious is going on in secret, sending more soldiers in will just make things worse. Kayden, you can't tell me I'm not in the right," Lira said strongly.

With a huff, Domika crossed her arms. "I know your brother is part of it, but that doesn't mean we should rush in."

Lira shot forward. "Don't tell me I shouldn't go! This isn't about just my brother, it's about so many others! If we go, we can do so much more. If you don't think it's a good idea, then you can go with Magnus to inform *your* brother, and I'll go alone to find mine," Lira said sternly. The fire flickered so brightly in her dark eyes that it almost seemed like the flame was real, burning within.

Kayden hadn't seen such intense eyes on Lira before. Her anxiety over her brother's life was getting to her, and she wouldn't back down. Kayden rubbed her forehead and let out a sigh. "Okay, everyone be quiet. I can't think with everyone yammering." In the silence, she could finally work things out. The unpredictability of Jirah's presence was a problem—she was already concerned about that. Callidan said 'it' was nearly finished, and that put a rush on their arrival. Disobeying orders wasn't Kayden's first choice, but it was the best choice.

They had to act. Lira was right.

"Callidan said whatever is being done, is finishing soon. We don't have time to go back. We can't force Lira to do anything.

She's going, and I'm going with her. Domika, you go back to camp and inform Jirah."

"I'm not letting you go without me," Domika said boldly. She let out a long sigh and shrugged. "You're right. If it's finishing soon, you may need all the help you can get."

"I won't let you go alone," Mags said as well.

Kayden looked back at Vesper, who returned a confident nod. "Fine, it's decided then. We're disobeying orders. We head toward Solmarsh at dawn." Kayden walked to her things and rummaged though to ensure everything was there. *Jirah was so adamant on having us return, but why? That doesn't matter anymore. We're going.*

Kayden felt a light tap on her shoulder. When she turned, Lira was crouched behind her.

"Thanks. They ganged up a little," Lira said quietly.

Kayden patted Lira's shoulder and nodded with a proud smile. "You stood your ground. Don't worry. We're going to find him. I promise." *I just hope we aren't too late.*

Chapter Thirty-one

The Temple of Titan's Rock

Zaedor Nethilus

It had been ten days since their departure from Zenato. It was a quick, straight route to Titan's Rock. Zaedor sat on the cart since they left, not having much time to move around. His back ached and his legs grew stiff and were in need of movement. The merchant moved his caravan quickly, traveling for almost all daylight hours. They passed through the desert for days, mostly barren wastes, rather than dunes. *Thank the gods, if they even listen,* Zaedor thought. If there were dunes, crossing would take twice as long, if that.

Zaedor spent his time listening to his gleeful comrade, whether he liked it or not. Nargosh talked for hours on end in his whimsical voice about all the places he'd been, to anyone who would listen.

Grom Kanda, the Terran who owned the caravan, listened sometimes, but sat on the front of the cart and tuned them out for the majority of the time. Terrans were a curious bunch: they were bland in their voice, and had brown to grey or white rock-like skin that moved as little as the mountains.

Zaedor listened to Nargosh carefully, as he knew he had a lot to learn. His universe was Amirion, and without it, he only had the mysterious outside world now. He still resented the deserts, though. It was possibly the dry heat he disliked, or the fact that he was kidnapped there. *Damn brigands.* The west was said to be filled with lush forests and marshes, which Zaedor never saw. It was home to a mixed people, with many races and personalities. Last time Nargosh was there, the late king Bracchus still ruled the land, before it was split into three.

He worried things may have changed now, more than he would have preferred. He told of the beautiful Lilac Lake, a massive fount of water in the middle of the region, north of which was the burned forest of the Treants, which has slowly re-grown since the war against the brute, savage Broken ten years ago. Zaedor did not know much of the war with the Broken; he only heard stories of their chaotic, conflictive nature, and their defeat.

The new nation of Orinas was the most appealing to Zaedor. They were an orderly society, with an emphasis on military training. Pristine, stone streets lined the capital, filled with people, and banners flying on all the houses. Freya, Kindro, and Rodrick were there, as well. He hoped he could see them again. He knew the town they went to, northeast of the capital, in the mountains. However, Zaedor had a mission to complete first.

"Mr. Zaedor, might I ask why you wish to go to Solmarsh?"

Zaedor was taken aback, as he realized he never mentioned it. "I believe there is something there I can do to help people. Something connected to what happened in Amirion." A shiver shot down his spine. *I still can't believe it's all gone.* He curled his legs in close. He worried that he was one of the few of his people left, with no people to call his own. *I promised I would fight for justice, not a people. But I can't just forget about my home.*

"Oh my. I hope you are right, old bean. It is quite the journey for a hunch!"

"I have no home, Nargosh, I am but a nomad, now."

"Ah, it is best not to think that way. I may not live anywhere in particular, either, but I find home in every friend I meet." Nargosh may have been a bit odd, but his words were wise. Through rugged, rotted teeth came sweet words that gave him restitution.

Yet Zaedor was alone. He still felt his death was waiting for him—a mission a god of evil did not finish. Lilanda, Lothel, and so many more were gone. "I don't have any friends."

Nargosh gave him a swift slap on the shoulder. "Nonsense, old bean! You have *me*!" Nargosh guffawed loudly, followed by a rough cough. "*Ahem*, excuse me. Don't forget those three nice people that we parted with. Just because they are far away, doesn't mean they are not friends, my boy! We have a new destination in the west, and many more people to see!" He was undeniably optimistic, and Zaedor supposed he needed it. He wondered how many years Nargosh had under his belt.

Despite his own many years, Zaedor was isolated for so long. At the age of thirty, he finally left his home to explore the world, and not on his own terms. "How old are you, Nargosh?" Zaedor asked.

"Oh, old enough, my friend. I'd rather not say and be a target of laughter! I'm younger than I look. It must be the sand aging me," he said, chuckling. "Age is but a number. Everyone grows at different rates, and explores at different ages. I've been seeing the world as long as my old noggin can remember!"

Zaedor understood and left it alone. The old man was possibly sixty years of age, but maybe he was fifty, considering what he said. Though in Amirion, he did learn that good nutrition kept one looking better longer when he was young, and Nargosh didn't live a fabulous life, it seemed.

It had been a couple of days since Zaedor paid attention to where they were. The sands receded, and they came into short, sparse grassland, leading up to a massive grey rock formation—the largest he ever saw. Titan's Rock covered the sky in their direction. He knew the bonebound gate was the most direct route, so this concerned him. "Which route are we taking?"

"Ah, worry not, my boy. We aren't going to the gate—we're taking another route." He leaned in close and whispered in a devious tone. "Can you keep a secret?"

A secret? What secret? Zaedor grew suspicious. He didn't like information being withheld from him. "I suppose I can. Although, I am a tad weary of mountains—"

"It's a path that my friend and I found years ago. There are a few hidden tunnels through the mountains! The gate is surrounded by armies and war, and we don't need those kinds of problems, do we?"

Zaedor definitely didn't want to encounter Rawling's military strength. He didn't know whether his people were being hunted, imprisoned, or let free, and would rather not find out the hard way. The mountain was massive, twice the size of any other in the land. It was staggering to even look at. "How long will it take us to get through?"

"A few days. It'll be dark, but we have torches. Luckily, Grom here can see quite well in the dark."

The mountain took up more and more of his view as they approached, with a snow-covered peak so high it reached above the clouds. Atop it a tall, mighty tower reached so high he felt it could not be real; it was a monument to the gods, the tower named Eternum. Zaedor heard stories that no Human nor any other race reached its doors. It was surrounded by a massive canyon at the mountain peak, with devastating winds and slick walls no man could climb. It was said if one made it up the canyon wall, through the doors and up the tower, they would be granted a wish.

"Where's this entrance?" Zaedor asked.

"Up ahead! It doesn't look like it, does it?" Nargosh laughed. "Just wait, old bean!"

As they approached the massive grey, rough wall, the shadows turned ever so slightly, revealing a small opening. It was almost unseen, camouflaged by the rest of the rough-hewn mountain wall. It went deep into the dark, and given the size of the mountain, Nargosh's prediction of time would be right, if not shorter than reality.

They pushed on into the blackness of Titan's Rock. The sound of trickling water echoed from the ceilings, dripping onto their backs once and again. It was cold as well, but nothing compared to the season of Air.

Snow crept to Amirion, but not further south. Amirion had the blessing of seeing all seasons—Water, Fire, Earth and Air—unlike the northern icelands, which hardly experienced the season of Fire at all. The season of Water was riddled with snow, and the season of Wind was unbearably cold. So cold, a man's blood and bones would freeze within minutes away from fire or warm clothing. There was often much death during the Wind. If the season was much longer than it was, it would likely wipe out much of the population, aside from those that ally with the season, such as the Frozelias and Frost Giants.

Zaedor wondered how a mountain so large could form. The legend, as Nargosh told, was that in the first age, the land was filled with mountains and rough, desolate rock. A Titan—a massive being sent by the gods—pushed the lands around it to the center of Renalia, leaving fertile land below, and creating the massive mountain in the middle. Legends also said it was the path to the lowlands and the heavens through the sky tower at its peak, Eternum. It also split the land in two by smashing its foot where the Risen Isles lie, leaving the other half across the sea far from Renalia, the land named Kathynta. While Zaedor found his stories hardly believable, they were entertaining nonetheless. *A massive being? Where did it go, then?*

Zaedor wondered what awaited him on the other side of Titan's Rock. He imagined a new land filled with trees, lakes, and swamps. He hadn't known it in truth and was interested to see a land of luscious plant and flora. He heard there was a conflict within the region and hoped it wouldn't cause him any issues.

Zaedor also pondered the new life he was entering here. The world was filled with fast-living people. The three leaders of the land engaged in a war, and Zaedor was not excited to get swept up into the conflict. Amirion stayed neutral to avoid unnecessary conflicts of warring states, each eager to have more land. Since his kingdom was gone, Zaedor had been pushed into the combative world beyond.

After what seemed like an eternity and a brief sleep, they came to a grand opening in the cavern. A hollowed wind passed through his hair, and the sound of the caravan echoed far in the distance. A light was seen from the opening, warm and inviting, yet it made Zaedor anxious.

They soon came to a massive stone dome, the walls smooth and built purposefully. There were magical lights surrounding the room, and a central pillar set in white stones, with several runes and ancient carvings in it. Most noticeably, there were many statues in different sizes of a peculiar metal, surrounding the wall of the pillar.

"Ah, here we are, Mr. Zaedor. The inner room of the mountain!" Nargosh called out. "You see there? That's the mighty Eternal Column, it's named. Those brilliant Golems guard it, and you can see that there is trouble getting by. There are lights all around the center, and outside, as well! No one knows how those work, either."

There *was* trouble getting by. A mass of skeletons surrounded the Golems. The statues seemed to be a mix of metal and crystal, shining from the dim lights surrounding the pillar. Grom guided the camels and horses leading the caravan around the edge of the large room, as they felt the gaze of the Golems linger on them.

"What do you think it is?" Zaedor asked, his eyes not leaving the engraved pillar. There were tunnels out in the north and south end, also. Zaedor wondered where they led.

"I'm not sure, my friend! I've heard it's the path to the tower above, but some say it's the path to the underworld! No one knows how it works, as no one can get close!" Nargosh said, chuckling.

Zaedor felt drawn to it, yet the allure was almost nauseating. He found himself crawling closer to the edge of the caravan, and before he could react, he was halfway off the cart and tumbling off—until something grabbed him from behind. He felt a hand grip the back of his neckline, pulling him back up.

"Mr. Zaedor, I would not suggest running off! I wouldn't want to lose you on this journey of ours! I would feel very responsible." They slowly went back into the black halls on the other side, seeing the light of the room fade.

Zaedor's mind cleared once more. He shook and rubbed his head. "What happened?"

"I'm not sure, my good man! You almost crawled off the caravan toward the pillar, possibly to an unfortunate end, seeing the others around the Golems. You gave me quite a scare!"

He shook it off, trying to forget about that room. He had to focus on his plan. The halls became dark, moist, and cold once more. They were halfway out now. The dark must have been getting to him. He wasn't sure how long he'd been in there, as there was no way to tell time inside the mountain. Several hopefully short days after they exited, Zaedor would be at his destination. He hoped he could find something in Solmarsh—and also hoped he was not too late.

Chapter Thirty-two

The Path of Life

Lira Kaar

Lira and the others rushed into Solmarsh through the vicious rain that hammered the ground. Lira's blistered and calloused feet groaned with each step. She was not used to walking much, let alone for days and days on end. She was disappointed in herself for disobeying orders, but she had to come home. There was no telling what went on, and if they waited another fortnight…

They barely made it across the lake using the rickety boat; it almost sunk from the raw water falling from the sky. It had cracks and rotted spots, but at least it carried them across. Lira felt as though she actually fell in the lake, though—the rain was torrential.

Her robe was soaked through, hair like a wet dog's. Even Kayden's knotted mane of hair was flattened and drenched. She retrieved her keys from Soghra, the Hydris who owned the inn. He kept it safe while she was away.

He kindly gave the key and asked a few questions of her new friends. Lira was sweet and polite, as she always tried to be. She carefully asked about the disappearances, but Sohgra knew almost nothing about it, save for strange markings in the center of town.

"Markings? What markings?" Lira asked.

Soghra ran his azure fingers through his white, ratty hair. "A circle carved into the cobblestones in a language none of us know. They showed up two days ago." His voice was like a hiss, but his words were polite and solemn. "The disappearances started a few weeks ago, and have only gotten worse. A scout from the Scions came and asked about 'em. She was a mountainous woman, 'round seven feet tall, with fiery red hair. Not too bright, though."

"What?" Lira said brittly. Only one individual matched that description that she could think of. "Alexandra? Sh—she knew?"

"What, did she not tell the boss?" Kayden wanted to know. She crossed her arms and leaned against the wall. She shook her hair wildly, attempting to get rid of some of the water.

Lira saw the look in Jirah's eyes as they left for Deurbin. *He was reluctant to send us, but why? Why hide it?* "He didn't want to send us to Deurbin to begin with—" Lira looked to the floor and picked at her fingernails. "Why would he do that?" *He knew my brother was among them. How could he?*

"There must be a reason, my dear Miss Kaar," Vesper said. "Surely there was."

"What, he *lied* to us? Does he think he can just keep secrets and send us on whatever idiotic mission he wants? Did he know who was in Deurbin? I swear, if he did—"

"Kayden, please, I'm sure he wouldn't do that," Lira said, leaning on the counter in front of Sohgra. She hoped Jirah didn't know. He prided himself on his honesty, and this made her feel like it was all a lie. "He must have had a reason. I can't believe he would hold back, though." She rubbed her arms nervously.

"Well I don't like being lied to. When we finish this, I'm going to make sure he doesn't forget that," Kayden growled, turning her gaze to Sohgra. "How many people have disappeared?"

"I'm not sure, missy. Twenty, maybe thirty."

Lira gasped, bringing her hand quickly to her mouth. "Oh no." She felt sick to her stomach. She knew many in town. If anyone were to have passed due to this, she would feel responsible. She had to find out what happened. Lira wouldn't be able to forgive herself if something happened to the people in her town. She was glad the others came with her, as she wouldn't be of much use all alone.

Domika held Lira's shoulders. "Don't worry, Lira, we'll find them."

Lira sniffled and nodded.

"Lira, whatever the case, it's good that you're back. We've missed you, and—Calvin's been asking about you," Sohgra said with a sigh. "As usual."

Calvin was *always* asking about her. He attempted to court her multiple times, but Lira never accepted his advances. He was a gentle man, but not quite Lira's type. He was much older than Lira, and ever since she turned sixteen, he was constantly attempting to court her. She was glad Loughran was restrictive in their marriage traditions toward eighteen—next year. She delayed marrying as long as she could, as she never found any interest in anyone yet. She hadn't told anyone, save for her brother. He told her to still try to marry, as it was best for her. She resisted as much as she could, though. Calvin didn't let it go, however.

"Lira!" The door slammed open. There he was. Calvin. His smile was wide as ever. He was ecstatic, and absolutely drenched by the storm.

"I saw your group enter town as I was taking some alchemy materials to Shamra! It's been so long!" He rushed in for a hug.

"Whoa, there. Better slow your pace," Kayden said, stopping him quickly.

Kayden was protective and didn't know anyone in town. Lira smiled and lowered Kayden's hand. "It's all right, he's a friend."

"Just a friend?" Calvin asked. He never gave up.

"Just a friend." Lira did her best to fake a smile, but was still overcome by the dark news of the disappearances—and potentially Jirah's lie.

"On your way, now," Kayden said with a frown. "Wouldn't want your bad luck to rub off on us."

Calvin's arms dropped and he looked to the floor. "Oh. Well, In either case, I'm glad you're back, no matter how long. I hope you can stay. I have exciting news to tell you!" He blinked twice. "I've been so worried since you left town."

"I don't think I can. I have responsibilities elsewhere. Cheer up, okay? We'll be here for at least a night or two. Maybe we can have dinner together tomorrow? As friends."

"Sure, I'd love that! I'll talk to you tomorrow." Calvin smiled again. He happily bowed and walked out of the inn.

Kayden swatted Lira's shoulder. "You really have to learn to let someone down hard. He's going to keep asking. Dinner might give him the wrong idea."

"Being brash isn't always the answer, Kayden," Lira snapped.

"Sometimes it is." Kayden looked to the others, each nodded in agreement. "See? Even Domika agrees with me. Of course, you can do whatever you want, you're a grown woman. But if you want to stop being annoyed with him, that's what you have to do."

"Oh, stop it. He's nice," Lira replied. Each of the others gave her a sarcastic nod of agreement. Lira rolled her eyes. "I've made it clear to him several times. His interpretation of how I feel isn't my responsibility."

Kayden's expression grew sullen. "Didn't say it was. It's just the reality we live in."

Motioning to the door, she said, "Come on, let's go to my home. There are two beds and two small couches."

Lira led them back into the heavy rain. Their feet squished loudly in their shoes, and even louder on the muddy ground as the rain hammered them. They soon arrived to her home; she had not seen it in a month, and it hadn't changed a bit.

The gardens, while soaked, were well-kept by Soghra. She unlocked the door quickly and ran in, water dripping everywhere from the five of them. Lira snatched some absorbent linens and wool blankets for them to dry off and warm up with. The roof echoed with the sound of what seemed like a thousand drums, pounding in unison. The main room was the same as before: a small fireplace fit with quite a few logs, the plush, red cushioned oak couch, and the two wooden chairs with thick wool blankets. Those, and Lira's vast wardrobe of crafts.

Lira just stood at the door, waiting for them to finish up. She didn't want to wait to get to work. She had work to do. "Are you almost ready?" she called to the others. Each glanced toward her with a raised brow.

Domika drew her mouth to the side. "Don't you need to rest? We've been traveling all day and it's pouring out."

She shook her head. Not backing down. "It's just rain."

Vesper shot off the chair, hand in the air. "I shall accompany you, my dear. It is not quite late, so we should not wait!"

Kayden gave Vesper a playful shove. "Sure, let's get to work. We can at least go check the markings, and then to that one friend the boss mentioned back at camp. Heard about it while I 'wasn't supposed to be listening.'"

They visited the markings around the center of town—a large circle around twenty feet across, cobblestones that had always been there, but now were carved into. It comprised of runes or letters with sharp, jagged lines and curves, none any saw before. The rain lightened up a little, so it was a tad easier to see.

Magnus stared long and hard at them with his arms crossed. "They have accents of the languages of Devils and Demons—but it is neither."

That sent an unsettling pain through Lira's stomach. "What do you mean?" Lira asked.

Domika poked her head in. "It means this language has similar dialects to both, but isn't either. It's probably evil or something. No offense," she said, looking to Magnus. He seemed unaffected.

Kayden just shrugged, trying to cover her hair. "This is a waste of time. It's pouring out still. Write it down, Ves. We'll check that other place next," Kayden commanded. Vesper took out a small piece of charcoal and parchment and scribbled away vigorously under the cover of his broad robe.

They made their way to the south end of town. Dilapidated blackwood buildings and shacks lined the street, as well as a small, quiet market of shoddy booths and tattered-clothed merchants. Kayden motioned for them to keep their eyes open and hands on their coin purses. A few hooded individuals sauntered through the marketplace then. The narrow streets slowly became cloaked in shadows as the sun set behind the horizon beyond the rainclouds.

Knightly Knowledge, the place was called. It was a large, raggedy old blackwood building with a door almost off its hinges. Pieces of the door were rotted and broken off.

A trader? Why did Jirah suggest we go here? Lira wondered.

The group entered to see a large man in a velvet robe sitting behind the counter. There was only one candle burning beside him as he read from a large book. Lira could barely make out the features of his face, except for thin crescents accenting a dark visage under his velvet hood.

The man looked up with his dark eyes, crooked teeth lining his lower jaw, and sported a suspiciously wide smile. "Oh my, what do we have here?" he spoke with a rough, yet honeyed voice. He gingerly turned the page of his book, and the white ring on his finger shone brightly in the candlelight.

With every step, the floor creaked loudly. "Jirah sent us. We're looking for information about the disappearances," Domika said.

"Oh, did he?" the dark man chuckled. "I'm glad. I told him to send for you a few weeks ago. My my, he certainly takes his time."

"Yes, I suppose so," Lira said quietly. "May I ask your name?" Lira didn't know this shop; she didn't even remember it being in town. *How long did Jirah know about Solmarsh? she wondered.* Lira couldn't believe it. He wouldn't do such a thing.

"My name is Krogar Steeltooth, a merchant here. I'm an old friend of your fiery superior."

"Are you able to help us?" Kayden asked. It had been a long day of knocking on doors and talking to victims, and Kayden was not in a patient mood.

"Oh, I might." Krogar chuckled.

"What do you mean 'you might?'" Kayden replied harshly.

"Depends on your mood, my mood, how much coin you might have—"

"Are you serious?" Kayden scoffed. She leaned to whisper to Lira. "*What's with this guy?*"

"Knowledge is my trade, miss."

Kayden got visibly flustered. She scratched both sides of her head. It had been a long day, and she was on her last limbs. Krogar looked at her as if he knew it and wanted to make it worse for a bit of fun.

Lira was confused. *Why was he not being straight?* She had to be patient, as the suspicious man across from them seemed to want to toy with them. "Well, Mister Krogar, we were wondering if you knew anything about the markings in town?"

Krogar exploded with a loud guffaw. "*Mister* Krogar! My, that's a good one, dearie. I like you," he said, barely stifling his laugh. "I wouldn't know anything about markings since I'm not in front of them, but I might know if I had something to read." It was hard to believe he hadn't seen the markings themselves. It was clear he was playing a game with them, and Lira had to win.

She looked toward Vesper, who walked forward with his scribble-covered parchment and placed it on the dimly-lit counter. "Might this be of help, my friend?" Vesper said.

Krogar looked up to him with a sincere smile. "Thank you, my dear entertainer."

How does he know Vesper's history? Lira wondered. She supposed it was because he saw a show. Vesper had done quite a bit of traveling in his day, and Krogar *did* say information was his trade.

"*Hmm*—" Krogar scratched his scruffy beard. "My, I haven't seen this language in a long while."

Lira's eyes widened, "You know it?" She was surprised, and relieved. Now they just needed him to tell them what it meant, if he felt like it.

Kayden laughed from her lean against the wall. "Wow, that shot in the dark worked out."

"Especially because it's dark in here." Krogar looked at them with a side-smile, and everyone was bewildered. "Never mind."

"Is this a game to you?" Kayden groaned.

"Kayden, be more respectful. He's helping, right?" Lira said, returning her look to Krogar's dark eyes.

"Oh, that depends. I don't like my feelings being hurt. What's wrong with having a little fun?" The shadow-faced man smiled widely and winked.

"Fine, fine, I'll leave. I'm waiting outside." Kayden grumbled and stormed out with a *slam* of the rickety door.

"*Hmph*. Well, remember not to put her in the corner," Krogar laughed. "She's a tad upset with me, what ever did I do?" he huffed with a grin. "Now, where were we?" His voice was sweet, but his words were convoluted. He seemed to enjoy irritating people—at least those easily frustrated.

"The markings?" Lira quipped. "Do you know what they say?" She watched Krogar's expression. It was a curious, analyzing stare. It was also oddly intimidating. "Please, I'm concerned about the people in this town. My brother was among a group of prisoners moved here as well. We have to figure out what happened."

Krogar leaned back with his large, puffy hands interlocked behind his head. "Well, you do seem like a nice bunch. Let me think for a moment." He slowly turned to Magnus with a grin. "Say, I have a message from your grandfather, if you want it."

Magnus's red pupils quickly turned to glare at him. "*What?*" Magnus did not put much emotion into many of his words. Ever. So her ears definitely perked up in response. Everyone's did.

"I know him. We talk here and there. Is it something you wish to hear in private? He did say you were a secretive man."

Magnus walked forward. His eyes bore into him, analyzing every part of Krogar. He leaned on the counter, looming over him. "Yes, I will hear it afterward. Will you help us?"

Lira wondered why this was so significant. If it helped them get information, she was satisfied. Every moment counted toward potentially saving her townspeople.

"Yes, I think I will. I'm interested in you young folks," Krogar said, eyes lingering on Lira. "It means, Miss Raelira, 'The harbinger comes by the path of life.'" The name alone set her off-balance and confused the others. Knowledge. She never went by her full name.

"What does that mean?" Lira poised. *What harbinger? What life?*

"If I had to think, I'd say it was a summoning circle," Vesper said. "Although, I have no experience with divine magic."

Lira gasped at a sudden realization. "Oh no! You don't think they're—they can't be hurting them to summon some monster? They can't!" Lira couldn't bear the thought.

Krogar raised his eyebrows in surprise. "Isn't that a fascinating connection." Krogar spoke with a light tone, almost as if he was impressed.

Domika gently placed a hand on Lira's shoulder. "Lira, don't worry. We'll find them. We'll figure out what's happening."

Lira leaned into the counter, causing Krogar to jump back for once. "Do you know anything else? Please, we must know!" she pleaded.

He paused for a moment, then spoke deeply. "I'm sorry, my dear, but I can't help you any further than that. The rest is up to you." He smiled again. "Now, out with you. My friend here asked for privacy." He waved his hands at them, ushering them out of the dark room, toward the gathering storm outside. Lira obliged, as did the others. Domika needed to give her a little nudge to get her moving. As they left, Kayden was waiting.

"Good, finally. I thought you were all going to get conned by that weirdo."

"Kayden, you don't have to be mean. He helped eventually—and for free," Lira jabbed. *But what is he hiding?* Lira felt he knew more than he'd said, or could add something else, but he refused to continue. Lira needed more information, more help, but she had nothing. *It's up to me.* Maybe Calvin would help.

But she thought about it. There was an inkling in his voice, a twinge to his eye, and the double blink that told a tale. Lira had a plan.

"Yeah, well, he kept dancing around the point, and it bugged me. Say, where's Mags?"

"Krogar said he had a message from his grandfather. I'm not sure what it was, but he wanted to hear it in private."

Kayden dashed to the door and pressed her ear to the frame. "Damn it, I can only hear muffled mumbles. Mags seems *furious*."

The mumbling went for a minute, and then stopped abruptly. Heavy footsteps approached the door. "Whoop!" Kayden yelped, jumping back.

The door slowly opened, and Magnus glanced over the four curious pairs of eyes looking at him. "Let us return so we can rest. We have another day of investigation tomorrow," he said bluntly. His brow was furrowed and tight.

"You aren't going to tell us what that was all about?" Kayden asked in a silvery voice.

"It is my business." He frowned, clenching the black scabbard on his left hip.

Kayden huffed, crossing her arms. "Fine, I get it. Let's go. I need a rest, and I need out of this damn rain. It's getting heavy again."

Lira wondered why he was so private about it. They knew nothing of his family, or his history. She hoped that eventually he would open up to them and wondered if he was ashamed of his past. He had been called a monster, given dirty looks from many they encountered on their past few missions. Some threatened him with a blade or violent means, but he was unfazed. Lira worried that he'd heard those words for many years of his life. She also worried that he felt he deserved it. In Deurbin, he admitted that he knew the normal state of Half-Devils, a race of men and women who killed, stole, and defiled the innocent.

Magnus was different. Of that, Lira felt was certain. *But why?*

But that didn't matter now. With each step back home, one phrase repeated over and over.

The harbinger comes by the path of life.

Which life?

Chapter Thirty-three

Laced with Crimson

Lira Kaar

Running inside Lira's home, they could finally rest and dry off. Domika went into Noren's room to look around. Lira almost called out for her to stay out but relented. She couldn't restrict her friends from their home—especially when they were here to help her save the one that used to live within.

"Wow," Kayden said, as if she was speechless. "Check out all these clothes." She looked through a plethora of linen and wool shirts and all other clothing articles.

Lira chuckled. "I wasn't a liar when I said I was a clothier by profession, Kayden."

"Your clothing is always so well-made, but I didn't think you made *this* much." She popped out of the racks, realizing she was still soaked. "Ah, sorry."

While she was distracted by the clothes, Domika popped out of the room wearing a new, drier outfit. "Why aren't you interested in that guy earlier, Lira? He seems nice." She wiped at her damp, obsidian-black hair until the flame slowly returned to flicker over it once more. "A little strange, but nice."

She just shrugged in response. "I don't know. I just never felt any interest. Is that so odd?" It's not like she wasn't attracted to people. She eyed Domika once and again; she had a beautiful figure, and her hair was strangely attractive with the subtle flame flickering above it. There were a few men in town she thought to like, but they were arranged for.

Kayden stuck her head out of the clotheslines. "Nope. I know when I don't like someone. I can smell it." Magnus gave a nod of agreement. She took her soaked armor off quickly, wrung out her teal scarf, and wrapped it around her neck again. Even without her armor, she was cloaked full in linen.

"What, are you a dog now?" Domika said in a snarky tone.

Kayden glared in response. "Don't test me." She turned her head and raised her chin. "Call it 'women's intuition.'" Kayden wrapped herself in the blanket, put a towel around her hair, and walked into Lira's old room.

Lira walked in behind her to make sure that Kayden didn't make a mess. Lira may not have lived there anymore, but she was a little particular. She walked in and sat on her small, oak feather-cushioned sofa. Kayden pulled out *elemental attunement* and read quietly. Lira dropped into thought as the others got ready for sleep in the other room.

Kayden was always alert. She always judged each person she met very quickly and acted on it. Lira wished Kayden gave people more of a chance, but it couldn't be helped. She had a mind of her own—especially with the magic her and Vesper practiced.

Each time they went to work it was a hilarious sight; Lira could barely stifle her laughter and could see why Kayden didn't want anyone watching. She would scream at Vesper for making her do it, telling him to stop, but he only ever had one response: 'Make me.'

Kayden confided in him more, now. She talked to him in camp and reveled in stories of his performances and magical teachings.

Lira felt her hair, still wet, and combed it into a ponytail. She reached into her bag, and took out the yellow scarf from weeks ago and examined the detail. She took more care with it than usual.

"What's that?" Kayden asked, pointing to the scarf.

Uh oh. Embarrassing. "*Ah,* nothing. Just something I made."

Kayden got up from the bed, meandered over to the couch beside Lira, and pulled her legs in. "You don't wear scarves. Listen, princess. While I appreciate flattery, I don't like being copied." She gave Lira a joking nudge. After Lira gave an embarrassed, awkward laugh, Kayden said, "What? C'mon, it was a joke."

Lira looked into Kayden's eyes, which showed confusion more than anything. "Well, I, *ah,* kind of made it for—uh—you." Lira held out the bright yellow scarf in her arms. "I thought I'd make you one. Because you're important to me." She wanted to give it to her ever since the night on the roof. Something changed between them—like they were sisters.

"Me?" Kayden stuttered. She covered her mouth as her eyes analyzed the scarf for a prolonged moment. Her hand shook as she grabbed the soft wool and felt it in her hand. "It's lovely," she stuttered. With a gentle grasp, she carefully accepted it. "The one I wear was given to me by my mom, before—" her voice dropped off. A tear crept from her eye, slowly dancing down her cheek like a fleeting memory.

"Oh, I'm so sorry. I didn't—" Lira felt horrible. *Who am I, thinking I could replace her mother's scarf?* "I had no idea. I'll take it back—I'll make something else. I don't want to replace something that important. I'm so sorry, I'm—"

"I'll wear it," Kayden said softly. She intertwined it with her mom's thin teal scarf. She looked back to Lira with a different shine to her eye. Belonging. Appreciation. With a gentle smile, she said, "Thank you."

Lira just shrugged. "It's nothing." It was only a scarf. She took a lot of care in making said scarf, and took a while to give it to her, and Kayden meant a lot to her, but...

Kayden's smile spoke a different message. *It's everything.*

As Kayden analyzed her new gift, Lira went to check on the others; Magnus sat on the floor by Domika, and both stared into the stone fireplace. Vesper was out like a torch, lying in Lira's chair in the corner by the door. It seemed as though the pounding of rain put him right to sleep.

Looking back toward Kayden, she seemed lost in thought, touching the new scarf. "What's on your mind?"

Kayden's face was blank. She glanced out the window. "When my parents died, I felt I didn't have a home anymore." Her grip on her shins tightened. She looked to the others, then back to Lira. "Maybe I have one, now." Kayden stared at the door and frowned. "I don't like that Calvin guy. He's strange."

"You don't like a lot of people." Lira sighed. "We've known each other for a long time. Just because someone is nice and insistent doesn't mean I'm attracted to him like that." Lira's voice trailed off. Something about his double blink told her something was up, even though their meeting was brief. She could feel it.

"I could tell. You weren't sending any hints. You shouldn't go along with it. When you ask him out to dinner, he takes that as a chance."

"I don't want to be mean. Like I said, it's not my responsibility since I've already declined his proposition. Also, he might know something about the disappearances."

"Sometimes you have to be mean. They should 'get it', but some people just don't. We could ask for info at his door, or at his work. You don't have to ask him out to dinner," Kayden said with a glare. "Just be careful, all right?" She bounded off the couch to the bed and lay down. "Damn, I'm tired. 'Specially since we kept going after arriving. Listen, I'm gonna take this bed, if that's all right," Kayden said, rolling up in the blanket.

Lira crept out of her room and closed the door.

"Having some girl talk?" Domika asked. She was sitting in the chair by the fire, wearing a pair of bright yellow wool pants and a white linen shirt that outlined her womanly figure.

Lira walked over and sat beside Magnus in front of the fire. "Not necessarily. It's my room, so I'm very particular about it."

Domika just shrugged. "Letting her sleep in your bed? My, you're brave. I'd be afraid of her cutting me in my sleep."

"That isn't very nice. I'm sleeping out here, anyways." After a pause, she said, "Why are you two always at each other's throats?"

She held up her hands. "I don't like being accused of things. When my brother left home, they accused me of helping him get out, when I wished he'd never left," she paused. "Kayden thinks I'm a bad person." Domika looked to the floor and fidgeted with her feet. Her voice turned brittle, barely heard over the crackle of fire. "It's not like I hate her. She just doesn't understand where I'm coming from. I—" Her voice cut off as she stared into the soothing blaze. The flame's light dimly danced across her face, accentuating her soft features. "She's just frustrating. You know what I mean?"

"Some simply need time," Magnus said quietly.

Domika sighed. "Maybe you're right. Maybe we all just need time," she said brittly, gazing into the fire with a stony expression.

After a pause, Lira looked at Domika's ringmail dress hanging over the chair, and her scythe leaned up against it. It was a strange and exotic weapon to use. It simply seemed specialized. Her and Kayden seemed so different—but both fought with such passion.

The fire and candles caused Domika's bronze skin to glow; but it accentuated the marred sections of her back and arms that bore scars. Old ones. "Where did you learn to fight?" she asked.

"What?" Domika said, looking muddled.

"You don't fight like most that I've seen. It's like a dance—almost hypnotic. I think it's a beautiful art." Lira fumbled with her hands. "I've never really been able to fight."

Domika chuckled. "Yeah, I saw Kayden trying to teach you a few things. It was pretty funny." She looked over to Lira, noticing her gaze at the floor as she rubbed her arms. "Sorry, I didn't mean to be unkind. It's good that you're trying, and it's good that she's trying to teach you a few things." Domika sighed. "I developed it myself. I learned to dance when I was young, growing up in Zenato City. It made me happy. Some told me my dancing was fiercer than others'—and through a few stumbles, I found a way of fighting that complemented my style."

"Stumbles?" Lira asked.

Domika's expression turned blank as she glanced at a long scar across her arm. "I'm sure Kayden told you how tough it is living out there. She isn't wrong."

"She did mention that. I never got the chance to travel or learn about the other cultures." Lira bit her lip.

Domika shrugged. "You'll learn about some of them, I'm sure. Some I hope you'll never have to." She rubbed her shoulders and looked toward the other bedroom. "I'm exhausted. I better hit the hay. Do you mind if I take the other room? Vesper is already out." His loud snoring echoed through the entire house. Or town.

"I prefer the floor. I have my bedroll," Magnus said. With how silent he was, she barely noticed his presence, despite his size.

Lira nodded with a smile. Domika went to the other room, briefly looking back before she gently closed the door.

Lira chuckled, staring at the fire as Magnus got his bedroll out with a strange silence. "Magnus, why do you prefer to be so quiet?"

He paused for a moment but continued unraveling his bedroll without looking over. "Over time, I have learned that listening teaches me far more about someone than speaking."

"Wise words, *Master* Magnus."

He looked so young—twenty-one, maybe. Yet he was One-hundred twenty-six. Lira wondered where he lived, and where he had been. "I am no master—I am still learning. Every wise person has a path of mistakes, my lady."

What kind of mistakes? Lira wondered. She knew so little about him, but he listened to everyone for so long. Lira felt good in him, but a darkness, as well. She didn't know how to explain it; it was just a hunch. He turned toward Lira's room as if checking on someone in particular.

It was a silent protective sense—as if he knew she could care for herself and dared not question her sense of independence. "Do you favor her?" Lira asked, motioning to Kayden's room.

Magnus looked to her with no reaction. No tells at all. "My feelings are not important, whether I do or do not."

Lira remembered she left her rucksack in her room with Kayden. She got up and gave a sly smirk. "Everyone's feelings are important. You should talk to her. Not necessarily about that sort of thing, but sometimes you must let others know more about you, too." Lira went to her bedroom door. "She has that flower pressed in her book, you know. Don't tell me that wasn't from you." Lira narrowed her eyes at him.

He simply nodded in response.

With a chuckle of victory, she said, "Rest up. We have work to do tomorrow," she said, trying her best to be cheerful. With a smile, she tried to stay strong. But each day broke her bit by bit.

She crept into her room and picked up her bag. Kayden was out cold, towel off her head. Kayden slept curled into a ball facing the middle of the bed, clutching her two scarves.

Lira tip-toed back to the door and cracked it open.

"Don't go," Kayden mumbled in her sleep. "Don't."

Lira curled her lip in, feeling as if she knew what that meant. Kayden was always reluctant to let anyone go anywhere dangerous without her.

"It's all right, I'm not going anywhere," Lira responded. She walked back to the couch that was barely long enough for her, and laid down under a blanket she had in the room.

"Okay," Kayden mumbled. She returned to deep breathing.

She wondered how much time they would spend in Solmarsh. She missed her home, and worried for the ones that vanished. Sohgra told her a few: Darryl Godron, the blacksmith, Terra Longworth, the head fisher for the docks, and many more. More wold come, she was sure, if they did not act quickly.

Lira fell into a deep sleep shortly after quieting her thoughts of concern, tired after a long day of traveling.

* * *

The next day, the group went house by house.

"Kidnappings! Armored folk carrying them off!" one said.

"A quick, crash-bang, and they're gone!" another supplied.

"Disappeared into the night!"

Lira wondered what 'they' were.

Kayden followed footprints from what she could find them, but the rain washed out the majority. The most peculiar thing was that at a point, the footprints would vanish. They were plate, some leather—not bare…

Less people wandered about the streets than usual. Some of they spoke to said the townsfolk avoided being out at night time, now.

Lira felt for the victims. She shared a few tears with them, but the others with her didn't shed a single one, and Lira couldn't see why. She always tried to empathize with others, yet Magnus, Kayden, and Domika stayed adamant the whole way through. She saw a glimpse of sadness in Vesper, but he calmed down quickly and returned to the strange man that he always was, except he mumbled and murmured less in recent days. Kayden always kept a strong demeanor when they meant business. She kept her soft side in check until they were behind closed doors.

But after their first day of door-knocking, they found nothing.

On their way back to Lira's house, Lira spotted Calvin walking into the centre of town alone, scratching his head in an awkward fashion. "Could we keep going?" she asked.

Kayden sighed. "I'm done. Too many people. I'm exhausted."

The others nodded and grumbled. She was tired as well, but something dug at her. "I'll meet you at my house. I'm going to look around a little longer."

"All right. Mags, keep an eye on her," Kayden said. Domika and Vesper walked with her, and Magnus stayed behind.

Lira crept around the corner of the road toward the center of town. Calvin scribbled on a piece of parchment, walking toward the markings. He scratched his head, analyzing them.

Lira glanced to Magnus, who raised a brow as well. By the time she looked back, Calvin was already walking away. She tried to keep out of sight, knowing if he even caught a glimpse of her he would stop what he was doing and come for a chat.

The previous night, something was off. Calvin was a peculiar man, but he always blinked twice when he was up to something, silly or not, and he had multiple times. Her gut feeling told her to follow him.

On his way, Calvin met with a few individuals in the town. He spoke to Harvey Trent Jr., his father's apprentice. They shook hands and spoke about a few ingredients needed for a couple concoctions for the alchemy shop. After he left, Harvey rubbed his head and sat down, as if exhausted.

Lira wanted to ask Harvey a few questions, but felt following Calvin was a better pursuit. As she kept her distance, the same thing happened twice. Calvin met with Porra Shiel, a fisher in Solmarsh, and Laura Pollard, the tanner. They shook hands, they seemed to tire, and then Calvin left.

"Peculiar. They seem to tire," Magnus whispered.

"Strange—" Lira's voice dropped off. Normally she wouldn't see it as an issue, but something didn't sit right with her. Calvin walked out the north gate of town, oddly enough. Lira rushed after him, until she saw something that stole the breath right out of her. Calvin spoke to a knight in crimson armor. She shot back behind the wall and motioned for Magnus to stay back.

Crimson armor. She feared the worst: Malakai. *Callidan spoke the truth.* "—and the girl?" a deep, resounding voice said.

"She won't be a problem. She's a good friend of mine and I assure you—"

"That *girl* was on our trail in multiple places." The knight cut Calvin off. "Kill her. Or does she mean something to you?"

"She is part of the arrangement, my Lord," Calvin said in a nervous tone. "She was the one promised to live should I endure these tasks. Lord Asheron said—"

"My brother gave me this task, and I shall not have it wasted on a whimsical decision. Should this fail—you cannot imagine the repercussions. Obtain the information about her that I have asked, should something falter. When we prepare, my brother will be here to ensure it moves forward. Keep that in mind."

"Yes, my L—" Silence. Then a gasp. Heavy breaths. "Where did he—" A sigh. "Again. He always does this." After a pause, he said, "Don't worry, I won't let anything happen."

Lira carefully checked around the corner—Calvin held his head, panicked. Nearly looking behind, she shot back around the city wall. Looking toward Magnus, his eyes only showed fear. He shook his head.

Without a pause, Magnus whirled around the corner, drawing a sword—but Calvin was gone.

"What? Where did he go?" Lira asked, peeking.

Magnus stood stoic. "I do not know. It concerns me—it could be some form of magic."

Lira sighed. She didn't know what to do next, and night was beginning to fall across the town. Malakai. Asheron.

Magnus' tone turned cold. "Kayden will not like this."

Lira shook her head. "You can't tell her."

He narrowed his eyes. "And allow this treachery to continue? He is clearly culpable—and you are part of this supposed accord."

Exempt. She was exempt. She remembered what the guards said when her brother was taken. She didn't understand then.

She shook her head. "It's too risky. If he and Malakai panic, who knows what could happen. Please, no mention of this."

After a pause, he relented and nodded. "Until your meeting."

The sound of slamming doors, parents rushing their children inside, as well as others running through town attempting to make it home, echoed through the gate to town. The sun began to set.

Disappearances occurred by night, and no one wanted to be outside, including Lira. "Come on, let's go home. I don't want to be outside after the sun is gone."

Magnus nodded. "The others will worry."

As they walked briskly across the dirt roads, Lira thought over and over in her mind about today's happenings. *The harbinger comes by the path of life*, the markings said. She worried for the town, at least, for those who were left. Many families traveled to other cities and towns for the time being, but some stayed in dedication to their work. Many didn't have the funds to stay in inns, or they didn't have family nearby.

Lira didn't understand Krogar's motives, either. He knew the markings were in the town, and even knew what they said. *Why hasn't he investigated anything?* she wondered. Knowledge was his trade.

She would find out more tomorrow. Perhaps she would have dinner with Calvin, to figure out what he was up to, and what Malakai's plan was. He was in Grandis Prison. He even mentioned his brother tasked him with this work. *They're working in this together for the King.* The knight said his brother would come to assess the situation...

But the next day, Harvey Jr., the young man Calvin met with, went missing along with two others.

The next, so did Porra.

Laura was gone the day after that.

They couldn't track Calvin down, until Lira finally found him. "Dinner tomorrow, just the two of us, at Sohgra's inn?" he said. "I'm very busy until then. Sorry that I've been absent." He hurried off before Kayden and the others arrived.

To meet the knight in crimson? she thought. Her village smelled of the King's plot. Of Asheron's deception. The Knight of Shadows was here as well, she was sure.

Lira had to tread lightly.

Chapter Thirty-four

A Plateau of Progress

Saul Bromaggus

Saul examined at the map Thalia gave him. It was zig-zagged and inefficient. *No direct path. This is ridiculous.* "I cannot believe we must take this blasted path. We should just walk straight through." He was suspicious of the path, but Saul had a choice: trust Thalia's guidance, or walk through the Plateau at the risk of running into the Stormwardens. *And probably death, as they would be the kind of Hydris that would kill us on sight.* Saul came to consider that not all Hydris were the same—just like the Broken. When he awoke in Rhoba's prison, Saul's ideal of a 'people' shattered.

"Didn't Lady Thalia say the civil war was occurring in the central cities? She gave us that map to keep us safe," Drof stuttered. He fiddled with his small hands and scratched his narrow jaw. His nerves were barely intact in past weeks.

Saul grumbled, "You may be correct, but I do not like it. They have us moving through forest, at least. Living off the land is of no concern of mine, but I am no master of mountains."

They walked for two days, and it felt like they went nowhere. They left their Ravagers in Shi'doba, since the beasts could not traverse the mountain ranges in the south end of the plateau. Their plan was to move south west, then move through the Thistleweed Forest. Then, to Saul's disgust, they would move through the Blackcore Mountains. The Terrans held up in there since nearly the dawn of the land. The Draconians sought to smoke them out, but nothing could match the Terran might within. They knew every tunnel, nook, and cranny of the mountains, which gave them a significant advantage. All the Hydris could do was trade with them and leave them to their mining. They were said to be somewhat peaceful, but stubborn as all hell.

"I have never seen a Terran," Saul said. Somewhat untrue; one visited him in his dreams. "How would they defend mountains from Broken, Hydris, and even the Draconia?"

Drof stumbled up. "They are mightier than any thought. Their arms are well made, bodies powerful, and they know the tunnels."

"I should hope they let us through freely," Saul said.

"What about the small woman? You seemed to take to her," Drof said. Saul scowled at him. "I—I mean, you d—didn't have a problem with her—"

"She's a magician, and a Hydris. I am uncertain of whether I trust her or not." He felt he could but wouldn't admit it.

One of the shorter Broken with yellow marks stepped forward to speak. "Yet you took her map and decided to follow it," Korren said.

Saul only returned a frown. "I take an opportunity when I am given one." In truth, Saul did indeed take to her. She was not as he pictured a Hydris, displaying an interesting strength of personality. She decided not to join them, therefore Saul probably would never see her again. It made no matter.

Looking toward Korren, he raised a brow. "Why did you stay? I would have thought you would go with Fae," Saul asked. They were siblings before exile. She had a strong personality in contrast to him, which Saul found peculiar. He was closer to Drof, in truth.

"My sister has a mind of her own. I do not wish to recklessly move for my goals. I believe that slow and steady wins the race."

Saul cringed at being called slow. The path was long, and more arduous than a direct route. He did not know which path the others took. He only knew that they also took a map as they left—but without a guided route. Saul wondered what came of the other twelve Broken, hoping they did not get captured. While Fae was a rough-willed Broken, she was still one of them.

"I'm glad you took Lady Thalia's advice. Her map seems safer, having marked the opposition's current controlled areas," Drof said.

"Well, I'm concerned about the line across Bolerra's Flow. It isn't over a bridge." Saul growled. "She had better not betray us. I've had enough of that in the last while." He chose to follow her advice. It challenged many of his beliefs, but that's what his journey had been all along. His choice to run challenged his sense of honor. His experience in Rhoba challenged the ideal of his people. His stay in Shi'doba challenged his view of the Hydris. *So much has changed. Before my father burned, I would have run to my death, or run to the Hydrian capital, Serpentarius, as recklessly as Fae did.* Saul wondered how his father would feel if he saw him now.

"We have to trust her. We won't know until we get there, or when the armies find us. What do you think we'll find in the capital?" Drof asked.

"Purpose," Saul said bluntly.

In truth, he did not know. He spoke with confidence so his fellow Broken would follow him with confidence themselves. He wished to know more about the Stormspire, the monument to his goddess. He wondered what secrets it held, what it really was, and how it was built. It fascinated him, and he felt drawn to it. He thought it had some meaning in his dream. Every night when he slept, he was struck by bolts of lightning from the dark sky. *A storm is coming,* Gadora had said to him.

* * *

In two more days, Saul and his group made it to the north end of the Thistleweed forest. There was a path paired with fields of spikebush shrubs in large bunches, with high-top Thistleweed trees behind, branches thin as corn and leaves long and spindled, just as the map described.

Curious that only a few fields of spikebushes would be along a forest ridge, Saul thought. The forest path was black as night, even in the middle of day, and they could hear a constant sound that reminded him of the grass whistle he played as a child in the Vale. The sounds made it hard for them to sleep at night, but eventually it dropped into the background like a soft wind.

Once more, the dream visited his slumber. He was atop the tower, but it grew smaller. The lightning crashed down on him, and he agonized in pain, slowly. The pain was less than before, but it eventually grew until he couldn't take another second.

He awoke with his heart racing. The rest slept soundly. The snarl of wolves came from around them. They were, however, behind a massive stone wall that rose thirty feet high, surrounding the small campsite. The stone was sandy brown, an accumulation of the rock that surrounded them.

What is this? The others were out cold, and his mind was still fogged, exhausted from the long journey they endured. He was very concerned as no one was on watch. *Who in the gods fell asleep?* He wondered if he was still dreaming, and where the wall came from. Saul attempted to stay awake to watch over them, but he couldn't resist slipping back into a sleep once more.

The next morning, the wall was gone. The others got up with loud yawns. "Did any of you see the wall last night? Someone was not on watch." Saul asked.

The others looked to him with raised brows. "There's no wall here," Drof said.

Korren let out a loud yawn as he stretched his shoulders. "What're you on about? I was on first watch, Drof's on second, and Torra was on third." The others nodded and said they didn't sleep a wink while on watch.

Saul scratched his head, wondering if any of them lied. "Must have been a dream." Better tom dream of walls than agony from the skies.

On their way through the woods, they hunted coalboars for food. Korren was a skilled hunter, despite his nervous personality. He was as he liked to be in life—patient, waiting for the perfect moment to kill. Every day was the same within the forest: hunting, listening, and walking. It was a calm place, but every night he had the same dream. Lightning struck, he awoke, and the wall was there. He tried to wake the others, but they slept like stones.

They finally saw the open plains once more, and with more days behind them, massive mountains climbed the sky in the distance. They moved swiftly, hoping to not be detected. It was more than a day's trip to the mountains, and they didn't want soldiers ambushing them.

When they slept, they did so in a valley, or in the shadow of a hill or mountain, attempting to avoid detection.

Morag and Korren did the majority of hunting—they were hunters and trackers for the Kannakash and Urikar clans. One day they brought a stag back from the hunt, and it was split amongst all. Saul did all the cooking, attempting the best meal he could with what little they had.

Over time, they approached the black, towering landscape beyond. Blackcore was a vast mountain range. They luckily had a fairly straightforward path through it, but the Terrans would stand in their way.

Saul was wary of them, not knowing their personalities or customs, as well as how they would react to Broken. As they drew closer, there was a large crevice between two mountains leading into a wide valley. The sides were gravel-filled, and wrought with gnarled, dead trees that struggled to live, cracking the earth around them. At the bottom of the valley lay a large cavern, opening at the base of a black mountain, with several figures standing at the entrance.

They were strongly built and armed to the teeth in black plate, hammers, and axes. One had a strong brow that looked as a stone ridge, and another seemed to have their face decorated with soot as a man would have stubble.

"Halt! Who goes there?" the stubbled one roared gruffly in the common tongue. His lips were large and slate-colored, and his chin had chips all along it, as if scars from battle.

Saul saw no need to meander about the point. "We are looking to travel through Blackcore peacefully, to the other side."

The guard's expression stayed as a stone monolith. "Well, I'm not sure, Broken," the Terran said. "Do you have any coin? We can't just let anyone through here. Especially you folk—I hear the civil war's boiling over you people."

"We don't have much coin. We were told your people were willing to let us through if we respected your laws and didn't cause trouble," Saul said.

Saul hoped Thalia wasn't wrong. Or lying.

"I don't think that's how we do things around here. Some of your folk came through here and gave us what they had to get through. If you have, say, fifty gold pieces, we can let you pass."

Saul knew they didn't. Even before their keeper of their money went with Fae. Saul didn't think to ask him to split it, foolishly enough. "We only have ten. We need it for supplies in an emergency, so we cannot give it to you." Saul growled. "A woman named Thalia sent us. Does that ring any bells?" Saul realized she never gave him her family name.

The Terran's eyes widened. "*Hmm*. I'll be right back." He slammed his hammer onto a switch, and the massive, dark steel door slowly swung open. He clomped his way down the tunnel, leaving the others to guard it.

"How do you know her?" the large browed Terran asked.

"She's a friend," Saul said suspiciously.

They looked to each other, nodding and whispering. After a time, the soot-covered Terran returned, along with a taller one with a rocky face covered in scratches, big eyes, and a long nose, wearing bright red plate.

"What is your name, Human?" he asked in a husky tone.

I am no Human. "Saul Bromaggus," Saul said.

"I am Frondin, son of Grond," the Terran said. He turned to the others, frowning. "You crags. You tried to tax them? If the Lady heard of this, you would be thrown through the grinder." His voice was cold. "Come with me, all of you."

Saul and the others followed Frondin down the tunnels and heard the large door close with a *slam* behind them. *Does Thalia have influence here? If so, how? And why?* Saul wondered. Rods illuminated the way with red light, causing the black walls to glow red as well. They seemed to walk for hours, it felt—left, right, up, down, down a hole with a peculiar lift contraption, and farther still. As they walked, they heard a rhythmic *tink, tink, tink* sound far in the distance, along with the *fwoosh* of forges.

Deep within the mountain, they came into a massive, open cavern. It was as if the outer rock wall of the mountain was a parchment-thin shell. Saul and the others stopped before the scaffolding the Terrans built. Vast steel grating extended from platform to platform, chained to the mountain wall with large links, each the size of a man. Hundreds of feet below laid rock floors with shining black ingots, intermingled with rivers of molten lava flowing into various steel-domed structures, smoke and steam rising from the chimneys.

"What's wrong, Broken? Afraid of heights?" the Terran said plainly. "Come, it's safe. Don't tell me the brave Broken are afraid of a little heat."

It *was* hot. Saul could feel the sweat trickle down his forehead, and his arms began to glisten as well. He knotted his forehead into a frown, staring the Terran in his wide, dark eyes. "I am not afraid," Saul said bluntly, taking the first step onto the steel bridge. It had short railings on either side—hardly high enough for him. Saul gripped them tightly as he stepped forward again. The others reluctantly followed behind him, each sweating a bucket of their own.

The network of steel bridges, scaffolds, and chained structures were vast, some at such an angle even Saul would have difficulty walking on. Terrans on pathways above and below sauntered by, stopping to stare at the intruders before continuing. He could hear the clashing of picks on stone in routine intervals from above and below. Machinery roared from all around him, machines he never knew existed or even fathomed. Metal beasts with belts carried large pieces of rock into a grinder, then to molten heat pressers, which then spat out refined ingots of iron, gold, and copper. The smell of ash, flame, and soot filled his nostrils. It smelled of the old blacksmith's quarters in Gadora's camp in the Vale.

"What are all these machines?" Saul asked. "They seem quick to work on ore, yet I've never seen them used in the Vale."

Frondin gave a subtle chuckle. "We've had these for ages. It's a secret of the Terran. It makes us strong, and our secrets keep us alive. Understand that I cannot tell you how they work, but they do make the best weapons and armor in the land." Frondin carried a large mace on his side, almost the size of his head. It shone orange and gold from the fire and lava lighting the grand chamber.

Each building was like a spire, with stairs circling the outside to the top, stabbing out of the steel-hung platforms they stood on like a blade. Formed with sharp edges, it was as if every corner could slit a man's throat. Ash fell constantly; Saul found himself brushing it from his arms and hair. It made a slimy mix with the sweat.

They came to a grand building, a hundred feet wide and deep. It was comprised of multiple levels, with stair-like steps leading to the tip of a pyramid.

"Come, he would meet with you. What is your oldest parent's name?" Frondin, son of Grond asked.

"Makari." A strong name. His mother was strength incarnate.

Frondin nodded to him, leading them inside. Saul and the others followed him to find a grand inner sanctum, with low chandeliers of black and grey steel, and candles lit aflame with the wax almost melted to the base. A massive, square table sat in the center, formed with black iron. It was hot and smooth, with a large map in front of it with many curves, turns, and tunnels all over, possibly totaling thousands. In the center laid a miniature stone structure, a pyramid resembling the one they stood in now, labeled, *Blackcore*.

"Dorneth, son of Morne, this is Saul, son of Makari, and his allies. He is a Broken, sent to travel through our city by Thalia, daughter of Kovos." Frondin spoke in the common tongue, to Saul's delight.

There were many Terrans standing around the table, each glancing up to the Broken in their presence. One Terran was especially tall and dark-skinned, as if he was made of obsidian. His round eyes fell to pupils dark as night, watching them closely. They all spoke in strange turns of the tongue and deep, hoarse tones—the language of the Terran.

Dorneth looked up from his large, iron map, analyzing Saul carefully.

Drof leaned over to Saul in a panic. *"Didn't Miss Thalia say Kovos was the King?"* he whispered.

Saul nodded. "I wonder why she never said anything. Maybe it is a coincidence." But he thought not. She was commanding, but apparently quite modest. Saul was surprised he didn't see it. He wondered what her plan was—and why she said nothing of it. Being a princess was no forgetful matter.

"Welcome, Saul, son of Greln," Dorneth said in a hoarse voice. "You are traveling through our fine city of smiths, and Frondin speaks of your alliance with Lady Kashral?"

Saul didn't think 'alliance' was the right word. She had good advice and spoke true words, and Saul took them. Nothing more. "She advised us to pass through here. We wish to make for the capital."

"*Hmph*. You Broken are always so antsy to get moving."

Saul drew his mouth to one side. "We move with purpose and meaning."

"Meaning, *hah*. Purpose, *oh*," Dorneth said. "Purpose is what you make of it. If you move in such a hurry, you miss details." He scoffed. "Do you even know why you came this way, and who you're avoiding?" His face moved little, but his eyes told a story.

Saul didn't have an answer but tried as best he could. "We're moving around the main force of the Stormwardens and joining with the capital."

A smile crept across Dorneth's stony lips. "Should we not turn you over? They'd pay me more."

Is this some kind of trap? Thalia wouldn't betray us, would she? Saul felt Thalia was honorable, but it was just a hunch. She was still a Hydris, after all. She talked of the rebels with a hint of disgust and spoke to the man at her door with a bold tone. He felt they took what they pleased without regard for others.

If it was a game of bluffs, Saul was going to win.

Saul spoke with an unmoving tone. "They would refuse to pay you. They're traitorous drakes."

The Terrans around the table laughed and chuckled, nodding to one another, then murmured curses and hateful words. "They tried to penetrate our iron doors and steal our machines before, so you aren't wrong. But they cover much land from the Valley to the Neck and have a lot of gold to meet that. We don't care about your politics. If the Lady hadn't referred you, I'd have sold you out. What makes you think you can stop the Soldier of Storms, *hmm*? Well? I bet you don't know who he is or what it means, Broken."

Saul growled at his words. *He refers to my people like that, expecting respect in return?* Saul clenched his fists and leaned on the iron map. "No, I cannot say that I do. I do not expect to stop this 'Soldier of Storms' myself—surely the capital can handle itself, but we might damn as well *attempt* to aid them. At least we will provide aid, and not mining our lives away. Who is this 'Soldier of Storms?' Some god among fools *we* can't stop, yet *you* can, holding your ground within these mountains?"

Dorneth coughed up a chuckle that added emotion to a blank slate. "My, you're bold, speaking to me that way." With a nod, the King said, "He is the King's son, one of three. What do you know of the royalty down here, boy? You certainly speak as if you know everything, yet you know nothing. You lived your life in a forest believing a Dragon was your King, the Hydris were evil, and nothing is more important than your people," Dorneth said in contempt. "We love nothing more than mining. We know more through the earth than you will ever know of the air. You strut around like a leader of a small troop of broken that think they rule the land, but you don't. At this point, the 'Soldier of Storms' does." His tone was harsh and loose. He coughed as he ended. "Aye, I'm getting old."

Saul saw through his words. They knew no more than the mines, as he knew no more than the Vale. "I see what you're trying to say. But I demand a little more respect, as you do."

"Aye, I'll give it to you. Works better than bantering endlessly, and I have work to do." He let out a long sigh. "The 'Soldier of Storms' is the King's son, as I've said. The Hydris royalty are linked by blood, and the family is blessed with the power of the circle."

"The circle?"

"The four towers, Broken boy, following the four elements. When a child of royalty is born, the seers at the central tower predict an element, and the child is blessed with its power, making him or her a shaman. It is promising to have four children, and Kovos did. One son disappeared after the war you folk had. I can't remember his name. Been too long, he's probably dead. Zitark was his second son, chosen for water. He and his blasted bastard brother started this war against their father, the crags. The insane bastard Ithaca was the one who received wind. He believes himself to be the 'Soldier of Storms.' Many others believe the same—that's why many joined his cause. He's insane, I can tell you that much. I knew it the moment Kovos brought his children through my halls twenty years ago. The only sane child was the one not yet born."

Thalia. "What element is Thalia?" Saul asked.

The Terran King raised a brow looking left and right, he met murmurs from the others. "Can't you tell? She's earth, you nitwit."

Saul remembered that she wore nothing upon her feet; bare—no shoes or sandals. *I prefer the feeling of the ground. It's sort of soothing, don't you think?* she had said. "She did not mention that fact." Saul wondered why she never told him. Another secret. He would be sure to get some answers if they ever met again.

Dorneth coughed hoarsely. "Ithaca spreads lightning from his hands, electrocuting anyone who disobeys him. He was never the favorite, and resents his stepmother and father for it. I don't know whether it was the reason he fell out of favor, or if he became insane as a result. I just know he's a selfish crag who destroys anyone he hates, especially Broken like you."

Saul's mind immediately went to his dream. *Struck by lightning, shocked into agony until I awake each night. Is this my purpose, to be killed by such a snake?* His mouth drew in displeasure as he contemplated his destiny. He grew weary in recent days from the restless nights he had. He looked back to see sullen eyes, shuffling feet, and fidgeting hands from his Broken. Saul then looked to the council of Terrans armed with warhammers, proud eyes, and stony words.

"Are you afraid, Broken?" Dorneth inquired.

"No Broken is afraid of destiny," Saul surmised. In truth, he was afraid of not fulfilling his destiny, and of disappointing those that depended on him.

"*Destiny?*" Dorneth yelled. He blew up in laughter. The others of the council joined in a lengthy guffaw. "You are driven by destiny? Destiny means nothing, boy. There is no destiny. A man chooses his own path. If it ends up where a prediction lies, it could be destiny, fate, a prophecy—whatever you make of it. It's all a load of craggen foolishness. Down here, a man makes his own steel, his own weapon and armor. No gods rule us, except the anvil and forge. We survived the Draconia, the Broken, the Hydris, and we can survive anything else."

"That's not my business," Saul said gruffly. The Terran's rambling grated on his fraying nerves. First, he insulted his people, and now, his beliefs. "I believe in gods, and that is my right. It matters not if you think my goddess useless; I care whether I get through your mountain alive and reach my destination. I ask you, are you willing to let us through?" Saul commanded. He could feel Drof nudge him. Saul didn't acknowledge it. This was a game of words, test of wits, and Saul was tired of it.

Dorneth smiled widely. "*Heh.* You remind me of her. I'd be surprised if you weren't acquainted with her. Lady Kashral helped us out on a few occasions expecting nothing in return." The Terran analyzed Saul and the others closely.

"And what exactly is that supposed to mean?" Saul said. Thalia gave him something, a map, a route, shelter, and expected nothing. *Or so she would have me believe.*

"It means we'll let you through, boy. We're sizing you up. Checking your potential. Seeing your honor. Hearsay of a Lady's word is one thing, but a meeting is another. I like the cut of your jib. You make for some good banter. With arms like those, you'd make good use in the mines, too. But, I wouldn't want to upset our gracious shaman. What say you, friends? Shall we let these *Humans* through?"

"*Broken*," Saul growled.

Dorneth laughed, running into a hacking cough. With a nod, he looked left and right, receiving confirmation from the rest. "I can't turn our Lady down, can I?" He smiled widely, exposing his mottled grey teeth.

Make friends, not enemies, Thalia had said to him. It seemed Saul made one of the former, which benefitted him greatly. "My thanks, Dorneth, son of Morne," Saul said reverently. It seemed that they spoke with their fathers' names out of respect. Saul decided to oblige, as he wished to gain an ally.

Dorneth chuckled, "Good, you've learned traditions already. Frondin, show them to the eastern gates of the mountain pass, and give them a detailed map. Lady Kashral would not have it any other way. You know what happens when she is displeased."

Another to hint at what happens when Thalia is 'displeased.' He wondered how fierce she was in a battle. Part of him wished to see it—as long as they were on the same side.

The other Terrans shuddered at the mention of that. Frondin nodded and went into the next room. Saul heard the shuffling of papers and books before the Terran returned with a map in hand.

"Be gone, we have more to discuss here in the mines. Major changes are occurring, especially with the unrest in the north. Did you hear? The Dragon's forces are readied at the knives. Or so the Watcher said."

"Who is the Watcher?" Saul asked. The damned Terran spoke as if Saul knew everything, or he attempted to teach him that he knew nothing. *The Dragon tried to storm the shores already? A fool, but they turned around—why?*

"A person they call the *Watcher* is in communications with many individuals. Eyes far across the land. The Leaders exchange information with him—or them—so that they may gain some, too. It's a small price for an eye to the future." Dorneth smirked. "Now, be gone with you. Good day, Saul, son of Makari." He shooed them away with a wave of his hand.

Saul and the others turned to follow Frondin as he walked. Saul always heard Terrans were selfish, treasure-hungry, and uncaring for the causes of others. *It's not a lie, it seems.* If it weren't for Thalia, he and the others may be locked in the mines below, sweating and striking ore until they died. *She neglected to tell me anything about her father, her powers over earth, or the fact that her brothers were the causes of the war. Let alone that a fabled warrior was a part of it, who happens to be one of the brothers.* Thalia was strong-willed and bold, and despite her lack of forthcoming behavior, he had a difficult time disliking her.

They walked along the unsteady scaffolds once more. Each Broken seemed a little more comfortable with the heights now, but most were still wary of the molten lava below. The sounds of mining picks clattered in unison; Saul felt he would go mad if he lived there from the heat and sounds alone. The massive chains hung embedded in the mountain walls, keeping the large steel platforms steady and unyielding. He wondered how many fell to their deaths every year in the hell they walked through, and inevitably wondered how Terrans did it. They lived and worked in these mountains non-stop, faces wrought with dirt and black dust. He wondered what other kinds of professions they even had, and how they ate. He supposed they may leave once in a while to hunt.

"What do you do here, Frondin?" Saul inquired.

"King Dorneth's scribe. I maintain order in the paperwork and mark our place in the history of the mountains."

Tales and edicts should be spoken by the word of mouth. He wondered about what they were getting into. The 'Soldier of Storms' that sought Broken blood was concerning, especially when he could shoot electricity from his very hands.

"What do you make of this 'Soldier of Storms?'" Saul asked. He worried for the dreams he had, now. Dreams of his skin burning away, as he is struck by lightning until he can't endure the agony any longer.

"I think he's a bastard. He's a real one, in truth, but he's a crag. Treason is a burnable offense in Blackcore. We wouldn't work with him even if he blasted down the door. We don't always keep to ourselves. Fight when we have to. There's a reason the mountain has never been taken from us." They walked to a large steel door at the end of the scaffolds on the eastern wall of the mountain hall. Frondin *smacked* a handle beside the door embedded in the rock wall, shooting the door itself up into the stone wall. "I met 'im before—Ithaca. He always walked around like he owned the place. Spoke to our King with no respect, although you and he had a bit of a tizz there, *heh*? Luckily the Lady saved you on that one."

Saul frowned. *I don't need her help.* But it was appreciated. "Hopefully we can make it to the capital in good time. There are others on their way there now." Luckily their own passing was quick. They had much ground to cover.

"Well, you're going the right way. Why go to Serpentarius?"

"They are fighting about us, after all. We wish to aid in the conflict," Saul replied.

"Aye, they think you're scum. With you thinking you own the land and another continent, that's a good word for it."

"What did you dare say?" Saul growled, stopping abruptly. He grabbed the damned Terran by the neck of his armor.

Without flinching, the fool said, "Do you think you belong in the Vale, or do you think the Broken should reign in Renalia?"

Saul's expression darkened. "We ruled Renalia for centuries; it belongs to us."

"No, it belongs to the royal family. Things were prosperous, I hear, before it went to shit recently. I'm a bit of a history buff, so why don't you tell me who ruled, and why you deserve it?"

"Icarus," Saul proclaimed. Icarus was the first Broken ruler, aided in the conquering of the Dark Ones and freeing of the land.

"A bastard. He enslaved all other races and forced them to make idols of him. Who else?"

How dare he insult the heroes of my past. Icarus was a grand warrior, finding glory wherever he went. "Aggaroth," Saul tried again. He was the hero who defeated the frost giants and the mountains were named after him.

"A bastard. Murdered innocent, harmless giants in his wake, and the giants kept to the mountains, as we do here. Are you going to keep choosing those that conquer, rather than those who lead?"

Saul growled, tightening his grip. "You—" he clenched his teeth, moving in close. "I idolized them for years, How dare you insult the war heroes of our race? If it wasn't for Icarus, the remaining Dark Ones could have risen after Gadora's ascension. And if it wasn't for Aggaroth, the giants could have risen up and destroyed everyone."

"*Could* have." Frondin took Saul's hand off him and continued walking. They soon came to a three-way split in the cave. "Give me your map." Saul obliged, handing it to him. He traced his index finger around on it and pointed to a specific tunnel. "We're here. Make your way in this direction, then turn here after a day's travel, and follow the rest of the path to this gate. Tell them that Dorneth and Lady Kashral sent you through. They'll know." Frondin walked back toward the main hall of Blackcore, stopping to speak one last time. "Don't attach yourself to stories, there are always discrepancies. Good day, son of Makari. Beware the *storm* that comes."

"And you, Frondin, son of Grond," Saul replied. Thinking of the potential fight to come, it was as Gadora told him in the dream.

A storm is coming.

TIDES OF FATE

* * *

The Broken walked along the heated tunnels for days. They came to sections of small—and much cooler—settlements in large regions of the rock, blasted and mined.

Drof grew more nervous as the days passed. He shook at night, he walked slower, and he questioned their route more often. He was a cowardly man, afraid of combat and confrontation. If a wolf ran at him, he would either run away, or fall and die. He was a kind Broken, but most of all, tactical. He belonged in a war room. It would suit him best.

Saul and Drof discussed the war that occurred ten years ago, back when he was but a young Broken. Drof was slightly older than Saul at that time, but not well suited for battle. His frame narrow and muscles tired, his clan did not deem him fit to fight. Drof knew much of what tactics the battalions used, the ways they moved their ships, and travelled along the mountains.

He mentioned an orb that appeared above the main force when they were crippled and devastated. The tactics were horrid, and the movements were all wrong. They were lambs to the slaughter, yet no one dared speak of it. If it weren't for Saul's mother, thousands more would have died. She brought her ships to battle as a decoy, so the others could retreat back to Kathynta.

Saul wondered why the armies were defeated so easily. He only pictured Obelreyon, who seemed unaffected by the loss. *We will return and take Renalia for ourselves*, the dastardly Dragon had said. *He said the same to my father before he died.* Frondin said the dragon's forces were readied at the knives...

What is Obelreyon planning? Saul wondered.

He knew nothing of the north anymore, hoping his people were alive and safe, and not taken to war using foolish tactics.

Chapter Thirty-five

Nefarious Kindness

Lira Kaar

Lira was exhausted after another day of knocking on doors and questioning witnesses. She worried often for her missing friends. The group was lucky that Krogar helped, but days still passed with minimal progress. She wished to get more information from him, but it was like pulling teeth. An interesting fellow, and nice enough, but everything was a game to him. Lira learned to play along, and Kayden stayed outside. She decided on meeting with Calvin, despite the group's opinions.

"Are you sure that's a good idea?" Kayden had said to her, over and over.

Lira reassured her and the others multiple times. *It's just something I sense, and only I can get the right information safely,* she thought. It had been a week, and they still hadn't discovered where the missing people were held. Or anything about Asheron or Malakai.

So, Lira sat down to dinner that evening in Sohgra's inn with Calvin. The warm, russet wood walls shone dimly in the lantern light. There was no one at the inn except them. *Sometimes I feel there's no coincidence that only him and my group are out in the daylight, and under the moonlight. The others are keeping away from the streets. Especially at night.*

"So, how are things in town?" she asked. "Aside from the sad news of disappearances, of course." Lira and the group hadn't found much, just a bit of information on 'The Figures' as the residents called them.

"Things are pretty different, actually. Ever since they closed the mine and took all the miners with them." Calvin's eyes widened, looking from his stew to Lira. "I'm sorry, I didn't mean to bring it up." She noticed something strange—his eyes blue as the sea were now flecked with violet.

"It's okay," Lira said brittly. The thought of her brother being dragged away entered her mind and vanished quickly. *I have to find him before something terrible happens.* "I really miss him. I wonder how my father is. He's still at the Orinde monastery to the south, most likely. I'll visit there when I'm done here. My mom is buried there, and I would like to pay my respects." Lira heard the clacking of glasses as Sohgra organized his dishes at the bar, and the wind howling from beyond the door.

"Your father was here a week or two ago, actually. He came to the shop to visit. He misses you, as do I." Calvin said, analyzing her reaction carefully.

Lira knew he would keep trying. She drew her mouth in regret, and Calvin's face knew the truth.

"I wish you would care for me, Lira. I could take care of you."

Lira's face screwed into a frown. *I don't need to be taken care of.* She didn't need protection. "I know, Calvin. I just don't feel that way. I care for you as a friend, but it won't be more."

"Is it my profession? I can do more—there is much more to me than you think! Maybe you'll be impressed."

Or maybe I'm onto something. "As impressive as you may be, that isn't how it works," Lira said bluntly. A bit of Kayden's voice came out, with Lira's light touch. "I'm sorry."

Calvin's expression drooped, but his eyes were eccentric as always. They went wide, cow-like, then narrowed, and sullen; there was no true consistency to them. They were usually wide and excitable when he and Lira were alone.

"What are you doing in town that's so impressive?" Lira asked.

Calvin paused. His eyes lingered on Sohgra, and he waited until he walked to the storage rooms. "Oh, I'm thinking of repurposing the mine into something beneficial to the town. I worry about the people here, and I want to help things get better. The miners aren't coming back, so I thought of something new." He blinked twice.

Lira stood up straight, leaning forward. "Oh? What is it?"

"Ah, it's a secret! I just don't want people to know until it's ready. It will help the progress of the town, I guarantee it! I just don't want to be embarrassed if everyone gets excited and it doesn't work." Calvin laughed, looking up as he spoke. Lira noticed two more blinks.

Lira wondered what he had in store. She knew he was up to something. Calvin had a tell when he was being nefarious, silly or not. He always blinked twice when something was up. "Oh Calvin, don't bring me in on something and then push me away!" Lira giggled and playfully slapped the table. She kept her eyes on his.

Calvin smiled devilishly. "Well, maybe if you watch the stars with me for a night, or decide being with me isn't so bad—"

Watching the stars would be okay. What could go wrong? Lira thought. She knew information was coming, and knew she had to push further. "If I say yes, will you show me? I am so curious! I'm glad you're doing something nice for the town."

"I am, too! I feel it will help everyone. What do you say—I show you, and you and I have dinner again together? I've waited ever so long to hear you say yes!"

Lira knew it had to be done. "Yes, I will. I'd love to!" She smiled sweetly. She played with her hair and shuffled her toes in her shoes as they talked. He was so vague about all of it, but she felt it had to be him. "I can't wait, Calvin. I'll support it if it helps the town! I'll see you tomorrow night by the mine?"

"Of course! I'm so glad you're coming. It's great, I promise. I feel like we're entering a new age. Oh, it just makes me vibrate in my seat," Calvin whispered. He jiggled from side to side and bobbed up and down. The lantern light danced in his voracious eyes. It took all her energy to not viscerally cringe when he acted so odd—or nice, but that type of nice was—unwelcome.

Sohgra came out from the kitchen and storage rooms with their meals: a crisp bread loaf and vegetable stew with fish freshly cooked in duck fat. The smell was invigorating. Lira wasn't the biggest fan of fish, but she happily ate it. It was much better than the food she ate while traveling with the others. She was surprised Sohgra had any good food left, considering many of the hunters in town left, or went out much less often.

Lira never saw Calvin so jumpy. His vision of roses clouded his judgment. They changed the topic of conversation to the fishery, then the comings and goings in town, and to what she had been up to. She failed to mention the rebellion; she felt that safety first was the best play.

They slowly ate their stew talking about old times: the mishaps of Grafa the clumsy Terran blacksmith, and the never-ending stories of Gregory Thol, the other alchemist in town that Calvin collaborated with. Gregory would talk non-stop from when you entered and left, barely pausing to tell you the price. Some would get away without paying, as he wouldn't notice that they even took anything off the shelves.

At the end of the meal, they got up and hugged tightly, and he leaned in for a kiss. Lira pushed him gently away on the nose with her finger. "No, not just yet, you! You'll have to wait for that."

Calvin shot her a sly eye, as if he liked it. He was shuffling his feet where he stood but nodded quickly. "At midnight, then! The moon is ever so beautiful at that time, just like you."

Lira giggled. "Thanks, Calvin. You're so kind!" she said, her nose perking to agree. "I'll see you tomorrow night!" Lira strolled out of the inn after paying Sohgra, who shot her a suspicious look.

It was past dusk, but Lira didn't fear the night. She said a final goodbye to Calvin and strolled through the north end of town. *I lied through my teeth. Was that wrong?* she questioned herself. *No, it wasn't wrong.* Lira knew it had to be done, and she was the only one who could have pulled it off. Lira wasn't shoved into it, either; it was her idea. Even Kayden gave her a nod for it. Domika was reluctant, as her safety may have been in danger. *Calvin wouldn't hurt me.* He was an odd man sometimes, but if there was anyone he dared not harm, it was Lira. She had a feeling nothing bad would happen. The Figures wouldn't get her, not tonight.

She passed by the markings in the center of town. *What did the spell mean, what harbinger was it?* Lira couldn't recall anything in particular. She read many books, but none jumped out to her. Lira feared for the townspeople. She hoped she could save some of them, any of them, from a possible death. She knew nothing of summoning magic, but definitely knew the path of 'life' indicated something nefarious.

Something she feared.

At last she came to her home, where the rest of her team was waiting patiently for her.

"*Finally*. You had me worried!" Kayden blurted out, stepping forward from her lean. After a brief, awkward pause, she said, "I mean—well? What happened?"

"Kayden got here just before you. She followed you there and back," Domika said.

Kayden shot Domika a dirty look, holding her index finger to her thin lips.

Each member of the group stared at her with eyes widened, leaning far forward. Lira looked to the floor and shuffled her feet. "It has to be him. No doubt in my mind."

"I can't believe it," Domika said. "He just seemed nice, even though he was kinda weird. Are you sure it's him? I feel like we should wait on this, rather than jump in." Her eyes lingered on Kayden, then went back to Lira.

"No. We do this tomorrow," Lira said. "Now we're on a time limit."

Domika nodded, fidgeting with her fingers. As she analyzed Lira with her eyes, a wash of concern came over them. "You're right, we can't wait. We should do it before something happens to you."

Lira *was* in danger. If she missed the meeting, there was no knowing how Calvin would react. He was clearly unstable, and even happy about what he had been doing. It was downright strange. Lira felt for him, but the townspeople came first.

A smirk grew across Kayden's face. "You're insane for going there and lying to his face. Didn't think you had it in you, princess."

"I'm just glad he bought it. But I'm sure," Lira began, placing her hand on her cheek. "Something about his meeting with the Knight in crimson told me all of the disappearances revolve around tomorrow night."

Kayden raised a brow. "Knight in crimson?"

Lira fumbled with her hands. "Well, Magnus and I saw him speak to a knight that looked like Asheron a few nights ago—"

"You saw Malakai. One of the Hunters. Asheron's brother. A few *nights* ago?" Kayden shot out of her chair. "Lira, we could have done something!"

Magnus shook his head. "We may have startled him. It was too dangerous."

Kayden opened her mouth as if to yell, and closed it, then opened it again multiple times. But something held her back. "I hate to agree," was all she could spit up. She picked at her short nails. "Backing someone insane into a corner has consequences."

Vesper stuttered a few words. "Lord Malakai is here?"

Kayden paced back and forth clutching her head. "Gods be damned. This is bad," Kayden sat down and shook her head. "Why did this guy make a deal with them?"

Magnus' gaze drew toward Lira, and she fumbled with her hands. "It has something to do with me. The first time I looked in his eyes before I left Solmarsh—" Her voice trailed off as she shook her head. "He's definitely the one. I can always tell when he's doing something nefarious. I just wish he hadn't. I wish I knew then what I do now—I could have done something."

Not only that, but it was the fact that he seemed so confident about his 'work' that made her so uncomfortable. The one she knew became something else. Something wrong.

But the cogs turned rather than halted from a wall of anxiety. She had a hunch about Asheron's way of thinking. She glanced toward Vesper, remembering the day she watched his display, weaving element to element—and the one that could have killed her. Lira had an idea for how to make sure the Knight of Shadows couldn't set the rules of engagement.

Chapter Thirty-six

The Half and the Whole

Lira Kaar

Lira and the others stood before the entrance of the Solmarsh mine. What was once a core piece of the economy there now lay dormant. She heard drips of liquid spilling through the cracks; the walls were wet with the sinew of ground water.

Vesper drew back, nervous as could be. He hadn't used much magic lately, aside from his practices; Lira wondered why. Kayden didn't seem to bother him much about it, as she would the others about their own skills. She badgered Lira constantly about her divine magic, probing and attempting to get her to work on it. Lira knew every magician had her ceiling, a height which she couldn't surpass. The gods determined it, but everyone was different. Lira's was low, and she knew it. Jirah was so interested in *The Great Vesper*, but Vesper dismissed him immediately. He did not seem that fantastic any longer—just a polite, mumbling middle-aged man who wished to help. With Lira's plan, help he would.

"Are you kids ready?" Kayden asked, walking forward. "Keep back a little bit, flame-breath. No offense, but your hair might get us caught."

Domika frowned. "I hate covering my hair. I shouldn't have to."

Kayden looked back with a glare. "This has nothing to do with your damn culture. It's because we don't want to be discovered."

"Fine." She sighed and wrapped her hair in a yellow shawl. Magnus cut in front of them, taking the lead. Kayden's hands shook as she placed one on Magnus's back. Humans were blind in the dark, but even Vesper seemed calmer than her now.

Domika rubbed the sides of her arms nervously as she looked over at Lira. "Are you sure you're ready to do this?" she stuttered.

Lira was ready. She had to be. "Yes. Let's get this over with." *I hope Noren is alive.* She feared the power of Lornak was in this place and feared for her own soul. She feared for Noren's even more. She slowly started into the dark mine. A hollow wind came from deep within. All that could be heard were their steps of plate and leather, and the drips of the cavern.

Lira could somewhat well in the dark, despite being Human. She could hear Vesper stumbling close behind Domika, who led him along.

"Which way?" Magnus whispered. There were several paths before them, splitting off into different mine shafts.

"Damn it, Mags, I can't see. Damn it, damn it. Just find a path that has a light!" Kayden whispered harshly again.

Lira couldn't see a single light but listened carefully for voices. She heard nothing. She wished Vesper could conjure a light but knew that would expose them all.

"Lira, are you sure he was talking about the disappearances and missing prisoners?" Domika asked.

"Yes. The prisoners were moved here, Callidan said. The people Calvin had contact with disappeared soon after, and it's the way he was talking. He must be involved," Lira replied. She couldn't bear the thought that her brother may be part of the disappearing townsfolk. She hoped he was there, still alive, so she could save him.

"Well, you better be right, princess, 'cause I don't like this *one bit.*" Kayden hissed.

The source of the dripping water came from far down the path, echoing through the mine. They tip-toed through tunnel after tunnel. Iron veins cut through the rock walls with mighty gashes surrounding them on all sides, now left alone when all the able-bodied men left with the commanders. Lira could hear Kayden's quickened breaths from in front of her, and saw her hands vibrating subtly, gripped into fists.

They passed by bags of stone and metal, and mining picks left behind by the miners in town. Jara, Matthew, Kari, Paul—so many miners taken from the town, taken from their homes. Lira missed Noren.

"Did anyone hear that?" Kayden whispered. She looked back, analyzing the mine behind them.

"Hear what?" Lira responded.

"I guess it's nothing. I swear I heard something, though."

They continued on. Lira hoped they weren't too late. She couldn't believe Calvin would do such a thing, but at the same time, she wasn't very surprised. He always had an odd way about him, and it unsettled her a little. As nice as he was, something always felt off. She knew it was him—there was no doubt in her mind.

"Now I definitely heard something!" Kayden whispered. "Go forward. Tread light, Mags." Magnus's footsteps became strangely silent.

Lira saw a light down on the end of the cavern they traveled through. The dew shined with the glow of fire, far from them. They crept down the way and looked into the room.

Several large, natural rock pillars lined the vast cavern room, with veins of ore all around the outer wall. A stone altar sat at the end of the room, partially stained crimson.

The smell of death lingered across Lira's nostrils as she noticed them. To each of the hundred pillars, there lay a man or woman chained.

"Holy hell," Kayden muttered.

They all seemed lifeless, but their eyes slowly shifted over to the group. Their eyelids shook, as they struggled to even blink. Their fingers twitched and their breathing was hoarse and labored.

"Darryl, Terra, Matthew—" Lira ran to them. "Wake up, wake up!" she shouted, shaking them. Their pupils slowly drew to her. Their mouths did not move, nor their limbs. They were pale, veins fully visible beneath their skin, each black as the ore in the walls.

The harbinger comes by the path of life, Lira remembered. *Their lives. Their souls.* Innocent people from the small town she came from, and more from the towns surrounding it, like Deurbin. If Lira stayed, she could have been one of them.

She got up and looked around frantically, searching for her brother. "Noren? *Noren?*"

"Lira," a hoarse voice said.

Lira saw him. It was Noren, after all this time, he was alive— barely. His dark skin paled to a bronze, his cheeks were gaunt and hollow, and so thin that she could see but a skeleton of what her brother was. His pupils were dark with black in the veins where red should have been. She gently cupped his cheeks with her shaking hands. "Noren, *no*. What happened?" She tried picking at the lock but didn't know how. Noren's wrists were caked with dry blood from the chains. "Kayden, open these. Pick the lock!"

"On it." Kayden ran over without complaint and worked at opening the manacles.

Lira caressed his face, trying to hold back her tears. She finally found him. The two halves were whole once more. "What did Calvin do? What happened?"

"They're—stealing our life. I don't know why. Please, get us out. If you don't—he said it would be—over soon."

Calvin, how could you? Lira backed off from the pillars, dropped to her knees, and cried quietly into her hands while Kayden worked. Magnus tried cutting chains with his weapon. Domika was next to him, asking him what he thought. *Is this Lornak?* In her lessons, Lornak was imprisoned, but fated to return…

Noren struggled to blink. He closed his eyes and let out a slow, weak sigh.

Every emotion in existence flowed over her at once. "I'm so sorry. This is all my fault. If I stayed inside, this would have never happened." She wiped what tears she could from her eyes. "Please, stay with me. Don't leave me," Lira pleaded.

"I'm here," Noren said in a brittle tone. "It's their fault, not yours. I would do—anything to keep you—safe—" He coughed hoarsely. He struggled with every breath. "I can't believe you're here but—I'm glad you are—please help. There were so many others, so many."

The patter of Vesper's steps sped around the mine hall. "What do we do? Do we wait for him? Do we let them go?" he wondered tremulously. His hand shook as he bit his nails fiercely, scratching his head with the other hand.

Lira kept her hand on Noren's cheek. "I won't let them hurt you anymore. I promise," she said, sniffling. She couldn't believe she finally found him. But he was drained. "Please forgive me."

Kayden opened the manacles. She placed her hand on Lira's shoulder. "Hey, don't worry. We'll get them out of here. We just have to stop him, first. Maybe we can get a few others before—"

"Lira," a shrill voice called from behind them. "Why did you bring these people here?"

It was Calvin. His clothing was decorated by sprays of crimson matching the splatters along the floors and wall. His hands shook feverishly, pointing to each one of the newcomers. "They—they are not—they are not welcome here," he said weakly.

"Calvin, stop this!" Lira screeched. "These people are being hurt! How could you?" She still couldn't believe it. "Why do this, what is this for?"

"I am *helping* everyone," he said. "With this, our town will be safe. This is for the greater good." He pointed to a man with a thick mustache, and then a weathered woman with greyed, straw-like hair. "This man steals from family. *This* woman rips off newcomers and travelers. We are better off without them."

How could he become this way? How didn't I see it? His eyes were his normal ocean blue but flecked with violet; a new tint she hadn't seen. "What about my brother?"

"Your brother won't be harmed further, I swear it. He's been here longer than the others. I've been sure to keep him safe."

She shook her head. Not enough. At all. "Let everyone go." Lira stood strong. Looking over toward Kayden, who nodded, Lira said, "If you let them go." She swallowed hard. "I'll let you live."

Calvin turned a shocked eye toward her. "You would kill me?"

She didn't budge—only gave a nod that took all her courage.

He shook his head in disbelief. "How could you reject this, Lira? We can save the town. We bring the Harbinger, and the town is saved. Someone else would take over. If I hadn't made the sacrifice, then the harbinger may be brought forth in the next town over, and he could have crushed us! How can you be so ignorant? Do you think I wanted to do this? Of course not! I never wanted this!"

"*I'm* ignorant?" Lira said in a shock. "These people," she said, drawing an arrow from her quiver, "are innocent."

The torchlight of the mine flickered amd waned. Slowly, a cold, eerie wind passed between them all among the tension that could break steel. A cold, resounding, and familiar voice echoed through the mine. "Innocence is simply a matter of perspective."

Lira looked around for the source—but the tone was more than familiar. From the shadows emerged the dark armor of the one set to inspect these horrid deeds.

Captain Asheron Highwind.

Expected, this time. But he was alone. Lira wouldn't be caught off guard. "You didn't bring your brother?"

His visage turned as if to look toward Calvin. "Now what would you know of him, silly girl?"

Calvin shook his head.

Lira frowned. "I've seen him. Don't mock me. You're just a monster with nothing but evil intent."

Asheron's words came with a tone of jagged ice. "You know *nothing* of my intentions."

"Then what are they, shadow-boy?" Kayden snarled. "You don't have the benefit of surprise this time."

"I see." Asheron paused for an extended moment while the pits of his eyes analyzed each of them. "This is serendipitous. I do enjoy reunions—a shame our little fiery friend could not be here." After a lengthy, horrifying silence, the Knight of Shadow spoke. "I am a fair individual. Back out of the mine, and you will live. Your brother will live, girl. Leave—"

"No," Lira cut him off. It took all of Lira's strength to keep still. To not shake in fright. To not be paralyzed. She wouldn't. Not now. "I don't want anyone else to get hurt, so I want you to leave and forget your plan."

Silence took them for a moment, until Lira pointed toward Calvin. "He'll be busy. You're alone. You captured us once, but that was half a season ago." She pointed toward the entrance to the sacrificial chamber. "I'm asking you now to leave."

Asheron let out a laugh marked with befuddlement. "You wish to convince me, girl? Are you that foolish?"

Lira shook her head. "I give everyone a chance. This is yours."

"*Lira what the hell are you doing?*" Kayden hissed.

"I'm waiting," she said, eyes locked on the abyssal pits of Asheron's helm.

"Seems even peasants have honor, unlike your leader, girl. But we've come too far for diplomacy—and I can smell your fear."

Lira drew her hands into fists to keep from shaking. Lira swallowed tightly. Preparing. Praying. She knew this was to come. It was inevitable. "I'm not afraid of you." She returned an icy tone. "I don't fear darkness."

Asheron let out a deep cackle that echoed through the hall. "You should."

The subtle *crack* of Kayden's neck echoed from across the harrowing hall. "So, are we going to wait?" she said, drawing her blades. Her voice turned low and cold. "Or are we gonna start?"

The pounding of heavy feet running echoed through the halls as dark warriors clad in black armor appeared from the cavern walls. Asheron's entourage. Expected.

"In the shadows," Asheron said cooly. He swished his hand in a circle, causing a swift, black wind to soar around each light-giving torch. "You are blind." He closed his dark-armored fist, and he stole the light from the room to leave them all in darkness.

All that remained was a profane command.

"*Kill them all.*"

Chapter Thirty-seven

A Simple Choice

Lira Kaar

As if she hadn't considered shadows.

"Vesper, now!" Lira yelled.

She barely heard a mutter before snakes made of fire flew from Vesper's hands throughout the room, passing each pillar and part of the wall, re-lighting all the torches, and staying on the walls to create light.

"And you're powerless in the light!" Lira yelled.

With a vicious growl, Asheron said, "Clever! Finish it, boy! I'll take care of them," Asheron snarled. He vanished in a burst of black mist and appeared at Kayden's side, slashing downward. She barely dodged out of the way and sliced the dark knight across his side in a gap in his armor. With a grunt of pain, he kicked her against the stone wall.

With a cough, Kayden steadied herself. "Nice try."

Chaos ensued. Lira drew arrows to shoot them at the guards, taking extra care to avoid the prisoners. Vesper focused on the snakes of flame, coursing them throughout the room, ensuring the battle was in the light, as well as sending one or two off to strike soldiers attempting to strike an ally in the back.

Kayden fought toe-to-toe parrying Asheron's blows. She sliced his right arm, causing blood to drip upon the stone, joining with that of the innocent. He roared out in anger, causing the room itself to shudder—and smashed her across the face with a gauntlet. He stabbed downward for her chest, missing as she rolled out of the way.

Domika circled and slashed the necks and legs of multiple dark-armored soldiers but grew overwhelmed. She took a slash on her arm, causing her to screech out in pain.

"Damn," Kayden said. She rolled behind Asheron and jabbed the back of his leg, causing him to crumple—giving her an opening to dash for the others to aid them.

Calvin began speaking in a strange language with harsh twists of the tongue and guttural sounds. She didn't recognize it.

Asheron's force was quickly exhausted, but so were Lira and the others. Domika was barely able to rise from the ground, Vesper gripped his head and bled from the nose, and Asheron took on both Kayden and Magnus—and he was winning. He punched magnus under the ribs, causing him to back off to catch what air he could. Kayden dodged his strikes left and right, but barely kept him off as he disappeared and re-appeared to strike.

Lira shot what soldiers she could, but Asheron pivoted left with incredible grace to keep Kayden and Magnus between Lira and him for cover against her shots.

The chanting grew louder, echoing through the mine. *He's summoning it. He can't. I can't let him!* "Stop this! *Now!*" She drew an arrow and aimed for Calvin's neck. "Don't make me do this!"

She heard Magnus and Kayden exhale in pain and a bash against stone.

Asheron's cold voice called out to her. "Shoot, and he dies." The room broke into silence save for the chanting.

Looking toward the voice, Asheron stood with a blade across her brother's neck. "Noren," Lira stuttered. His eyes grew fearful with the blade near his neck. *Help me,* they said.

The hall grew still as a graveyard. Asheron's brigade crumpled. But Kayden and the others were too far. Magnus was disarmed, Kayden stood twenty feet away without a dagger, and Domika was against the wall with Vesper.

There was only Lira, her betrayer, her brother alongside the knight of darkness—and an arrow.

Calvin didn't stop. As he chanted, the prisoners began to gasp for air. Their skin paled further, veins turning black as night. After a moment, Kayden and the others crumpled to the ground as well alongside Asheron's soldiers. The fire snakes began to fade, but the torches remained lit.

Calvin's voice was almost mesmerizing, twisting from word to word. His arms spread wide as a small orb of violet mist appeared before him. Streams of white mist led from each person chained to the pillars into the orb, save for her, Asheron, and Noren. With each word, blood dripped from Calvin's nose more and more.

Lira flinched forward.

Asheron brought his dark blade closer to Noren's neck. "One movement, girl."

She didn't cry. Rather, she grew angry. Her friends were dying in front of her, all from the folly of someone she trusted.

So she let the arrow loose.

Asheron roared out in pain as the arrow pierced his left hand, forcing him to drop the blade. She ran at him as he picked it up with his right hand. While shoving a bare hand forward, she yelled "Fhor!" and the brand on her hand glowed a bright blue; a burst of light blasted from her hand and threw Asheron back against the far wall causing the rock to crack and room to shudder. She nocked another arrow, and as she let it loose, he cut the arrow from the air with lightning-like reflexes using his blade. He waved a hand across his vision, and he was gone in the darkness leaving behind a few choice words: "More will die for this."

Leaving the two alone. But the chanting continued.

Calvin looked to Kayden and the others; his chest grew soaked with his own life, blood pouring from him. "I must do this. I will let your brother stay. You can save him. All I ask is that you stay out of the way. I can't guarantee his safety otherwise." Calvin spoke again in the language with harsh, guttural twists of the tongue.

She gave enough chances.

He would die from chanting, or from her own actions.

She let an arrow fly before Calvin realized what happened. It struck true with a *thunk* and guttural chokes. She stared back at her brother's body, and with a growl from Calvin, Noren's body, as well as the other prisoners, flashed with a bright light that left their bodies and into the violet orb above the altar. Each body screamed with an unnatural, horrifying wail. "It is done," a disembodied voice said—and the violet orb disappeared.

Calvin bent forward, choking on blood and arrow. His robe was now soaked with his own blood.

Lira ran to her brother as the others gasped for air. "Noren?" she whispered with a cry. He gasped for breath as if the air was filled with water and poison. His eyes lay open, lifeless, and pitch black. "Noren!" she yelled. His skin crackled and pulsed as the color slowly faded away.

Noren's eyes receded into pits and teeth dissolved into black dust. His breaths sounded as though someone breathed in sand and rock. He grew rough and granular until his entire body and soul shattered into ash that passed between her fingers like sand in the final moments of an hourglass.

"*No!*" She hit the ground, seeing innocent lives turn to dust and wind all around her. Her whole body felt aflame with shame and hatred, feeling her faults and failures all led here. She gasped for breath, trying to keep herself alive in a room filled with the dead. "How could you do this?" Lira cried.

She backed off from Noren's remains and stormed toward Calvin, who barely had breaths left to make through the blood clogging his throat. She grabbed his neckline and shook him. "*What have you done?*" she yelled in a thin voice.

Calvin could barely speak as he choked, the arrow still lodged in his neck. Blood soaked his upper lip and chin, neck, and chest. "It's too late—our people are safe—it's done. You chose them over him. Things have only begun," he said weakly. "Solmarsh is safe. It was destined, but I put destiny in our favor." He shuddered and coughed, shaking his head. The flecked violet in his eyes faded, and his eyes grew wide. "Wh—what have I—" With that, he faded into the next life.

Lira growled and bared her teeth. She got up, clutched the arrow in his neck and ripped it out violently. She wiped it on his robe and rushed to check the other prisoners. Their eyes were all black as night, veins dark—bodies lifeless. Each one she checked, every man, woman, and child. Laura, Terra, Matthew, Darryl, Gregand—dead. After a few moments, the rest dissolved to ash.

No. I didn't save them.
I failed.

Lira dashed to her brother's body and embraced what was left. She bawled into his withered chest. Wished it was a nightmare. Wished she could wake. He was an empty shell for the harbinger...

She didn't know what it was. But the circle lay in town.

Her friends gasped for air nearby. Kayden lay on her back, coughing, hands on her throat. "What the hell was that?"

Lira ran to her and helped her sit up. "Kayden, get up." After a moment, she shook her again. "We have to move! Let's get to the markings. We have to do something!" Lira yelled. There was no time to bury the dead.

Slowly, Kayden regained her life. With an exhausted nod, she said. "Let's go." She clumsily ran toward the cave's entrance while picking up the daggers she threw. "Everyone, *move*. Lead the way, princess!"

With every step, Lira shed tears for her brother, but she had to act now. *I won't fail again.*

But as the ground shook beneath her feet, she feared what came to her small village of Solmarsh—as it not just bore the scent of a king, but a god.

Chapter Thirty-eight

Bound by Fate, Freed by Passion

Saul Bromaggus

Saul and the Broken with him marched for days and days on end. All were relieved to finally enter the clear air of the outside. The Badlands were a welcome sight in lieu of the mountains they had been encased in for days prior. As they reached Bolerra's flow, they veered south of the Snake's Fangs to find a broad stone bridge leading over it. It was one massive block—no cracks or frays or scorches or slits from blade, flame, or smashes of catapult fire blemished its surface.

How is this bridge so unmarked during a civil war? Saul thought. It was fifteen feet wide, crossing the river of magma coming north from the dark mountains of Blackcore. Rumors said the river came from the old skeleton of Bolerra himself—a colossal hundred-foot long, red-scaled dragon, flame still clutching to the ancient bones flowing out endlessly across the Plateau. He was said to have burned a billion men in his time, protecting his mountains long before the Terrans came.

The Terrans stormed the mountains, striking hard and fast. They lost innumerable stalwart warriors to claim the mountain for themselves. *A brave venture and a glorious victory. It's no wonder they stand so adamant within it.*

"Try not to slip," Saul scoffed to the others.

They were but eight now; the majority went with Fae to Serpentarius. Saul had no knowledge of their whereabouts, only hoping they made it there safely. He resented their abandonment. Thalia alluded to his fault in it. *I am rough in my rule, but I never led before. They had not given me a choice and left without offering thanks for saving them.*

"Why is this bridge not marked on the map? Are you sure we should go this way?" Drof asked weakly.

Gods man, speak confidently. "I do not know. Kashral has not steered us wrong yet. We need to press on," Saul surmised.

"What do you think awaits us there? I don't think we should just walk in the front door," Korren said.

"Don't be a coward. If they support us, we have nothing to fear. We are Broken—and should not fear the face of our enemy."

The Broken kept quiet during their travels. They spoke at times, and they learned some about one another as their journey went. Drof was a good individual, Saul knew. As the Terrans would put it, he was a crag.

He was a coward, afraid of confrontation, but no fool. Saul was wary of walking in the front door, but he was not afraid. Saul was only afraid of fighting with him by his side, as a Broken is only as good as the comrade beside them. Saul was powerful alone, but with each weak ally, he became more vulnerable. If Drof were to rise high in rank, Saul would name him a tactician, where he belonged. There was little room for full tacticians in Broken society, as all were measured by their fighting status alone. Drofar was exiled for failing his training for leaving his allies vulnerable. He was banned from battle teachings but studied to compensate.

Saul thought of Thalia, remembering her eyes watch Drof. She thought the same but said nothing of his involvement. She was a small woman of strong opinions, and apparently a shaman of earth. She walked like a ghost in bare feet, as if she didn't wish to disturb the earth below. He had no capacity of how powerful an ally or enemy she was and was irritated that she failed to mention the involvement of her brothers in the war.

She was eerily attractive, and Saul mistrusted it. He gave no care to weak individuals, any compliant individual who wished to woo him in the Vale. If there was anything that retracted him from a woman's touch, it was weakness, and a lack of self-reliance. Thalia had none of those traits. But she was still a Hydris.

* * *

Over the bridge and past the highroad to the Fangs, they came to the Cligar Mountains. They moved south and went around, which was a pain. Several mountain villages and towns decorated the mountainside, but Saul made sure they gave no notice. He did not trust them, especially with brutal rebels prowling the Badlands. The heights and paths within were red, sun-scorched, treacherous, and filled with Manticores, mountain lions, and small populations of basilisks. While Saul did not fear those alone, he felt he could not slay a hundred beasts and get everyone out alive.

A strange thought. He felt the will of Highwind, Othellun, and now Thalia in his decisions.

Before his banishment, he would go through the mountains with no fear, feeling each Broken should fight and were not his responsibility if they failed. Now he avoided certain dangers, knowing that even one deaths was wasteful and cowardly on his part if they were unnecessary.

The trip took weeks since Blackcore, and one more wouldn't hurt as all the others would have to make the same trek. The mountain range was a steely grey, with frosted tips miles above. He never climbed a mountain and found himself wondering how truly cold they were. Saul saw many seasons of Air, each as deadly as the next, but luckily short enough so not all crops were lost in the Vale. Each crossing of the Air felt like death came ever closer, but with thick bearskin cloaks they survived. Soon the Air would come once more to Saul.

He heard the Plateau saw little of the elements changing, at least nowhere nearly as prominent as the Vale. He wondered how it was possible, not understanding why. In the north, the Fire grew hot, the Air froze the land, the Earth was desolate, and the water was laced with torrential storms. But here, the Air was rarely ever cold, and the fire was far hotter—or so he heard.

Feeling his sword arm itch, Saul yearned for combat. *Soon, we will come to Serpentarius. There I may find combatants to fulfill my need for the clash of blades, and a society I may war for, to fight against those who persecute my people.* For years he fought every day, and since exile he only spilled blood through the death of those in Rhoba. He wondered if he would spill blood alongside the Hydris, a race that were the Broken's sworn enemies. Since his exile, he'd encountered a betrayal of his own people, and a surprising alliance with a perceived enemy that potentially saved his life. He sensed that he could trust Thalia, but she still hid some information from him.

As they passed around the mountains heading east, A deathly black cloud hung over the southern skies, covering the horizon. The Plateau declined into the ocean, as the map told. South laid the Striker's End and, off the coast, the Stormspire. Thalia said only those with permission from the King could seek it.

Saul would get there, no matter the cost.

The recurring nightmare still plagued him—being struck by lightning, electricity enveloping him in agony until he finally awoke. Slowly but surely, the nightmares grew longer and more painful, as the pain grew slower, as if he became accustomed to it—but grew to a horrifying height when he awoke.

The bags beneath his eyes grew larger as well. A voice spoke right before he awoke, saying, '*Rai soli moria, gadoras faust.*' The very words Gadora taught him. He thought of the 'Soldier of Storms,' Ithaca—Thalia's brother. *Am I to face him? Will that be my time to die before the gods?* he wondered. He looked to the dirt-covered, muscular arms that bore the drop. He was fated to die—yet, his father had been fated to live. Fate played a game with the mortal realm, and Saul was going to win.

Days passed as they travelled off the highroad; fields of bloodweed and long moongrass flitted across the plains like a million feathers floating in the wind. Korren hunted daily with a new partner, so each could learn the ways of survival, and he would not be the sole provider for them all.

Drof read books he carried with him, some which were given to him by Thalia in Shi'doba. Saul routinely practiced his combat training, sparring with anyone who asked, or who he could get to fight with him. It was what he lived for—either in training or in real battle. He enjoyed cooking the meat and vegetables and fruits they would all find, but combat was his truth.

The day came where they saw a massive city in the distance. It was high noon; the sun gleamed bright and hot overhead.

"This is it, Serpentarius," Saul said.

The land I saw as my enemy, but may not be anymore.

He could hear quivers and mumbles behind him, but he paid them no mind. The city was built with rounded stone walls, each wrought with embrasures, bastions, and large sculptures of Hydris atop each tower. Engravings portrayed men and women battling with spears and blades, others commanding Earth, Wind, Fire, and Water to their will. Pillars lined the path as they approached, each with the sign of the local gods, the Glories. He bowed his head to the three crashing winds as they passed. They were all tinted green from venomstone, but also strewn with moss and lichen, blown in from the seas off the monstrous cliffs to the east. Saul could smell the salt in the air; the moist leaves and moss also added their own musk.

Yet, more than anything else, he heard yelling: commanding, the roaring of soldiers, but no clashing of blades. Saul broke into a run, not caring for the ones behind him. He looked back to see them falling behind but following just the same. There was a battalion of guards at the entrance, skins of deep green, blue, and in between, fins of different sizes, and many piercings on their ears and faces. They drew blades and pointed them at the arriving Broken and narrowed their eyes.

"Who goes there?" the head guard yelled with a hiss in the common tongue. His skin was a dark black-blue. Each soldier wore the sigil of the Kashral bloodline, the black serpent on a field of azure.

"We're here to join the effort against the usurpers, or at least want more information. Is something happening?"

"The Stormwardens have barricaded themselves in the inner castle. They snuck past our defenses and attacked all at once. They have Broken prisoners, hostages, and threaten to kill them and our King. We're forced to stay here, in case of a frontal attack. They're led by Ithaca, the Soldier of Storms!"

Oh gods, no. Fae and the others! Those fools, they should have waited. Saul feared the mention of the Soldier of Storms. Not only had Saul dreamt of being struck by lightning until he awoke from agony, but the Soldier of Storms was supposedly meant to unify the land. *But how could such a traitorous wretch unify anyone?* "How long has this gone on? We must enter! We must stop them!" Saul roared, drawing his blade. "Let us in, or we shall *fight* our way in!"

"No, *Broken*, we cannot let you in. Letting more in will only make things worse, and there could be a frontal attack coming. We aren't sure."

Saul drew his blade up to the guard's neck, which caused the entire battalion to raise blades and bows toward him. "Don't test me. My allies are in there, and I must stop those wretched knaves from killing my people!" Saul could feel the stare of the whole battalion, including dozens of archers above. "I must go. My fate commands it. Thalia Kashral told us to come here from Shi'doba, and now you dare reject her rule?" Saul hated using her name for his gain, but he had to get through.

The head guard hissed at Saul. He looked to the others and reluctantly gave way. "Be on your way. If you cause any problems, we'll throw you to the rebel dogs ourselves. You five, escort them."

Saul ran past the foolhardy guards, waving for the others to follow. His legs ached, his joints throbbed, and his trusty shield felt heavy after marching for weeks. The city was lined with large, well-made wooden and stone buildings, with signs hanging above shops and inns, and signs delineating different regions. Saul registered no words or symbols, only wood, stone, and people running. He had no time to think, no time to wander or smell any damned flowers. *I must save them. I must. This is what the dreams told me.*

A large inner wall encased the castle ahead. Saul ran with no sense to stop; blood pumped through his veins without relent. He tired but did not pause. He worried but did not falter.

The Broken approached the inner wall. Soldiers upon soldiers stood around the perimeter, wearing azure cloaks along with the black serpent of Kashral running across them. They yelled at the Hydris up on the wall if the inner castle, each aiming bows at the others. The ones on the wall all wore white cloaks, yelling, "The storm has come! The storm has come!" and, "The Soldier of Storms is upon us!" *The Stormwardens,* Saul thought. His destiny was at hand. Saul knew the name of their leader in the western Plateau, Ithaca, Thalia's bastard brother.

Saul banged on the massive, steel-studded oak door again and again, roaring to let them in. He took out his bow and fired at the usurpers above, one, two, three, and finally hit one. One guard beside him smacked his bow away, yelling at him for possibly hitting innocents still inside the walls.

The chanting stopped, and then the disgraces above yelled, "Broken! Broken! Traitors!"

Saul could barely see the men above with the sun blinding him. Before he could react, a crosshatch of shadows flew over him. A net hit him quickly and closed tightly as it dropped. Then a great force pulled him upward. The other Broken and some Hydris tried to pull him back down, but it was no use. He ascended into the light in the net, bringing him to the top of the inner keep's wall. The last image he saw on the ground was Drof and the others backing away, fearing to be netted with him. Strikes of cudgels and maces battered him from outside the net, and he struggled and dropped into the fetal position, covering his head.

He was still in his plate with blade and shield, but there were too many. He wouldn't die struggling in a net. He would die standing tall. "Bring me to your leader!" Saul yelled.

"*Hah*! You hear that? The beast wishes to see the Soldier of Storms! I knew Broken were stupid, but this is new. Bring him to the Lord with the others." The Hydris's laugh slithered and hissed, mocking Saul.

Saul was dragged along the ground, slogged down a seemingly infinite number of stone stairs. "Let me out of this net, despicable beasts!"

They simply laughed at him, spouting slithering curses and mockery in the Hydrian tongue while he was dragged down the stairs. He couldn't count how many as his sight shifted from the sky, to stone, to men, to the dirt, unable to focus on anything for too long.

By the time they stopped, he felt the dirt ground. The net opened and Saul writhed out immediately, struggling to his feet. His back ached and his arms hurt from the stone steps. His ears rang from the beatings, but he stood as strong as he could. His arms and legs were bound, however.

The circular inner courtyard was lined with warriors wearing the same white cloaks, a sigil of an ocean blue snake on a field of cream, with long fangs painted on their steel. Innocents, eyes wide and filled with fear, lined the wall around them, with several white cloaks standing with blades pointed at captives.

An old, wrinkled Hydris with ratty white hair was tied to an elaborate wooden chair. Behind him lay a set of steps leading to a massive stone dwelling fit for the gods. The old man had a white, finely trimmed thin beard, and was clad in a velvet and magenta silk doublet with blue cloth for a lower robe. His brow was furrowed, yet eyes sullen, and every muscle in his body tensed.

"Look here, beast," a gruff, slithery voice called. The Hydris stood with short, hunter green hair and forest green skin, with bronze piercings all along his eyebrows and his ears. He stood before four Broken that Saul recognized, including Fae. Her arm was broken, and her eyes burned with rage. "Look at what your people are. I tell you, *all* of you, that these people are a curse to ours. They have pushed us to the south, and now we must move north. We must not ally with them, but *crush* them, so they may not betray us later! I am Ithaca, the Soldier of Storms! Obey me, and we shall come into an age of freedom from tyranny, I will take my rightful throne, and move to claim what is mine from the Spire, *the blade that carves the skies*! My father denied me that which is rightfully mine—the Serpentarian throne. I have come to claim what is deserved, and I will bring an age of peace!"

The blade that carves the skies? He doesn't mean—Gadora's Edge? That's impossible. "We *never* betray! That is not our way, Hydrian fool!" Saul yelled.

"Silence, you dirty Broken!" Ithaca roared.

One of the white cloaked soldiers beside Saul threw him to the ground and kicked him in the stomach. He growled in pain and attempted to catch his breath. Saul could smell the cooked flesh of men and looked past the kneeling Broken to see the blackened bodies of his other comrades.

Saul struggled in his binds, attempting to get back to his feet but the soldier beside him forced him down again. *Damned coward. Unvind me.*

"Now, watch as these traitorous people, who entered our great city unannounced, pay for their crimes so that we may be free!"

Ithaca raised his hands dramatically. White bolts of electricity flew out from his fingertips, meeting the bodies of Saul's allies. Wails of agony filled the inner walls of Serpentarius, causing all within to shudder. Slowly, the screams turned to weak yelps—and soon, the other Broken subtly writhed upon the stone ground.

Saul could do nothing but watch as the electricity burned their bodies. "You weakling! Fight me without your foolish tricks! You are weak—*nothing* without your foolish power!" Saul yelled in desperation, hoping to provoke the despicable leader before his allies died. He felt it was too late; when the lightning faded, the bodies of his fellow Broken were black and burned. He hoped they still had a little life left.

After a brief, shocked pause, Ithaca cackled in hilarity. "You dare challenge me, beast? I am the Soldier of Storms, the Warrior of Light, the one who will unify our lands!" He calmed himself and narrowed his eyes. "Unbind him, I will slay him myself." With a maniacle grin, he said, "I'm going to enjoy this." Ithaca drew two long blades, one in each hand. "No one can stop a storm of steel."

Saul was let free. Their biggest mistake. He grabbed his maul from his back and smashed it on the ground. "Nothing but a petty spit of rain." *I am strong. I can defeat him. A Broken warrior with all his limbs and armaments is unstoppable,* he thought.

The other Stormwarden soldiers separated into a large circle around them, laughing at and mocking Saul. "No one challenges the god that lives! The Soldier of Storms!" The surrounding warriors chanted his words, over and over.

Saul stormed toward Ithaca, swinging his great maul round and round. The Hydris dodged backward once and again, barely staying the heavy strikes. Ithaca took a blow by the maul and toppled to the ground, but quickly kipped up and slashed at Saul's leg. One slice made contact, cut through his greave, and drew blood. Saul staggered back, and then moved in with haste to smash him from above, but Ithaca dodged sharply and slashed Saul's right shield arm, causing him to let go. Ithaca smacked the maul's haft to the ground and jumped forward to kick Saul back.

Saul fell to the ground, seeing the dishonorable fool saunter toward him with blades ready. Saul ripped his blade from his scabbard and jumped for his shield still by the net. Saul donned it with haste and deftly swung his blade, clashing with both of Ithaca's. Slashing high and low, he attempted to keep up. Ithaca struck from both sides with lightning speed. Saul guarded his deadly slices with his shield and bashed him back. Ithaca reared and soared in, swinging high and then spinning for Saul's legs. Saul barely parried the strikes, getting pushed back time and time again. He bashed when he could, barely blemishing Ithaca's right arm.

Boos and mocks came from the Stormwardens around them, but Saul's concentration stayed strong. Saul retreated behind his shield, running full force into Ithaca before he could react, causing him to topple like a fool. He dropped one blade, and Saul deftly kicked the other away.

"You have lost!" Saul yelled, bringing his sword down like a mighty bolt of lightning himself.

Ithaca rolled out of the way and flipped up with a stagger to his step. He wiped blood from his mouth, growling at the stronger Broken before him. "My blade!" Ithaca demanded with a hand outstretched. Saul attempted to run in for the kill, but the white-cloaked wretch was too quick. Ithaca grabbed a two-bladed sword gilded with gold and black iron wrapping out of the air and blocked Saul's sword with a *clang*. The other swished around for a carving of flesh, but Saul dodged out of the way.

"Coward! Fight me without the help of your underlings!" Saul took up a new weapon and shield, but he rolled and dodged to get it on his own. The damned coward Ithaca had an ally give him a weapon.

Ithaca only laughed. "Your race is *full* of cowards. Now you shall die, beast!"

He swished and swirled his two-bladed sword around like a staff, with death spelled at each point. Saul ran for quite a time and was already tired. His blade slowed as he stopped blows and dodged Ithaca's dual strikes. Ithaca's stance was low and strong, blade quick and elusive as a hurricane's eye. Their blades clashed to the sound of silence; not even the other Stormwardens hooted or hollered anymore. Saul bashed one end of Ithaca's blade, only to have the other slash his sword arm. Each strike from Saul only made the bastard swing around harder and fiercer.

Ithaca retracted back, making a mighty double swing at Saul's blade, causing it to fly far from his hand. In the shock, Saul paused, giving Ithaca the chance to elbow him across the chin, throwing his shield arm out. The glint of steel passed into the center of his vision, and Saul felt himself contort his back to bend to a far tilt, only to feel the blade sever the close stubble on his chin. With a violent, upward pull of his other blade, pain fired across Saul's forearm like a violent fire that boiled his blood. Ithaca carved through Saul's shield arm flesh and bone all at once.

Saul roared in pain as he was kicked to the ground, gripping the bloodied stump that remained of his right forearm. *No, my arm, my shield arm…*

Ithaca drew back and let out a frantic laugh. "You see, *this* is the weakness of Broken! Only a fool would challenge the Soldier of Storms!" Ithaca threw his two-bladed weapon away far from the battle as his lowly Stormwarden grunts cheered. He threw his arms forward for his final note, as vile lightning spilled from his hands like a thousand blue-white threads of death.

The lightning surged through Saul's body, forcing his grunt to wails. His veins exploded in pain, and he yelled and screamed in agony. He could barely hear the muffled laughs around him now. *This is the way I die?* Saul thought between the shocks of death. *Armless, a waste of a Broken…hardly a warrior. Just like the dreams, I die now. It is my fate, it was foretold.*

No! I can't give up. I make my own fate! Saul thought frenetically.

As the moments passed, Saul struggled to remain conscious, and slowly, he felt less and less pain. *As in the dreams, I feel it less. I can't let the pain overtake me. I can't surrender to this fate. I won't let it stop me!* The light stayed and laughs continued, but Saul opened his eyes to see the lightning surging all throughout his body with little feeling any longer. Instead of pain, he felt an energy he never experienced before. Slowly, he fought to his feet to challenge his enemy once more.

Arm or no, I will never surrender. "I'm not finished!"

Gasps and roars came from all angles. "No, this can't be! I am the Storm! Die, you filthy monster!" Ithaca roared as the lightning grew in brightness and strength, but it only gave Saul more drive to rip the head from the bastard's shoulders.

Saul ran forward with a powerful charge and grabbed the Hydrian traitor's hands before he could run or find another weapon. Lightning flowed around both of them, but now it was not Saul who screamed, it was Ithaca. His power was fading; electricity sprawled over his skin, leaving behind burns and blisters.

"You are not the Soldier of Storms!" Saul yelled. "*I am!*"

Ithaca's screams filled the air as he fell. The electricity faded, and Saul grabbed his weak, thin head with his sword hand, and bashed his skull over and over into the hard dirt ground. Blood spouted from Ithaca's nose and mouth, until the wretch slowly stopped struggling and screaming. The final screeches of Ithaca and Saul's roar of rage echoed through the cylindrical inner castle, followed by a deafening silence in the crowd.

As Saul lifted his hand, it was covered in blood. He slowly rose to his feet, hearing only still air. No hoots, no hollers, no mocking words, no screams, no laughs, and no cheers rang out. Slowly, murmurs rose in the circle around him. "The Soldier of Storms," he heard whispered around him.

Is that what I am? Saul wondered. He said it in a moment of passionate anger, but he did not know the truth. Saul stared at the burning pain in his arm, the screaming nerves telling him that his hand was severed. *A man without an arm is useless. How could I be the Soldier of Storms with this?* Saul kicked the body of Ithaca over and over, knowing that even in death he would mock Saul's stump of an arm. A Broken with this deformity was useless. They were banished from home or banned from combat. Moments passed, and he stood staring at his arm seared by electricity. Gradually, soldiers in white cloaks descended from the wall, coming to join the circle around Saul and his defeated enemy.

Sand seeped in from below the massive oak door, soaring and sifting with the wind. It blew past Saul and the corpse of Ithaca, forming into the body of a person: a tiny Hydrian woman with sharp gold-pierced ears, a perky nose and flowing hair as the Vale's dark canopy, running toward the King.

"Father!" Thalia cried. She fiddled with the binds, freeing the King.

Saul heard the scrape of steel on scabbard, then murmurs of curses and growls from around him. A circle of white armor slashed with azure and green skin slowly converged on him. The soldiers reformed, seemingly unaffected by their leader's demise. Lightning or no, Saul was not immune to the scrape of steel.

"Soldier of Storms or no, he has no sword, and no shield arm! The Broken are a blight, and we will snuff them out!"

Thalia turned a sharp eye and spoke in a cutting tone. "Don't be stupid, Kraid. You approach him, and you know what happens next."

The fool shrugged, tightening the grip on his blade. "Shut up, frail girl. The great Ithaca told us about your power. You are weak—nothing but a small woman. You can't stop us all. This—this *beast* must have cheated somehow, sold his soul to one of the Four!"

The others nodded in agreement.

There must have been forty of them. Hydris ran down from all angles wearing white cloaks and armed to the teeth.

Kraid rushed at her in a flash, but Thalia rushed forward, arm now the color of pewter, and smashed him across the face with a vicious *crack*, setting his neck aside in an unnatural manner. His body crumpled to the ground, dead.

The rest ran toward her. Thalia hissed and frowned. "So be it." She walked forward and winked at Saul as she passed him. "Stand back."

She raised her hands and opened her eyes wide. Earth from all around—dirt, rocks, even stone from the walls—swung around her in a cyclone. All drew back in fear, and Saul watched as she formed into a twenty-foot tall stone Golem, wielding a giant blade of rock. An earth-shattering, guttural roar came from it. She swung in mighty whirlwinds, barely missing Saul's head. White cloaks flew left and right, smacking against the stone wall of the inner castle. The soldiers attempted to slash and maul the stone legs, but to no avail. One man tried to jump and climb her back, only to be ripped off and thrown to the wall with a great *crack*.

The King stood up strong with hands behind his back as he watched the carnage unfold—as if it was expected, or as if he judged her form. One by one, the men flew and broke under the weight of Thalia's stone feet, arms, and blade. The last man attempted to run, only to be caught under a large stone foot with a *crunch*.

Such a small woman, but with such power, he thought. Saul found the fact oddly endearing.

When the supposed new leader, Kraid, ran towards Saul, he came with a great blade held overhead, and Saul was unarmed. Saul reached for a blade that fell from another stormwarden, only to see

Kraid be caught by Thalia's massive stone hand, raised into the air, and *smashed* to the ground like an ant under a boot.

After the last traitor died, the stones fell from Thalia like sand, returning her to her short, slender form. Strangely, she approached Saul with an exhaustive expression, rubbing her head furiously. She glanced to Saul, eyeing his arm with a gasp. "This is going to hurt, but it's necessary. Give me your right arm."

Healing magic couldn't regrow limbs. Saul knew what came next, and obliged. Her hand grew red-hot, placing it on his pathetic stump of a forearm. Saul growled in pain as she sealed the wound closed. "My thanks. You have interesting timing—and you're late." She conveniently arrived after the battle. Saul wondered how she even came to be in Serpentarius, as they'd left her in Shi'doba, far across the Plateau in the Neck.

"I was just a bit behind you the whole trip, Saul. You're bad at seeing a tail. It isn't my fault you rushed in here." She passed by him, gracing him with a sly wink.

Saul did rush into the city and challenge them as quickly as he could.

She grasped the old man's hand, and spoke softly. "Father, are you okay? I was worried when I heard the news of their plan."

"You always know how to make an entrance, daughter. If only you were born a man."

Thalia scrunched her face into frown. "Stop that. I'd rather not have been. The 'men' you bore became traitors." She glanced at Saul, whose jaw was still dropped. "At this rate, I might have to be your successor."

The King frowned. "Don't patronize me. My bastard son just tried to kill me. I have no need for attitude from my daughter."

"Well, aren't you lucky Saul came? You should at least thank him—and oh, don't forget I sent him here."

As they spoke, Saul shook his head and came back to reality. A hoarse breath echoed from nearby. *Fae is alive.* He limped over to her, still injured from the battle. She could barely croak a word.

"No, you cannot die. Your symbols show victory!" Saul said.

Fae coughed up a laugh, "Blind to the end, Saul. Idiot—don't you see? We did win. Soldier of—*storms*. Heh—wouldn't have guessed." Her words faded, and her eyes turned lifeless.

He was too late. *Ithaca, I would kill you again if I could*, he vowed. He closed her eyes and saluted her and the others who died. *They were brave, but did not think before they acted.*

"Saul, it's too late." Thalia called softly from behind him. "We will give them a proper burial, to your customs."

"Thank you," Saul said bluntly, still staring at the bodies marred by electrocution. "If only we arrived earlier."

"That can't be helped. He would have killed them all if he could, the scum. He was hardly a man—nothing but a monster." She paused for a moment, growing reflective. "I had a feeling it'd be you."

"Why didn't you tell me?" Saul asked, turning a narrowed eye toward her.

"It was only a hunch. Plus, sometimes people need to find out who they are on their own. It's a part of discovering one's destiny, wouldn't you agree?" She grinned pointedly.

Saul didn't like her reply, but knew she was right. His destiny had drawn him south. He got up and turned toward the King. "Your Grace, may I have an audience?"

Kovos laughed hoarsely. "Oh, I suppose you might as well, boy. In time, I'll grow busy, and newcomers can't take precedence, even *if* you killed my traitorous, bastard son. Kith, Rhaena, unseal the door and let these people out. We will speak on the morrow about our *security*." He sighed, waving some of the guards away. He walked slowly to his castle door, which was ripped open, but attached. "Boy, we shall speak now. I'm certain my daughter will see to your accommodations afterward." The guards went to open the door, and all left outside spilled in. The King sauntered back into the massive royal structure alone, waving the guards away.

Victory had been attained, but Saul's mind didn't linger on the King, Thalia, or the fools killed. It lingered on the words of Ithaca. *If the blade that carves the skies is there, I will seek it atop the Stormspire.* "Thalia, would you come with us?" Saul asked.

"Oh, come now, Saul. I was coming along, regardless of your invitation," she laughed. "I can't leave you alone. You'd get into trouble without me around." Thalia walked ahead with a swagger, and Saul followed.

Chapter Thirty-nine

Risen from Ashes

Zaedor Nethilus

Zaedor and Nargosh finally arrived in Solmarsh late into the night. They entered from the North gate, finding an inn nearby made of tattered black maple planks. The town shone with the mystifying white glow from the moon. They strolled into *Sohgra's Inn*, looking for a room.

"Well, that's a face I haven't seen in a long while," a Hydris said in a slithery voice. He was cleaning the deserted bar near the end of the night. "What are you doing down here, my musical friend? I thought you went east." He was like one of the men Zaedor met in the pit. His skin was azure, and fins ran over his head and through his thick grey hair. His voice slithered like a snake. Zaedor didn't know what to make of him.

"Oh, I'm just traveling, my good man. I can't sit still! I do love exploring. I have a friend here who wanted to visit this small town of yours."

"Oh? Odd. Why're you in this town? It's a little odd for—" he paused briefly, "—someone to be here out of the blue. Although you aren't the only new person here, I suppose."

Zaedor looked up with wide eyes. "There are others? Who?"

"She left town some time ago but is back here checking some things out. A sweet girl, but you'd best keep yourself in check. I see that look in your eye."

"Do you mean Miss Kaar?" Nargosh asked.

"Yes, that's her. She's changed a bit since she left after her brother's arrest."

Nargosh closed his eyes and nodded. "Oh dear, that's very sad. I'm sorry to hear it, old bean. Why did she leave?"

"No clue, but she's with a bunch of rough-and-toughs now. They're investigating the—well, the disappearances."

Zaedor's ears perked up. It could have something to do with the orb, or Cloaker, or anything. He needed to know more. "What disappearances?" Zaedor asked.

Sohgra explained what he knew. He mentioned how many disappeared, and the markings in the center of town. Apparently Zaedor was late to the investigation, and another group were at it for quite a few days. He wondered how it could possibly connect to Amirion; Zaedor feared he traveled far for nothing.

"Who is investigating, where are they? I must speak with them. I came a fair way," Zaedor leaned forward on the bar and picked at his fingernails.

Sohgra leaned back. "You can't just ask for details like that. How do I know you aren't from the state?"

"Mr. Zaedor isn't that kind of man, old bean," Nargosh interjected. With a strong pat to Zaedor's shoulder, he said, "He wants to help. He seems to believe they have a connection to his home," he said in his hoarse voice.

Sohgra's forehead tightened. "Oh? Where are you from?"

Zaedor saw his city in his mind, burned. Broken. "Amirion," he said bluntly. "It was destroyed by Zenato almost a season ago."

Sohgra nodded with a somber expression. "Yes, that news reached here not long before you did. A true tragedy. I prayed for them to the Four. I thought there was no one left."

"I am one of who even knows how many. I used to see my people every day, now I never see any," Zaedor said, looking to the bar counter. He felt he was alone. His wife, Eryndis, had gone to Zenato to speak with the new King of the Eastern lands of Zenato, Rawling Tirilin, the late King's brother. He missed her. *Did she arrive in time? Eryndis, what happened in Zenato?* "Please, I must know. Who are they?"

Sohgra described the newcomers to town that went with the one called Lira. There was Kayden, a short, rugged woman, a Blazik woman named Domika, an old wizard in a violet robe, and a massive Half-Devil.

Sohgra mentioned that the wizard was *The Great Vesper*, a previous conjurer of the traveling circus of Renalia, but the Half-Devil worried Zaedor more. Devils were abhorrent beings who enslaved and tortured those who came near the pits of hell, and Half-Devils were monstrous hybrids who stole from innocents, murdered carelessly, and ravaged women and men alike. *How could these people be helping?* The view of Half-Devils in the north was apparent, as well as in Amirion, but was the west different?

Sohgra spoke without a wince by the mention of 'Magnus.' Zaedor wouldn't accept help from one of his kind, even if he needed it.

"An odd group. The Half-Devil, especially," Zaedor said.

"Lira seemed to trust him. Thus, so do I," the Hydris spat.

Nargosh nodded, quietly sipping a cup of water.

Is that good enough? Just one girl's trust? He couldn't take Sohgra's word for it. He sat quiet on his stool for a short while, paying no attention to Sohgra's slithery growl.

"Is there anything else you can tell me? Is there anything else out of the ordinary here? I do wish to help and, if they are the ones to go to, I would like to speak with them."

Sohgra surrendered his frown. He let out a long sigh, leaning forward. "All right. They're in town trying to find out what's been happening. But somethin' last night was really out of the ordinary."

Zaedor leaned in closer, seeing Nargosh sporting a sly smile. "What happened?"

"Well, this one eccentric in town has always been after Lira's heart, and I mean *always*, ever since she moved into town," he said, looking left and right. "She turned him down time after time— she's too sweet of a girl to let him down hard. Last night, though, she finally agreed."

Zaedor crossed his arms. "So? What's the wrong with that? He was persistent, and she gave him a chance." *Was this the Hydris' big tip?* Zaedor didn't have time for wasteful comments. *I hope he is taking this seriously.*

"No, you don't understand," Sohgra hissed. "The little lady doesn't say yes to things like that. She was acting as if she always wanted to, was suddenly more excited, more interested in this 'mine business' he has going. If you ask me, she was interrogating him. Impressively, I might add. He didn't suspect a damn thing," Sohgra said, leaning back. "She was supposed to meet him at the mine tonight. It's past that time, so I'm not sure what you can do now."

"What are you going to do, Mr. Zaedor?" Nargosh asked.

"I'll check where they are staying. I would rather not run into the Half-Devil or the robed man, but I'll take my chances," Zaedor said, rolling his eyes.

"They're staying at the small blackwood home with the light brush garden out front, just west of here, closer to the water. 'Kaar' is on the letterbox." Sohgra leaned in close, his forked tongue flicking subtly. His small fins tightened to his head. He bared his teeth, same as a Human's, but with two sets of sharp fangs. "If harm comes to her because of you, you'll regret it."

"Su—sure." Zaedor said with a cracking voice, backing off. This woman was important to him, that much was obvious. He did not know where she was, or what to expect. He sauntered toward the door of the inn.

Nargosh gave him a parting comment. "Do be careful. There is an ominous wind tonight. Old men like me can smell it."

Zaedor nodded, turning to open the door. He walked a few houses down, finding the blackwood house with lovely little shrubberies around the door. The soil was dark and moist—someone kept them going while she was gone. The house was dark and silent. He knocked on the door quietly.

He thought of his old home. Zaedor still couldn't get the images out of his head: the burning banners, the screaming of men, women, and children as their souls were stolen from their bodies.

No one answered the door. He felt sadness overtake him once more, as it had throughout the past days on the road. When left with his own mind, he couldn't keep the thoughts away. For once he truly appreciated Nargosh's rambling stories. He knocked again. No answer. *Please, answer the door,* Zaedor thought. He pounded on the door with all his might. There was no one home.

Moments later, he heard screams and wails from elsewhere in town. He saw people running past him, yelling for him to run away. He had to see what was happening. He feared it was a repeat of that fateful night in Amirion. Zaedor dashed to the origin of the sounds, seeing a bright, violet aura emanating from the south.

He ran to the center of town, the source of the violet aura. *What are these markings?* They were lit in bright violet, the same as the orb. The light from them pulsed slowly, as if counting down to the inevitable end. Zaedor felt a light from above. He slowly raised his eyes to see the fateful sight: the darkness consuming the light of the world, the wind that snuffed out the lone Torch. The violet orb of mist was there, fifty feet above.

He was back in Amirion, he felt; the spirits of hell came to take innocent souls away. The guttural, disembodied voice spoke once more. Zaedor again heard the mysterious, vile words that lived in his nightmares.

"No, it cannot be, not again!" Zaedor yelled, drawing the gifted greatblade upon his back. White spirits flew from within the orb and swished around it. Ten, twenty, fifty, a hundred—the faster they swirled, the more plentiful they became. Round and round, they soared above. Zaedor felt helpless; he didn't know what to do. His blade shook in his hands as he backed away slowly.

A deafening clap of thunder came from the skies; black clouds quickly surrounded the town, swirling over where Zaedor stood. Townspeople ran from the scene, though some curious enough to stay stood beside him. So many spirits flew around the orb that he couldn't count them anymore. With blinding speed, the spirits looked like halos around the omen of death, forming a white, glowing sphere around it.

The spirits froze in the sky like a million stars. They rushed one by one into the center of the markings, and each *slammed* into the ground and shook the foundation of the land. *What is happening?* Zaedor asked himself. *What evil is at work here?* The pain of a million men and women surrounded him, overtaken by pure evil. The ground shook so wildly that Zaedor stumbled and fell.

As the final souls crashed to the ground, a dark violet portal opened within the circle of markings. It was colored with violet, magenta, and azure tints. Three serpentine beasts emerged from the ground, each with black wings and a long neck and tail, as if to be a Dragon. Each was as large as Zaedor, with veins of magma pouring down their arms, eyes alive as an inferno that burned the realm. They dashed at Zaedor and the townspeople. Zaedor sprang to action, cutting and slashing at them with his blade, but their skin was thick as hardened leather, and their claws like steel.

Others in town came armed with axes and blades and cut away at the three beasts. Zaedor cut off the arm of one and it bit at his arm with sharp teeth, piercing through his scale mail. Zaedor kicked it off and backed up, raised his blade, and cut the beast's head clean off. The creature staggered about as if it still lived. Its black skin began to rebuild and reform. Zaedor kicked it again and pushed it back over the portal, and it fell back through before it could regenerate. He looked around to see the other two beasts biting and slashing townspeople, but with a charge from Zaedor and a swing of his blade, he quickly overwhelmed the two beasts and shoved them back down as well.

Zaedor panted and gripped his arm; he could feel that it was wet with blood. Some of the people around him staggered away and limped from their injuries, others stayed, and some ran as fast as they could. Zaedor couldn't leave.

He wouldn't fail this time. Alone, but he stood his ground.

His ears popped with a strange pressure in the air. A swelling sound rose around him, the dust rising and falling across the street.

A massive, scaled arm the size of a tree reached out from the portal and smashed upon the ground and shook the land. Another reached out from the other side and cracked the earth beneath it. A monstrous being emerged, climbing out to view its new land. The vile creature was twenty feet tall on two legs, with black, scaly skin and a powerful tail flowing out the back. Its body oozed with magma as if it flowed through its veins, body made of corded muscle, with arms extending to hands with claws like scythes. Its head was protected by a large exoskeleton skull that shone like steel, with bright, fiery pits for eyes like the depths of hell, leading to a destructive maw. Smoke flowed out with each breath, forming a harrowing haze all around him.

Zaedor never encountered such a monster before. *Oh gods. I don't know if I can challenge this,* he thought. He needed allies.

"Holy hell!" a raspy voice yelled.

Five figures rushed onto the scene. A tiny woman with a great mane of hair, a massive pale-skinned man clad in rusty plate, a tall, dark-skinned woman, and he couldn't see who else. He recalled their names and hoped they would aid his plight.

The massive creature turned to them, commanding, "My thirst for life has been quenched. I have risen from the ashes of one million corpses. I command your worship of Him, the one who freed us from the abyss. To resist means your death. Your soul is mine—a feast for eternity."

"What are you to command us, beast?'" Zaedor yelled. As the monster's fiery gaze turned toward him, Zaedor swallowed tightly. *One million souls, devoured? My people. More than just them. Many more,* Zaedor thought.

"Valikar, foolish mortal. I am the Harbinger of his coming as he, Lornak, summoned us; I move to smash the stones that bind his soul. To bring Him forth to this plane to claim the realm. Kneel now or I shall devour your souls—leaving nothing but a hollow shell. Kneel, and you live."

Zaedor couldn't move. His knees clattered at the sight of it, and he wasn't alone. The Blazik woman, Domika, and the Wizard in the violet robe, Vesper, also backed away, shaking wildly. The others did not budge.

Kayden turned to Zaedor. "What are you doing, idiot? *Run!*"

I cannot run. I have to face it. My people would never forgive me. Zaedor wanted to run, he did, yet he was unable to move. He felt paralyzed by fear.

"Bashira!" Lira yelled, holding her hands toward the beast.

A spittle of light flowed toward the beast and around its arms, but it shook the spell off and laughed. "Pathetic magic of pathetic gods. Your pitiful power cannot shackle a being as powerful as I. You will die for your insolence! Behold the power of the Dark!"

The beast inhaled deeply and blew a vast flurry of black flame across the ground and buildings, lighting the straw roofs on fire as the five barely dodged out of the way in time. He breathed the flame again, bathing townspeople running for their lives in a vile inferno. Screams echoed through the streets as flesh boiled and burned. Kayden ran around the outer ring as Magnus charged at the beast, shield raised. Lira raised her bow, shooting arrows wherever she could, but barely fazed it.

The Harbinger swung its mighty claw and bashed Magnus to the ground, causing him to tumble. They came in with a final strike, but Zaedor charged into action and struck the monster's side, causing him to miss and rear around. Backing away, Zaedor barely dodged the beast as it ran full-force into the building where Vesper and Domika stood.

It crumbled under Valikar's might with a *smash*. Domika and Vesper barely dodged out of the way, scrambled to their feet, and ran in opposite directions.

Kayden jumped on its back before it turned and climbed up. The beast flailed but couldn't shake her off. She ripped two blades out from scabbards and jammed them into the back of the beast's neck.

Valikar roared in pain, caught Kayden in his monstrous grip, and threw her to the ground, motionless, along with her blades.

Magnus snuck up from behind and sliced behind the monster's knees, causing it to turn around in a violent rage.

Zaedor watched, paralyzed, as if a spectator. *I'm a coward. I couldn't save my king, I couldn't save Lothel, and now I can't save them.* The beast exchanged blows between the four still up. The Half-Devil protected his allies as they struck his limbs.

Zaedor watched closely, the wounds in the monster's neck and behind its knees—were *healing*. *They need help, but what am I capable of?*

"It's healing! The beast is healing!" Zaedor yelled.

The Wizard, Vesper, carefully shot small balls of flame and shards of ice at the beast, doing nothing. *Is he even trying?* He seemed afraid, and nothing was pushing him to fight. Domika swirled and sliced, barely able to gain ground against the beast, whose long arms swiped and threw her against the stone wall of a building with a loud *thud*, bending her arm in an unnatural fashion, and leaving her unconscious.

Vesper backed off indefinitely, leaving Lira, who shot arrows from afar, and Magnus, who was then fighting one-on-one with the massive beast. The fool's armor was weak and rusty, yet the bladelike claws of Valikar slashed and swiped, unable to pierce it. Magnus' movement slowed, bit by bit, tired and breathing heavily from dodging claws and flame. The beast, instead of swiping once more, grabbed Magnus with both hands and smashed his steeled skull into the comparatively puny man. Valikar threw him down and knocked him unconscious—or dead.

The monstrous demon turned his gaze to Lira. He ran at her with a massive claw raised. Zaedor moved without thought, he saw no other option. *I must do something!*

"Die, beast!" Zaedor yelled, running with his blade overhead. Zaedor leapt at Valikar, bringing his sword down with all his strength, nearly carving through Valikar's entire arm. Zaedor swung again, causing the monster's limb to fall to the ground, and it roared in agony. Zaedor deflected the other claw strikes, but was slammed against the wall with raw force, and with a sharp swipe, both he and Lira were smashed aside. Lira's side was bloodied from the slash, as was Zaedor's chest. It hurt to breathe. Ash and blood filled his nostrils. As his ears rang and vision realigned, he could see the beast turn toward the unconscious Kayden. Valikar deeply inhaled, readying another breath of mighty flame. Kayden awoke; her eyes opened wide as she saw her time come.

The breath of flame flowed over her like a raging river but split in half where she stood.

The violet-robed man appeared before Kayden, splitting the flame breath around them with his bare hands. The beast stepped back in shock, and without pause, Vesper swished his hands back and pushed forward, unleashing a fury of lightning, encapsulating Valikar in a violent electrical storm that nearly blinded all around them. The beast writhed in pain, slowly moving toward the slender man. Vesper threw one hand forward with a mighty gust of wind and pushed the beast back against a building with a *crash*, caving it in.

"Vesper, what the hell?" Kayden yelled.

Vesper raised his hands to the air, forming a transparent, blue-tinted ice-like shell around him and the demon, separating them from everyone else. Valikar exploded off the building, rushing at the wizard once more. Vesper spread his fingers wide, cutting them around like knives, slicing off the limbs of the beast like a sword through butter with an invisible blade.

The beast laughed. "Your magic means nothing to gods." The beast grew alight with violet and regenerated its limbs within moments.

"Demon, you know nothing of this land! You shall feel the power of *The Great Vesper*!" Vesper yelled in a gruff voice. In an instant, he teleported from place to place within the transparent shell, delivering bolts of lightning and storms of ice spears to the beast's leathery body. With every spell cast, Vesper grew more tired, and the beast healed himself, over and over again.

Zaedor stood back, gripping his chest. The blood soaked through his clothes, and he felt weak. Lira was in tears beside him, huddled into a ball, her own robe becoming laced with blood.

Zaedor knelt down and attempted to staunch her bleeding.

"Vesper! God damn it, stop this! Let us help, you moron! You're going to get yourself killed!" Kayden screamed, bashing on the transparent shell. She slammed away at it with hand and blade, unable to penetrate it. The beast hammered at it as well but was also unable to break the wizard's mighty shield.

Vesper appeared before Kayden, facing the demon. He held one hand out to his right and formed a mysterious red orb above his open palm. Small, sun-like spheres shot out from each of his fingers to orbit around the larger red one.

"I'm sorry, my dear, but I won't let him hurt anyone!" Vesper said. His beard was accented by lines of dark crimson—blood, hemorrhaging from his nose. With his other hand, he maintained his powerful cuts, lances of ice, and flurries of lightning. Sweat poured down his forehead like a river, and his breath escaped him.

The red orb gathered more mass in its orbit. It was eerily beautiful, almost mesmerizing. Vesper dropped to one knee, but orb after orb emerged from his hand, adding more to the orbit. He panted and wheezed but remained adamant. *What is that spell?*

Magnus was back on his feet. His eyes were wide, seeing the orb in Vesper's right hand. "You do not have to do this! We must find another way!" he yelled.

"It is my only option! *Our* only option!" Vesper called to him. His gaze turned to Kayden with tears flowing from his eyes. "I may have failed my family, but I won't fail you!"

Vesper turned back to Valikar, who was regenerating once more. Vesper reflected his flame breath with his left hand. The red orb still gained size and spheres in its orbit in his right.

"Vesper, you idiot! No, I can't lose you. It's not fair—it's not *fair*! You can't do this!" Kayden bashed the shell again and again, helpless. She bawled uncontrollably while bashing her arms against the invulnerable shield Vesper created.

The shell's light began to flicker; Vesper's power was fading. The beast sauntered toward him. The lightning in Vesper's left hand quickly weakened and faded to nothing.

"Now, your soul shall be mine." Valikar chuckled mockingly.

"Take care of her for me!" Vesper yelled. His front became drenched with blood pouring from his nose like a fountain. "I'm sorry, my dear, but it must be done. I will be with my family now!" Vesper said, staring the demon down. "Your will is strong!"

With regaining its strength, the beast charged at Vesper with the power of a thousand bulls.

He brought his right hand to his center, using his other hand to stabilize the small sun-like object. He spoke a few short words in a language Zaedor did not understand then opened his hands wide. Each yellow orbiting sphere stopped dead around the large red sun as the world grew completely silent for a moment.

Vesper opened his eyes and yelled, "*Annihilus!*"

The smaller spheres shot at once into the orb. Following a deafening screech, a bloom of blinding fire shattered his body as a devastating explosion of red and blue flame filled the shell; the shield smashed into a thousand ethereal shards and blew everyone back and to the ground with a powerful shockwave.

Valikar writhed on the ground, body half-melted and massive breaths hoarse and foul. "A spell of—fire cannot—kill one borne of—it," the beast stuttered. It roared to the night sky, readying to heal itself once more. Crippled and broken, the beast rose to it's feet. I may be—weakened, but you have nothing left to—stop me."

Lira struggled to her feet and spread her hands wide with eyes bright like the sun. She spoke in an angelic, echoing voice in a language he couldn't understand, finishing with a final word yelled at the top of her lungs: "*Bashira!*"

Massive golden chains sprouted from her hands as a violet portal appeared behind the beast. With one end in the violet, the chains wrapped around the beasts arms, legs, and neck before it could escape, and dragged it backward.

Valikar struggled against the chains and charged forward with all its might toward Lira. It thrust a claw forward within a moment of her. Lira swished her hand and pulled backward; the golden chains threw the beast back to the ground and dragged it toward the portal.

It scraped the ground with its mighty claws, screaming like a rabid beast. Zaedor heard the Valikar's voice call out as the violet portal sucked him in, body half incinerated by the blast of flame. "Fate will come for you. *We* will come when the vile star falls."

As the golden chains pulled the monster through, they left to swirl around the violet orb above, pulling it toward the portal it opened. As the orb slammed into the ground, the earth below shook as the million souls burst from the portal, screeching so loud Zaedor was forced to cover his ears.

They formed into the violet orb once more and shot toward Lira in a split second with her chains, bashing into her chest. With a scream, she flew into the stone wall behind her, barely conscious as the violet energy surged and screeched across her skin before vanishing.

The beast was gone. Zaedor's enemy, vanquished.

As silence took the town centre, the portal vanished leaving nothing more than a small pile of ashes, and a set of charred black bones with a skull on the ground.

Chapter Forty

A King's Proposal

Saul Bromaggus

King Kashral led Saul into the grand stone keep within the inner walls of Serpentarius. Saul walked beside him, standing a couple inches above, although the King was hunched over from old age. The walls were barren, glowing with the subtle green tint of venomstone. The ceilings were rounded, absent of cracks or frays as if a battle never took place within the city walls.

Saul slowed his walk to keep pace. He could feel Thalia's presence behind them, despite her silent steps. It was pitch black, but Saul could somewhat see the outlines of arched doors with no color to them. Paintings and statues were placed along the walls, but he could barely make them out. Hydris could see well in the dark, while Broken had limited sight. At least they weren't entirely as blind as Humans were. He hoped not to walk into any walls or statues.

"Oh my, how could I forget," the King said hoarsely. With a weak snap of his fingers, a small ember appeared in his open hand.

The warm light filled the hall; Saul could see murals and statues of Hydris in full armor, robes with tomes, blades, and staves. "Sometimes in my old age I forget your people don't see in the dark as easily."

He *was* old. Saul thought maybe seventy, or even older. The most peculiar aspect was Thalia was not even twenty. He was undoubtedly her father; he could see his eyes in her, and her authoritative presence.

Saul couldn't wait any longer. "I must ask—"

"Not until I sit. Have patience," Kovos interrupted, slowly swaying his hand in a circle.

Saul felt a slap on his shoulder. He glanced back with a frown, only to see Thalia shake her head. They passed many rooms of statues of Hydris, young and old, some warriors and scholars, some kings and queens. Libraries were filled with books large and small, with intricate cashmere rugs and pelts of wild beasts.

They ascended a high staircase with steep steps. Thalia took her father's arm, slowly coming up to a large room with many books, as well as a set of six oak chairs and blackwood tables shone to perfection.

"Ah, here we are, my solace," Kovos said. He lumbered to a large silk and wool felt chair with a golden lining along the wood. Carefully lowering himself to onto the cushion, he shot the flame in his hand to the fireplace to produce a calming warmth. "Now, boy, what can a King do for you? I believe you may have many questions."

Thalia plopped into the seat beside the King with a leisurely cross to her legs. She sank into a lazy slouch before smoothing out her fiery orange silk robe reflecting the fire's light.

Saul chose the chair across from them and sat carefully on the soft cushion. *This is eerily soft. I miss my bed back in the barracks, but I am a long way from home.* "I do. I demand an explanation for what happened out there. My people are dead, and now we are but eight." *Seven and a half, really.* He looked to his stump of an arm with contempt, hardly able to secure a shield with it. If he donned one, there was no taking it off. Broken prided themselves on their versatility, and Saul had next to none now.

"Mine have died in much higher numbers, from my own sons. They were stupid to leave and challenge me. They betrayed their own father. It seems I have raised monsters, boy." Kovos sighed. "One son went missing ten years ago, and my daughter is the only one to not run or reject the laws of our people. Yet she is the only one who cannot claim the crown alone."

Thalia screwed her face into a frown. "Father, it's a ridiculous law. The people view me fine, it's you who put that restriction on the bloodline."

"You're a woman. Women cannot rule alone. You were not alone in Shi'doba, and I put you there to protect you. Your mother accepts the laws and respects my will, as should you."

Thalia grumbled openly. "I ruled there. Those other idiots did nothing. I kept them alive while Zitark ravaged the western plateau. Or did you not notice that, sitting in the city? Clearly you had no idea Ithaca was here. If Saul hadn't come, you'd be dead, and he'd be going south to the Spire, although he'd probably die there regardless."

"You *dare* you lecture me as I lose a son? What kind of child are you? You boast of your strength, and yet *you* weren't here. You boast and boast, yet what have you done?" The King's tone grew rough.

Thalia's face crumpled into a frown. "I cared about him, too, but he was rotten to the core. I have done much in my life."

"You have done nothing, girl. Don't act an artisan when you are but an apprentice."

Thalia huffed and crossed her arms. "Don't insult me."

The King ignored her. "Now, where was I? Ah, yes, the war. You come from the Vale, no? I have been considering unifying forces with the Vale. The Dragon seems willing to comply. His initial messages sent speak of a united fleet sailing to the shores of the Dragon's Archipelago. Have you come with a message from him? Curious that he would send a personal messenger this far."

Saul gritted his teeth and his heart sped up. *Obelreyon.* "He wouldn't ally with anyone. He follows a false god, goes against our ways, and sets fear into everyone who follows. It is clearly a trap."

"I see. Then what would you have me do? Destroy him? Stay isolated? The people are restless, and the Blazik Lords of Feyamin are stirring. Caught between Broken and Blaziks is an awful situation, and I'm convinced the damned Blaziks would never ally with us. They want this land, and always have. What would you do about the Dragon, boy? Would you lead my people against your own? Is that what you want?" Kovos chuckled. "Don't answer that, I'd rather not know. I suppose I should thank you for what happened. It was quite the spectacle. Unfortunate that you lost a hand. I hear Broken don't like that sort of thing. Nothing we can do about that, though. Your people are gone, too, but look at the result."

Saul raised an eyebrow. "What result?"

The King coughed up a chuckle. "People are talking. Did you not see the faces of the ones in the courtyard? The Soldier of Storms is a *Broken*. The legend has been whispered for centuries, ever since we were all banished here. Lo and behold, it's *you*. You found your own way here, somehow. It's a serendipitous and humorous truth."

"I gave him the path here," Thalia cut in.

"Don't take credit, girl. Now, where was I? Ah, the Soldier of Storms. Do you like your title?" Kovos chuckled, not waiting for his response. "I hardly believe in it. My daughter here believes in it wholeheartedly. No clue why, *heh*. I saw it myself—you walked away without being hurt by the bastard, that I'm sure of, aside from your arm." Kovos picked at his sharp nails and sported a sly smile. "What is it you wanted, boy? The people outside whisper your title, yet you don't seem to care." The flame flickered in the back of the room, barely illuminating the azure snake eyes of the two before Saul.

"Ithaca spoke of *'the blade that carves the skies'* being atop the Spire. Is it true?" Saul asked.

Kovos laughed, which led into a guttural cough. "Gadora's Edge. A fool's errand. No one's touched the blade since her ascension. I don't serve her. I serve Kannakash, hence the flame. He's more powerful and more influential, hardly what a woman could do. Goddess or not, I barely pay her mind."

"Don't insult the power of my goddess. Mortal women are not weak, either. Many of the Broken generals are women." Saul thought of Mirakia Othellun, the one who helped him escape to exile and the fiercest warrior in the Broken armies. He'd hated it then, but now knew it was the only option. Kovos was so against the abilities of women that it irritated Saul. Broken gave value to those who were strong. Some, especially Mirakia Othellun, were deadly on the battlefield. *I've seen her carve ten Broken, alone.*

"*Heh*, don't make me laugh. I may have wanted to align with them, but that doesn't mean I'll accept every belief they have. Listen, boy, you have to understand that women aren't as strong as men. They're smaller. Quick, maybe, but one lick of a blade and they're done. I've seen it. I fought a war against the Blazik Lords of Feyamin with women on my side, and they were crushed under the blades of men. We hardly survived back then, and next time they come, and they *will* come, things must be different."

Thalia tapped her foot quietly, rubbing the side of her neck. "Father, we aren't weak. How can you be so thick?"

"Silence, girl. I put you in Shi'doba to protect you—don't forget that. Now you come back into war, thinking you can make a difference? Don't be a fool. Why don't you find a man to marry and give me a viable heir? The others are disgraces, and, while a disappointment, you are the only one not a traitor."

Saul clenched his fists. "You shouldn't speak to your children that way," he growled. His father was rough on him as well. At least he gave Saul a chance to prove himself.

The air grew tense as the King's cold eyes turned towards Saul. After a moment, his cold, dead expression broke to speak words bold as stone. "I will speak to my child the way I please." Relaxing his shoulders, the King continued. "We are in the midst of a civil war, and who will lead us? You? *Heh*, maybe that's what you're here for. Everyone followed Ithaca around when he claimed a birthright to the title of 'Soldier of Storms.' Maybe they'll follow you around like a bunch of helpless cattle, as well. Although, you could hardly keep command of a small troop of Broken yourself, and now look at them." Kovos coughed and coughed, cleared his throat carefully, and narrowed his eyes at Saul. "I'm no fool. I know what you want. You want the Stormspire, don't you, boy?"

The Stormspire. Does the blade await me there? He put his fist to his chin, thinking. "I wish to go there. I will climb the Spire."

"*Heh*, I'd like to see you try, but I'm too old. Although, I won't die anytime soon. Every man who's climbed it was cooked like a meal in the process. Some even made it to the top, struck or no, but were fried by a touch of the hilt of the damn thing. Is that what you want, boy? Do you want to be cooked alive by the storm that gathers there? My son's power was one thing, but—oh, the blade is something else."

"I am not afraid." Saul felt he needed to go, but was worried about the story the King told. He caught a change in Thalia's expression, irritation toward the one beside her, to concern for the one across.

Kovos chuckled again. "I like your attitude, boy, but it's stupid and immature like hers." He motioned to Thalia, who scowled. He coughed and hacked before continuing. "I'm old, but I know smart politics. The people love royalty and they love stories." His eyes glanced from Saul to Thalia, who's now widened at his glance. "Normally suitors are much older, if anything never *younger* than a princess, but I know good politics. If I let you climb the Spire and you take up the blade, you shall marry my daughter."

Saul coughed after hearing those words. "Excuse me?" they both spat out. Age mattered not. It was her boldness.

Saul had not thought of such things. A couple of women attempted to woo at him in the Vale, valuing strength over all. They were weak—rough-hewn, Broken—but personalities that showed frailty. He found no interest in any fool of a woman. There were some he saw, but when they bent to his will, he lost every shade of interest. *Thalia is strong of mind, however.* With every statement he made, he felt Thalia analyze each with a critical eye. She corrected him when he was incorrect, she spoke out when she felt wronged, and she led with such command.

"Father, this is ridiculous. You can't expect me to marry someone because you will it. I refuse!"

The King turned a harsh eye toward his daughter. "You will do what you are told, girl. Marrying the Soldier of Storms should be an honor. Just think of what the people would see. That's my ruling—marry, or nothing. No Spire, no aid." Kovos's tone was gruff and hoarse. "Girl, you have denied many suitors over the years, for nothing. Each sir was as good as the last."

"No. They were weak, demeaning, and overbearing. I won't be treated like a child."

"You *are* a child. You killed Lord Shilen's son when he tried to court you." Kovos said, gripping the wood of his chair.

That surprised Saul. Not only did she refuse suitors she was displeased with but killed one—Saul was not unsettled by it, but intrigued.

"He tried to force himself on me. I had no choice. The wretch deserved the spike I shoved through his chest. I'm of nineteen years! How could you be so thick?" Thalia slammed the arm of her chair, leaning into him.

"And I have tried to marry you since twelve. A woman of your age is undesirable." A long, silent, and vicious glare was shared between them.

Saul saw no other option. The King seemed to be a difficult and unrelenting individual, unreasonable and irrational. Saul could see that age brought a coarse resistance to all around him.

But he did not think of it as an unfortunate option or choice. Thalia was oddly beautiful, but most importantly *tough*. She played a smart political game. While outwardly resistant, she followed his rule thus far, and stayed the only child in favor. However, her treatment of suitors was quite against the King's ruling.

A spike through the chest? Although, forcing one into such things deserved punishment. Only a disgrace of a Broken would force a woman into bed. A welcomed courting is an honor, and a forced one is pathetic and weak, Saul thought. He did like her boldness.

She'd killed a man for a disgrace, as he would have. It made her more endearing, if anything. Saul listened quietly, watching her azure-slit eyes grow harsh. He could tell her tone was sincere, but her anger was toward the King, not him. Saul felt they were more similar than he originally thought.

He acclimatized toward her since they met, and now he looked upon her with respect and interest.

After a harsh silence, the King scoffed and spoke out. "Lords run from the idea of marrying you. They hiss rumors of you eating the Lordlings when they come near, and now they're all afraid. I am the King, girl. I have to be unmoving, else I'm seen as weak. Do you want our family to be overthrown? Word is the fools in Renalia have that issue now. It has made them weak, and soon we may return in strength."

Thalia leaned back in her chair and crossed her arms. "We won't be overthrown. Make me Queen and I'll make sure our nation grows."

Kovos coughed loudly, letting out a weak but hearty laugh. "A sole Queen? Don't make me laugh. No woman will sit on my throne as long as I live. Then we would be overthrown for certain. You're a small, immature girl who knows nothing of power. You wreak havoc with your rocks, but true power lies in words. If I were to die, I would have Chorra hold the throne until you marry."

It's a combination of both tools. A King with a sword in hand is better than either alone, Saul pondered. He finally clued in to what was being said. *If you climb the Spire and claim the blade, you shall marry my daughter.* That would make Saul the heir to the throne, but he didn't care for a crown, or a prophetic title. He truly cared for his honor, his people, and the realm. Kovos didn't like Saul, he felt. But it was politics that drove the old snake's words. He saw the benefit of a unity of prophecy and royalty. While Kovos was an unlikable man, he wasn't stupid. It was logical.

"Lord Chorra is a stand-in puppet for you. Don't you dare insult my power. You were worse than me at my age," Thalia shot back.

"Yet I married for politics after Ithaca was born. Fancy that."

Thalia exploded out of her chair. "You can't force us into marriage!"

"I'm not forcing, girl. I'm telling. If he seeks the blade, swear to marry if he can claim it. You're aware that he may be cooked?"

Thalia turned around, her hair and robe swishing in a circle. "I'm aware," her voice grew brittle. Thalia pursed her full lips and clenched her fists.

People have married for politics for ages, and that's only if I survive. My dreams have plagued me for months, and I have grown tired from restless sleep. No matter my fate, I will choose my destiny here, Saul determined to himself.

He still struggled with the thought. He would potentially marry the race he was told was his mortal enemy. Yet every inclination showed the opposite from her. *Choose your people for their ideals,* Thalia had said to him. Her words were straight and honest, but everything seemed like a bit of game to her.

She jested at many things, but Saul knew that's all they were. Jests were not disrespectful mockery. She was as bold as he, and something about her pulled him to speak. He felt it necessary, and his choice was from more than just convenience.

"Thalia." Saul broke his silence.

She turned her face toward him, narrowing her eyes. "You've been quiet for once. What do you want?"

Saul stood up. *I must do it not for destiny, but for myself. I see strength in her, a boldness I respect.* He held out his hand to her. "Would you marry me, if I take the blade?" He barely believed the words would ever escape his lips. If it was purely for the blade, he wouldn't dare think to ask such a thing. But it wasn't just for the blade. Something else pressed him.

Thalia's mouth dropped open. She gasped and leaned back. She closed and opened her mouth time again, as if her words were lost. "You're serious?" she stuttered. Her eyes shot left and right, raising a brow. "I thought you disliked our people, Lord 'high and mighty, I am strong?'"

"I dislike *weak* people." Saul replied. *Is that what I sound like?*

"She's a weak girl. Don't be a fool, boy. Don't make me change my mind," Kovos scoffed.

Saul ignored the King's comment. His eyes didn't wander from Thalia's. As he waited for her words, he gave a subtle smile. Hand still outstretched, he waited for an answer.

Her lips trembled slightly, extending to a curious smile. There was a long pause as they stared into each other's eyes. Saul could see her processing the situation. He returned the sly smirk.

"Yes—I accept." She chuckled and took his hand gently.

"Good. That wasn't hard. Damn it, girl, I haven't the foggiest idea why you rejected so many before, and why you accept a Broken instead."

Both ignored the King, leaving their eyes on one another. "Do I have your permission to climb the Spire?" Saul asked.

Kovos coughed up a laugh. "*Heh.* Yes, boy, that's what we agreed. I will inform my riders to escort you to the Spire on the morrow. When you return—no, *if* you return, we will speak of unity. Now, leave me, both of you. I must mourn my son alone."

Saul and Thalia strolled out together, making no eye contact.

"And girl," Kovos hacked. They stopped, and Thalia's eyes looked to Saul. "Don't spike this one, even if he's one of them."

Saul smirked at her, but she didn't return it. After descending the stairs, Thalia whispered to him. "I can't believe this. I shouldn't have to marry you just so you can sit on the throne."

Saul shrugged. "I didn't speak of sitting on the throne. I am a warrior, not a politician."

Chapter Forty-one

The Calm

Saul Bromaggus

Thalia chuckled. "I can't imagine you sitting on a council, but maybe one day I will." She sighed, glancing back. "My father has always been that way. Always treating me like a child as if women are weak." After a long, drawn-out sigh, she said, "I can't believe you agreed to those terms. I thought Broken favored strong people."

"I cannot disagree with that," Saul said. As she turned with a glare, he continued. "I dislike weak individuals. Weak-willed. You have a strength of character I admire, and I do not find you repellant, if that is what you are inquiring about." Saul challenged himself in this endeavor. He grew up learning that the Hydris were hateful and traitorous. He saw none of that in her.

With a laugh, Thalia leaned in and grasped his arm. "Oh, Saul, you really know how to woo a woman."

"I did not mention that I would attempt to woo you. I said I would wed you," Saul replied.

She gave him a light shove. "*Tsk*, not even going to try? How depressing. Here I was, thinking I was a catch." She sighed.

Saul stopped abruptly and turned to her. She stopped after another step and turned to raise a brow. He said, "You are."

He turned back and continued walking toward the keep door.

Thalia bumped him with her hip. "You're funnier than I thought. Careful now, your romantic side is showing."

Saul frowned, not looking toward her. "I never said I would be romantic. Do not assume that."

"I think I'm going to like this marriage, if you make it." Her giggling continued. They arrived at the keep door. She opened it, and natural light finally filled Saul's vision. "Next I'll find out you have a soft side."

"I said *stop*," Saul growled.

Guards stood at attention outside and put hands-on-hilt at his outburst. They relaxed once Thalia's laughter grew.

She was lucky Saul's mind was in another place, wondering what the Spire was, and how he would climb it. He hoped it would have steps, fearing he would have to climb with one hand, if it was even possible.

With a relaxed tone, she said, "I suppose it wouldn't be so bad. As long as you treat me with some respect, I won't have to stab you like the last one." She spoke lightly, as if it was nothing. "I have a feeling you will. You wouldn't make the decision to marry unless you're committed to it, and you respect the other fully. It's endearing."

"That is concerning—but forcing one into things is a disgrace. I am no monster, nor a fool," Saul reassured her. She snorted a laugh, but Saul paid it no mind. "Why did you think it was me?"

"A hunch, silly. I told you. Dreams of storms and lightning, it was in the tome I had. Do you read much?"

"No. I have not learned to read well, nor has it been important. Broken commonly learn through word of mouth."

"*Mmm.* We'll work on that. At least you aren't terrible with your mouth." She snickered.

Saul didn't respond. If it was a joke, he didn't understand it. He felt that question was coming considering how many books lined the wall at her home in Shi'doba. The prophecy implicated him; it was no wonder she sent him to Serpentarius. *Although, I did wish to go. She simply gave me a nudge.* His whole journey led him to this place—and she aided him without question. But one thing remained. "What do you know about the Spire?"

She shrugged. "It's a large structure, a wide bottom slowly thinning as it reaches the sky. The waves around it crash and roar to sink boats that approach. A storm of black clouds stands over it constantly but has grown more vigorous in recent years. Many have tried to climb it seeking the blade, but have been burned by the strikes of lightning, as my father mentioned. He wasn't lying, or exaggerating. None have survived."

Saul shifted in his boots. *Burned alive by lightning, like my dreams. My goddess said a storm was coming.* "I suppose we'll see. I won't fail." Saul said strongly, pounding his fist to his chest.

"Such confidence. The mighty Saul—oh, I am the strongest, most glorious fighter of all!" She pretended to unsheathe a blade and hold it above her head. Saul grumbled in response, and she shoved him playfully, making no ground. "As for failing, I should hope not. Lest I meet more suitors dirtier and older than I would care to." She chuckled and rolled her eyes. "Some of the damn families in the Plateau are horrid. The Krellars are demeaning, the Grolanis are forceful and dominating, and the Fireks are downright insane. Some families aren't so bad, but they all married off early, and no one wants to marry the man-stabbing prude of the King who eats Lordlings. Gods forbid a suitor can't take a joke or back-talk in general. Many came before, but they were all awful. I stabbed one just to make a point." She gnashed her teeth and laughed at her own play on words. "Needless to say that family supports my brothers—well, brother, now."

They stopped at the large gate to the main city. "I wouldn't call myself a high-born. I was, in truth, but an exile is seen as disgraceful. I have no title."

"Not like I care. One can learn proper manners and somewhat leadership, but you can't teach someone to garner respect. Stuff like that sticks to a person, like a disease. Parenting, am I right?" Saul took that as a compliment to his mother and father.

They opened the large gate, meeting a sizeable crowd. "It's him, with the princess! The Soldier of Storms!" one yelled.

The crowd was filled with Hydris, save for seven Broken at the front—his comrades, whom he traveled with. They seemed relieved to see him, eyes wide and mouths open. Korren's face was sullen; Saul placed his hand on his shoulder and nodded. They saluted each other in respect for his sister who died.

Mumbles and murmurs went over the crowd. "He saved the King. Do you seek the blade, my lord?" the man asked.

I am no Lord, Saul thought. "We move south on the morrow,"

"We will follow you!" many said, as others whispered and gasped. Some cursed and rolled their eyes.

Ignoring them all, Thalia leaned up toward his ear. "Come, let's go to my second home here. Helps me get away from the condescension of the keep. Your friends can stay in the inn nearby." She grabbed his arm, leading him through the crowd. Many touched his arms and back reverently.

"He's missing a hand," one said.

"How did he kill Ithaca?" another questioned.

Saul ignored them all as Thalia led him and the other Broken out of the crowd.

The city was vast. It reminded him of Chromata, the central city of the Vale. Most houses here were made of light-colored wood, pale grey stones carved into sharp ends, and gently curved roofs. The city was rather absent of people, and Saul assumed that many were either in the crowd or hiding in their homes. The walls of the city were high above them, each with massive carvings larger than the ones on the outside. He could barely make them out, but assumed they took centuries to craft. He wished to see the architecture, and wanted to investigate the city he would stay in. "Could we view the city first?" Saul asked.

Thalia scratched the nape of her neck. "That's a surprise. I think we've both had an exhausting day, but—sure, I'd love a stroll through town." She smiled. She motioned to the guards, who began to escort Saul's allies to their home, and to leave the two in private.

They strolled through long streets that seemed to go through circles, as if they were built to mimic the outer wall. Thalia told him stories of when she was young: where she learned to use her magic, where she went to learn as a child, and what she was forbidden from doing—of which there were many. There were many things to learn about her as a whole.

She took him to the outer walls, and they walked along them casually. Saul was fascinated by the engravings of various battles; Thalia spoke of the victory of Chaira Frauntis, who slayed three Dragons herself three thousand years prior in the wars between Feyamin and Kathynta, long before the Broken settled in the Vale. The wars crept back many times in history, though the last was fifty years gone. The Blazik Lords were as hotheaded as their people and not ones to budge. She told many stories of heroes of the past, and Thalia seemed enamored by them—reminiscent of him in that way.

They walked up a large set of stone steps on the city wall for almost an eternity, it seemed, to the top. Thalia sat on the edge of the wall, legs dangling over the side. "Say, we haven't actually talked about *your* history. It seems you know mine, now. Except about my Mother. She's been off in Feyamin on a diplomatic mission. She was supposed to come home some time ago, but it's been extended by the request of the Lords there. They prefer having a representative to deal with in person." After a pause, she said, "She was nearly killed by Ithaca after she rejected him. He was a bastard from before their marriage, and she denied his existence."

It was true—he hadn't talked about his past much. "I was raised knowing that the military was my life. I was strong, I was great, and I would bring my people to glory." The sun began to set near the horizon; the sky filled with slashes of oranges and reds, dancing across the blue.

Talia's eyes lingered on him. "Do your people have actual hobbies up there? Or do you train all day?"

"Each of us has one non-combat profession, at least."

"This is like pulling teeth," she said, sighing. "And yours would be—let me guess, knitting?" she snickered.

"Cooking."

"Oh my, I've bagged myself a winner. He fights *and* he cooks!"

Turning with a narrowed eye, Saul asked, "You have your own cooks, do you not?"

"Just because I have my own cooks doesn't mean I don't want my future husband to cook for me. I'm sure you're a lovely meal crafter. But you've run all day, and almost—well, fallen. You need a rest." She slapped his left hand loudly. "You can make me a meal when you bring that blade back." Holding her hand on his, she gave it a light rub. "Do you have any family?"

Saul winced, and Thalia leaned back. He simply shrugged and told her the truth. "Uncles, Aunts, Cousins. My mother died in the war ten years ago. She was a Warmaster, and a brave woman. She pushed forward in the battle to distract the armies, allowing the others to retreat. My father was a member of the Council of Fangs, but was burned for rejecting the Dragon's new laws. It was the reason I was exiled."

"I'm so sorry. I didn't mean—"

"It is all right. My mother died fighting for her people, and my father died for what he believed in. They died well," Saul sighed. *He told me to choose my own fate. Just like him.* "I could only hope to do the same."

"Dying can be honorable, but remember, there are always some you leave behind." She gave his hand a light squeeze. "There is honor in living to fight again. If I could die and save ten, or live and save a hundred, I'd save the hundred."

I think that's what they tried to teach me. My father, Warmaster Othellun, and Highwind. "That's why I'm here. The night I fled, the Dragon searched for me, calling me, 'the heathen.' With the help of another, I escaped, rather than fought. I hated myself for it then. Perhaps it was the right choice," Saul smiled subtly. "Perhaps it helped me maintain my honor."

Thalia jumped back. "Oh, a smile. I think I do see a soft side."

Saul growled and glared at her.

Thalia sighed. "I apologize. Sometimes I can't help it. It's another reason I've chased off so many so-called suitors. They see a disrespectful Hydris, not a funny one."

Saul didn't mind it. She didn't take herself too seriously, unless she had to. She was bold enough to make the jokes, which said enough. He did find them funny once in awhile, but he wouldn't dare admit that.

"What was your mother like?" she asked, staring at the sea.

"Bold. She was a hard Broken, tough and respected. She didn't let others walk on her, even in the face of death. She never gave up on her people."

"Like mother, like son," Thalia said. "You shouldn't give up, either, no matter what happened to your arm." She stared deeply into his eyes. "She wouldn't want you to."

Saul knew she was right. His father was strong and raised Saul to be the same. Even with a severed arm, his sword arm remained, possibly for the blade atop the Spire. He unhooked his plate slowly and rolled up his right sleeve, glancing at his marks of the Oracles. *What is my purpose?* he wondered. Saul heard the markings held little truth, and simply gave one a guideline to live his life, with no guarantee of truth. He saw a failure in Gorum, in Fae, and even his father. *Were their markings false?*

Are mine?

Thalia looked down at his arm. "I know your people have these markings, but I know little about them. What do they mean?" she asked, examining his right arm.

"There are the colors, the god, the subject, and the outcome," Saul said. Thalia raised a brow, making eye contact with him again. "These are red, implying the purpose of a slayer. The three crashing winds are Gadora's mark, the sharp-hooked wing resembles the Dragon, and the drop represents—" Saul's voice dropped off for a moment, revealing his emotion. "The drop represents death. To die for one's cause. But I have seen fates fail." Saul sat, thinking. "My Goddess came to me in a dream. We spoke of fate, it—left me believing as if a being makes their own fate."

"Then there's hope."

Saul smirked. "Hope." *What hope do I have, now? Only time will tell.* "The one on my other arm—well, I do not know. Blue is the protector, and the circle resembles all people. The god's mark, the six-pointed sun, I do not recognize."

Thalia shuffled closer. "It's kind of funny. Your sword arm is the slayer, and your shield arm is the protector." She chuckled. "If it's the one I'm thinking of, the six-pointed sun is the mark of Shiada, a goddess they worship in Renalia."

Shiada, the opponent of Lornak? The dastardly Dragon serves him. Does she aid my cause? "I do not know her."

"Not all gods care to be known." She carefully led her finger down his arm, along the markings. "You make your own fate." She took his chin and drew his eyes to hers. "Don't forget that."

Her eyes were the color of the northern seas, the slit of black dilated subtly. She leaned in, giving him a prolonged kiss on the cheek.

It felt like silk on his skin. His heart beat sped up to a charge, never reacting as such from a woman's touch before. She backed away and looked down with a grin, and he returned it. While he did not prefer softness, hers was welcome.

She slowly stood up and walked to the stairwell down to the city once more. He smiled but added a burning question that was a little out of place. "Why did you not mention being the princess?"

Thalia winked. "You never asked," she said with a sly smile, turning. "It's okay, I appreciated it. It's nice to be seen as a woman instead of a princess. Then again, you don't seem like the title-hungry sort of man." She gnashed her teeth. "Speaking of hungry, come on, it's nearly time for dinner. My cooks are on their way."

Saul followed her back down the wall and through a market where the merchants yelled for business and told of their special prices. Saul walked alongside her, and they drew glances and a few wandering eyes. Saul still couldn't believe he could be some fabled warrior, and hardly cared for it. If a blade would bring him the strength to free his people, he would acquire it if his goddess willed it.

They soon came to a large, slate grey stone home with wooden siding. It had a steep roof with wood curved into sharp points at the end, with large bush gardens and flowers all around it. Saul spotted lilies, roses, nightrain flowers, and dragoncallers.

Thalia motioned to the inn down the way. "Your allies will be staying there. Don't worry, I spoke to the guards and sent the message along." She led him into her house, which was modestly decorated, slightly messy with many books and weapons, along with armor sets strewn around the living room. "Are you ready to consummate the marriage?" she asked, sporting a side-smile and narrowed eyes.

"Excuse me?" Saul said, surprised.

Thalia burst out laughing. "It's a jest! Come now Saul, you have to *work* for it. You can't just ask me to marry you and suddenly hop into bed." She sighed, rolling her eyes dramatically. "I have a guest room upstairs. My chefs bring food here every day when I'm in town. They'll be here soon, and I bet you're starving. We have a big day tomorrow. I'm going with you, of course. There's no way you'll be getting to or climbing up the Spire without my help." Saul wondered how he could even climb it. "I'll be back. Sit tight, oh-stormy-one. You can change if you want, and there is a bathing room right through there." She pointed beside the stairwell to a small door. "There won't be any fighting tonight."

Saul sat in a broad, dark wooden chair with no cushions. It was hard, but Saul preferred it that way. He stared at his right forearm, severed down the middle. It still burned like a flame, feeling as though his hand still lived, and it was itchy as the hells.

He sighed and slowly removed his plate armor. He unhooked the pieces one by one, the weight dropping off his shoulders like the stress of the journey. He rummaged through his bag, finding a pair of fitted, dark brown cloth pants and shirt. Before changing, he looked to the stairwell, thinking he should bathe to remove the smell of stale sweat for his potential bride. A ridiculous thought, at least would have been ages ago. But alas, he entered the bathing room, finding a small granite bath that seemed carved by a master.

He bathed quickly and changed as fast as he could as to not make his princess wait. He threw on his spare outfit and waited in her largest chair that still only somewhat fit him.

Saul lost all hope of a breath the moment she appeared. Thalia delicately descended her staircase wearing a fitted silk robe the same azure color of her eyes. Her hunter green hair spilled down past her left shoulder like a coursing river over her chest. She perked her nose up subtly. "Oh my, he wears something other than armor. I'm honestly a little surprised—and you bathed, I must say I'm flattered." She grinned but lost it as her eyes drew toward his malformed limb. "How is your arm feeling?"

"It burns and itches as if the hand still remained there," Saul grumbled. He didn't understand why it itched. The hand was gone, and yet it still had feeling. It screamed in pain, despite the wound closed with a burn. He was lucky it didn't fester.

"I've heard that happens. Just because you're missing part of your arm doesn't mean you can't fight. We can strap a shield on."

"That is simple to say. You still have both arms. Your people don't see a one-armed warrior as half of one."

"Jests aside, you can't let it drag you down," Thalia said, biting her lip. "People respect bravery and leadership, not just combat prowess." A long pause followed. Thalia looked toward the door. "The cooks should be here soon. I'm going to get some reading done. Your comrades can come, too, *if* they don't wreck the place." She plopped down on the couch beside him, and began reading a large leather-bound book. "Would you like me to teach you?" she asked.

Saul winced. "I'm not so sure that's necessary."

Her eyes grew sullen, a strange sight to behold, considering how Thalia reacted since their first meeting. "Stop that. Learning to read is important. Some cultures find a lack of literation a disrespect." She patted the cushion next to her and signaled for him to come sit closer. After a peculiar pause in the air, she spoke quietly. "Would you read with me?"

While he was not proficient with it, he saw no reason to reject her. If reading was something his wife-to-be enjoyed and wished him to participate in, he was wrong; it was necessary. He would do it without question, as a stronger bond meant for greater things within their lives. Thus, he got up from the chair, and sat beside her. He felt her posture relax, and she let out a strange relaxed breath the instant he sat down.

To his surprise, it was a book about the history of Broken. "I did not know you had books like these."

"I thought it'd be nice to teach you using things you knew."

"Is that the only reason you decided to read this book?"

"Yes and no. I want to teach you, and I think it's important to learn about one's spouse's culture," Thalia replied casually.

Saul respected and appreciated her effort. She led her finger along the lines, reading as she went. Saul did recognize some of the words, but also missed many. She stopped and explained them, the structure and the lettering, and asked him questions about some of the story details that the book didn't explain.

By the end, he did learn quite a few new written words. Part of him disliked it, but she was going out of her way to teach him.

She asked if he would teach her a few things with a blade, too, as she did want to better herself. She was small, but Saul had seen a small Broken kill a ten-foot tall beast once. It all came down to skill of the weapon, just as reading came down to skill of the mind.

After a time she closed her book, and grew silent. Saul probed her with a few questions about her mother, since he hadn't met her. She had been gone some time to Feyamin on a diplomatic mission. But she made no jests, which was a surprise.

He gazed over to her, seeing her eyes divert away from the page, to the door, the stairs, and other random locations. "Is something the matter?"

"No, nothing's wrong."

"You don't seem to be laughing as you always are," Saul said.

With a deep sigh, she said, "I don't laugh all the time."

Saul shifted in his seat. She laughed much since she arrived, despite the occurrences. Her brother Ithaca, despite being insane and a traitorous murderer, died. Saul struggled to believe that she would actually feel for a death of such a disgrace. Her father also pushed her into marriage, although she agreed. *Had she given up? Or is it me?* "You worry about what being wed to me could mean," Saul surmised.

"No. I worry about my mother because she's away, but that's normal. I'm worried about my father since my bastard brother tried to kill him—and you—and I arrived too late. I'm worried about having to marry you. You clearly respect for me, even though I can feel the reluctance you were born with. Frankly, I'm surprised you took my father's ridiculous offer because deep down, you hate our race. You all do."

Saul leaned back, not expecting that sort of response from her. He struggled with his beliefs for the past season. He traveled out of the Vale, and he was forced to challenge fate itself. In Rhoba, he challenged his beliefs on his people and purpose. In Shi'doba, he challenged his beliefs on the Hydris. He doubted himself throughout, but he didn't doubt himself any longer. It irked him still, wondering if he could trust the other Hydris, but he finally felt like he could trust her. "I don't know about the Hydris as a whole. I don't know if I trust them. It has been ingrained into my being ever since I was young." He placed his hand on hers. "But I trust you."

She turned to him with a strength in her eyes. "I know." She nodded and perked her sharp gold-pierced ears. "If you didn't trust me, you might have ended up like the others. It's just—" After a brief, teary pause, she said, "It's hard for me to believe that of all people, a Broken, one of the people that hate us, one of the people that dislike books as a whole, is the first one to sit with me to read," she gave Saul a subtle smile, and said, "When I was left alone with whichever suitor it was, they would call me stupid for wishing to spend time with them doing something like this."

Her reaction was peculiar. Certainly, reading may be strange to him, but if it aided the bond between those to unify, it was a priority. "You asked me to read with you. I see no reason not to participate in activities you enjoy."

She gave a light chuckle. "It sounds so simple when you say it that way."

Saul just stared plainly and gave a subtle shrug. "Strong bonds are simple. My mother and father participated in the enjoyment of the other. She was a war-singer, and he helped her practice as well as watched every one of her performances. She always helped him form his speeches for his work as well as plays he performed in. The happiness of the other brings happiness to yourself in a strong unification."

Voices came from outside, and the scents of food tricked in.

She looked deep into his eyes and placed a light hand on his thigh. "Are you saying we have a strong bond?"

Saul didn't smile, nor flinch in any way. "We have a bond," he said plainly. "And bonds are strengthened when treated honor and respect, and live with a sense of equity."

A warm, relaxed smile grew at the corners of Thalia's lips. She simply nodded, as no words were needed. A knock came to the door, to which she rose and went to it. Before she opened it, she looked back toward him with the same smile—a smile of mutual understanding.

The chefs brought a meal fit for a lord—fresh, succulent stag meat braised with duck fat, various roasted ground vegetables, and more. Sweet fruits from the jungles of the northern plateau, spiced tea, and wine were served, as well. Saul ate rough game, fruits, and nuts for months, with a meal in an inn once in a rare while, so this feast was a treat. The seven comrades from the inn came to get some, as well. They gave the Hydris a watchful eye but voiced no complaints. The horror in Rhoba changed their belief of a 'people' as it did for Saul. Especially when they were taken in by the city of Serpentarius, there was something less than evil about the Hydris. *Perhaps it was a lie of the Dragon*, Saul suspected.

Saul caught a look from Drof here and there, seeing a hint of concern in his bright yellow eyes. Saul sat and ate quietly, thinking of the danger to come. Thalia sat beside him the same way, not speaking a word, but her presence came with a sense of comfort which was needed. For in the days that approached, his life was in the hands of the gods.

Chapter Forty-two

Burning Hate and Scorching Light

Kayden Ralta

Kayden's screams and wails echoed throughout the core of the town. She dropped to her knees, hands shaking, holding the black skull that lay where Vesper stood. She heard only dead silence and nothing more. Vesper's murmuring was gone, and the smell—*the smell*—of burnt flesh and ash was all that was left.

Her shrill screech brought forth onlookers from the town, watching Kayden's pain flare up like the buildings still aflame from the beast's breath. She hated everything, and everyone. Anyone she cared for died. No matter who she met, it was only a matter of time.

Lira, Mags, Domika, all of them—they'd die because of her.

Vesper was like a father to her. They only knew each other a short time, but his kind gestures and strange personality were comforting. She felt he was family, someone she could talk to and relate to, and someone who understood her. He always said she reminded him of his daughter, too. Kayden wondered what Nala was like, having never met.

Vesper was with them now, but Kayden cursed him for his sacrifice. *There had to be another way. There had to be.*

"Kayden, I—" Lira's voice came from behind her.

"Get the *hell* away from me." Kayden snarled, sniffling.

She didn't need them. She didn't want advice, or help. She bawled and bawled, not caring what they thought. She came to Loughran to do something good, to change what she was, and yet all she did was kill another. She was *bara marai*, just like Sheeran always said. She was a born killer.

"How could you let this happen? How could you?" Kayden yelled. She shot up and turned to Lira. "You and your divine—*powers*." She shoved her, again and again. "This is what I was talking about! This is what happens when you don't have any god damn self-confidence!" She shoved Lira and slapped her bloody side wound.

Lira began to tear up, clutching her side. "Kayden, I didn't mean—I didn't want—"

"Oh, of course you didn't! Can't you seal things like that right away? Send it back to whence it came without his help? We could have saved him!" Her gaze turned to the blond-haired idiot that stood there dumbfounded. "And *you*," she walked over to him. "Just who the hell are you? Someone who sits back 'til the last second? A lot of help you gave!" She pushed the drake and he stumbled back, stunned. His buggy blue eyes gave away his idiocy.

"I swear to the damn gods, I'm gone from this insane rebellion as soon as I get the chance. This is a waste of my time, and people just end up dying everywhere I go! Maybe Domika is right—maybe I don't belong here. I'm just a runt with no real purpose. I've had it with all of this. I hate all of you. *Every single one of you*!" She walked back to Lira. "Now do you see the consequences of not trying? Of having no confidence? You'd better watch yourself, or you'll get yourself killed—or others might sacrifice themselves because of your shortcomings!"

Lira started to cry into her hands, but Kayden couldn't have cared less. The others stood there like muddled cows.

Kayden took a flask out from her sack, carefully squatted, and scraped what ashes she could into it. *I'm sorry, Ves. I'm so sorry…*

She carefully picked up the skull and the few bones there were and carried them off. Kayden walked past the group, bumped into Lira, and caused her to fall. She could hear townspeople running to the lake to gather water to put out the flames. The moonlight lit her way back as the flames dissipated.

No one followed her, and she wanted it that way. She looked at the charred bones cradled in her arms, unable to stop the flow of tears. Vesper told her his family was buried at the crossroads, and thought she might bring them there, to have him rest with them. He made her feel like he was important, like she mattered. All of it was gone.

All she had left was his advice and his bones.

She arrived at Lira's home. She picked the lock with ease, slipped inside, and gently placed the bones in a thin leather bag she had. She locked the bedroom door, changed out of her armor, and curled into a ball on Lira's bed, clutching her scarves. She wanted to leave, she really did, but she was frozen, paralyzed by anger and fear. She felt her mind receding to what it once was, one enveloped by anger—*the Shadow of Death*. Her life in the north—something she promised to discard once she left for the western forests.

'There's no proof that you're the Shadow of Death,' Richard said to her. 'But I want you to go west and do good there.'

He was wrong. I'm not good. I can't handle this life. I bring death wherever I go. In Deurbin, in Solmarsh, in Orinas…it never ends. I'm better off being the agent of it, rather than trying to prevent it. She thought over and over how the battle could have gone differently, but she had been unconscious for most of it. She remembered Lira, Domika, and that other blonde idiot sitting around while Vesper protected them from the grotesque beast.

She hoped no one would come in, that everyone would stay away from her forever. Maybe she would be the Shadow of Death once more. She cried and cried, hating everyone and everything for what happened. Another person she cared about, dead before her eyes. She eventually cried herself to sleep, passing into a dream.

* * *

She awoke in a small, hard bed, in a room all-too familiar. The blue moonlight shone through the tiny window and illuminated the surroundings. She saw the old, rotted wood walls, a small wooden cabinet with her clothes, and the drawings in charcoal. There were three drawings: one of flower beds in front of a house, another with three people: one man, one woman, and one little girl with large, happy smiles, and the last was the warrior she always drew, standing and raising her blade in front of her allies in command. It was her room, ten years past.

No, not again.

A soft knock came to the door. Looking down, she realized she was the smaller, skinnier, eight-year old version of herself. Her mom and dad entered the room, with tears in their eyes. They were just like she remembered: her mom with pale skin and blonde hair, and her father was human with dark olive skin, dark, chestnut brown hair, and a thick beard that she pulled as a baby.

"Azra, honey, we have to talk to you," her mom said. "We love you very much. We do. I'm sorry, but we must go. We'll be back, we will." Azra. The name she told no one. Not since then.

Her father looked to his wife with sullen eyes. "We may not be. I'm so sorry. We have to tell you that we do this because we love you." He looked down, kissing Kayden on the forehead. "It's for your safety. We'll always love you."

He got up as Kayden's mom kissed her and caressed her cheek. "You'll be safe. Don't answer the door, honey. Please, trust us." Her mom broke into tears as they carefully closed her door.

Kayden uncontrollably broke into tears. "Don't go—don't—please—" Kayden muttered, sniffling, and gasping for air. She put her face into her hands. "Don't leave me." She couldn't bear to open her eyes again. She waited what felt like an eternity, wishing the pain would stop. Wishing they would come back. She feared looking up from her hands, but she had to see if it was over. Hoping they came back to her, her eyes stung from closing them so hard.

The dream changed when she looked up. She could smell it. She stood upon the dirty, sandy road in the desert town of Kwora. Her feet were bare and covered in sand, cold from the desert night. She went to town to search for them. It was a week later, she remembered. The warm light flew upon her. The flickering reds, oranges, and yellows caused her tears to shine brightly in the glow. The smell filled her nostrils, and it wouldn't go away—the smell of burning flesh. The old inn was lit aflame. All of the residents escaped safely. Each tenant and bystander looked in horror to the rafters of the porch overhang. "Who are they?" one voice asked.

"I have no idea. I've never seen them before."

Her parents' bodies each hung from a noose, tied to the inn rafters, an image she never forgot. There were more, so many additional bodies since her nightmares began. Tonight, there was a new one, an old, thin man wearing a violet robe lit aflame. Even without the flesh, she knew it was him. She closed her eyes so tightly they hurt. She felt her chest burn from smoke before she blinked them open again.

***

Kayden awoke from her dream with a fierce gasp. She could barely catch her breath. The birds were chirping outside. By the angle of the light, it was just after sunrise. Her door was still closed, bed undisturbed. Kayden supposed they let her be. She needed time to think, in a place that was quiet from others.

Out the window, the waters were gentle. The sun sat on the horizon warming the town, and the cool breeze sifted through. She felt the need to sit by the water. She waited until her breath slowed before going outside. When she felt calm enough, Kayden tiptoed across the room, and carefully cracked the door open.

Mags was asleep on his bedroll. Domika was not present, probably in the other room. Lira was in the chair where Vesper slept previously, close to Kayden's door. Surprisingly, her wound was wrapped and healed. Perhaps she found another healer or did it herself. She was curled into a ball on the chair wearing a new, long white linen robe. Kayden wasn't ready to talk to anyone just yet; she was still furious. With feathered footsteps, she crept out of the house.

The streets were busy; a few townsfolk ran by her, with slats of wood, some dragging trolleys with large bricks, others with buckets for mortar. A haze still hung over the center of town from the fire the night before. Where the markings were, townsfolk chipped away at the multitude of broken stones, reformed walls, and worked together to rebuild the damaged homes. The markings disappeared with Valikar. Their voices were tremulous, but they spoke of rumors of the night before. Most wouldn't have seen the battle, if any.

"I heard a group of travellers killed it," one man said.

"No way, I heard a god stepped in and destroyed it himself!"

"I heard an all-powerful Wizard slayed the beast!"

With the damaged buildings and the burned bodies of men and women it was hard not to talk about, Kayden supposed. *A powerful wizard, hiding behind a guise of self-consciousness,* she thought. Vesper said everyone had a ceiling of power in magic, but rarely mentioned his own. He had to know what he was capable of. The red orb, the spell so destructive it melted and banished Valikar to whence it came. She worried about the vile beast's final words. If Valikar's threat was real, in time it would bring its fury back when *the vile star falls...*

Kayden came to the water a bit north of the pier, looking east. The wind blew softly through her thick, mousey hair. Seagulls and prinobirds flew over the water with their black and plum feathered wings, cawing happily. Sometimes Kayden wished she were a bird, free to fly wherever she wanted. She could go to the Aggaroth Mountains, to Krot'ahk's valley, the Risen Isles—anywhere. She felt the need to flee to the Isles. It was neutral territory, and she had never been before. Jirah told her that refugees fled there, yet it was difficult to get a boat, as security was tight. Kayden could hide. She knew how to go anywhere undetected, if she wanted to.

That's why I'm the Shadow of Death. It was a horrid name, a title she no longer wanted to hear. The public named her that, whether they knew who it was or not. There were suspicions once she was arrested, but there was no evidence to convict her.

She took the flask of ashes out from her bag and stood it up in the sand in front of her. *Maybe I can save you now,* Vesper had said. His power was so vast. Before the battle, Vesper's strength was minimal, conjuring only small fires and spells. Intense emotion and confidence in oneself revealed a Wizard's true power, and his had shown through the night previous. She was angry, so *angry* that he sat in a pile of charred bones and ashes. Worst of all, he died protecting her. If she hadn't gotten knocked unconscious, he may have been alive. Vesper died to protect her, and Kayden couldn't forget it. Wouldn't.

He lies above the tavern now. I did this to him.

She felt caught up in something much more than a miniscule rebellion. *What was that beast?* Kayden wondered. It claimed to be a harbinger of a god, coming to sweep the land into chaos. *Who would they tell? That drake, Fillion, a sickly old man sitting on the throne in Loughran, orchestrated it.* He hired the disgusting torturer to send people to Solmarsh, to feed the demon. *But why?* Kayden's mind was muddled at the thought. A time of gods was long past, and Lornak was supposed to be dead. She wondered what kind of web she was caught in. *Is there even a way out?* She wondered if she could run now, after all that happened. Kayden wasn't needed here. *They wouldn't have someone insulting them all day anymore. All I do is yell at them.*

Kayden sat and pondered her purpose in the rebellion for what seemed like hours. Wondering what use she had, and whether a runt really belonged with such a group. She brought death wherever she went, and the last thing they needed was a *bara marai*. A born killer.

A loud *plop* sounded from beside her. Mags found her at the waters. Probably came to comfort her. She didn't need comfort. "What do you want?" she grumbled. "I don't want to talk about it."

Mags didn't look at her. He instead looked to the waters as she did and crossed his legs. "Have you ever heard the name Gallan Foldrin?" he asked.

She had, actually. A name from over a hundred years past, yet it hadn't been forgotten there. It was a disgraced name, never forgotten by the icestone cities. "The man who loved a Devil," she replied weakly.

"He was my father," Mags said. He sighed quickly, and he *never* sighed. His plate gauntlets trembled and his eyes gave a slight wince. "My mother was different from other Devils. She may have been a devil, but she really loved him. She refused to kill him, as was their way. They kept their love a secret and got her with child—me."

Mags looked to the sky with a wince, fidgeting with his nails. "Years later, they were found out, and my father was imprisoned and tried for blasphemy. He denounced the existence of a child, denounced the existence of his love for my mother," Mags looked to the ground. After an extended moment, he said, "They found him guilty and executed him. My own father denounced my very existence. I was angry. Uncontrollably angry. I gave in to what the people thought of my race."

Kayden shuffled her feet and brought her knees in closer. "I heard the powers of darkness killed the ones who tried him, calling it the 'Grim One.'"

"The Grim One." Mags repeated her words in his hoarse tone. "They did. I did. My father denounced me, but I hated them for taking him away. I killed every individual who denounced my father at the trial." A long, somber pause followed. "I was twelve."

Kayden didn't say a word, only listened. His tone was filled with pain, something she had not heard in his voice before.

"I hated them. I became what they wanted me to be."

I want to be more than I'm told, Mags told Jirah once.

Does he seek redemption? Kayden wondered. She did. That's why she came to the west.

"My name is Talon Foldrin," he said after a long sigh. "I hate my name because it resembles the people I belong to, and the one who denounced me to the world." He paused for a drawn silence. "I hate what I am."

The wind passed over them from the water, and the sound of waves was relaxing. Mags's neck muscles were tight, and his brow furrowed. It was clear he hadn't told anyone that before. *Why now, why me?* Kayden wondered.

"We all make mistakes. It is up to us to redeem ourselves. Sir Vesper left us on his own will. He cared for you and wished to make up for a mistake he made by saving our lives. He was correct. There was no alternative."

No other way. Her heart broke at the thought. "What was that spell?" Kayden blurted out. She hadn't heard of it or seen it before.

"As the command implies, it is a spell of total annihilation. Only a few gifted individuals know the spell, and it's only taught to those of sound mind and of great power. The last man who was known to learn it was Sandro Chora, the head magister in Orinas. He's been dead for several years."

She already knew his history. The moment they shared.

"He was afraid of his power. In his final moments, he chose to use it to protect, the very reason why it was taught to him. Your connection with him drove him to believe in himself."

Kayden let the information process slowly. She waited a time to speak again, thinking about Mags' past. She wondered what else he had been through. He blamed himself for what he was. *Just like how I blame myself.* "You shouldn't hate what you are."

"I am half a minion of Hell, and half a man who denounces his own son."

Kayden bit her lip and looked over to him for a moment and watched his somber gaze scan the horizon. She felt something different about his father, and thought of an answer other than a betrayal. *Why would he denounce his son if he loved the mother?* A Half-Devil may have been executed under such blasphemy. "You're half a man of love and order, and half a man who protects his son."

Mags turned his head toward her. "What do you mean?"

Kayden just shrugged. "The worst of Hell is the evil, the best is the striving for order—and you said it yourself, your mother loved rather than strived for lust. Your father may not have hated you. Maybe he protected you from them by lying." Kayden placed her hand on his. "The best of both worlds."

With a lengthy sigh, he said, "Maybe so."

Another long silence followed. She hoped she could help him. Kayden hated what she caused but couldn't hate what she was. But she hated what she became the night prior.

She yelled at her best friend with words meant for herself. She was helpless, unable to do anything to save Vesper. She picked up the ashes in her hand and examined the flask. She blamed everyone else for not doing anything, but they were as helpless as she was. Lira may have divine power, but everyone had a ceiling of strength.

"When you left, she cried until she fell asleep," Mags added. "Krogar, the individual you clearly disliked, came to her home and healed up her wound." He was simply giving her the facts, as if he knew not to say he told her so.

Kayden rubbed her shins nervously. She touched her scarves, thinking of her parents. They would stay with her when she was sad, and Lira reminded her of that. Kayden finally remembered her harsh words. She blamed Lira for her own shortcomings.

Lira's mind was already filled with self-conscious thoughts. She wasn't forced into adulthood as Kayden had been, yet she knew social convention better than Kayden did. "I didn't mean to yell at her."

"But you did," Mags said bluntly. He didn't fluff his words. Kayden respected it, barely. She didn't like being told what she already knew. "Even after she, not us, forced Asheron to escape. After watched her friends and brother die."

A pain swelled within the pit of her stomach. Self-disgust. Lira experienced something Kayden knew all too well—and she yelled at her selfishly, putting her feelings in front of others. "I don't belong here, Mags. It's like Dom says—I'm a runt. All I do is cause problems and yell at everyone."

Mags raised an eyebrow. "You shouldn't be self-defeating," he said. "I don't want you to go."

She lightly gripped his hand. His red eyes widened. "I know, but sometimes people just don't belong."

Quick footsteps ran up behind them. Kayden quickly released her hand and brought them both back to her shins.

Domika panted and bent over, one arm in a sling.

"Where have you guys been? Lira ran off! Some monk crawled into the town all bloody, she healed him like it was *nothing*, and ran south! Zaedor chased after her, but she was too fast! Something about a crimson knight!"

Kayden shot to her feet. Mags did the same. "Shit, that's gotta be Malakai. He must be at the monastery!" She reasoned that Zaedor must have been the other random individual they met last night.

"What monastery? Where?" Domika questioned.

"South. Orinde. Her dad's a *monk* there, idiot!" Kayden bolted to the southern city gate, running at full speed. "C'mon!" Magnus fell behind wearing his rusty full plate. She passed bloodied bodies of robed men with the mark of Orinde sewed into the breast. Kayden paid them no mind. Her breath escaped, but she pressed on. She passed knights—one, two, three—with arrows in the neck, through the eye, in the heart. Many more had armor blackened by burns and faces melted by flame—or so it seemed.

Was this her doing? Kayden wondered. She ran, and ran, and ran... Until she finally saw the monastery. Kayden saw that blond knight, clunking away in his armor, running slowly. She passed him with ease, breathing heavily and wheezing. Domika and Mags were a hundred feet behind. She saw Lira in the distance, bow-in-hand. She ran like the wind through the large, wooden monastery door.

Kayden could barely see a knight clad in spiked crimson plate, nearly identical to the dark-armored Asheron they met in combat over a month previous. He was versed in blood magic, which made him especially deadly and sadistic. He held a long blade encrusted with dark rubies in black settings to the neck of a man with dark skin.

The door closed just in time for Kayden to be shut out. She shook and pounded it, to no avail. It was unlocked, but the door wouldn't budge; it was either pressed closed, or magically forced. Her heart was threatening to bust out of her chest, it felt.

"Give my father back!" she heard Lira scream.

"Oh, my dear girl, I'm afraid that's not possible. These fools have helped the Scions of Fire, so they deserve nothing less than a painful death. You have intervened in our plans, and you have something I need, as well. Where is the rest of your little group?" a gravelly voice replied.

Kayden frantically looked at her surroundings. The broad temple was made of limestone, fifty feet high with tall inch-deep steps above the door leading to the roof. Stone pillars ran all along the outside. Kayden saw many skylights before the door closed, hoping they could be of use for entry. The windows were no more than a few inches wide; Kayden couldn't fit through those.

"Please, I don't know. Please just let him go!" Lira yelled.

Mags and the others arrived on the scene. Kayden jumped for the first stair above the large door, but she was two feet too short. The stone was smooth, and there was nothing to grab onto.

"Mags, throw me up!" she yelled.

"Pardon?" he said, shocked.

"I said throw me the hell up there!" Kayden commanded, pointing to the thin stairs.

He grabbed her by the waist and hoisted her up. She threw herself up with her arms, climbing nimbly from stair to stair. It reminded her of her escapes in Orinas, but that was a different time, a different woman. She found a skylight on the roof. It was a small window less than a foot wide—they all were. She peered in and saw Malakai looming over Lira's father, who was bloodied and breathing heavily. Lira was not, surprisingly. She wasn't hurt, or even out of breath. Lira's eyes were wide and teeth bared; every muscle in her body tightened. Kayden could only see anger in her eyes.

"Give him back, now!" she yelled.

"No," Malakai said. He sounded eerily similar to his brother. "I think I might kill him. I don't need him. I just need something from you, something you stole last night—and one of your little friends."

Something she stole? Kayden thought. Lira hadn't stolen a thing. *Though there was the strange impact that hit Lira after she shackled the demon, where the souls and orb shot toward her...*

Mags and the blond soldier called from beyond the door.

"Go ahead, girl. Let them in," Malakai chuckled.

"Go to hell," Lira growled.

Why is he asking her? Kayden thought. *Is she closing them in? Lira, what are you doing?*

Four knights surrounded Lira as her bow was readied.

The bodies of monks surrounded them. Their green robes were covered with slashes of crimson, and punctures filled with pools of their lifeblood. The limestone floor was stained crimson. Blood dripped from Malakai's sword, echoing through the temple.

"Maybe I'll kill you, too. You've killed some of my knights, caught my brother off guard—I think I'll drain your life. Then you will beg for death as you watch your father die." Malakai outstretched his hand toward her. A vile, red mist led from his fingertips to her chest. Lira groaned in agony and dropped her bow.

"No, Lira!" Kayden screamed. "You can't die, you can't! You have to fight! Let them in, do something! Anything!" She slammed her hand onto the rough stone temple roof until her hand couldn't feel the pain anymore. She regretted not bringing her daggers.

"Let—my father—go!" Lira growled.

"What are you going to do?" Malakai gave a mocking laugh. His hand pulsed with energy, causing Lira to groan in agony. "Since you temporarily disabled my brother, this task falls to me. I do enjoy my work, and no pathetic maid will stop me." Malakai raised his blade for the final strike. "Any last words for him?"

Lira fell on her hands and knees and muttered quiet words under her breath, and Kayden barely made them out. *Mortanai Shala*, Lira whispered between cries—Kayden had no clue of what it meant. *Mortanai Shala, Mortanai Shala, Mortanai Shala...*

Malakai stepped toward Lira with his blood-covered blade. "What's that, girl?" With a laugh, he said, "I can't hear you."

Lira's voice raised to a hiss through her teeth. "Mortanai," she said. She rose her head to stare at the vile knight with eyes brighter than the sun. "*Shala.*" Lira screeched louder than Kayden ever heard; it was eerie and unnatural, shrill and deafening. Her whole body shone with blinding light. An immense shockwave flew out and blew Kayden back from the skylight, causing her to tumble off the roof.

Screams of desperation and absolute agony echoed from the monastery—and they weren't Lira's.

Kayden caught herself on the last set of thin stairs, but then fell to the ground on her back, causing her to grunt in pain. The doors blew open. Mags, Domika, and the blond knight were all thrown back twenty feet to the ground. Kayden sat up, shook her head, and looked to see Lira still on her hands and knees, breathing heavily. Blood dripped from her nose to the stone floor, joining the stains already present.

The four knights that surrounded her were on the ground, charred as if aflame for hours. Malakai staggered back screaming in pain. His crimson armor was half-melted. He ripped his helmet off and spoke an incantation to draw the life from the dead around him—but the wound refused to heal. He cursed under his breath.

Lira's father lay there, too, injured and burned, but not as badly as the others. His breaths were weak—but he was alive.

"Wh—what the hell are you, witch?" Malakai roared. "You will pay for this, girl! With more lives than you know!" He ripped a black crystal from a small bag at his side, crushed it, and vanished. All he left behind was a sinister cackle.

"Father!" Lira yelled, running to his side.

Kayden heard him weakly mutter a few words to her, and she responded, but Kayden couldn't hear details. *What the hell was that? Is this Lira's power?* It seemed as such. Seeing the result of Lira's spell, she recalled what those words meant—Mortanai Shala—*the light that sears flesh.* Perhaps weak healing was not Lira's ceiling.

Perhaps there was more.

Much more.

Lira let out soft cries as her father closed his eyes. Kayden approached with caution. She passed the charred bodies of the knights and the sliced corpses of the monks, smelling burned blood. She placed her hand gently on Lira's shoulder, and Lira didn't move.

She held her father tightly, slowly attempting to calm herself. "I'm sorry, Kayden, I'm so sorry—"

"No, Lira. *I'm* sorry. I shouldn't have blamed you for what happened. After what happened with your brother, I shouldn't have acted like that. You didn't deserve it. I was—I was yelling at myself." Kayden spotted breathing from Lira's father. "I'm sorry for what I said." Apologizing took a lot. She looked around at the surrounding bodies. Blackened.

"I guess—I'm more powerful than I thought," Lira whispered. She released her father and turned. "I burned my own father. I didn't mean—I didn't mean to. I don't understand."

"We know you didn't," Kayden said. She released her grip and looked into Lira's sullen eyes.

A drop of blood crept from Lira's nose down her chin.

The cost of magic. Vesper barely finished his spell before his mind sundered from the raw pressure of magical energies.

"Look at me. You saved his life. If it weren't for whatever that was, he would be gone, and you may have been, too. I would take a burn over death." Kayden paused, and let the information sink in. "Is he okay?" Kayden asked cautiously.

Lira nodded. "He's okay. It'll take time, but he will heal, I think. He needs to go to Solmarsh for help. He can't stay here." Lira originally wanted to come to the monastery to visit her mother's grave, and Kayden needed to remind her.

"Mags and the others will carry him back, okay? Why don't we go and see your mom? I'll go with you." Kayden smiled sweetly, trying her best to stay strong, and to be nice. Lira almost lost her whole family in a day—Kayden knew how that felt.

"I'd like that." Lira tried to smile. They got up as the others approached. They carefully took up her father, nodded, and began their trek back to Solmarsh. Lira led Kayden to a small cemetery surrounded by a three-foot high ornate stone wall. A bright green, grassy plot was filled with headstones of various shades of black, grey, and white, each with its own inscription and name of a departed loved one. There were many with fresh as well as dead bouquets of flowers. "Kayden, I'm worried. What was that thing, Valikar? What happened? What can we do?"

"I know you're worried. I don't know what it was. We stopped whatever it was, at a great cost." She bit her lip at the thought of Vesper passing once more. It was still so fresh in her mind, and a cost she felt she brought to the group.

"Maybe I can do more, now. I don't know how I did it, but maybe I'm stronger than I thought. I still can't believe what I did. I don't remember it at all."

Kayden smiled. *I'm glad, princess. I'm glad you feel stronger. I just wish I could be,* she thought. "I'm sure in time you'll figure it out."

"That Demon, whatever it was, I worried about it. I'm scared, Kayden. What if something like that comes back, what if there are more of them, what if—"

"Don't worry, Lira. We need to take this one step at a time. We aren't gods, right? We need to find a way to stop these things from returning, and the ones who sent it."

Kayden pondered her own words. She wanted to encourage Lira, but still felt it was herself that endangered them all. *His death is still my fault. I bring it wherever I go. Lira brings happiness and kindness, Magnus brings protection, and what do I bring?*

Insults and death.

Lira had confidence. She didn't need Kayden anymore. They were safer without her.

"I'm sorry. I'm so sorry, I know I could have done more. I just didn't know. I felt useless. I could have come quicker or found out more faster. I could have saved him. This is all my fault."

I think we all felt useless. "Look, Lira, you put a hold on your own power. Sure, the gods or whatever set their limit, but you never know your potential until you try."

"I didn't think you believed in the power of gods."

Kayden sighed. "I don't. Let me try to help, at least. My beliefs don't matter right now."

"Thanks. I'm going to try." Lira carefully strolled around the plots, while Kayden paid no attention, not realizing where she stepped. "Kayden, you shouldn't walk on graves."

"Sorry," Kayden said quietly. They stopped before a pearly-white gravestone, *Aya Kaar*—Lira's mother.

Aya's read, *Lived true end, kind to all, optimistic in darkest times.*

Lira told Kayden about her brother. It reminded Kayden of her parents, who said they did the same, in the recurring dream she couldn't leave behind. They said they were protecting her when they left, and Lira's brother went to the military to protect her— only to be arrested to protect her again. Kayden knew Lira felt entirely at fault, and she was, but couldn't blame herself forever.

Lira's mother grew sick, passing away peacefully in her sleep. She always said she took after her mother, always finding a bright side and kindness in everyone. She only regretted not being there when she passed. Temples were restrictive.

It was foolish to think everyone had good in them. Kayden trusted certain people, and no one else. Lira trusted too many.

"So much changed," Lira said. "I killed these people. I prayed and prayed, but in the end all I could think was that I had to stop them, and part of me knew that I could." Her voice dropped to a whisper that met the gentle breeze. "I had to stop them no matter what."

"And you did." Kayden crouched beside her. "Don't think for a moment that you didn't do the right thing. I'm proud of you."

Lira's voice trembled as she knelt before her mother's grave. "Thanks. It's hard."

"It always is. You'll learn to live with it." Kayden sighed. "I'll leave you be." Kayden backed off.

"I'd like it if you stayed," Lira said. "I won't be long."

Kayden nodded. Lira interlocked her fingers and prayed. A light breeze blew through Kayden's hair; it smelled of newly bloomed damp lilies from the monastery garden. Lira's onyx hair blew with the wind as she whispered words of devotion to her goddess. Kayden stood behind her, not pushing to hurry. After the past days, they all needed a rest.

She watched the quiet, meek Lira pray to her goddess. The same woman who seared the flesh of six men—including her own father—just a few moments prior. One's potential showed in times of intense emotion. Kayden hoped Lira realized how powerful she could be, as it seemed a time of rebels and knights would soon turn to gods and kings.

"We have to stop them, Kayden," Lira whispered. She turned her head with sharp, glistening eyes. "I won't give up until we do."

Chapter Forty-three

Darkness Comes

Jirah Mirado

"I don't know why you are all staying here," Jirah growled. He paced back and forth at the entrance of Wolf Camp. The damn fools stayed, even after they knew. He hated it, but he chose them for that fact; they were loyal to the end. The crickets sang the song of the night, and the owls hooted in the distance, *hoo, hoo, hoo...*

"We're not leaving you. We can't abandon our leader when he needs us most," Gorkith said.

Jirah winced. *You're going to get yourself killed,* he thought.

"Sir, why did you not tell us about this?" Gorkith's rough voice called from beside the fire. "We could have helped."

No, no one could help with this. It was inevitable. And it's all my fault. "I can't believe I left this for so long. I must wait for the other scouts to arrive. *None* of you should be here. It's too dangerous!" Jirah commanded. "Who knows what could have been found there. All I know is that they're coming. I know a bluff when I hear one, and this wasn't."

"We are here to help," Alex said in her deep voice. "To the end. You taught us that. Fight for our freedom."

Her words were simple, but she was right. Jirah brought them in and taught them to fight for good, freedom, and honor. Their honor brought them here, and it bound them to stay. He wished for them to abandon their beliefs, just for a short time, so they would survive. Jirah did not know their fate, but feared what was to come.

"I hope that whatever was happening in Solmarsh was worth it," Jirah said weakly. "It may cost us more than we know."

Only four remained in the camp: Alexandra, Pali'ah, Gorkith, and himself. Jirah sent Serafina to Solmarsh on horseback to follow the group and discover their fate. She was their fastest rider. He still worried about Steven Felkar, who hadn't come back from the crossroads.

"What of your friend, sir?" Gorkith asked. "Did he respond to your message?"

"No, he didn't. I hope to the gods that he was forgetful to respond, as he always is. I can only hope he will come. I sent Felkar to retrieve him, but he still hasn't returned."

Richard was a very forgetful man, but if he got the message, he would come. Jirah had no doubts of that. It just depended on whether he could arrive before *they* did. Ever since the set-up, Jirah traveled endlessly between the camps, giving out orders and missions on his own. He didn't reveal his plans to anyone, save for a select few. He could feel bags beneath his eyes sagging more with every day. Perhaps this would be an end to it—but he hoped not. His men, in all camps, waited on his orders and leadership. *What would happen if I were to die?* He could not think like that. He needed to persevere for their sake, and for Loughran as a whole.

Quick hooves could be heard from the southern path.

Jirah and the others were armed to the teeth, ready. Serafina's white hair blew wildly in the breeze. Her horse neighed loudly as she brought him to a roaring halt, almost kicking Alexandra in the chest.

"Whoa!" Alex yelped, stepping back. "We thought we lost you, Sera," she said with a sigh.

"Sorry to worry you. It's tough to catch me." Sera laughed. She hopped off her black mare and patted him roughly. The horse was exhausted. She brought him to the small stable they set up and set it to feed before reporting. Her eyes shone like the moon, a clear white with pale grey pupils. She was delaying her reporting now.

Most of the time, Jirah wouldn't mind, but when the hunters were on their heels, he had little patience left to give. "Well?" Jirah commanded, still pacing and scratching his fiery scalp.

The others were taken aback. Serafina looked to him with a raised eyebrow. "What's the urgency? At least let me feed the poor thing before I report." She stood up and winced, gripping her lower back. "Speaking of which, you better have a seat."

Jirah didn't sit down. The others did so slowly, carefully eyeing Serafina as she meandered toward them. Her brow furrowed and tightened. She scratched the back of her neck with her sharp nails, pacing back and forth in front of them while trying to form a sentence. She gently scratched behind her broad, floppy ears. "A Demon was summoned in Solmarsh."

All eyes widened, and Jirah couldn't believe it. "What?" He froze like the dead. "What about the others? What Demon? What happened?" He pummeled her with questions.

Serafina put up her hands toward him. "Please, calm down. Word is, a giant Demon came out from the ground in the middle of town. What actually happened is hard to tell with all the rumors. Some say it was sliced to death, some say a god came down and burned it, and most say a powerful Wizard defeated it."

"A powerful Wizard?" Jirah questioned.

"The group was gone the day before I arrived. The innkeeper there said that one was missing. None of them would talk about it, but their eyes looked more sorrowful than any he'd seen before. The old man was gone. Vesper. He's—he didn't make it." She shuffled her feet and her voice grew scratchy "He cast some spell that incinerated both of them."

"Oh no," Alex said in her deep voice. "He was nice."

"Yes, and talented. It seemed *'The Great Vesper'* went out fighting, to save the others." Jirah silently saluted him.

"The thing was twenty feet tall. It claimed to be a harbinger of a god, a corruptor, and gods know what else." Serafina continued to scratch the nape of her neck.. "What do you think it means?" Light slowly began to fade in the camp, save for the fire.

Fillion made a deal with the devil, Jirah thought. "I think it means we're fighting a war against more than we bargained for." Jirah fought wars against men and Broken alike, but no Demons. He did not know what to expect. A good man died to defeat the monster, if the rumors were true. Jirah did not shed a tear. He bowed his head in respect for the sacrifice Vesper made for his friends. He didn't know what it meant but felt whatever they were wasn't good.

"That girl's father was there—Lira, was her name? He was unable to talk. He was burned. Badly. No one knows why. They paid the healers in town to take care of him and took the boat back across the lake. I may have passed them, due to my—talents." Serafina was attuned to the shadows.

It reminded him of someone specific. She could ride and walk over water as she pleased, so that may be how she passed by them.

Jirah nodded. "Thank you for the report." Jirah looked to the allies that remained. All great men and women, and each fools to stay in camp with him.

TIDES OF FATE

Asheron's words were clear. *Everyone in your camps will die.*

Jirah wished it were a bluff, he truly did. One scout was still out, and Jirah dared not leave without him. Steven Felkar was sent to the crossroads to wait for Richard, and he still hadn't returned. If Richard arrived in town, he would contact Felkar and head to the camp, in case Richard forgot. While Jirah trusted Richard, his old friend was terribly forgetful. *Hurry Richard, please...*

Jirah hadn't told Serafina about Asheron's words yet. She was a skittish person, always wanting to stay safe, and not willing to take on high-risk missions. She spoke of the home she lived in long ago, but travelled across the surface of Renalia since then. She said there was no way to the underground; a massive earthquake caved in the column of Krot'ahk's Valley shortly after she arrived on the surface. Jirah heard there was a fabled entrance far in the north continent of Ormont, but none had ever gone there. Many tried, but none who sailed there ever came back. She never wanted to go back there. Jirah took her in, and promised to keep her safe, but it wasn't safe in the rebellion any longer.

As she took time to feed her steed, Miri, he knew he had to tell her—but feared her reaction.

"Sera, there's something I must speak with you about."

Sera's floppy ears perked up. She looked to him with narrowed eyes. "What's the matter?"

The others looked to him and her awkward glances. The owls hooted nearby, *hoo, hoo, hoo...*

"Asheron came to me some time ago and told me that he would come for us if we intervened in Solmarsh."

"What?" Sera exclaimed. "You knew this, and you didn't tell us?" She looked around to the others, seeing drawn-in lips and lowered brows. Slowly, a wash of realization passed over her face. "You knew? You *all* knew? Why didn't you tell me?" her tone grew

515

fierce. She faced each member, swinging her arms in an accusatory manner. "What in the hells? I can't deal with this!" she yelled in panic. "You can't just lie to your followers!"

"Sera, calm down!" Jirah commanded. He slammed his fist on the tree beside him, demanding her emotions rest. "This is why I didn't tell you!"

"Yeah, no shit, boss! You think that justifies not telling me? I followed you because you got me out of trouble, and now I'm back in it! What, do I just wait here to die? Why don't we just run?" Her hands shook as the stress set in. She had been caught for breaking into homes and stealing from nobles before the war began. Jirah was a prominent figure in the military then, and he pulled some strings. She had done good with the things she stole.

"We stay because he's staying," Pali said plainly. "We don't fear them." He spoke straight to the point.

Sera just scoffed. "Yeah, well, I do. This is impossible. You don't understand. Do you want to die in vain? For *honor*? Why die now when you can live on and fight again? I swear, you sent *Felkar* to the crossroads? That guy never took anything seriously. Boss, you may not trust everyone with knowing everyone else's plans, but you still need to be wary of the ones you *give the plans to*!" Her voice shook, and her breath sped up to match.

"I'm waiting for Felkar and Richard. What if they come to a destroyed camp? Or just nothing? We would lose them! You have to trust some people!" Jirah yelled.

"Why can't we just go to the crossroads?" Serafina was ever adamant on questioning everything.

Alexandra shrugged. "Danger there. Too many guards. They will know us."

"I can't stay here." Her tone was tremulous and brittle. Jirah knew she would go, and he couldn't stop her. "I'm not brave."

Jirah walked to her, placing his hand on her shoulder. "I know, Sera," he said, looking into her dilated grey eyes. "I've told them to leave, and they haven't. Now I'm telling you. Go."

He and Sera shared a long, lingering stare of understanding. After the moment ended, she hugged him close. As they separated, she wiped a tear from her pale grey eyes. He calmly watched as she frantically unhooked her mare once more. Her hands shook the reins, clicking and rattling. She jumped back on and kicked spurs to flesh. He looked down the path as she rode into darkness. Jirah didn't shame her, nor did he hate her for leaving the cause. One less sword made no matter, and it may have saved her life.

A coward wasn't the most honorable of soldiers, but in dark times, the only surviving one.

"Why did you let her go?" Pali asked.

"I'm not a tyrant," Jirah told him sternly. "She's a fearful girl. She doesn't know how to handle facing consequences." He strolled to the fire and looked around the camp. The others left to other camps, in hopes that they wouldn't be found. Abandoned lean-tos, bedrolls, and tents stood wanting, and the last four left were sitting around the fire. "It's only a matter of time. I hate to be pessimistic, but I don't think Richard is going to make it."

No one responded to him. They stared blankly into the flames. Gorkith's bow sat with an arrow ready to be drawn. Alexandra had her great hammer sitting in front of her. Her leather armor was thick, covering from head to toe. Pali'ah never wore more than a white cloth tunic and shorts, although no one could hit him. Jirah's armor was as tired as he was, the bags beneath his eyes matching the burns and cuts in the steel.

Hours passed and the moon rose high in the sky, bringing with it a small light through the trees. The owls hooted, the crickets sounded in the night, and the fire crackled quietly. But soon the flame faded, slowly but surely. The colors around them shifted from vibrant to a muted grey scale. Jirah felt his life and the wars he fought were just that: shades of grey. The moonlight grew dim above them, the flame turned cold, the forest grew silent as the dead, and Jirah knew what came next.

Gods help us.

Chapter Forty-four

The Storm

Saul Bromaggus

Crack went the skies, as thunder rumbled above them. Days of travel passed with many Hydris behind as Kovos's riders led Saul to the Stormspire. They came to cliff hundreds of feet over the sea, with a steep slope around the hill going to the rocky, mudded shore. Inhabitants of Serpentarius journeyed to watch the spectacle, whether it be a victory for the ages, or a failure beyond measure. The rain poured down like a sheet of rocks, stinging to the touch.

Every crack of lightning struck the Spire, the light revealing a structure reaching hundreds of feet above the crashing water, both gnarled and orderly at the same time. At its base, massive lance-like rocks spiked out like a sea urchin, with a small opening facing the mainland. From the cliff it seemed needle-thin; Saul felt that a rogue wave could cause impalement of an unsteady fool. A stone path swirled around the gnarled Spire, ending near the top.

The last hundred feet were left without assistance. *Rai Soli Moria.* Warriors fall. *Gadoras faust.* Heroes rise.

"I am unsure if I can climb with one hand," Saul grumbled. His clothes were soaked. He didn't wear his plate, coming only in beige cloth pants, a tunic, and his father's tattered, beige cloak.

"Don't worry about that. I'll take care of it," Thalia reassured him. "Many times these people have come, each believing that one day the soldier would rise. Do you think it is that day?"

"I do not know. I only care that I can use the power to change the fate of many."

Thalia chuckled at that. "Good. No one likes someone who is bound to what they're told. Come, let us descend." She led him down the side of the cliff. Her hair was drenched, a black-green mop flat as could be against her skin. She wore a thin black robe, starkly different from the bright magenta, azure, or orange he had seen her favor before. As they came to the water, the eyes of many stared down at them. "Are you ready?" she asked.

"We aren't taking a boat?"

"Don't be silly. A boat could get us killed. This will be a little strange. Walk straight beside me."

Saul stepped into the water as she did.

Crack went the lightning. With hands out flat and beneath her waist, she raised them to belly-height as stone pillars emerged from beneath the waves, pushing them into the air. Thalia stepped forward, and Saul followed. He almost fell from the first. For every pillar they passed, another one rose in front. *What power,* Saul thought.

"I won't climb with you. That is your task. Whenever anyone climbs it, the lightning intensifies, striking more often. After I take you to the base, I will return to the cliff." She placed her hand on Saul's arm. "I'll be watching."

Crack went the lightning. Over pillars they stepped, side by side. Saul could make out more detail now. The swirling spire's path was broken, thin and steep. Every step closer made the Stormspire seem more monstrous and intimidating. *I am not afraid. I will not falter.* His clothes felt heavy from being waterlogged. It was still better than plate. He felt as light as a feather without his armor. Rain filled his boots, drenched his hair, and lightning *cracked* and shot down around him, yet he walked on. A mighty whirlpool swirled around the structure. It was clear ships would be swallowed whole the moment they neared the spiraling beast.

Every turn of the tower narrowed the path, spiraling to the sky with walkways cased with metal, iron steps, and rungs just asking to be struck by the storm above. Saul and Thalia soon arrived at the path, sliding up the side. It was cracked and broken, with accents of iron veins all along it.

"Are you ready?" Thalia asked once more.

When he turned to her, there were no side-smiles, raised brows, or laughs. The pouring rain flowed over her soft face, and all he saw beneath were wide-eyes, quivering lips, and shaking hands.

Saul looked to the Spire and the swirling storm, and felt Thalia wasn't alone in her fear. Saul reached out to grab her hands, holding them together, close to him. "I must do this. You know that. I would not be here if it was not for you."

Thalia nodded. "I know. Give me your arm." Saul obliged, a mere blunt forearm showing his obvious weakness. She placed her hand gently on it, slowly creating a hand made of a thousand black rocks, flying in from all around them.

Saul felt the ability to clench the fist once more. Moments later, he was able to move each finger individually. "What did you do to me?"

"It's an ability I have. This will help you climb," she said plainly. "It doesn't last long, so don't take an eternity."

Saul smirked at the gift. *Perhaps this venture isn't a waste. And maybe magic isn't as cowardly as I thought.* "I will return. You have my word. By flesh and rock, I shall reach the top."

"I'll be on the cliff. Don't die on me," she said, narrowing her azure eyes.

Saul simply nodded, carefully nudging her back toward the shore. She walked on the pillars, raising and lowering as she went, glancing back with every few steps. As she arrived at the shore, Saul's gaze returned to the Spire. *Mighty Gadora, grant me strength.*

Crack went the lightning. Saul walked around and around the Spire, carefully stepping around the breaks and across fissures, keeping close to the wall to avoid rogue bolts of electricity. The rocks were black as night, some deep grey or silver. There were metal veins embedded in the walls and steps, more than he saw in any mine.

With another *crack,* a bolt flew in front of him, causing Saul to jump back. Blood pumped through his veins in panic, but it invigorated him. He began to run and jump, yet still managed to tiptoe around the cracked pieces. Rock flowed down from the tip of the Spire like a thousand rivulets, intertwining with iron helices encircling the Spire.

Crack. The lightning hit the Spire, again, and again, and again. The bolts struck more and more often as he ascended. He passed leagues of skeletons, some pale, and some charred black. *Is this my fate?* Saul wondered. Others expired more recently, their heads wrought with red-black burns, exposed skulls, and rotted brain splattered on the stones. The smell of burnt flesh passed through his nostrils to accent the damp stone and lichen surrounding him.

Crack. There was another turn of the Spire he walked. Steeper it went, and harder the rain fell. Below, the water swirled like a vortex that would swallow the pride of a fleet. *If I fall, I am gone.* A set of stones fell out from under him; Saul jumped to the next and held on with both hands and pulled himself up by flesh and rock to continue his journey.

Crack. Up another turn of the Spire he ran. Saul jumped across broken paths and sidled along thin ledges, wobbling from the wind that soared up, down, and around the Spire. The rain felt heavy, and his breath escaped him as he went. His heart beat faster with every rumble of the skies. He felt vulnerable, looking to the sea beyond Kathynta, south at the horizon, with nothing but crashing waves for miles beyond to the land of Feyamin. The rain fell so hard he felt the continent would be swallowed whole. *This storm is unyielding—but it is me. I am the storm. I will conquer it.*

Crack. To the top of the tower he came. The spiraling path ended, and before him laid a tower with rough-hewn rock walls and broken handholds. Anchors and spikes laid jammed in still, left from heroes long passed who attempted the climb. A hundred feet it reached into the air, winds buffeting the walls to force even a strong man to fall to his death. The scent of wet stone and iron were all he found, coupled with the view of the black skies above and equally dark waters below. Saul turned to see hundreds on the cliff in the distance, barely making out the grey in the center, with a hint of forest green. *I will not fail you,* Saul thought.

Crack. His final climb began. Saul's hand of rock clasped the handholds with great strength, even more than his hand of flesh would. He gripped the spikes and anchors, taking the aid of his predecessors, those who desired strength, yet failed. Where they all fell, he would survive. Lightning struck the metal linings in the rock, sending a jolt through him and weakening his grip.

It only drives my will more. I cannot be stopped!

Lightning *cracked* and struck him again, with a jolt so strong it sent him to the floor below. His back hurt from the rough stone, but the rain cooled his hot, reddened skin. *I can't give up—I won't give up. Get up. Get up*, he thought. Saul lumbered to his feet, shaking his head to steel himself.

He gazed up again. "Gadora, give me strength. I must do this for them, not just for my own need!" Saul felt the soaked, tattered cloak his father left as it dripped heavily around him. *I will lead, Father. I will rise from your ashes to lead with the strength of our god.* Saul took a long breath to relax and calm his nerves. He could feel energy flow through his veins, as if the gods blessed him once more.

Crack. His climb began once more. He soared up, handhold to handhold, rung to rung, spike to anchor. The wind buffeted him, but his hand of rock held like a Dragon's jaw. With each break, he climbed further up with vigorous intent. The holds were wet, and he came close to slipping, but held on. As he ascended, the holds were less broken and spikes fewer, marking the small number of those to reach the top.

Crack. He pulled himself over the wall. He came to a flat surface on the top, with intricate stonework of bricks and metal veins particularly placed in circles around the centerpiece—a black hilt, reaching out from the stone and metal of the Spire. The mark of Gadora was set in the base of the pommel, with each wind set with bright red rubies, and coiled gold and silver encircled the black steel neck coming to a Dragon's head. The maw opened to the ground, hiding the blade below. Saul carefully walked around the center, reading the runes he recognized from the teachings of Gadora. *The blade that carves the skies,* it read. Saul stopped in front of it, looking to the cliff with the mass of people that stood watch.

He looked to the black sky with its torrential rain plummeting to the rough seas. Saul's breath sped up to meet his heart that charged like a thousand bloodthirsty ravagers.

He reached out to the blacksteel hilt above the stone with his left hand and closed his grip.

Crack. A spiraling column of lightning crashed down upon his hand that touched the blade. His markings shone bright red and blue all around him as he was coated with powerful electricity. Saul roared in pain as his skin felt aflame, and he fell to his knees in agony. His vision flashed to his father burning, then to a Terran with the blade atop a massive demon, and a violet orb above a sea of Broken galleys.

His body shook wildly as the electricity passed through his veins, but he refused to give up. He had one final vision: a woman with yellow and blue markings coated in flame surrounded by shadowy figures, calling for help, and then a storm of lightning striking all within.

He wished to release the blade. He wanted the agony to stop. *No, I won't let go. I must claim the blade. A storm is coming,* Gadora had told him. The nightmares trained him for this moment. His blood boiled, his brain felt to burst, and his eyes bulged out.

"*Gadoras faust!*" Saul roared, rising again to his feet. *Heroes rise.* The electricity flowed from black cloud to hilt, burning him like all the others that came before him. He could see the skin of his left hand begin to crackle and blister. The white bolts splayed out from the hilt, connected with his arm, and seared it black all over. The blackness crawled up his arm as he slowly pulled the blade from the Spire.

He growled, building up to a guttural roar, slowly gaining strength as the burn reached his shoulder. With a violent scream, Saul brought the blade out from the stone and pointed it to the sky with its fire-orange steel burning bright like the sun.

The black burn reached his neck and part of his face, but he felt no more pain.

Energy surged from the blade—*the blade that carves the skies*—as the lightning above *cracked* again and again into it. But with every strike, Saul felt more powerful.

Saul heard the chants of the crowd from afar, in unison yelling, "The Soldier of Storms, The Soldier of Storms!" They yelled it over and over, with arms thrusting into the air.

Saul gritted his teeth, knowing his destined path. As the storm raged around him, he roared to the sky, echoing through the hills and lands beyond. "*I am coming, Obelreyon!*"

He was an inexorable storm that would sweep over Kathynta, and Renalia was next.

"*I shall give you something to fear.*"

Chapter Forty-five

Queen, Knight, Pawns

Domika Mirado

Night took the camp, and it was under Dom's watch.

Every moment since she arrived in Wolf Camp for the first time, her soul bled. But she had to persevere.

Lira tossed in her sleep, writhing each night since her brother died. Each thrash reminded Dom of their own decision. Her own motives.

Family—or part of it. Lira chose her friends and sacrificed family. Dom did the the very opposite. The one who raised her came before all others. Her mom came first.

It was the first time Kayden slept in days since Vesper died. Finally alone on watch, Dom crept out of the clearing. The wolves howled in the distance as if warning the others.

She knelt in a small clearing of dirt and spoke the incantation to activate their connection with the one she obeyed.

They slowly scraped each symbol in a circle around her as instructed. Placing the deep violet crystal into the dirt, a vision appeared before her.

"I have awaited this report for days," the Cardinal hissed. Her fiery orange hair felt aflame itself, and bright green eyes grew more vicious by the moment.

"The harbinger was banished, your eminence," she stuttered. "The girl and the magician. He cast a spell of annihilation, and she banished it while it was weak."

"Don't act as if I have not heard this from the brothers. The foolish boy summoned it too early in a panic." The cardinal shot up from the broken throne of Amirion, her dark armor casting a shadow over her despite it being magical communication. "They, along with the puppet king, have informed me of their failure— and that the girl *somehow* absorbed the essence in the altercation, and that you *helped* the rebels."

Dom shuddered at the Cardinal's sharp tongue. Fearing what awaited her. "I'm sorry, your eminence," Dom whispered. She assumed death came next. Or torture. Or worse. "I could not reveal myself. I felt it was too risky."

A deafening silence took them. The traitor's eyes stayed at the ground. Dared not look into the cardinal's eyes now. It was said the Cardinal's gaze could steal one's very soul.

"Look at me, Domika," the Cardinal snapped.

A rush of ice charged up Dom's spine. She drew her eyes to her leader. If only she failed by mistake. But she didn't. She wanted to help. Part of her wavered from her path.

The cardinal looked down at her subject. "Remind yourself of why you took your pact. We have all made one."

Family. Something Jirah never understood. He left and never came back. Dom took a pact to save the only family she had. *Mom.* If she betrayed it… She didn't want to think about that.

"The brothers and king are not pleased."

A test. "They are pawns, your eminence."

A smirk crept across the Cardinal's lips. "Quite right. It is good that you know their place—and your own." Her expression returned to absolute ice. "Do you have a plan to correct these mistakes you have made?"

It was far worse of a plan than she wanted. It bore a battle of morals within her. But her decisions were beyond good and evil.

"Domika." Her tone was laced with poison. The Cardinal's cold voice drew quiet. "Do not make me ask again."

When one would normally ask a second time, the Cardinal brought forth the lash instead. Or the sword.

"I do, your eminence."

"I will grant you this chance. Should you fail, I should not need to remind you of the consequences. I would not want to send Cloaker to assist you. He has been—occupied." After a brief moment, the Cardinal waved her hand across her form, whispering an incantation under her breath. As the vision faded, she said, "Do not disappoint me again."

The mountain on Dom's shoulders vanished, and she took the first breath in a year, it felt. Dom wretched and heaved, and finally, threw her stomach contents upon the dirt. She slowly drew her hands into fists, breathing heavily, trying to keep her composure. She would not sleep tonight, even after her watch ended.

"Domika?" Lira's kind, but horrifying voice called out from behind. "Are you okay?"

Looking forward to the darkness, Domika spoke between heavy breaths. "I'm okay. Just—feeling sick after what happened."

As a hand touched her back, Dom shivered. Lira said, "I understand. I've felt awful since Vesper's passing, and—" Her voice cut off, but her eyes said, *my brother.*

A tear crept from Dom's eye. "You did what you had to do."

Just like me.

A brittle smile grew from Lira's somber expression. "Thanks, it's been hard." She looked up to the stars above, and her posture relaxed. "It helps knowing I'm with people I care about, and trust."

Dom's heart shattered in that moment. Trust. Care.

Dom trusted them. She cared about them.

And she betrayed them.

"Lira, can I ask you something?" Dom said, rising to her feet.

Lira tilted her head in response. "Sure, what's the matter?"

"If—if you chose your brother, and we—" She paused for a moment. "Died—would you feel you did the right thing?"

Lira watched Dom for a moment with eyes that glistened in the moonlight above. It wasn't regret in her gaze. It was a strange sense of sadness—and confidence. "There was no right answer." She slowly shook her head. "I just have to live with my decision."

Me, as well.

Grey. It's all Domika saw in life.

Good and Evil were constructs made up by those with excessive pride. Every evil decision had an outcome that some would see as good. Every good choice came with a consequence that had evil results.

At least, that's what Dom told herself to stay sane.

She walked the line between savior and horror. Should she fall, it would mean her soul—or that of the one who keeps her alive. She only wished her friends weren't caught in the balance under the blade of the executioner.

Under her scythe.

"All beings make mistakes.

In the span of my existence, I have made one.

What a grave mistake it was."

- The Forgotten One

Sean J. Leith is the author of *The Origins of Life and Death* series, beginning with *Tides of Fate*. He writes both fantasy and science fiction, with many stories to come. When he isn't writing books, he can be either found in a biochemistry lab, or playing D&D through homebrew campaigns or character classes he creates.

For maps of the world of *The Origins of Life and Death*, visit: https://www.seanjleith.com.

Made in the USA
San Bernardino, CA
08 January 2019